# GABRIELLA

*By the same author*

Under the Tricolor

# GABRIELLA

*Mary Medawar*

HarperCollins*Publishers*

HarperCollins*Publishers*
77–85 Fulham Palace Road
Hammersmith, London W6 8JB

Published by HarperCollins*Publishers* 1992
1 3 5 7 9 8 6 4 2

The Author asserts the moral right to
be identified as the author of this work

A catalogue record for this book
is available from the British Library

ISBN 0–246–13470–4

Set in Bembo by
Falcon Typographic Art Ltd, Edinburgh & London

Printed in Great Britain by
HarperCollinsManufacturing Glasgow

*For my brother,*
*Norman T. Collins*

*and in memory of our parents,*
*Caroline and Sam Collins*

# Acknowledgements

I thank for their help and encouragement:

Kay and Alan Anscomb

Prof. Elisabetta Brusa – Composition Department, Conservatorio
G. Verdi of Milan, Italy, who responded to my enquiries on the
historical background of the Conservatorio with enthusiasm and
generosity of her precious time.

Penelope Isaac, my Editor, for her skill and that sparkling sense of
humour!

Jerry Kirk MS, FRCS

Ian Lyle, Head Librarian, Royal College of Surgeons

Tony Medawar

Clelio Moretti and his niece, Maurizia Moretti, Villa Giuditta
Pasta, Blevio; and their friend, Gertrud Muller

Municipal Silk Museum, Garlate, Como Area

Barbara Shirlaw

Hadyn Collins

For hospitality: June Leoni, Hotel du Lac Bellagio; Clara
Fantoccoli, Blevio; Angelo Fanto, Rome

For musical inspiration: the fine tenor voice of Dr James Dooley
MD, BSc, MRCP; Anne Harding, whose sharp eyes and steady
nerves guided me across Rome's busiest roads

Low Visual Aids Department, Moorfields Hospital

For unravelling the mysteries of the word processor:
Mike Williams and Derek Jenkinson

The London Library

His Honour John Byrt QC for encouragement

And, of course, I thank my husband!

I go to prove my soul!
I see my way as birds their trackless way . . .
In some time, His good time, I shall arrive:
He guides me and the bird. In His good time!
*Paracelsus*
Robert Browning

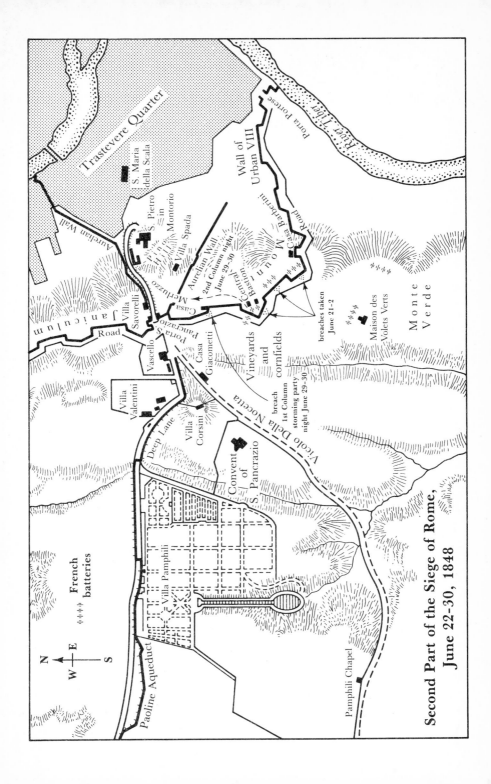

**Second Part of the Siege of Rome,
June 22-30, 1848**

# Chapter One

Yesterday, the assassin had threatened the life of the Queen, but the small pale face which looked out of the carriage window was serene and smiling. Gabriella's young heart bounded with admiration and she threw back her head and shouted with the rest.

'God save the Queen!'

The Italian Opera House in London's Haymarket was full, its audience a-glitter with jewels: diamonds and luminous pearls which had sparkled and glowed from within a seemingly endless line of carriages bringing the rich and noble to the first production in Italian of Mercadante's opera, *Elena Uberti*.

On tiptoe, Gabriella tried to catch one more glimpse of the young Queen Victoria and her German Prince, but others, taller and just as eager, blocked her view, and all she could see was the flight of the caps and beavers of men shouting their hurrahs. Moments later, as the hubbub quietened, she heard for the second time that evening the strains of the National Anthem within the Opera House. Outside on the pavement they began to sing, uniting briefly their voices with the aristocracy in homage and thanksgiving for the life of the Queen.

'Rather 'er than me!' joked a man in a loud voice as people began to move away. 'I'd rather face an assassin's pistol than listen to the horrible foreign jabbering in there!'

His comment brought laughter from all around, but Gabriella flushed scarlet and, unable to restrain them, the words tumbled from her lips. '*L'Italia è bella!*' but the man was already a dozen people away and did not hear, and those who did only laughed all the more.

'A sweep's brush talking?' joked a young fop, pointing to the girl's short, spiky hair. 'No, I do declare, it's the prima donna Madame Frezzolini herself, only instead of an orchestra she has a concertina around her neck. Play us a tune then, Madame!'

From long practice, Gabriella's hand automatically shot up and caught the coin. She wished she could throw it back at the smirking faces, but with hardly more than three other coins in her purse to take back to her master, the penny might well save her later from a whipping; so with a nod of acceptance, Gabriella made to drop the coin into the purse at her waist.

'Oh no, it can't be!' she gasped, turning pale with fright as she saw the empty loop from which her purse had hung. As her desperate fingers clutched at the severed thong, she realized that usage and old age were the culprits and not the knife of a pickpocket. Hopeful that it might have dropped nearby, Gabriella crouched down and began to search the area, ignoring as she went the indignant shouts of her recent benefactor. But there was no purse, and soon all she had to show for her frantic efforts were cuts and bruises on her shins and hands. With a deep sigh, Gabriella turned away from the Opera House and the bright lights and, filled with fear and apprehension, walked towards Blackfriars.

At the entrance of the alley which led through to the street where she lived, her brother Nico was waiting for her.

'At last, Lark, what kept you?' he grumbled. 'His Highness is threatening to leather you, so I hope you've made a bit.'

'I've only a penny, I lost the rest.'

'Lost!' gasped the boy, his brown eyes widening in horror as he stared at the young girl. 'How could you be so stupid? He'll be furious!'

'I know,' whispered Gabriella miserably. Then, unable to bear the desperate look on Nico's face she forced a laugh. 'I did see the Queen though, and Prince Albert, and earlier I stood by the stage door and listened to the singers rehearsing. Oh, it was marvellous!'

'Sounds as if you didn't spend much time playing that,' snorted Nico, pointing to her concertina. 'You know Menotti's temper, yet you go wasting time listening to singers – and now you're looking to me to get you out of it.'

'Well, you always think of something,' she smiled tentatively, despite the dark scowl on Nico's face. Her brother's expression remained grave, though, and her mouth went dry as he shook his head helplessly and gave a weary shrug of his shoulders. In subdued silence, dreading what lay ahead, Gabriella followed Nico through the alley, out on to the street and towards the Three Bells. Within the soft pool of light cast from the alehouse window they paused, peering through the clear glass which spelt out the word 'Ales'.

'Perhaps he won't come back tonight,' murmured Gabriella wistfully as she caught sight of the large grey head of their master.

'Some hope!' said Nico, pulling her away. He was turning disconsolately towards the alley, when suddenly his fingers tightened on her shoulder. His eyes had brightened. 'The tide is out and there's a fog coming up: there'll be few mudlarks at work. Kate always needs coal – it's your only chance.'

Filled with hope, they ran to the back door of the alehouse. Inside, Lizzie the serving maid stood washing dishes.

'Hello beautiful,' said Nico with a broad wink. 'Kate about?'

'There's nothing she can do for you that I can't,' said the wench, responding with a sly smile and a flick of water in the boy's direction.

'Ah, but have you got sixpence, Lizzie?' asked Nico, giving the giggling girl a slap on her bottom. 'Now run along and get Kate . . . and if you-know-who asks, you haven't seen us!'

One only had to see the shrewd expression in Kate O'Reidy's lovely green eyes to realize how she had acquired enough money to buy an alehouse. As a prostitute she had been much sought after, and whilst fortune had not cast the gentry her way, the factory owners and merchants had been generous. Now she had customers who drank her ale and others who enjoyed her girls. She entered the room in a flurry of skirts and scent, her sweet pungent smell instantly vanquishing all kitchen odours.

'Well, and if it isn't the devil herself,' the Irishwoman joked. 'I hope you've a cup of silver for Paolo Menotti, he's in an ugly mood.'

'I've made nothing, Kate. I lost my purse,' confessed Gabriella. 'Nico thought you might need coals.'

Kate O'Reidy looked at the girl's dark blue velvety eyes. Hard though she was, she could not help but respond to the wistful appeal in them. Besides, before her was a girl who would shortly have a very bright future in Kate's establishment, and she had no intention of allowing Menotti to damage the goods with a beating.

'Very well,' she said. 'Bring back two baskets . . . and tomorrow, Lark,' she added, using everyone's nickname for the girl, 'it'll be time for you and I to have a little chat.'

A thick acrid yellow fog had settled over the river. Ankle-deep in mud, Gabriella and Nico moved slowly forward along the shoreline, probing with their naked toes for the pieces of coal which fell overboard into the river during unloading at the wharves.

'The tide will be on the turn soon,' exclaimed Nico after a time, 'and we'll not have filled a quarter of a basket. There's a Geordie barge came in today. Hang on to my basket while I go and see if it's been unloaded.'

'What about the Peelers?'

'They'll not be out tonight,' he laughed. 'Likely be in an alehouse.'

Gradually the sound of his feet sloshing through mud and water died away and, soon afterwards, two short whistles signalled Gabriella forward. Eventually the dark outline of a barge appeared, and she heard her brother's excited shout from the beached boat.

'What luck!'

'Do you think they'll mind?'

'Mind!' he exploded. 'Who cares? It's better than a beating. Come aboard, me heartie, and keep an ear open for pirates.'

But apart from the distant mournful alarm of the fog horns, there was only the gentle slap of water against the side of the barge.

'The water's starting to rise, Nico!' she said, as the boat lurched gently to the right.

'So is our pile of coal. Jump down and I'll hand the baskets to you. Look lively, me lad!'

Seized with the giggles and lightheaded with relief, Gabriella obeyed. She raised up her arms for the baskets filled with their precious contents: the lightermen on the Thames often stole bales of silks and such to make their fortune; tonight, for her, each of the coals was like a nugget of gold.

From the Three Bells the sound of raucous singing had increased. Inside, quite deaf to it, the girl Lizzie slept before the kitchen fire.

'How can she, with such a din?' said Gabriella, setting down her basket.

'Used to it,' said Nico, munching a scrap of cheese left on the table. 'Look, this sixpence here must be yours. Let's scram.'

Home for Gabriella, Nico, and the other organ-grinders was next to Kate O'Reidy's alehouse, in a tumble-down stable behind the house where their master, Paolo Menotti, and his wife lived. It was to this house that Gabriella went to hand in her money to the master's wife.

'What did she say?' asked Nico, when Gabriella caught up with him in the yard at the back.

'Told me off for being late and slammed the door in my face.'

'No offer of supper?'

'No.'

'Then it's a good job I saved you a drop of mine,' laughed the boy, opening the rickety door of the long wooden shed where they slept.

'What would I do without you, Nico?' said Gabriella, smiling up at her brother in the darkness. 'I'll come up in a minute, just as soon as I've said goodnight to Pepe.'

'You and that bear!' scoffed her brother. 'One day he'll give you a big hug! Don't be long now, or I'll eat the lamb cutlet myself!'

Gabriella laughed: lamb cutlets were unknown to anyone here. Their only luxury was the odd fresh egg stolen from

Menotti's hen coop, but that was a rarity, for a sharp watch was kept by the signora from her kitchen window.

As she walked past the boys' barrel-organs and towards the caged monkeys and squirrels which they used to amuse the Londoners, Gabriella wrinkled her nose in disgust at the smell of urine and droppings. For as long as she could remember this had been home, yet the fetid smells still made her want to retch. Nico and the other boys didn't seem to mind: they said they had always lived next to animals in the countryside back home.

Where was her real home? Nico never talked about it, or about their parents, and all he had ever told her was that he had run away with her when she was small to make his fortune in England as an organ-grinder. All the boys who arrived from Italy had expected to make their fortunes; instead they had been contracted to a harsh master who granted them only the barest necessities of life. Gabriella gave a deep sigh as she arrived at Pepe's cage.

'Well, at least he is kind to you,' she murmured, reaching through the bars of the cage for the furry head of the dancing bear. 'Hello, my friend, did you think I had forgotten your little treats?' she crooned. The pointed snout of the black bear pushed vigorously through the bars against her arm as she took out a little paper bag from her pocket and shook the contents on to the palm of her hand.

'Two wasps and enough ants to make your stomach ache,' she said, laughing as the bear's rough tongue licked across her hand. With a final pat and a tickle behind Pepe's ears, Gabriella whispered goodnight and walked wearily away to the wooden ladder which led up to the loft: it had been a long day. As her foot touched the bottom rung, she paused and listened to Nico and the boys above laughing and talking. Outside, from the direction of Kate's, men's voices disturbed the night like howling dogs. Though their singing masked all other noises from the nearby streets and gloomy courts, Gabriella knew well the cries of poverty and they were terrible, ugly. As though to banish this wretched world in which she lived, she sang a few of the notes she had heard at the stage door

14

of the Opera House earlier that day. Instantly, the snatch of music dominated all else, transforming the grey scene like sunshine. Within, Gabriella felt a powerful surge of energy and excitement. Her rough hands reached upwards and took hold of a high rung.

'I will not stay here always!' she vowed. 'I will not!'

As though it had come to her in a dream during the night, Gabriella knew the next morning what she was going to do. Filled with impatience, she told Nico.

'Are you mad?' he said. He set down the battered tankard from which they had been taking turns to sip the ale they always had for breakfast. 'You know what he has said about the school. Anyone who goes there is out on their heels – do you want to end up as one of Kate's girls?'

'I likely will in any case if I don't do something about it. You heard what Kate said last night. We're all getting too old, and Menotti will throw us out like kittens when they're too big to appeal to people.'

'Well, even so,' said her brother, tossing the tankard up into the air, 'school learning is no good to me, unless they teach house-breaking and such. If Menotti finds out where you've been, don't ask me to protect you.'

As they left the yard to head for their own individual patches and another day of begging, Gabriella continued to try and persuade Nico to accompany her that evening. But her brother refused to contemplate coming with her after work to the school in Hatton Garden. Indeed, he became very surly as they parted company.

'I am making plans for our future. Your going there will ruin it all,' he snapped at her as he pushed his barrel-organ away.

It was the first time that Gabriella had heard of any plans; throughout the day as she sang and played she wondered what he meant. Still, her resolve to go to Hatton Garden that night did not weaken, for she had the uneasy feeling that if Nico was planning anything for their future it would include his friend Angelo, a pickpocket and thief.

It was after nine o'clock in the evening when the young girl ran from Blackfriars after handing in her money. As she walked towards Leather Lane she felt rather dizzy, for there had been no time to wait for the green-grey soup which Signora Menotti served up each evening. She hoped her absence wouldn't cause suspicion, for unappetizing though the food was, at the end of a long day it was gobbled up by everyone.

The school, she knew, had recently moved from Number 5 Hatton Garden to further up Leather Lane. However, even if she hadn't known this, it would have been impossible to miss where it was, for the whole area was crowded with organ-grinder boys pushing their organs towards the free school run especially for them at 5 Greville Street.

'Why, nearly all the organ-grinders in the city must be here,' she laughed, seeing the long line of instruments parked outside the building.

'Are you coming to our school?' asked a small boy curiously as she entered with him.

'Yes,' she smiled.

'But the Signore runs it for us.'

'Well, I live with organ-grinders, and I could work with one if I wanted to,' Gabriella explained. 'I was too small to push one when I first came to England, so the master gave me a concertina. I always kept with it, but I am still one of you,' she added, beginning to feel a little anxious lest she be turned away. Her fears proved groundless, though, for the moment she peeped shyly around the door after the youngster had entered, a striking, bearded man, who was talking to some of the pupils at the front of the classroom, caught sight of her. He walked towards her with a welcoming smile.

'*Buona sera*, welcome, you wish to learn with us?'

'Yes, yes I do,' replied Gabriella fervently. 'I play the concertina for Paolo Menotti . . . I'm not really supposed to be here, for he said we were not to come.'

The slim, dark-haired man sighed sadly and fixed his intense gaze upon the ragged girl, noting the beauty that no dirt could hide and a hunger that was not of the flesh.

'I am Giuseppe Mazzini,' he said softly. 'Do not worry about being here, it is every human being's right to learn. Tomorrow

16

I shall visit your master and make everything all right.' Then, taking her by the hand, Italy's famous exile led the new pupil to a vacant stool at the front of the room.

The man's words astonished Gabriella, yet though his manner was mild, there was a power about him that she had never seen in anyone before. Nevertheless, the thought of him going to see Paolo Menotti filled her with dread, and she knew before leaving she must beg him not to, not only for her own sake but for his. In the meantime, though, her anxiety soon disappeared, for there was so much to look at, from a large blackboard on an easel with a drawing on it which looked like a large boot, to the unexpected sight of a large basket of apples on Signor Mazzini's desk. Their red and golden skins made the juices in Gabriella's mouth run, and she was not the only one whose gaze never left the fruit, for though the boys around her might have kinder masters who let them come to learn, they were no better fed.

'Now children,' Giuseppe Mazzini said, picking up one of the rosy apples. 'Tonight we are going to talk about the land you came from. Do you know where you lived before you came to England?' he said, looking at the boy who sat next to Gabriella.

'My family live in the Papal States, Signore,' whispered the boy shyly.

'And you, Signorina?'

Under the intense gaze, Gabriella flushed with embarrassment.

'I don't know,' she said, turning a deeper colour as laughter broke out. 'Lombardy I think,' she said, dredging from the depths of her memory some name which Nico had once mentioned to her.

'Lombardy, the Papal States – and Liguria,' Giuseppe Mazzini added, as another boy spoke out. 'All different places,' he said with a smile as he took a penknife from his pocket. 'Now, before I start to cut this up, do you all know what it is?'

'An apple!' chorused the whole room, breaking into laughter at such a silly question.

17

'Of course,' smiled their teacher, cutting the fruit into three pieces. 'And I'm going to give one of these pieces to our young lady from Lombardy, and the other two pieces to the boys from the Papal States and Liguria. Now what will they have?'

'A piece of apple,' chorused the other children enviously.

'And what do you get if you put them all together?'

'An apple!'

'Yes,' laughed the Genoese exile, distributing the rest of the apples to the children. 'It's very simple, and that is what one day we must do for Italy. We must rescue all the pieces from the foreigners and cruel tyrants and put them together to make Italy one nation and one people. But before you can help me to do this, you must all learn to read and write, for tyrants are frightened of children who can read and write.'

'Will we learn to read music, Signore?'

Giuseppe Mazzini started with surprise at the unexpected question and beamed approval at the eagerness and anxiety on the young girl's face.

'If that is important to you, of course! On Sundays the boys come here to learn to draw, so, if you wish to read music then I shall arrange for one of my friends to come and help you . . . but first I think you should make a start on the alphabet.'

For the next hour, under Giuseppe Mazzini's guidance, Gabriella and the boys scratched away with small pieces of chalk on their own individual pieces of slate.

'Your letters are very well formed,' commented Mazzini, stopping behind Gabriella. 'I see you have written before.'

'No, Signore,' she replied shyly, her heart nearly bursting with pleasure at his praise.

'Curious,' he murmured, fingering his fine beard as he looked down at her slate. 'It hardly seems possible.'

'Signore,' said Gabriella, more anxious about the next day than the teacher's curiosity. 'Please don't visit Signor Menotti tomorrow. It would get me into trouble and he might hurt you.'

Once again, Gabriella experienced the strange power which seemed to shine from the man's eyes.

18

'Don't you worry, my child,' he said, laying a reassuring hand upon her hair. 'Other masters forbade their workers to come and they relented when I went to see them. So shall yours.'

'But he's a very violent man, Signore.'

'He will do his duty for his fellow human beings and for Italy,' said Giuseppe Mazzini firmly. 'And tomorrow, you shall make a start on arithmetic.'

Afterwards, as she walked the short distance home to Blackfriars, Gabriella's heart sang with happiness. She felt she had achieved so much: she must persuade Nico and the rest of the boys to come with her the next evening. Just a few minutes listening to Signor Mazzini would be enough – he made one feel that anything was possible. And though he was half the size of Paolo Menotti, the light in his eyes and that strange inner power made her believe that even their bully of a master would not dare disobey him.

On the way home, glowing with happiness, she sang; but as she opened the gate into the yard she fell silent. The chink of light from the Neapolitan's bedroom window showed that he and his wife had retired for the night, but she knew that the slightest noise might bring him to the window.

'Stay where you are!'

The harsh voice rooted Gabriella to the ground as, lamp in hand, the heavy bulk of Menotti appeared around the stable door. 'I can guess where you have been,' he snarled, 'but let me hear it from you.'

Paolo Menotti's face was filled with menace; his words left the air heavy with the reek of rum. He lurched towards her. Trying to halt him, she blurted out an explanation, 'I took a walk, Signore, to Hatton Garden.'

'You missed supper to take a walk – do you take me for a fool?' he roared, seizing hold of her by the collar. 'No one disobeys me. People shall see what happens to those who do, as your friend Nico found out earlier when he tried to lie and cover up for you.'

In an agony of mind as she watched him set down his lamp, Gabriella considered whether she could escape; but the absurdity of the notion struck her at the same time as Menotti's fist. One after another a rain of vicious blows descended about her head and shoulders.

'You went to that school, didn't you? Didn't you?'

'Oh please, please stop. I won't go again, please. Don't, please . . . Oh God, help me . . .'

From within the confines of his cage, the bear growled as he heard the voice of his friend screaming in pain. In the darkness the occupants of the other cages took up the bear's distress, the monkeys' strident gibber adding a high descant to his deep thunder. Above, in their long dormitory, the organ-grinders whispered fearfully.

'Mother of God!' exclaimed Nico, clutching his throbbing head. 'I must go down, he's killing her.'

'We'll all go,' said one of the older boys.

As the buckle of the master rose and fell, Gabriella could no longer scream. Limp and unresisting, she felt herself falling away from lamplight and pain into blackness. Her piercing cries stopped as the bear's protective fury erupted and his massive weight crashed against the cage. The quivering structure swayed a moment on its supports, then it toppled sideways. Freedom called to Pepe the bear, then his neck snapped as the heavy roof above crashed down.

On hearing the noise within, Paolo Menotti flung aside the inert body of the girl and raced into the stable. His howl of grief hung in the air like a wolf's on a snowy plateau, halting those boys who had followed in his tracks. Then, as silence was followed by the more human note of sobbing, one of the boys moved forward.

'What happened?'

'He's dead!' wept the Neapolitan, his tears soaking into the warm fur as the boys stole away.

'You'd best get the Lark out of here,' they warned Nico, who was kneeling beside the body of Gabriella.

'Yes, he'll blame it on her,' agreed the boy, tears glistening in his eyes which he wiped away roughly with the ragged cuff of his jacket. 'I'll have to take her to Kate's.'

At the sight of Nico entering her kitchen with the inert body of Gabriella in his arms, Kate O'Reidy stopped counting that night's takings.

'Lord preserve us!' she gasped. 'Menotti?'

Nico nodded.

'One day he'll swing,' commented the Irishwoman, shaking her head in dismay at the battered appearance of the youth and the moaning girl.

'He's been mad from toothache all day – he even took it out on the bear this morning. Now he's blubbering his eyes out because the roof of the cage has fallen and killed Pepe. He's bound to blame it on the Lark . . . will you look after her for a while?'

'Of course, it's something that I've been intending to do,' said Kate O'Reidy, touching the spiky tendrils of Gabriella's hair. 'Don't worry, Nico, when this has grown and the bruises have faded, I'll transform this girl's life with a little satin and lace. Men like Menotti will not be able to afford one single hour with her.'

As the Irishwoman's hand lifted away from the cut cheek of Gabriella, Nico's eyes blazed with jealousy and outrage. His hands clenched into tight fists, then he turned on his heel and left.

Outside in the street, the boy leant his head against the rough brick of the alehouse and ground his teeth as he wondered what he could do, where else he could take the Lark. Then he had it, and with a jubilant kick at the wall with the heel of his boot he sped away.

The classroom at 5 Greville Street was empty, but hunched like a student himself, Giuseppe Mazzini was writing away furiously on one of the many essays destined to reach his native land. At Nico's whirlwind entrance, he immediately put down his pen and rose to his feet.

'What is the trouble, my boy?'

'You must come with me, Signore . . . you are the teacher?'

Mazzini nodded.

'Then you must come, it's the Lark, Menotti beat her for coming here!'

21

Mazzini looked at the wild desperation on the boy's face.

'I will come with you at once, and you shall explain everything to me as we go!' Mazzini said, turning out the lamp.

As the older man and the boy hurried from Hatton Garden towards Blackfriars, Nico explained what had happened.

'None of us told on her, Signore, but our master saw her turning in to your school himself. He's always hitting us – we're used to it – but he's never hurt Pepe before. That's why he's in such a state now – he really loved that bear. Gabriella can never go back. You have to take her in.'

Giuseppe Mazzini halted.

'You expect me to take her?' he exclaimed in amazement. 'But, dear child, that's just not possible. I have barely enough money to exist on myself. And my landlady would not permit . . .'

Nico's expression hardened and his eyes were full of accusation. 'If she had not come to your school this would not have happened. If she stays with Kate she will end up with the other girls at the Haymarket, if you get my meaning. There must be something better for her.'

The Genoese wanted to say, 'It's impossible,' but as he looked at the boy's desperate expression, he realized that he couldn't crush his only hope. Even in the midst of squalor and deprivation this peasant boy wanted to save his sister from what would not only be acceptable, but also highly lucrative employment hereabouts. Well, if this might prove the only aspiration in his life, then he must help him realize it.

'Very well, my son,' he said, patting the boy's shoulder. 'You have done your duty, and you have shown me mine.'


Though her body ached and smarted from the beating she had received the night before, Gabriella awoke to a life which she had never thought might be hers. There was warmth, the smell of bread baking and a remembrance of gentle hands bathing her face and body. Perhaps the fact that one of her eyes was too painful and swollen to open made her think that she had dreamt that the room to which she had been carried was full of birds, but here they were, at least a dozen of them, bright yellow canaries flying free, perching on the backs of the chairs and pecking at a mass of papers on a wooden desk.

'So, you poor mite, you're awake and smiling,' said a friendly looking lady bustling into the room. 'Though it's no wonder you didn't sleep on with all these chattering birds. Why Mr Mazzini has to have so many of the creatures, I don't know – he says their bright colours remind him of Italy.'

'Is this Signor Mazzini's room?' asked Gabriella slowly, for it pained her to move her lips.

'Yes,' replied the lady, sitting down beside the couch and lifting up a spoon of bread and milk towards Gabriella's lips. 'I've made a bed up for you in the attic. Mr Mazzini needs his room for writing. He writes all the time, you know. He tells me this wicked man hit you because you wanted to learn. May God forgive him, for I never could. Anyway, Mr Mazzini has gone to see him this morning.'

The woman's words filled Gabriella with horror, and she struggled to sit up, crying out as she did so, 'Oh Madam, he must not. Please, you must stop him from being hurt.'

'Now you lie back, and don't you go worrying about Mr Mazzini: your master is not the first he has dealt with. There have been others, and they were brought to court for their cruelty. Like your bruises, child, this Menotti probably will turn all the colours of the rainbow with rage, but in the end our Mr Mazzini will have his way.'

As the landlady predicted, Gabriella's bruises changed during the next few days into a multitude of horrific hues.

'Gosh, you look terrible,' declared Nico, swopping the stool which the landlady had shown him to for the edge of the bed. 'How are you feeling?'

'Terrible,' Gabriella mumbled. 'You don't look too good yourself.'

'It is a bit of a shiner,' grinned Nico, fingering his own black eye. 'But he did a better job on you,' he grinned, taking a closer look at the green and yellow swelling over Gabriella's eye. 'He didn't do so well with the teacher though.'

'Signor Mazzini hit him?' exclaimed Gabriella in surprise.

Nico laughed. 'Hardly. If he had tried that he would have been flung clean over the shed roof. No, he just talked.'

'Talked?'

'Yes, it was that easy,' laughed the boy again. 'Like calming down a mad bull. I hid behind the shed door, and when your Mazzini approached he made some kind of sign and then I heard him mention the Carbonari.'

'What is that?' asked Gabriella.

'It's a sort of secret society in Italy – well, it did the trick. He calmed down and, you'll not believe this, he started to cry. To cry! Now we're practically ordered to go to school and we've all been given another blanket – not new, but quite thick and warm. Perhaps you could come back.'

Gabriella heard the wistful note in her brother's voice and she touched his hand. 'I miss you all already, and Pepe of course,' she said, waiting for her brother's usual impatient snort. But it did not come, and instead he coloured and looked away. Then he reached into his pocket and, still avoiding her eyes, he thrust a fine embroidered handkerchief into her hand.

'Oh Nico,' she scolded, 'you've been picking pockets? Why, there's an initial. Is it a P? P for Pepe?' she asked with a smile.

'That was just luck,' Nico mumbled awkwardly. 'There is something in it . . . You mustn't cry, Lark, because . . . he is at peace.'

Gabriella's expression became grave as she unfolded the linen. 'Pepe,' she whispered as her fingers touched the dark ball of fur inside.

'His neck broke . . . he was trying to rescue you – perhaps I shouldn't have brought it.'

Gabriella's fingers closed tight around the soft dark fur and tears welled up inside her as she thought of the faithful bear. Then, as Nico put a comforting arm around her, she carefully knotted the handkerchief around the fur.

'Thank you, Nico, I'll keep it for ever – it will remind me always to be brave; and one day it will remind us of Blackfriars,' she said, taking her brother's hand between her own rough ones. 'We are going to get away from Blackfriars,

24

Nico . . . No, don't laugh,' she urged, tightening her hold on him. 'I just know it!'

For a whole week, Gabriella was made to rest in bed by Giuseppe Mazzini's kindly landlady, after which she was allowed downstairs to sit quietly in a chair by the kitchen fire. Sometimes, when he could spare time, her new protector invited her to his room where, with his pet canaries whirring yellow sunshine around them, he played his guitar and sang to her. Such times Gabriella loved, for the music which came from far beyond the shores of England seemed to stir some half-forgotten happy memory of warmth and colour.

During the first days of her stay, Gabriella had assumed that Signor Mazzini must have quite a lot of money, for in comparison to where she and the boys lived, his lodgings were very grand. But the bustling landlady, who was herself married to an exile from Italy, soon acquainted her with the truth.

'Oh no, child,' she commented one morning, when showing Gabriella how to darn the heel of a sock. 'Mr Mazzini is grand in the sense of being a fine person, but often I know the poor man can hardly find the money for my rent . . . he sometimes takes things to the pawn shop,' she whispered, nodding in a secretive way to indicate a confidence.

'But how does he manage to run the school?' asked Gabriella. 'When I was there he brought a huge basket of apples for the pupils.'

'That sounds like our Mr Mazzini,' sighed the good woman. 'Always giving and then having nothing himself; although things are not as bad for him now. He writes for the journals, you know, and he has many generous friends who have helped to start the school. They hold bazaars and famous people have given concerts to raise funds. He comes from a good family in Genoa, but dare not return there: he is under the sentence of death for planning a rebellion against the government. Just see the state of his cuffs, dear: if it weren't for his mother sending him things, why he'd walk round in rags.'

'Just like me,' smiled Gabriella.

'Not for long – I believe Mr Mazzini is bringing back

something from his friend Mrs Carlyle. That sounds like him coming in now,' she smiled. 'Perhaps he will have it with him.'

Filled with excitement, Gabriella ran from the room and almost collided with Giuseppe Mazzini as he entered the small hallway.

'There you are, young lady,' he said, his face beaming with pleasure. 'I was just coming to find you, I have this parcel for you. Let's go in and see my little birds. Whilst I feed them, you shall unwrap your present. Come in, come in!' he cried, as excited as she.

Fingers trembling with anticipation, Gabriella took the brown paper parcel offered to her and, as the slim bearded man walked towards the canaries' cage, she began to undo the paper. Inside was a brown dress, grander than anything she could ever have imagined wearing, and trimmed with velvet! For a moment Gabriella stared down, so overcome that she could hardly speak, and though she knew this was hers, she still had to ask the question. 'Is this really for me, Signore?'

'Yes,' said Giuseppe Mazzini with a smile. 'My friend Mrs Carlyle says it is a little heavy for summer, but she will soon send you something for hot days. I think she promised a bonnet and cape too.'

'Oh, it is too much!' said Gabriella, shaking her head in disbelief at so much kindness from a stranger.

'And now for my gift,' the exile said, shooing away one of the little birds which was trying to land on his head. 'They have no respect,' he laughed, brushing his hand over the large dome of his forehead. 'Or perhaps they want your stick of candy.'

'Oh, Signore, you should not have, not when you are so . . .'

'So poor!' smiled Mazzini, finishing off her words as she blushed with embarrassment. 'Well, not today, Gabriella, for I have just received payment from a review for one of my essays, so we shall share this stick of candy together as a symbol of our change of fortune.'

★   ★   ★

26

As the days passed, no mention was made of her leaving. The Madre, as Signor Mazzini called his landlady, began to give Gabriella housework to do. She usually finished by six o'clock in the evening, after which she was given a good bowl of stew or such. It was with the warm comforting feeling of the landlady's cooking inside her that Gabriella set out one evening to resume her lessons at Signor Mazzini's school. Just like the first time she had come, Leather Lane was alive with boys, but this night the sight of their tired pale faces filled her with guilt, for she knew they had empty bellies.

'I should have brought something for Nico,' she whispered under her breath, cursing her thoughtlessness, for she had been so excited at the thought of seeing everyone and showing them her dress that she had not remembered the hunger pangs which only two weeks ago she had known all too well. 'How easy it is to forget,' she murmured as she entered the house. Yet, looking at the number of boys milling around, Gabriella knew the gesture would have been hopeless, for generous Nico would have shared it with all of them: how could one do otherwise? Gabriella bit her lip at the enormity of the problem.

A shout from the open door of the classroom diverted her attention. It was Luigi, one of Menotti's younger boys.

'Why look at the Lark!' he squealed, loudly enough for everyone to hear. 'Just see how she's gone up in the world.'

Gabriella giggled as the thin urchin swept off his cap and bowed, and in return she dropped him a low curtsy as she entered the room. Still laughing as the whoops and cheers broke out from her old companions, Gabriella glanced up to see if Nico had come; he had, but he was not joining in with the fun. Instead there was something fearful about the surprised expression on his face.

'I'm glad you've started to come here,' she said, sitting down on a stool next to his. 'What do you think of my dress, isn't it fine?'

'For something from a Dolly shop, I suppose it's not bad,' he commented with an indifferent shrug.

Gabriella looked at the broad, handsome face of her brother

27

and she knew that he was being deliberately difficult and hurtful.

'You know Signor Mazzini is poor, he couldn't afford to buy anything like this, even from a second-hand shop. This came,' she said, lovingly touching her brown dress, 'from an English lady, Mrs Carlyle, who had one of her own dresses cut down for me. I thought you would be happy for me,' she said, reaching for his hand. As if she were attempting to burn him, Nico snatched his hand away and averted his head. Nonplussed at this reaction, all the joy Gabriella had felt when setting out drained away, and her eyes filled with tears. As if sensing them, her brother spoke, though he still did not look towards her.

'I'm sorry,' he said gruffly. 'I am glad for you, it suits you fine . . . it's just that you seem to be moving away from me. When are you coming back?' he asked, looking sharply at her; the brown of his eyes jealous and possessive between the thick fringing of his lashes.

Filled with dismay at the thought that they might grow apart, yet not seeing how it was possible to return to Menotti's, Gabriella groped for an answer.

'We'll find a way, Nico. I know we will,' she whispered uncertainly.

But Nico scarcely seemed to be listening, and the brisk entrance of their teacher put paid to further discussion.

'Now my children,' said Mazzini. 'Last night you had a geography lesson. Once again there is a drawing of the peninsula of Italy on the board but, as you see, I have used coloured chalks to show where the different states and kingdoms are. Now, I want to tell you about your inheritance – does anyone know what that word means? An inheritance,' he continued, when no one answered, 'is when someone dies and leaves you something. You have all been left something – no, I don't mean money.' He smiled at the immediate buzz of excitement that went around the room. 'It's more precious than that, it is something that can never be taken away or stolen; it is the history of your people, the glorious past.'

Like a master weaver working with golden threads, Giuseppe

Mazzini began to weave the heroic deeds of ancient Romans into the grey fabric of their lives, transporting them far away from Hatton Garden to a land of artists, poets, and warriors.

'And to think London was part of our Empire!' laughed one of the boys as they all piled out on to the street after the lesson was over. 'Just wait 'til the next cockney boy cheeks me.'

'What'll you say, Luigi?'

'Help!' joked someone else, which made everyone laugh. With a smile Gabriella turned to speak to her brother, but he had slipped away. For the first time she appreciated how he must have felt during the last two weeks. How could she have been so bound up with her new life as to forget her brother? He had saved her, yet he was sleeping on a straw-filled sack still, scratching for pennies whilst she enjoyed comfort, warmth and security. They had never been parted before: the thought of a future without Nico terrified her. Gabriella looked towards Blackfriars and wondered if she dared go to him, but the fear of what Paolo Menotti might do again made her hesitate, and then Signor Mazzini had appeared and was taking her arm to walk back to Chelsea.

During the next few days, Gabriella waited for the right opportunity to speak to Signor Mazzini about Nico coming to share the attic room with her. And when she did, although her urgent pleas met with sympathy, her benefactor shook his head sadly and said the landlady would never allow it.

'But I will speak with my English friends,' he said, giving her a kindly pat on the head. 'And we will see if we can find him an apprenticeship.'

'And how can I repay you, Signore?' asked Gabriella anxiously.

'Time enough for that,' smiled Giuseppe Mazzini. 'You can help me make sure the school and our pupils look sparkling clean for our visitors next week. Madame Grisi and Mario have raised a considerable amount of money for the school, and I hope they will give another benefit concert on our behalf.'

'Madame Grisi! You mean Madame Grisi the famous singer?' gasped Gabriella in disbelief.

'Why yes,' laughed Giuseppe Mazzini.

'She and Mario are coming to our school – and I will see them?'

'Yes,' replied the exile, astonished by the blaze of joy on the winsome young face. 'And if you would like to, it shall be you who presents the bouquet.'

# Chapter Two

The intended visit of the famous tenor and soprano had filled everyone with excitement. On the day itself, Gabriella had risen early to give a final polish and scrub to everything in the school. Then she had returned to Chelsea to help bake small cakes which were to be offered to the visitors. Then, at last, came the time for her to pack the refreshments into a large basket and set forth.

'If only my hair were a little longer,' she sighed, tying on the bonnet which, true to her promise, Signor Mazzini's friend, Mrs Carlyle, had provided her with.

'Don't you fret about that,' smiled the Madre, adjusting the bow under the girl's chin. 'It will soon grow, and you look very pretty in blue. Now, off you go, and don't let any of them boys eat my baking until the visitors have had their chance!'

As if royalty were expected, the street outside the school was thronged with people: husbands and wives and their children from the small Italian community. Amongst them, Gabriella spotted the large grey head of Paolo Menotti. For a moment her heart raced with fear; but he did not see her as she scurried past, nor did his sallow-faced wife.

Inside the school, the monitors for the evening were handing out the slates and, in the first classroom, Mr Toynbee, one of Signor Mazzini's friends who also taught them, had started to write on the blackboard. But though all was in readiness, there was one pupil missing, and that was her own brother. It couldn't be work that had delayed him, for the others were here and Menotti and his wife were outside. The sound of running feet made her sigh with relief, until she realized that they were too light for Nico's.

'Luigi, have you seen Nico?' she asked as the boy rushed past.

'Gone off with Angelo.'

Outside on the street, the cheers greeting the two Italian opera stars drowned the sound of Gabriella's cry of fury. Then she too was caught up in the excitement as the famous prima donna swept into the school.

'Oh, how elegant she is,' breathed a member of the Ladies' Committee who had come to stand beside Gabriella. 'Go along, my dear,' she said. 'Go and welcome her to the school, just as Signor Mazzini told you.'

Gabriella moved awkwardly forward, thinking that this was the most terrifying thing she had ever had to do, even though the trio at the door were looking towards her with friendly, encouraging smiles.

'Welcome to our school, Signor Mario, Signora Grisi,' she stammered. 'If you would care to come this way,' she added, and then, not stopping to find out if they would, Gabriella fled to the first classroom. There, as instructed, she waited on one side while the celebrated guests moved amongst the pupils and talked to them about their work at the school. Many of the boys she saw were, like herself, quite overcome and could hardly utter a word in response, but no shyness could hide the pride which everyone felt to be spoken to by such grand people, nor the pleasure they all felt in seeing their teacher beaming with happiness.

At the end of the tour, the Ladies' Committee, together with the friends who taught at the school, took refreshments with the singers. Her own part, to hand out the little delicacies which the committee and she herself had brought, had seemed simple enough to Gabriella. However, when she approached each animated circle, no one seemed to be aware of her presence. She stood patiently, holding her tray, but she didn't like to interrupt them, so she passed the time by nibbling the snacks herself and listening wide-eyed to these clever, cultivated people. Everyone seemed to be talking about opera and no one about the school, except for their teacher, Mr Joseph Toynbee, who stood behind her. Gabriella turned around and, to make sure he noticed the treats, thrust her tray vigorously between him and Signor Mario to whom he was talking.

'Gracious!' exclaimed the famous tenor, as the glass in his hand tilted, spilling some drops of sherry on to his coat.

'Will you try one, Signor?' said Gabriella enthusiastically, not noticing what she had done. 'I made some of these myself.'

The eyes which were looking up at him were of the deepest blue: the irritated expression slid from Mario's face as he reached down and took one of the proffered morsels.

'Mmn, exquisite,' he said, thinking as he swallowed that the eyes were neither the deep blue of the ocean nor of the cornflower, they were more like the dark blue of the pansy and violet. 'Adorable,' he murmured.

Beside Gabriella, who was watching spellbound the plump fingers take up the contents of her tray at such a fast rate, Joseph Toynbee coughed nervously.

'Gabriella is our only girl pupil,' he said stiffly. 'She is eager to learn to read music.'

'Indeed,' said the opera singer, his eyes now swiftly taking in Gabriella as a whole. What he saw made him burst into laughter as he remembered the effect the eyes had had upon him moments before, for she had batons for arms, no breasts and was, in effect, a child.

'Are you laughing at me, Signore?' asked Gabriella, turning pink with embarrassment.

'No, my little colt, I was laughing at foolish fancies. So, you want to learn to read music? Why is that?'

'It is the most beautiful thing in life and no matter how sad I am or how ugly things are, well . . . when I sing I escape. That's why they nicknamed me the Lark,' she finished breathlessly.

'Not the Nightingale?' joked Mr Toynbee.

Gabriella gave the teacher a swift smile, then her face grew serious and her eyes came alive with an inner energy that held the attention of her listeners.

'I want to be able to make music like they do at the Opera House, like you do and like your wife does . . . she has such a voice!'

'You have heard my Giulia?' Mario asked in amazement.

'Well, not this season, because of her confinement,' said Gabriella matter-of-factly.

'But how?' asked both men at once, their features registering their astonishment.

Gabriella gave an impish smile.

'Well, if you promise not to tell, I sneak in at the stage door and sit in one of the laundry baskets.'

'So, you have never been in the theatre itself?' As Gabriella shook her head, the Italian slipped his hand into his pocket and withdrew a thin leather case. 'Here, take my card, show it to the doorkeeper and he will let you look around. And perhaps in a few years' time' – Mario murmured with an expression which produced another disapproving cough from Mr Toynbee – 'perhaps I'll let you have a seat in my box.'

'Perhaps,' said Gabriella thoughtfully, responding with great daring, 'perhaps, Signor Mario, I may have my own one day.'

The excitement of the evening had driven thoughts of Nico to the back of Gabriella's mind, but the next day, after her tasks were done, she went to speak with him at his pitch at Piccadilly. As usual, a small group of children were grouped around him, for he had taught the monkey he worked with to perform acrobatics on top of the organ as he turned its handle. On seeing Gabriella, the rakish smile which had been directed towards the children's young governess disappeared, to be replaced by a scowl.

'What are you doing here?' he asked. 'Shouldn't you be on your way to school?'

Gabriella ignored the sarcasm in her brother's voice and put out her arm for Jacko, the monkey, to jump on to. 'Why didn't you come last night?'

'I had better things to do.'

'With Angelo!'

'As it happens, yes.'

'Stealing?' she asked fiercely.

'Why not, isn't that what the Romans did? They took what they wanted, and so will I,' he snapped, his brown eyes hard and defiant as they looked past her. 'And I don't need schooling for that.'

'But you were doing so well, you're very clever at arithmetic. Signor Mazzini told you so, I heard him.'

Nico stopped turning the handle of the barrel-organ and looked directly at her, as if she were mad. 'I don't want to end up on some high chair looking at ledgers all day – I want adventure, excitement. Do you really want to wear other people's clothes all your life, Lark?' he said, his tone softening as he took the monkey from her. 'Angelo and I have just found an outlet in the carriage business: a girl would be the ideal lure and look-out. Won't you come in with us? It'll be fun, and we could all end up rich!'

'Or in prison,' she said. 'Oh Nico, isn't there some other way? There must be something else that we can do together. I couldn't bear it if you were sent away on a convict ship, or . . .'

'Ended up dancing on the end of a rope!' he laughed, his brown eyes sparkling with merriment. 'All this learning is making you lose your nerve. Don't forget you are a Bloodbrother of Blackfriars – you can't ever be a grand lady while you've got this,' he grinned, holding up his wrist on which was a small scar in the shape of a cross. 'Think it over, Lark. Have I ever failed you?'

With a cheery wave, Nico walked on, whistling as he went. Gabriella followed his progress with uneasy eyes. It was hard to resist his appeal: they had always done everything together, and she had never questioned his judgement, for he was quick witted and possessed a reckless kind of luck. As his lanky figure disappeared around a corner, she felt lonely once more, knowing that they would not be curling up next to each other as they had always done, ever since she could remember. And part of her misery was the realization that her reluctance to join with him and Angelo went much deeper than a disapproval of their plans. She had her own desires, her own aspirations which every day seemed to press more insistently on her consciousness: she knew they would laugh at her, whereas Signor Mazzini had not.

They had been walking back to Chelsea the night before when Gabriella, brimming with the excitement of the evening, had tentatively outlined her dream to him.

'If that is what your heart is set on, Gabriella, then you will find a way,' he had said, his voice grave and filled with encouragement. 'I will carry my own hopes to the grave. No matter how bleak things have been for me – even during my imprisonment, when my dear friend Jacopo Ruffini committed suicide in prison lest he betray his companions under torture – I have never surrendered that dream: that one day Italy will be one nation under a Republic. And to that end I will bend all my energies, make any sacrifice. And so will you if you want your dream fiercely enough. Your dream too can be one which, in its own way, may serve Italy one day. So we must find a benefactor for you, my child, someone who will pay for you to go to a good school for young ladies.'

Whilst a future benefit concert was envisaged to help pay the running expenses of the school, the Ladies' Committee were planning a bazaar in order to finance the customary Anniversary Supper to be held in November.

'They'll need more than one bazaar with all those mouths to feed,' commented Mazzini's landlady, when Gabriella brought home some fine linen for the making of pocket handkerchiefs. 'Why, there are nearly two hundred pupils Signor Mazzini says . . . and what do the good ladies expect me to do with all this cloth?'

'Well, they asked if you would cut out squares, and hem them, and then embroider something tasteful in the corner: I told them you're very clever with a needle,' smiled Gabriella.

'Did you now!' exclaimed the grey-haired matron fiercely, whilst her eyes twinkled with laughter. 'Well, I'm sure I don't know what they mean by tasteful, so you'd best go and look what they are selling in the smart shops. Then you can buy the same silks for me to work with.'

To be given a free morning to go and look at pocket hand-kerchiefs was a great treat, for she had never been admitted into any of the grand stores before. Now, though, with a clean face and a blue dress and bonnet, she felt confident enough to face the sniffiest of those superior ladies who assisted in the drapery stores.

It was the perfect summer day, with only the tiniest of fluffy clouds in the blue sky. In the park, the boys were hitting their hoops and chasing birds and each other, and, when she stopped to admire a baby, its nanny did not chase her away but smiled and allowed her to hold its tiny fingers.

'I'm not a dirty creature any more,' Gabriella thought to herself as she headed proudly towards Number 10 Piccadilly.

Everything which was displayed and laid out before her on the gleaming polished wood counter, it seemed, had come from Paris.

'The Rue Chaussée d'Antin decreed that the designs should be worn to the front and to the left,' directed the soberly dressed assistant, eyeing with distaste the shabby bag which Gabriella had placed upon the counter. 'Naturally they are rather expensive.'

'Yes, I'm sure they must be,' murmured Gabriella wonder-ing, now that she had seen everything, how to escape from the snowy pile of embroidery and the intimidating assistant. She pursed her lips, as if considering which one of the pocket handkerchiefs to purchase and, as she stood there, her brother's face flashed into her mind. She knew that if he were looking at her through the window, he would be bent double with laughter at her predicament. Almost hearing its mockery, she took a deep breath and stared into the expectant eyes the other side of the counter. 'They are not quite what I want. They are lovely,' she added hastily, 'but I am looking for something very special for Signor Mazzini. Thank you for showing them to me. Please would you direct me to where the embroidery silks are sold?'

Some time later, after much care had gone into the selection of the shades necessary to reproduce the bunches of grapes and laurel wreath designs, Gabriella emerged out of Swan and Edgar, bubbling inside with laughter as she recalled the outraged expression on the assistant's face when she had asked to look at the embroidery silks. 'I expect these grand ladies do it all the time,' she giggled, beating a hasty retreat.

Her route was taking her past Her Majesty's Theatre, and she stopped to look at the entrance through which royalty and all the important people entered to hear Italians sing. In there, Gabriella thought, it didn't matter about being different, not being English. In there Italians were not bullied and despised as they were in the backstreets; in there they were adored for making beautiful music.

'I want to be part of it!' she announced fiercely, clutching her parcel tightly against her thin chest as she looked up at the columns of the façade. The card which Signor Mario had given her was in her room at York Buildings, but she made her way to the stage entrance anyway and, after hovering for a moment, strode purposefully through the open door.

'Oh hello,' she said, giving the doorman her widest smile. 'Signor Mario and Signora Grisi came to visit our school the other evening and Signor Mario said you would let me look at the theatre. He gave me his card, but I have forgotten to bring it,' she added, with another smile.

Benjamin Lumley, in his first year as director of Her Majesty's Theatre, was waiting for the buffo bass, Luigi Lablache, to arrive. The last few months had been a nerve-racking time: whilst the pre-Easter season had gone so well, especially the production of *Giselle*, which had quite captivated the audiences, he had afterwards been beset by the kind of problems his predecessor, Laporte, had had to contend with. Madame Persiani and Carlo Guasco had pleaded illness, then, even more exasperatingly, Mario had refused to sing Pollione opposite anyone other than Giulia Grisi, who was unavailable because of her confinement.

Lumley shook his head and sat down a moment in the royal box as he thought about the very trying temperament of some singers. As he pulled at his bushy side-locks in vexation, he suddenly noticed a figure moving slowly into the centre of the stage below. It was a girl, of no more than twelve or thirteen years of age – no doubt she was a maid sent to retrieve something, and curiosity had brought her out of the wings. He half-rose to tell her to leave but, as her attention lifted to the box where he sat, the impact of her face, the yearning expression in the large, magnificent dark eyes made him pull swiftly back into the shadows. Let her make-believe for a while, he smiled, as the gamine curtsied to her invisible audience.

Gabriella had promised the doorman that she would not be long, but once on the stage, looking out at a silent void that seemed expectant and waiting, she forgot everything. She held out her skirt and began slowly to dance as she surveyed the rows of empty boxes, imagining them filled with smiling, applauding people. After a moment she forgot everything, and spun and whirled around until she was dizzy and breathless; still, as she regained her breath, Gabriella tiptoed quietly to the front of the stage and sang a note. It sounded terribly loud, but no one appeared, so she sang another, relishing the special way her voice sounded here and the excitement of hearing the note shimmer and hang in the air. With a feeling of joy such as she had never known before, she began to sing one of the tunes she especially liked on one of the boys' barrel-organs: she had no words for it, but that didn't matter. Suddenly a deep voice, as loud as an organ in a church, began to sing with her and, as she whirled around, from out of the wings appeared a large, friendly looking man who was gesturing enthusiastically for her to continue.

'*Pace, pace, o vita mia!*' he boomed. Gabriella shook her head in delight, instantly liking this impressive figure, whose plump rosy face looked exactly like the cherubim on the church ceiling. So, singing her wordless version unreservedly, she joined in until, near the end of the pretty tune, unbelievably, her partner seized hold of her hands and waltzed her around to the front of the stage.

'Did you enjoy that?' the stranger beamed, dabbing his

forehead with a handkerchief after they had come to a halt. Quite overcome by such outrageous behaviour in an adult, Gabriella could only look with adoration at this whirlwind of fun and laughter. 'I shouldn't behave so at my age,' he continued, 'but spring always makes me want to kick up my heels.'

'But it is summer, sir,' said Gabriella shyly.

'Outside, yes,' agreed the man with a fatherly smile. 'But you, young lady, are a small green bud of talent that, given the right gardener, should flower one summer into something quite beautiful. Can you be the reason why our director asked me to come here this morning?' he laughed, as hurrying footsteps sounded from the back of the theatre. 'You are starting your prima donnas young, Mr Lumley!' Gabriella's partner boomed to the bearded man approaching the stage.

From that moment on, Gabriella could hardly believe what was happening. The director of the theatre was not at all cross with her, but wanted to know who her parents were and where she lived. And upon learning her circumstances, he had requested that she call the next day with Signor Mazzini to discuss her future. Her future . . . Once outside the theatre she repeated the golden words over and over, walking for a few minutes in a complete daze, only remembering that moment when the man had stepped out of the wings and had sung with her. She, Gabriella, had sung with Luigi Lablache, the great bass, the toast of London. Gabriella stopped and, as if opening her eyes, saw that she was standing near to the spot where, earlier in the year, she had watched Queen Victoria drive to the Opera. And now she herself had sung with the man who had taught Queen Victoria how to sing! The ball of excitement erupted in Gabriella and, to the astonishment of passers-by she let out a great big whoop, then ran as if being chased by a hundred devils towards the British Museum, to wait for her guardian angel to emerge from the Reading Room.

'The wiser choice would be Paris, its fortunes are stronger than Milan's at the moment.'

There was a silence in Benjamin Lumley's office as Giuseppe

Mazzini considered the advice. Gabriella, who had been sitting quietly throughout the discussion, felt his eyes turn towards her.

'Well, Gabriella?'

'I am Italian,' she said simply, and was glad to see his eyes light up at her words.

From behind his large mahogany desk, the director of Her Majesty's Theatre chuckled. 'So, you would prefer to go to Milan? Well, in many ways that is the better choice for you. Your natural coach lives in Lombardy.' He turned back to Mazzini. 'I'll say no more about it for now, until you have received a reply from your proposed sponsor for Gabriella. And I from the principal of the Milan Conservatorio di Musica, to whom I shall write this very day.' He smiled at Gabriella. 'Perhaps your destiny lies in your native land.'

'There lies the answer for all Italians,' said Giuseppe Mazzini, rising from his seat.

News of her good fortune swiftly passed around the pupils at the school, and everyone was thrilled for her. Gabriella had not wanted Nico to hear it from anyone else but herself; but despite calling in at his various pitches she had not found him. Finally she had asked one of Menotti's boys whether he had been given a different area to cover, and was told he had left after quarrelling with the master.

'Didn't you know?' asked the lively Luigi in surprise.

'No, he never told me. Do you know where he is living?' she asked, shocked and hurt.

Luigi shrugged, wiping his slate clean with his coat sleeve. 'Never asked him.'

'Well, keep a look-out for him, can you, and tell him I need to see him and . . . don't tell him anything, will you?'

'All right,' grinned the boy. 'Anyway, you might be going nowhere, Gabriella. They might not want you in Milan. That's where the Austrians are, Signor Mazzini said. Who'd want to go there!'

Gabriella was well used to the boys' teasing. Affecting a disdainful air, she bent over her work again: she knew she had

41

to be able to read and write as well as sing for the Conservatorio of Milan to be willing to consider her as a pupil.

In the weeks which went by whilst she waited to hear from Mr Lumley and her teacher, Gabriella moved constantly between hope and dread. There was much to occupy her, however, for besides her lessons and housework there were preparations, first for the bazaar and then for the Anniversary Supper.

One morning, Signor Mazzini received two letters. She was summoned to his study and, even before he spoke, she knew by the delighted expression on his face that it was good news.

'You have a patron, Gabriella! And you have one who was prepared to use her influence with the Conservatorio on your behalf. However, I am pleased to say that Mr Lumley and Signor Lablache's recommendations were sufficient. Milano's Conservatorio di Musica is willing to accept you as a pupil.'

'Oh, I can't believe it!' cried Gabriella, her eyes wide with delight. 'You mean they don't even want to hear me sing first?'

'Well, they would have done, had the recommendations come from anyone else but the director of London's Italian Opera company and Luigi Lablache. They will have been influenced too, of course, by the assurance that your studies would be paid for.'

'But Mr Lumley didn't know that.'

Mazzini smiled and tapped the letter in his hand. 'I knew before I wrote that Christina Belgiojoso would not refuse you. Where there is an Italian in need, the Princess never stints her time or money. She is a great patriot, because of which she must live in exile in Paris, away from her home in Lombardy. Her pen never ceases to support the cause of nationalism and to speak against tyranny and injustice in our land.'

The meal in November was a simple affair of potatoes and gravy, but the finest roast beef or plumpest capon could not have made for a merrier occasion. Like the boys around her, Gabriella knew loneliness, not the friend of the artist or poet, but the desperate terror which surfaces amidst happy throngs on busy streets or in the darkness when all about are sleeping; the bitter envy felt on seeing children caught up within loving arms. But this night, each one of them felt they belonged: the room resounded to the babble of voices and laughter.

'Does he know what we're going to do?' asked the boy sitting next to Gabriella.

'He thinks I'm going to sing, that's all,' she said, turning adoring eyes on the man they regarded more as a father than a teacher. With a nod to the group of boys who were awaiting the sign from her, Gabriella rose and, with the handle of her spoon, hit the table for silence as the four boys slipped unnoticed from the room.

'Signor Mazzini,' she began. 'The boys have chosen me to speak for them. Before you came to us, none of us could read or write: we didn't expect to do such things, and we felt ashamed of not being English. Now we are proud to be your Italian children!'

From the far corner of the room, with his concertina, a boy punctuated Gabriella's last word with a random pleasing chord, and then, as arranged, the door opened and the four boys entered carrying the banner. As a tricolore it barely passed; earlier in the day, the boys had sheepishly confessed they had forgotten to make one, so Gabriella had frightened the wits out of them with threats that if they didn't appear with one that evening, each one of them would have to make a speech instead. It had proved more than enough to send them scurrying off in search of the materials. However, whilst they had come upon a piece of sheeting and some green paint, they had had to resort to a trip to Smithfields for the required band of red; now, what had initially met the desired crimson had dried to a horrid shade of brown. Gabriella looked apprehensively from the makeshift banner towards Giuseppe Mazzini lest the intended noble moment be making him laugh, but it was not and, as the tiny organ-grinder called Giovanni rose and started to read some words which she had copied from one of Mazzini's notebooks, their teacher nodded encouragingly.

'We must teach Mankind not Rights but Duty,' Giovanni

mumbled, his small face shining with pride as he sat down, for he was the slowest reader of all and had practised his piece for days.

'*Viva l'Italia!*' cried everyone together as the banner was handed over.

'*Viva l'Italia,*' responded Mazzini, accepting the tricolore which, beyond the Alps, had once been steeped in other blood.

She had sent messages several times to Nico, for Gabriella knew the boys must see him about the streets, despite the fact they denied knowing where he was. She couldn't understand his cruelty, especially when she would soon be leaving, for whilst the boys were obviously keeping his secret, she expected one of them had passed on news of what was happening to her. So this deliberate rejection must be Nico's way of punishing her. Well, it was working, she thought, crying herself to sleep one night after wondering how she could ever leave without him; even less without saying goodbye.

'I can't go,' she whispered to herself one day late in January, as she saw her landlady arrive back at Chelsea with a battered second-hand trunk for her journey. It was thought that the wild storms of winter had passed, so the booking for the journey to Paris had been made.

'So, you are to break your journey to meet your patron the Princess Belgiojoso,' said Mr Lumley, to whom Gabriella had gone to say goodbye and to thank for his support. 'You are fortunate that Mr Mazzini found you such a powerful patron: she runs a brilliant salon in Paris.'

'Yes, I am very fortunate, Mr Lumley,' said Gabriella, 'and I owe you and Mr Lablache so much. If you had turned me out that day . . .'

'I would never have done that,' smiled Benjamin Lumley fondly. 'Not even if you had sung like a corncrake: your lovely blue eyes had quite melted my heart. Aha, now I have made you blush.' The young director laughed, seeing the pink flush on the smooth olive skin. 'Don't forget,' he continued, as he took her for one last sentimental look at the stage, 'I shall expect

44

a letter once in a while. After all, in a way you are my protégée . . . I only wish I had been in a position to help you financially. Still, work hard and, when you are older, one of the world's greatest sopranos may take you for private coaching. Lablache and I saw a glimpse of something that marks you as Giuditta Pasta's natural pupil. If one day you can match her Norma, Gabriella, I'll put you under contract immediately! Good luck young lady,' Benjamin Lumley said gravely, shaking her hand as if she were the most important of people. 'God go with you! And if you should see my favourite rogue, Lablache, in Paris, tell him London is greyer without him!'

The day before her journey to Dover, Gabriella had become frantic to find her brother. All day she roamed the places where he might be found; then, as evening approached, and despite the fact that she must be in bed soon because of the early start the next morning she walked towards Blackfriars, filled with a certainty that he would be there. He was, just as he had always been, waiting impatiently at the top of their alley.

'You took your time!' he said laconically, though his eyes were intense as he examined her from head to toe.

'I have been searching for you all day, for weeks!' she exclaimed angrily, hardly able to control the emotion she felt on seeing him at last.

'Come on, let's get away from here,' he said, moving off towards the river. As she followed on behind, Gabriella saw how smart her brother was. Gone were the filthy coarse jacket and trousers. In their place were a frock coat and trousers which, though by the largeness of the fit she judged must be second-hand, were worn with the rakish air of a young blade.

'Why didn't you reply to any of my messages? Why did you stay away from me?' Gabriella asked, when at last he stopped at a spot looking down on to the silent, silvery-lilac river. For a moment Nico did not reply as he studied the movements of men further along the wharf who were preparing their barge for departure.

'I didn't want to give you the opportunity to explain,' he

said at last, swinging around to face her. 'I wanted you to know what it would be like if you left, how you will miss me. Did you miss me?' he asked harshly.

'Yes!' she whispered miserably. 'I'm pleased that you are doing well,' she added, not knowing what to say.

'I am. That was another reason why I kept away from you. When I next met you I promised I would have this – see!'

'Why, it's ten pounds!' she exclaimed, peering at the large banknote in the gathering dusk.

'You see, Lark,' said her brother, using her old nickname. 'You need not be poor any more. Surely you were not really going to go away and leave me? Surely not?' he said, his voice suddenly vulnerable in its tenderness.

Tears flooded into Gabriella's eyes as she heard the love, and remembered all the times he had sung and told her stories to make her laugh when she was cold and frightened.

'Oh Nico,' she choked, lifting her arms up to him. Her brother put his arms around her and held her close to him; then she felt his mouth move down on to hers. For a second it was filled with brotherly tenderness, but suddenly the kiss became desperate and hungry and his passion was spilling over and catching her up in the same madness. Horrified, she struggled to push him away as his hands sought her body.

'Stop it! You're my brother!'

'No, I'm not! I have the right . . . You're not my sister, you're Gabriella . . .' He stopped, frightened by his own words.

Uncomprehending, Gabriella reeled back in anguish and astonishment, feeling as though her world was caving in.

'Gabriella who? What are you talking about? You are my brother, you must be, you must be!' she sobbed, feeling she was losing everything.

'Say you'll never leave me,' cried Nico, catching her by the arms and pulling her to him. 'Fate made you mine!'

'What do you mean, Nico? You must tell me who I am,' she shouted desperately.

'Only if you stay, Lark. Only if you promise to stay with me,' Nico rejoined.

Hardly able to think or speak, Gabriella hung on to the one certainty amidst all the confusion. Her fingers dug into the youth's arms as she strove to speak the hurtful words.

'I have to go, don't you understand? I have to make something of myself . . . please come to Milan with me!'

With a cry of anger, Nico thrust her away and looked down at the dark shape of the barge that was moving slowly past them. In less than two steps he had jumped down on to it and he held up his arms to her.

'It's now or never, Lark . . . If you love me, if you want to know who you really are, jump. Jump!'

As though his command had plunged a knife into her heart, Gabriella gave a cry of pain. Yet she remained motionless. Wider and wider the dark space of the Thames stretched between them, its strong current bearing away the youth who was no longer her brother.

# Chapter Three

'Don't be afraid, come closer . . . within the light so that I can see you.'

The silvery voice urged gently but with an imperious note, and reluctantly Gabriella moved out of the shadows towards the tall thick white taper burning beside a black couch on which the Princess Christina Belgiojoso reclined. From her position at the door, Gabriella had thought she had been shown to a funeral parlour: the whole of the salon was hung with black velvet and, until a white hand beckoned, she thought the emaciated figure on the couch might be dead. After hours of travelling over a rough Channel, crossing this strange, star-spangled chamber claimed the last of her courage. Before her the lady in the grey robe pulled herself up into a sitting position, and Gabriella saw that, despite her wraith-like body and waxy pallor, the Princess Belgiojoso was very beautiful. Most prominent and striking were her large black eyes, which were filled with kindly curiosity.

'Please be seated,' she said, gesturing to a small chair which merged as one with the surrounding blackness. 'Welcome, Gabriella, I am most pleased to meet you. I have heard much good about you from dear Giuseppe – have you brought me greetings from Signor Mazzini?'

'Yes, Princess Christina, I have this letter for you,' she said, opening the bag which had been Mazzini's farewell gift.

'Excellent. I shall read it now, so I will not delay you further from your couch. You look exhausted, poor child. Tomorrow will be time enough for us to become better acquainted.'

Gabriella stared in surprise. 'Then I am not to travel onwards tomorrow, your Highness?'

'No, dear child,' replied the Princess, the large rounded pearls at the tips of her ears seeming like twin moons against the star embroidered hangings. 'I have just become a patron, and I intend to show off a pretty protégée. Besides, you cannot possibly leave without seeing something of Paris.'

After the Princess had summoned her maid, Gabriella found herself established swiftly in a bedroom. She was by now so tired that she barely took in her surroundings, or the fact that her trunk had been unpacked. All she was aware of was a warm nightdress laid out for her use, and bedding which the same kind soul had also thought to warm. Soon, with the sheet pulled over her head to hide away from the unknown room, Gabriella's thoughts drifted away from the Princess in her night sky salon to her sad departure from Signor Mazzini, and his parting words. 'You have been given a chance which other poor children will never have and, if you succeed, you will enjoy a liberty and equality which women, rich and poor, do not often experience. Do not let anything divert you from your chosen path.'

And indeed she had not: barely consciously, Gabriella began to cry, unable to contain any longer the guilt and pain of losing Nico. She pressed her face into the pillow to hush the deep sobs that were racking her body. She recalled again the expression of yearning on his rugged, handsome face as the moment of no return for both of them passed, as the barge had moved out into midstream.

'I am so afraid without you,' she murmured, as sleep closed over her troubled heart.

It was not so much the raising of blinds which awoke her the next morning, but a combination of sensations. Stronger than the sudden wink of wintry light and the comforting chink of china, was the rich smell of coffee. It was this which persuaded her to peep over the covers in delighted expectation.

'Good morning, Mademoiselle,' said a young maid whom

Gabriella vaguely recalled from the previous night. 'The Princess thought you might like to have your breakfast in bed – you must still be very tired. Did you sleep well?'

'Yes, thank you,' replied Gabriella shyly, as much in awe of the girl's crisp uniform as the exquisite offerings on the silver tray.

'If there is anything else you require, please ring. The bell-push is just there. No need to hurry.'

The delicate Sèvres ware on the tray was worthy of long perusal, but it was not until she had devoured a whole brioche and downed a cup of coffee that Gabriella felt able to examine both that and her surroundings. Like the salon of the night before, she saw here too a mood had been created: the black velvet had frightened, but here were lemon drapes and walls with a frieze of green leaves bearing oranges and lemons. The whole effect produced such a feeling of warmth and gaiety that when her gaze was carried upward to the ceiling of blue, she almost anticipated a large yellow sun. With a sigh of utmost bliss, Gabriella poured herself more coffee from the silver pot and then, taking up a silver teaspoon, she removed a whole strawberry from the preserve and popped it straight into her mouth. With the tip of her tongue, she touched the plump fruit, waiting in sensual anticipation for the moment of biting. As she flirted with it, her glance wandered over the green carpet towards her trunk: in one gulp the strawberry was lost as she saw with consternation that its lid was raised.

Mindful of the delicate china despite her alarm, Gabriella carefully set down the breakfast tray and scrambled out of bed. Nothing remained inside the trunk but the writings of Giuseppe Mazzini, now no longer concealed amongst her clothing but neatly stacked in a corner and visible for all to see. Gabriella sank back on to her heels, remembering the shock on her teacher's face when she had confessed to taking the papers.

'But dear child,' he had gasped, the high dome of his forehead wrinkling in anxiety. 'You don't know what you are doing, the danger you are putting yourself in. I cannot allow it, you must open your trunk and take them out.'

'There is no time,' she had laughed. 'I have never disobeyed you before, Signore, but I have to do this for you. It's the only way I have to thank you for everything . . . I know how important it is to you for your essays and pamphlets to reach Italy. So please, tell me to whom I should deliver them in Milan?'

Still he had hesitated, but with the hackney coachman becoming impatient outside, he had given the name and address of one of his disciples.

And now, even before setting foot on Italian soil, they had been discovered. Was the maid to be trusted? The Princess, she had been told, was watched by Austrian spies who sent their reports on her liberal activities to the governor of Lombardy-Venetia, and to Prince Metternich in Vienna. Were there spies within her household, and had Gabriella endangered her by bringing Mazzini's contributions to the journals? And if this maid were in the pay of the Habsburgs, might she not send word ahead of what Gabriella was carrying? With a shudder Gabriella pictured her arrival in Milan and the waiting Austrian soldiers.

'I took the liberty of having your cape cleaned, Mademoiselle,' the maid's voice said from behind Gabriella. With a guilty start, as though caught red-handed in some crime, she sprang up. 'People can be so careless on sea voyages,' continued the servant. 'It happened to me when we were sailing from Leghorn to Marseille. I made the mistake of standing next to someone with a weak stomach, though it's hard to tell beforehand,' she said with a cheerful grin over her shoulder as she shut the wardrobe door. 'And if you do not mind my saying so, Signorina, the papers you are carrying should be concealed with a little more cunning. Perhaps you'd like me to deal with it before you leave?'

'Why yes, thank you,' said Gabriella, relief flooding over her to discover an ally and not a spy. 'I've never stayed anywhere so splendid ever,' she confessed. 'I hope I will not make any blunders.'

'You must not worry about anything, Signorina. Just enjoy your stay, and I and the rest of the household staff will smooth away anything which might make you feel ill at ease. Our Princess is very unusual. She attracts all kinds of people to her salon. She has boundless energy; she writes for hours, day after day, yet still finds time to give lessons to the poor girls of Paris. You are very fortunate to have her as your patron. Now, if you will permit, I will help you with your toilette, after which the Princess will receive you in her boudoir.'

With memories of the funereal salon, Gabriella had hoped Christina Belgiojoso's boudoir would be ordinary, but such expectation was disappointed when she saw a huge white-turbanned Negro standing guard outside the door. Her immediate reaction was to turn back, for he looked very fierce and unfriendly, but the giant had already spotted her and was opening one of the large carved doors.

As day provides contrast with night, so did the boudoir to the salon: where there had been black, there was white; where soft velvet, silk; the whole room shimmered and gleamed with reflections from crystal and silver, mirroring the drifting clouds of white silk. There was no daylight in the chamber, but a blaze of light like that surrounding Christ's ascent into Heaven.

Between herself and the Princess, who was seated before a writing desk of a silvery metal, there stretched a virgin snow of white carpet. Should she remove her heavy shoes, she wondered – but to expose darned stockings! Gabriella moved forward with the lightest of steps.

'I hope you are comfortable in your room?' said the Princess, laying down her pen.

'Oh yes, thank you,' she replied, feeling conspicuous in the bleak landscape in her brightly coloured dress. 'When I awoke I thought the sun might be shining, for the oranges and lemons are so bright; then I looked through the window!' she said, giving a mock shiver.

The thin, delicate lips of the Princess Belgiojoso lifted into a smile. 'I wanted a room which reminded me of Italy. On grey Parisian days, I sometimes go in there to feel touched by the sun. It perhaps sounds fanciful, but it does work. Now Gabriella, I understand from Signor Mazzini that you were quite young when you arrived in England, and that apart from a brother, you have little remembrance of your parents or background, other than that your home was in Lombardy.'

'Yes, Princess Christina,' Gabriella replied, beginning to feel awkward and ill at ease, not only about Nico's recent revelation, but because the scrutiny of the black eyes had become rather critical.

'Do you usually dress your hair so?'

'No, Madame,' she flushed, touching the smooth bandeau which the maid had contrived. 'Your maid suggested I might like something a little more fashionable – it was very kind of her to trouble so.'

'But that is not at all what I want you to look like,' exclaimed the Princess. 'I intend to show off a young protégée, not a child apeing fashion. Go and tell Lucia to alter it immediately, after which we shall take a drive along the Champs-Elysées. Would you enjoy that?'

'Oh yes,' replied Gabriella, excitement sweeping aside her apprehension at facing the maid for the return of her plaits.

Before she could see the sights of Paris, Gabriella was taken first by her patron to a gown shop. 'I may wish to introduce you to some of my friends,' explained the Princess. 'And if I do, then you must look very special.'

In the hushed interior of her salon, Madame brought out her mannequins dressed in the latest Pompadour design, and Gabriella's heart filled with longing at the sight of the beautiful divided skirts. But as with her ability to create a mood in the rooms of her luxurious home, the Princess had definite ideas of the impression she wished her protégée to impart. Imperiously she waved away a further tempting array.

'Something young, in tune with spring!'

'But, your Highness,' declared the Parisienne, 'these are what will be worn and, if I may say so, there are none lovelier in Paris!'

'Not appropriate!' said the patrician firmly.

After this, Madame made no further attempt to seduce, and produced instead a simple gown of white organdie. With a glance of regret at the forbidden 'Pompadours' as she was led

53

through into a dressing-room, Gabriella submitted to being stripped, *like a doll*, suffering the added indignity of Madame's exclamations of disdain as her undergarments were thrown to the ground. With no one but herself the least embarrassed by her nakedness, soon the light brief touch of the two young apprentices was replaced by the steely grip of a corset, and Gabriella began to realize that fashion started several layers below a gown. She was thrilled with the corset, and with the long pants which, unlike the ones she had seen in England, were closed at her ankles with a little band. I could run and climb in these, she thought, trying not to laugh as she caught Madame's eye.

'Why, it's so light,' she murmured, touching with surprise the soft material of the petticoat as it was slipped over her head.

'*Tissu crinolise!*' Madame nodded, her shrewd eyes gleaming. 'It is new, the best, yes?'

Gabriella nodded and smiled. Ignorant though she was about the world of high fashion, she realized this flimsy garment, which could retain its shape as well as her old, cumbersome petticoat, and provide a base for a dress, was very special indeed.

'It's horse hair, the cashmere is padded with horse hair!' explained the Parisienne gleefully. Then, with a motion of her hand, she gestured for the apprentices to bring forward the dress.

As the white organdie slid over Gabriella's shoulders, she understood what her patron was trying to achieve: compared to the earlier gowns, the line was simple, with no attempt at coquetry. It had caught that brief moment between childhood and womanhood, that wistful threshold of youth that no paintpot or artifice could ever recapture.

'Ah, to be able to start again,' murmured Madame, her hard black eyes softening a little.

'Oh, it's wonderful,' Gabriella breathed, as the Frenchwoman circled around her and here and there adjusted the fall of the skirt. Then, with a snap of her fingers, a long scarf in blush pink was hurried to her.

54

'This!' explained Madame, 'is called *une écharpe à la Monte-span*. And to complete your ensemble, a bonnet. Have you ever seen anything quite so pretty?'

'Never,' said Gabriella, nearly swooning with pleasure as a transparent gimp bonnet lined with rose pink was placed on her head.

'There! What do you think, your Highness? Does this meet with your approval?'

Christina Belgiojoso looked at the transformation wrought by the skilled couturier. Mazzini's waif was lovely. When she was older – even without good birth – it would be easy enough to arrange an advantageous marriage with a man of the merchant class. Not that she would wish the girl to take such a course: her own marriage had been a sad disappointment, brightened only in the last five years by the little daughter she had borne. No, this girl, like herself, would do better to find fulfilment through her talent.

'You look charming, Gabriella,' she said, 'though I do not think the bonnet and scarf are necessary . . . Oh, very well, as a special treat for your first day in Paris,' the Princess relented, seeing the look of disappointment on the girl's face. 'You have done well, Madame,' Christina Belgiojoso said, turning to the Parisienne. 'Have them delivered, and please include some green and red ribbons.'

It would have been nice to have kept the new dress on, and she would have been quite willing to freeze to death for such pleasure, but with Paris before her, viewed from the carriage of a Princess, she soon forgot her appearance. It seemed to Gabriella that life had taken a turn which would make her old friends of Blackfriars speechless with amazement. The maid Lucia had declared the Princess to be bountiful with her charity, and this Gabriella found included her time as well, for the tall slim aristocrat had clearly set aside all her engagements in order to show Gabriella all the great buildings and the fine open boulevards.

'Oh, it's all so . . .'

'French?' laughed Christina Belgiojoso, as Gabriella grasped for a suitable adjective. 'Well, it isn't in there,' continued the

Princess, pointing out the Italian Opera House. 'In there, our French friends are treated to recitative the like of which only one nation can produce. Does it inspire you, young lady?'

'Oh yes! Yes!' exclaimed Gabriella, hanging out of the carriage and craning her neck backwards to memorize the building.

Intense by nature herself, the Princess nodded gravely as Gabriella, eyes shining, pulled back into the carriage.

'You asked me a little while ago how you could ever repay everyone's kindness. The money is unimportant: excel as a singer and you will have repaid Mr Lumley; love your country and use your gift on its behalf and you will have repaid Giuseppe and myself. And now,' smiled the Princess, 'I think it is time to return, before my little girl becomes quite jealous of you.'

Maria Belgiojoso's dimpled chubby fingers grasped for the silk roses and cock's-comb frill on Gabriella's new scarf as it was withdrawn from its box.

'Ah, she's so lively,' laughed Gabriella as Lucia, rescuing the delicate material, swiftly removed it to the safety of a drawer. 'The Prince must be very proud of her, Donna Christina.'

'Maria is a bright child,' replied Christina Belgiojoso coldly. 'If you will excuse me, I have rather a headache.'

Very much disconcerted by the Princess's abrupt manner and departure from her room, Gabriella looked enquiringly at Lucia. Then, as a thought struck her, she turned crimson with embarrassment.

'Oh dear, of course, the hangings in the drawing-room. Did the Prince die, Lucia? Little Maria is so young to lose her father.'

A closed expression settled upon the maid's round face and she started to fold the tissue paper which had been wrapped around the white organdie dress.

'Prince Emilio is not dead,' she said discreetly. 'But it would be better if you did not speak of him again.'

'Oh dear, I didn't realize, I . . .' faltered Gabriella, still not understanding. 'I didn't mean to make her sad.'

'You haven't, Signorina,' reassured Lucia. Then, indignation

56

overcame discretion, and she blurted out, 'It is Prince Emilio who is to blame for that – he has publicly humiliated her by running away with a married woman!'

'Oh, how terrible,' said Gabriella, feeling quite out of her depth.

'It's not as if he has not strayed before,' continued the young servant, abandoning all formality as she sat down. 'Why, in Geneva he adored the Countess Guiccioli, Byron's former mistress. Indeed he followed her here to Paris. But to run away to Villa Pliniana with the Duchess of Plaisance, Berthier's daughter you know, and she to abandon her children! It has scandalized Paris: her family have put their servants into mourning, declaring her dead to them. There,' said Lucia rising and gathering up the folded tissue, 'I shouldn't be speaking to you so, except that understanding often prevents the insensitive remark – and our mistress has been humiliated enough. Why, last year her dear friend the poet Alfred Musset severed their relationship and wrote a poem for all the world to see, and from what I heard there was no mistaking who his cruel words were aimed at; but to see her the next day at one of her receptions you would never have known: she was as sparkling and witty as ever. Sometimes I think she is too clever for the men: last year two volumes of her *Essay on the Catholic Church* were published and they caused quite a sensation.'

'And Signor Mazzini says she knows his friend – the lady writer who dresses as a man.'

'Ah, George Sand . . . Of course, everyone comes to her salon!' laughed Lucia. 'That might be very useful to you one day: you'll meet all the composers here.'

The next day, bearing in mind the maid's words, Gabriella looked beyond the Princess's bright smile and noticed the shadow of sadness in her patron's black eyes, even when, as now, her little daughter was covering her hands with kisses.

'Life must have been very hard for you, Gabriella,' said the Princess, quietening little Maria's exuberance, 'with no mother or father to guide you. Living with boys, too, it is unimaginable. Were you not living in a state of fear every day?'

'Well, we were all afraid of the master,' replied Gabriella, 'but I had Nico to look after me. He's very strong and the boys always listened to him . . . I suppose without him I would have been bullied,' she murmured, realizing for the first time as she spoke how different life at Blackfriars would have been if she had been there alone. 'I have never known a mother or father. Nico was everything to me.'

The Princess saw the pain in the girl's face. 'Now, Gabriella,' she said briskly. 'Have you a song that you might sing before a few of my friends this evening?'

Gabriella paled and looked apprehensively at her benefactor.

'I only know the song I sang for the second Anniversary Supper, and a tune which Signore Lablache told me was from *Don Giovanni*, but I do not know any words for it . . . Am I to sing at one of your soirées, Madame?' asked Gabriella, with a feeling of terror rising within her.

'Not quite,' smiled Christina Belgiojoso. 'For those you must glitter like a diamond, and that requires years of study. No, I have a few close friends coming for supper whom I am trying to interest in the fate of our country, and it will be interesting for them to meet a child of Italy.'

Though it was only to be an informal occasion, the Princess Belgiojoso insisted on a careful rehearsal of the chosen song. And whilst Gabriella still felt nervous, her patron had nodded with approval after she had finished.

'That was lovely. I never doubted your ability, of course, but Monsieur Lablache told me I would be surprised. I confess I am.'

'And the song?' asked Gabriella, wishing she knew something more dramatic.

'It is perfect – I shall tell them which exile, driven from his homeland, taught it to you. Now you may go and play with Maria. After that I think you should have a little rest before this evening.'

Later, an hour before she was to make her entrance into

the drawing-room, Lucia arrived to help her with her toilette.

'Your hair is not very long!' she complained, as after several minutes of brushing she began firmly to criss-cross the plaits.

'It's very much longer than it used to be,' laughed Gabriella. 'Oh Lucia, I'm so nervous. What if I make a mess of things, will the Princess change her mind about helping me?'

'Don't be silly,' said the young woman, tying a red ribbon on the first plait. 'Once you get going you'll be all right . . . though it might be better if you don't look at the pianist,' she giggled.

'The pianist?'

The maid's smile of secrecy deepened, making the round cheeks dimple. She made a great show of perfecting the green and red bows on the plaits and, despite Gabriella's pleas, would give no more details as to who the pianist or guests might be.

The embroidered silver stars gleamed dimly against their sky of velvet black, softly illuminated by a candelabra on top of the grand piano. Within this focus, Gabriella was to stand, though she wished as she walked towards the piano that she could also merge into the shadows like the seated guests who were talking in low tones to the Princess. Her accompanist, she saw, was already in position and, recalling Lucia's secrecy concerning him, Gabriella examined him closely. Could this sickly looking man be someone famous? And would there be important composers and well-known performers amongst her audience?

'So you are Gabriella,' said the man, rising from the piano stool, interrupting the speculations which were turning her legs to jelly. 'It was the ladies who persuaded me to play for you. It is not something I usually do, but they are very persuasive, and you are the young friend of an exile like myself. Do you have music?'

'No, Monsieur, it is only a simple country song,' said Gabriella, thinking that this man would be better off in bed than at a piano, for he seemed very pale.

'It's not important,' said the man, sitting down. 'Softly hum your tune through for me.'

Very quietly so that no one else should hear, Gabriella did as she was bid.

'It's very kind of you to play for me, Monsieur,' she said, before leaving to take up her position.

'We all had to start, and to accept a helping hand,' murmured the pianist with great charm. 'Besides,' he added conspiratorially, 'our efforts, I believe, are really meant to beguile the politicians present to champion Italy's cause, so we must both perform exceptionally well. Do you think, my young friend, you will be able to do so?'

'Oh, I'll try very hard!' said Gabriella fervently.

As soon as she took up her position, a hush fell on the drawing-room. As the young man had forewarned, he began to play an introduction to her song. As the first chords resounded in the room, a shiver of excitement ran up Gabriella's spine. Here was a master: instinctively her inexperienced ears identified what could not be mistaken, and she knew as she prepared to sing that this was a moment she should never forget and that, whoever he was, she was truly privileged.

At the end of the song which told of the peasant boy far away from home, just as though she were a singer at a real soirée, the small assembly of people politely applauded. Quite overcome with relief, delight and embarrassment, and forgetting what she was supposed to do, Gabriella bobbed a quick curtsy and would have dashed away.

'You must learn to enjoy your applause!' laughed the pianist, springing to his feet and leading her back by the hand to stand before the half-circle of people who were now quite visible as servants moved about lighting more candelabra.

'Why, there is Signor Lablache,' she cried, exchanging a smile of recognition with the portly singer.

'So you will now discard me for a Neapolitan?'

'Oh, forgive me,' said Gabriella, realizing that she had forgotten the man beside her. 'I am very grateful to you. I realize you have done me a great honour, Monsieur, Monsieur . . .'

'Chopin,' offered a woman's voice, brimming with laughter. 'You see, my dear Frédéric, not everyone has heard of you.'

'Oh, but I have, Madame!' gasped Gabriella, scarlet with embarrassment. 'And I knew at once, the moment your fingers touched the keys, Monsieur, that you were no beginner!'

As she finished speaking, the astonished expressions on the two faces before her collapsed into laughter, and for a moment Gabriella thought the composer would choke; but as their laughter dissolved and the bright, clever eyes of the woman settled once more upon her, Gabriella hazarded a wild guess that she must be George Sand!

'But you are not wearing trousers, Madame,' she blurted out in disappointment. 'And do you really smoke cigars?'

'So, I am discovered,' laughed Madame Dudevant, amused by the artless enthusiasm of the young girl. 'You seem to know a great deal about me.'

'You are very famous in London, Madame, and it was Signor Mazzini who told me that your writing is very important for women. We all learnt your words by memory,' she added shyly. '"There is but one virtue, the eternal sacrifice of self."'

Madame Dudevant lifted her eyebrows in amused astonishment, but as her gaze swept over the young, eager girl, her expression changed to one of regret.

'I think, my little sister,' she said, touching Gabriella gently on the cheek, 'that you should forget those words for a while. Enjoy yourself a little. Later, when you are older, the opportunities for self-sacrifice will be all too many. Do you not agree, Christina?' she asked as the Princess Belgiojoso glided alongside with Luigi Lablache in her wake.

'You sang very well, *ma petite*,' boomed the opera singer.

'And she has a silver tongue in more than one sense,' teased Frédéric Chopin. 'For she tells me I have some talent!'

After one small but breathtaking glass of champagne, given to her when the Princess's back was turned by Luigi Lablache, Gabriella bade goodnight to Christina Belgiojoso's guests. With wings on her feet she sped back to her room.

'Well, Signorina?'

'Oh Lucia,' laughed Gabriella, running up to her and pinching the first piece of soft flesh her fingers could contact. 'How could you not prepare me for Frédéric Chopin? Though it's just as well, otherwise I would have shaken with fright. Imagine, him, playing for me!'

'Yes, well, you have the Princess and Madame Dudevant to thank for that. I heard them persuading him, and if you had been a day older I don't suppose he would have. He has been quite ill, too, and soon I believe Madame and he will be leaving Paris for Nohant, so you just caught him at the right time.'

'Could you hear me, Lucia, did it sound agreeable?'

'Agreeable, what a word!' laughed the maid. 'It sounded as clear and lovely as the bell of Holy Office. I'll be able to say, when you're famous, that I heard you the first time you sang!'

'Oh Lucia!' giggled Gabriella. 'I shall miss you. And the friends of the Princess are so gracious; everyone was so kind to me, and a Monsier Thiers spoke to me for a long time about my life in London and at Signor Mazzini's school.'

'Ah, that will have pleased the Princess,' said Lucia, helping to remove the white organdie dress. 'He is one of the important politicians whose continued support she counts on. Of course he adores her – he even rolled his sleeves up to cook her omelettes when she first arrived in Paris with no money.'

'I wish I could stay to watch the guests attending her salon,' sighed Gabriella as she padded across to the comfortable bed. 'It has gone so quickly.'

'Yes, it is a pity,' agreed Lucia, 'for I have the perfect spyhole which I let Maria and her nursemaid peep through. Everyone famous comes: Madame Récamier, the painter Delacroix, Balzac the writer, Victor Hugo, Rossini too. Bellini used to come as well. He is dead now, of course.'

'I would like to meet Rossini!'

'Well, but for his gall stones you might have; but since arriving in Paris to seek medical treatment, he has shut himself away.'

'Lucia, do you know everything?' laughed Gabriella.

'It's one of the hallmarks of the good servant . . . the other is never to divulge to other visiting ladies' maids anything of interest. I'm always being asked about Her Highness's relationship with her friend, Signor Bolognini.'

'And?' questioned Gabriella, hugging her knees and relishing this female gossip which she had never known before.

The servant smiled and shook her head at the young girl sitting up in bed. 'I think it's time you had some sleep, Signorina. You have a long journey ahead of you tomorrow.'

Gabriella was to start early the next morning on the final stage of her journey. Once she was dressed, and before she left her room to go and bid farewell to the Princess, she had a quick peep into her trunk to make sure that the papers of Signor Mazzini were there. Of course they had been hidden, but after a quick, then more careful search, she could discover nothing.

'Lucia,' she said as the maid entered the room. 'You did remember to include the papers in my trunk?'

'I'm afraid I'm not allowed to say,' replied the maid. 'You'd best speak to the Princess.'

The young woman's noncommittal answer puzzled Gabriella, and it was the first thing she spoke of when she entered the shimmering boudoir.

'I am sorry to bother you with my travel arrangements, Donna Christina, but Lucia seems unable to tell me if Signor Mazzini's writings are in the trunk. I cannot find them; I do not wish to leave them behind.'

The Princess who, like the man in question, was always to be found with a pen in hand, looked up. Her magnificent black eyes gleamed with reassurance.

'Have no fear: Mazzini's words will be read, but that is all you may know. If your luggage is searched, and if anything is found, you must say your trunk was packed by servants of the Princess Belgiojoso – that will be sufficient for the Piedmontese or Austrian authorities to view you as my innocent dupe. As someone accused of high treason, I am well known to the Court of Vienna.'

'Will you ever see Milan again, Princess Christina?'

'Yes, it has been possible for me to return since the Amnesty in '38; but here I have freedom to write, I am able to influence French thinking in Paris: we need their support in our struggle for freedom. Ah, you will adore Milano,' she said wistfully. 'I shall expect you to write and tell me of your progress, Gabriella, and should you ever have special needs, you must inform me.'

'I am most grateful for everything. I hope I will not disappoint the trust you have put in me,' said Gabriella.

'Goodbye, my dear,' said the Princess, rising and extending her wraith-like hand. 'Your eyes will soon see the loveliest of provinces – Verdi speaks for all the estranged hearts: "*Oh, mia patria si bella e perduta! Oh, membranza si cara e fatale!*"'

'"Oh, my country so beautiful and lost. Oh, memory so dear and fatal!"' repeated Gabriella softly, as tears glistened in the eyes of the exiled Princess.

Outside in the hallway, Gabriella found little Maria was waiting for her with a large bag of bon-bons as a farewell present.

'I come too, Mademoiselle Gabriella,' squealed the little girl, jumping up and down with excitement.

'I wish you could, pretty one,' said Gabriella as she lifted her up in her arms to kiss her. 'But you must stay to look after your Mama. I, I must make my journey alone.'

Chalon, Lyon, Avignon, Arles, and then Marseille and the waiting sea! Oh how she wished she could be sharing this adventure with Nico, she thought, rushing about the deck, her bonnet ribbons flapping and fluttering high in the salty breeze as she peered into the horizon for her first glimpse of Genoa. Then, when all became busy on deck, her first sight of marble palaces and their terraced gardens held her spellbound until they entered the bustling harbour. Was this where she and Nico had sailed from? she wondered, seeing a group of roughly dressed boys embarking on to a boat. As she watched them she felt a resurgence of sadness, and her hand closed around the handkerchief in her pocket, her one keepsake of the past.

'Look to the future,' she murmured, pressing the soft ball

of bear's fur still within its embroidered kerchief. 'At least you'll never be forgotten, Pepe,' she said with a smile, then laughed, remembering the astonishment of her former companions when they'd heard her choice of a surname. 'Well, it was the least I could do for you – in a way your death brought me here.'

Down below on the quayside, she became aware of a group of policemen; but the moment her feet touched the quayside, she felt such a rush of excitement that she sailed past them with a nod and a happy smile.

'You've been away long, Signorina?' asked a young officer after he had checked her passport.

'Yes,' she laughed. 'And now I'm going home.'

Her stay in Genoa was overnight, at the home of Signor Mazzini's parents, where she was received with great warmth. They were delighted to meet Gabriella and to hear news of their son. Then it was onwards the next day in another swaying diligence until they left Piedmont and gained the flat plain of Lombardy. There, like spun sugar, rosy-tinged by the sun, the pride of Milan, the mighty shimmering cathedral, floated up before them on the horizon.

Within the ancient city walls, white Austrian uniforms were in evidence everywhere.

'There are a great many soldiers!' Gabriella observed, as their diligence was waved on through the Porta Vercellina.

'It's a garrison town: you'll see Croats, Hungarians, Tyrolese, Slovaks, Carinthians, Austrians and our own Italian conscripts,' said the gentleman sitting opposite her.

'So many!'

'Yes, and we're expected to pay for the roads they tramp up and down,' he said venomously.

Gabriella looked with added interest at the elderly gentleman of military bearing, and wondered if he had served as a young man with the Emperor Napoleon, or been a member of the Carbonari secret society. Or was his tone of disapproval feigned? Lucia had said Lombardy was filled with spies who would say nasty things just to lure you into indiscretions! So, mindful of what she was sure was in her luggage, and discouraging more dangerous talk, Gabriella returned her attention to the safer passing sights.

She was tired, she was stiff, but the thought of what Lucia had also told her about Milan had the effect of an oasis upon a weary traveller. She had made up her mind that before she sought Mazzini's followers she would go and buy sorbet! But as she stepped down from the diligence, a lady moved forward.

'Signorina Pepe. I am one of the inspectors from the Conservatorio della Passione. If you would please point out your trunk, our porter will put it on the cart.'

'Why, thank you, it's just being lifted down now. It's very kind of you to meet me,' Gabriella said, trying to hide her disappointment.

'We would not wish you to walk through the streets unaccompanied, Signorina,' said the woman gravely as she made a gesture for an elderly man to come forward with his handcart.

The magnificent duomo dominated all, so as Gabriella walked ahead of her luggage with the woman servant from the Conservatorio, she could not resist turning her gaze repeatedly upward to the thousands of statues and soaring marble spires.

'Oh, it is overwhelming, breathtaking!' she exclaimed enthusiastically, looking towards the silent woman at her side. A ghost of a smile passed over the reserved features and the inspector fingered the crucifix which hung down the front of her simple robe.

'I can never remember not seeing it,' she murmured.

'Well, there is nothing like it in London or Paris,' declared Gabriella cheerfully, all shyness swept away by the overpowering spectacle. 'I'll come back and look at it more closely when I've unpacked.'

At this suggestion, Gabriella's companion made no comment, and there was something about her silence which, taken with her earlier words about young ladies being escorted, began to make Gabriella somewhat uneasy about her future freedom.

Since 1808, the Convento dei Lateranensi had taken the name of Conservatorio della Passione, and here, boys and girls of exceptional talent were able to obtain a general education whilst studying for a musical career.

Led past the church of Santa Maria della Passione which was attached to the latter convent, they did not enter the main gate but walked on to a side entrance further along, whose ornamental gate opened into a large garden.

'The front entrance,' explained her escort, as the porter closed the gate behind them, 'is used only by the teachers and the male students: they live on the ground floor and naturally use the gardens at separate times to the girls. The female quarters are up here on the first floor,' she said, ushering Gabriella ahead up a flight of stone steps. 'As soon as you have refreshed yourself, I will come back and take you to meet Matron.'

'Thank you,' said Gabriella as the woman opened one of the doors on the long corridor. 'I shall be glad to wash my face, the road was very dusty,' she added with a grateful smile.

The room she was shown to had formerly been one of the convent's cells. It was sparsely furnished, and the only decoration on the bare walls was a wooden crucifix. After so recently experiencing the luxury of the Princess Belgiojoso's residence, her future home seemed austere and forbidding on first sight. At once she moved over to the window to see what the view was like. Down below was a courtyard, and stepping out into it from the cloisters opposite was a girl of about her own age carrying a violin case under her arm. As she watched the student's hurried progress, Gabriella's heart gave a bound and she started to unbutton her coat. Then she whirled around to face her room. She was here, and here there was music! As if in response, a bell began to toll.

For one brought up in the harsh world of street begging, the strict routine of the Conservatorio came as no great shock. To rise at seven o'clock in the winter and at half past five in summer did not seem unreasonable, nor to have to keep her room clean and wash and iron her own clothes.

'The bell must be obeyed at all times, and lateness for classes will not be tolerated,' said the matron, looking down an exceptionally fine long nose. 'You will of course wear the dress of the Conservatorio, but perhaps we had better leave that until you have taken your exam tomorrow.'

'Exam?'

'Students are not usually accepted without first sitting the exam. Whilst your case is exceptional, nevertheless the formality, I understand, will still be observed. For the rest of the afternoon you are free to unpack. Dinner is at half past seven, prayers at nine, before bedtime. If you are unsure of anything, Signorina Verenese is in the cell next to yours. Of course,' she added, as though knowing what was passing through Gabriella's mind, 'it is a long time until dinner. One of the inspectors will bring you some refreshment; you have had a long journey.'

On returning to her room, Gabriella found a tray with some light refreshments awaiting her. Her trunk had also arrived. In Paris, the search through her clothing had not produced Mazzini's papers; an hour later, with her possessions piled high on the bed and every inch of the trunk prodded and examined, Gabriella sat back on her heels defeated, feeling she had been treated like a child. With a sigh of vexation she picked up the piece of wood to rewind the length of dark blue wool given to her for a winter coat by the Princess. As she balanced its weight in her hand, her blue eyes suddenly gleamed. It took a little while, for her fingers were clumsy with excitement, but at last the end slat of wood slipped out to reveal a hollowed inside, filled with the missing papers!

Repacking the trunk with the clothes she could not use as a student, Gabriella considered when it would be best to deliver Mazzini's work. The convent bell was just ringing four o'clock which, according to what she had been told, meant that lessons were at an end and the students would be going to their rooms to prepare their work for the next day. Perhaps now was the time she would not be missed, for tomorrow onwards it might not be so easy. If only she had not been met, she would not have had this problem; nor would she, within a few hours of arriving, be about to break the rule about walking out alone;

but it seemed unsafe to keep the papers in her room, and anyway, for Signor Mazzini's sake the risk must be taken.

As she peeped out into the corridor she saw there was now quite a lot of activity, as young ladies in blue-grey dresses made their way towards their rooms. It was now or never, thought Gabriella, ducking back and snatching up her bag. Going the same way that she had been brought, she crept down the flight of steps, pausing on the bottom one. Very slowly, she peered around the corner to see if the attendant was still in the lodge at the gate. She was! For a while she considered whether she might creep past the woman on her hands and knees, but although she had had years of practice at such things when following Nico on his adventures, it would be so undignified if she were spotted. Besides, the woman would be sure to hear the gate open. There was only one course left.

With a confident smile, Gabriella approached the Conservatorio's watchdog.

'I believe, Signora, you know where the duomo is. Is it to the right or left?'

'Why, it is to the right, of course,' said the woman, surprise replacing suspicion for a moment. Before the latter could return, Gabriella slipped through the gate with a smile of gratitude. Then, as if she were back at Blackfriars, dignity suddenly forgotten, she was running like the wind. As soon as she was well clear of the Conservatorio, she stopped to ask directions to the Porta Tosa and found that she had in effect been running away from it and that it was very near to the Conservatorio.

The house to which she was to deliver the papers was built in the old Spanish style and situated on a crooked, winding street. Before stepping under its portico, Gabriella looked swiftly to right and left to make sure that she had not been followed, for her imagination was still full of the possibility of spies. Within a smallish courtyard she found a flight of worn stone steps which led her upwards to an unmarked door within the shelter of a gloomy landing. The sound of voices came from within. At least there was someone there, she thought, moving closer to knock; but as she raised her hand, she heard the speaker making some kind of vow: 'To constitute Italy one free, independent, republican nation; to promote by every means in my power – whether by written or spoken word or by action . . .'

'Listening at keyholes, spy!' hissed a voice.

Startled, Gabriella whirled around.

'I'm not a spy,' she gasped.

'Tell that to my friends!' said a young man, gripping her shoulder with his hand.

'Take your hands off me. Let me go!' she protested, kicking out wildly as the disturbed occupants of the room appeared and pulled her into the chamber.

'Who are you? Why were you listening at the door?' asked one of the circle of young men confronting her.

'My name is Gabriella Pepe. I am from London and I'm seeking a Signor Facini on behalf of a friend.'

'I am Enrico Facini. What do you want with me?' asked the spokesman of the group.

'I have brought you something, but I would prefer to give it to you in private.'

'I have no secrets from my friends.'

Gabriella bit her lip and wondered if it was safe, then her eyes lighted upon a sprig of cypress and she realized they must all be members of Giovane Italia.

'I have brought the writings of a patriot,' she announced grandly.

'Mazzini's?' cried the young men excitedly.

'Yes,' she smiled. 'Giuseppe Mazzini's!'

Within seconds, as if she were a liberator, a glass of wine was pressed upon her, a chair produced, and she was overwhelmed with a barrage of questions. Gabriella had never felt so important. When she opened her large velvet handbag to take out the papers, the waiting dark eyes glistened in anticipation like a circle of dogs expecting a bone.

With great reverence the young men received the cuttings from the *People's Journal* and the *Apostolato Popolare*. For some time Gabriella sat quietly, forgotten as Mazzini's disciples eagerly, emotionally devoured his essays. She thought of the writer: his supper forgotten, the candle burning low, his heart

70

and mind far away beyond the sea which separated him from his home, his people.

Until today, she had not really understood why he was doing it all. She had brought these papers to repay a little of his kindness: there had been nothing brave about it for, in the classroom at Hatton Garden, the tales of Austrian occupation had seemed as unreal as tales of ancient Romans.

At last, Enrico Facini looked up, his eyes moist and glistening.

'We live in blind ignorance here. Everything is censored. These words are bread and water to us . . . You are very young to have been entrusted with such a mission,' he added, with an envious note in his voice.

'I rather forced it upon him,' said Gabriella. 'I owe Mazzini a great deal, as do many others in London.'

'Have you just arrived in Milan?'

'Yes, and I've already stayed far too long with you. It's my first day at the Conservatorio and I don't think I should be out.'

'No, I don't think you should!' smiled a young man in a black jacket. 'The good matron would be very shocked to see one of her young ladies here. You must be very talented to have earned a place.'

'Are you all interested in music?' asked Gabriella.

'What else is there!' laughed the young men.

'Love!' sighed one of their number she had heard called Giovanni.

'Unrequited, as I understand it,' mocked his companions. 'Isn't the lovely Flavia Balziano developing a passion for your brother?'

Giovanni's handsome face flushed an angry red.

'You'll see tonight at La Scala!'

'La Scala!' exclaimed Gabriella. 'You go to La Scala?'

'Naturally,' replied the elegantly dressed Giovanni. 'I go every night, as does everyone, excepting Fridays of course. And tonight is the première of *I Lombardi alla Prima Crociata*.'

'The Lombards on the First Crusade,' murmured Gabriella wistfully.

'Giovanni will escort you!' winked one of the young men. 'And he might even take you for a sorbet in his smart sediole!'

'Oh no, really, I must be getting back!' said Gabriella hastily, noticing the look of irritation darted at the speaker. 'But I'd be very grateful for a ride back to the Conservatorio. It would save minutes,' she said, flashing a wide hopeful smile at this owner of a carriage.

'Very well, it will be a pleasure,' agreed the young man, answering the appeal in the beautiful deep blue eyes.

'Till Sunday, Signorina,' laughed the deep-voiced young man in the black jacket as Gabriella made her goodbyes. 'You'd better not tarry,' he added as, surprised by his words, she halted at the doorway. 'Our Conte is faster than his horse.'

Outside stood a thin horse between the shafts of a light carriage. It had not particularly impressed her on her arrival, but once out on the street, it shot off like a hare.

'I hope you won't get into trouble,' shouted Giovanni, applying his whip.

'So do I,' cried Gabriella with feeling. 'And I hope your lady smiles at you tonight.'

The young man beside her frowned, and Gabriella regretted the tactless remark, but then with an arrogant, dismissive shrug of his shoulders, her driver spoke with studied nonchalance.

'I think she is a little young for me, she is not much older than you. Besides, tonight there will be war at La Scala!'

'War?'

'Yes, the Austrians will be tugging their whiskers in fury. Temistocle Solera, the librettist, and Merelli have already had to answer to the Chief of Police over the Archbishop's complaints of sacrilege in the text. That has now been settled, but I hear from my brother Luciano that the libretto is very patriotic.'

'Who is Signor Merelli?' asked Gabriella as she stepped down from the carriage.

'If you're to be a singer you'd better find out!' shouted the young Conte as he raced away.

Like the dust settling back on the road, the excitement of her recent meeting and the exhilaration of the fast ride vanished, leaving her filled with apprehension about what reception awaited her on the other side of the Conservatorio gateway.

Relief rather than anger was etched on the old attendant's face when she opened the gate, and in a rapid stream of dialect of which Gabriella could only understand the frightening word, matron, she was bustled along the garden path towards the flight of stone steps. Before her the corridor which led to Matron's office stretched out like the road to the scaffold and she saw there was a solitary spectator to watch her unhappy progress. It was the dark-haired girl she had seen earlier carrying the violin case, and she was standing in the doorway of the cell before her own.

'They've been looking for you,' hissed the girl.

'Yes, I know,' answered Gabriella miserably.

'They think you went to the duomo. Did you?'

Gabriella shook her head. 'No, I went to see friends. One of them gave me a lift back in his carriage, otherwise . . .'

'A man!' exclaimed the young student, seizing Gabriella by the hand and pulling her into the room. 'Oh, you mustn't let them know that, you'd be sent away. You must say you went to . . . to pray.'

'But I didn't,' said Gabriella, knowing that she could never withstand the penetrating eyes of their matron.

'Then say them now, with me,' urged the girl, leading her before the crucifix which was also on her wall.

As with the elderly doorkeeper, Gabriella felt there was more relief than anger underlying the matron's reproaches.

'You must never leave here again without permission. All that we knew was that you had asked about the duomo. You are now in our care. What if something had happened to you, and just a few hours after arriving! What could have been so important?'

'I gave my thanks to God for bringing me safely to Milan,' murmured Gabriella, mentally thanking her new friend and crossing her fingers behind her back.

'That is understandable,' said the narrow-faced woman, her thin lips softening slightly. 'But you must make sure you know what the rules are, and if you break them I will be forced to report you to the principal. Now go or you will miss dinner. I have asked Signorina Verenese to show you the way.'

Giuseppina Verenese, Gabriella's new friend and neighbour, was a student of composition. She had been at the Conservatorio for one year.

'You'll still leave before me, Gabriella,' declared the student. 'You singers only have to do five years, whilst we have ten years of study. Still, I don't mind, we have the brilliant Felice Frasi as our professor. Oh, it's so nice to have another girl student: we're greatly outnumbered by the boys.'

'Do we take lessons with them?'

'With the boys, oh no!' cried Giuseppina, bursting into giggles, her girlish face for the first time losing its intense seriousness. 'Why, we have nothing to do with male students,' she said, laughing again.

So much was different, thought Gabriella, as later she lay in her bed after prayers. To her, boys were more familiar than girls, yet here the mere mention of the word set the younger girls off into fits of laughter. Yet some things were surprisingly the same. Blind ignorance were the words Enrico Facini had used to describe their state when he and the others had eagerly taken Mazzini's writings from her hand. Yet these young men, in their velvet suits, with their carefully arranged disordered hair smelling of cologne, were obviously not poor. In the slums of London it was poverty that kept you from learning; here it was the Austrians. With a sigh, as she thought of the harsh life of the children she had grown up with, Gabriella rolled over to go to sleep. 'I'm so lucky,' she thought. 'I'm not a beggar any more, I'm here to learn to sing.' She knew that at this moment, in this city, Erminia Frezzolini was singing Verdi. And, as her eyes closed, Gabriella wished with all her heart that some day she might be doing the same.

# Chapter Four

The next morning, Gabriella was introduced to the routine that would be hers for the next few years: fifteen minutes to get up, fifteen minutes for communal prayers, thirty minutes to wash and dress and then breakfast from eight to eight-thirty.

'I am sure all will go well for you,' said Giuseppina Verenese sitting beside Gabriella at the refectory table.

'Do I look nervous?' asked Gabriella in mock surprise.

'Yes, terribly,' laughed her new friend. 'You've hardly heard a word I've been saying and you keep dipping your spoon into your porridge and then forgetting it . . . There goes the bell. I have to go back to my room to prepare my violin.'

'It's becoming quite noisy here,' said Gabriella, as they walked back past cells in which wind and string instruments were being tuned for the start of classes at nine o'clock.

'You don't notice it after a time,' smiled Giuseppina. 'But the bell – well, that's quite another matter!'

Gabriella was quite confident about her reading and writing, for she had worked very hard on both at Signor Mazzini's school. Though the examining priest made no comment, his nod of satisfaction reassured her that all had gone well. Next came the meeting with the professors.

Robed in splendid gowns of green, lavishly decorated with silver, the principal, Felice Frasi, and the Conservatorio's professor of singing looked so imposing when Gabriella came before them that she felt she would never dare open her mouth in front of such illustrious gentlemen. Then the beaming cherubic face of Luigi Lablache popped into her mind:

he had said she had been blessed with a gift, so she must try not to be afraid and ruin things.

'Gabriella, this is Professor Mazzucato,' said Felice Frasi, introducing the gentleman beside him. 'Now, all we would like to hear is what your voice is able to do. Just relax and follow the piano.'

After her first two hesitant notes, Gabriella's heart stopped thumping and the butterflies faded away as the piano's flight of notes consumed her attention and took her higher and higher.

'Very good,' said Felice Frasi with a grave smile. 'Mr Lumley informed us that you were not certain of your age; thirteen or fourteen, he thought.'

'Yes, I've never really known. Am I too young?'

At Felice Frasi's side, Professor Mazzucato saw a desperate anxiety in the girl's eyes and this, together with the exciting prospect of nurturing a naturally fine voice, swept all formality away. He answered before the principal.

'Voices vary,' he said. 'But I can safely say that yours is ready for five years of hard work.'

'Oh, I will work very hard!' assured Gabriella, feeling that she could burst with relief and joy.

'You will certainly do so,' smiled Felice Frasi. 'And, had there been any doubt about that, or of your ability, you would never have travelled so far.'

In a state of ecstasy Gabriella departed from the green-gowned professors and sped to collect her uniform from Matron. Compared to the fashionable gowns of the Parisian salon, this long-sleeved, high-necked blue-grey dress was very plain, but as Gabriella fastened the belt around the coarse cotton, tears sprang to her eyes. She bit her lip, feeling a little foolish before the matron, but this moment had aroused so many emotions in her. She was now a student at the Conservatorio.

At twelve-thirty, the bell summoned everyone to lunch. A trifle self-conscious in her new dress, she entered the girls' refectory. Straightaway, the smaller girls of eight and nine rushed up to her and hugged her; then Giuseppina and other

76

older students in their final years approached and warmly congratulated her with kisses on her cheeks. Never before had Gabriella known such easy, spontaneous warmth of affection, nor such a feeling of security.

Italian literature was the first lesson that afternoon, followed by an hour of French and afterwards an hour of Religious Instruction. As the days went by, besides general subjects like History and Geography, Gabriella was introduced to many specialized subjects for the students of singing: Ballet, and the art of Gesture and Mime, and training in diction for good Declamation. It was all very exciting, absorbing, and tiring too, for she had never, even at the evening classes at Hatton Garden, had to concentrate for such long periods: hers had been a wild, free life, and to sit quietly was at first a great strain. The physical demands of singing surprised her even more.

'Did you think you just stood and opened your mouth and it all poured out with no effort on your part?' teased her teacher, Alberto Mazzucato, when she expressed surprise that she should have to learn about breathing. 'Not so,' he declared. 'If those lungs of yours are going to be able to express what the great masters have written, they must become as if made of iron. Before you go, let me show you what I mean. Notice when I finish how I still have a reserve of breath.'

In a mixture of surprise and disbelief, Gabriella watched and listened as her professor sang up and down a scale three or four times with comparative ease.

'Are you sure you did not cheat just a little, Professor?' Gabriella asked mischievously.

'Indeed not!' expostulated Alberto Mazzucato, shocked to be so addressed by a student. But, unable to resist the sparkling, admiring eyes, he dismissed her with a wave of his hand. As he watched the flying plaits disappear around the corner, Alberto Mazzucato shook his head and smiled. After all, he thought, we have here a wild cat from the English slums, whose rough patois, like her manners, will take a little while for the good priests to polish. Whilst I must be careful not to crush that which will make her unique.

Caught up in the scholastic whirl, Gabriella had forgotten

77

about her meeting with the followers of Mazzini, but on Sunday morning, as she and the rest of the young lady students were leaving the church of Santa Maria della Passione after Mass, Gabriella suddenly glimpsed, amongst the rows of black-jacketed male students, the young man she had met in the house at the Porta Tosa whose words about seeing her on Sunday had puzzled her so much at the time.

'Why are you staring?' whispered Giuseppina, giving Gabriella a nudge. 'Why,' she gasped, 'that young man just smiled and winked at you. Do you know him?'

'Only a little,' replied Gabriella, turning her head to return the young man's smile as her friend in a state of alarm dragged her down the aisle. 'I didn't realize he was a student here.'

'I think he lives with his parents outside the Conservatorio – some students who are paying their own fees do – and I think he is training to be a singer, whilst the young man beside him, the one with the long fair lashes, is studying composition.'

'For someone who says she knows nothing about the male students, you seem to know a great deal, Giuseppina,' teased Gabriella, laughing with delight as her friend turned quite pink.

On Sundays, between one and two o'clock, the parents of the students were allowed to visit. Gabriella chose this time to write her letters, so as to feel she too had a family. Her patron, the Princess Belgiojoso, was first on her list, after which she wrote to Giuseppe Mazzini, enclosing a little note for Nico in which she described the journey and the sea voyage and things which would interest him. She didn't write a great deal about the Conservatorio, except to say that arithmetic at eleven o'clock on a Sunday morning was absolutely hateful, and she wished he was there to help her with the answers.

Milan was quite different to London, encircled as it was by its high rampart wall rising thirty feet above the plain. Where in London one might wander freely from city streets to village meadows, here there were the gates and Austria's police to deny at will such passage to the Lombards. Instead of St Paul's, there was the filigree fantasy of the marble duomo; in place of

78

the Thames was the elegant canal of Leonardo da Vinci. In each comparison there were gains and losses, yet no greater gain, Gabriella decided, than the air she breathed; for here there were no clouds of belching, sooty smoke from countless factory chimneys, nor did acrid yellow fogs swirl around the piazzas and fine palaces, or shroud the galloping horses on the façade of La Scala. La Scala – it was where they all wanted to be, so no matter how many times she wanted Piermarini's Opera House to be included in their supervised walks, no one objected to her request.

Like some plant long denied sun, Gabriella revelled in each cloudless day of spring, but as the weeks passed and the temperature soared to produce a stifling, fierce heat she, like the other students, abandoned playing in the garden during free time to rest in the coolness of her cell. Autumn provided relief, tingeing the trees with red and gold, before colder weather divested them of all covering. For the students, there was some respite from the gruelling daily schedule, with a performance of the Nativity and the end-of-year concert, when the most gifted senior students left her and her young friends shiny-eyed with admiration, despair and determination. Then, unbelievably, spring had come again, a year had passed, and she too could glide up and down scales and end with breath to spare! She had learnt about her maxillary sinuses, nasal cavities and frontal sinuses, and how they affected the sounds she made. Every day, for a whole year, she had performed what her professor described as vocalizing, which required her to hold her mouth in a smiling position and send sounds to the three different registers: for the medium the breath must be directed against the upper teeth, for the chest the breath sent forth freely, not striking mouth and passages, as the least rubbing of glands would spoil the vibrating quality, whilst for the head register she had to direct sound to the frontal sinuses.

Though day to day her progress had seemed slow, now Gabriella realized that she had achieved quite a lot in her first year. Even so, she was startled to learn that she would be going so soon to meet the famous prima donna Giuditta Pasta at her villa at Blevio on Lake Como.

'Oh, don't look so fearful, child,' said Professor Mazzucato after he had delivered the unexpected news. 'You are not ready for her coaching yet. Signora Pasta merely wishes to meet you, and permission has been granted by the principal and by Conte Renato Borromeo, the president of the Conservatorio, for you to go and stay for a few days at Blevio.'

Her news provoked sighs of envy from her close friends as they paused on the city walls during one of their walks and looked north across the green, tree-clad plain towards the glistening snow-capped chain of the Alps.

'Oh, how lucky you are to see the lake in spring,' said Clara who was studying pianoforte. 'And Blevio is so pretty. I have seen it from the steamer. My uncle has a villa further down the lake at Bellagio.'

'And are you to stay with Signora Pasta?' enquired Giuseppina.

'No, I am to stay with a retired professor and his sister who live at Blevio. And guess which of the inspectors is travelling with me to make sure I do not get into any mischief,' asked Gabriella, pulling a face as her friends burst into laughter when they learnt it was the bane of all their lives, Signora Mathilde.

Since leaving London, Gabriella had seen much spectacular countryside. Como might have been a disappointment, except that by the time the diligence arrived, the lake had wrapped itself in one of its sudden, impenetrable veils of mist, as if holding itself aloof from competition and comparison.

'So you'll keep me waiting to see the loveliness that I've heard so much about,' Gabriella whispered as she boarded the ferry with Signora Mathilde.

'Is Blevio far?'

'No, Signorina,' laughed a young boatman sympathetically, as the inspector reprimanded Gabriella for speaking to him. 'It's after Cernobbio.'

'Thank you,' smiled Gabriella, earning a further look of disapproval from the devout woman beside her. But Signora Mathilde's nagging restraints were like the bite of an ant compared to what she had experienced in her childhood. Earlier she had politely heeded warnings about dust in eyes and ladylike behaviour whenever she had hung out of the coach window to catch for her memory the approaching mountains. Soon, however, Signora Mathilde would be returning to Como to stay with her family until it was time for the return journey to Milan. Then, with luck, thought Gabriella as the dark misty outline of Como disappeared behind the ferry, with luck she might enjoy a little more freedom.

The Villa Rosa – where she was to spend the next three days – was built on a slight elevation, which gave a splendid view of the lake and the gentle slope of its own garden. In the first hour of her arrival, Gabriella's attention was taken up mainly by her hostess, Signora Agnese Prioni; for, after greeting her, Professor Prioni had withdrawn rapidly to his study.

Signora Prioni was not a pretty woman: her features were too strong, especially her nose which, like that of her brother, dominated her face like a curved beak. This feature, together with their lack of height, had immediately reminded Gabriella of two little owls. But as if she were the greatest beauty, the middle-aged spinster bore herself with an air of supreme confidence and her quick and lively glance constantly darted with approval towards her reflection in any mirror that she passed.

'My brother is well known to the professors at the Conservatorio,' the dame said, as she showed Gabriella up to her room. 'That is why we were happy to have you here, especially as I understand your patron is the Princess Belgiojoso herself . . . Such a pity about the Prince . . . I suppose she is, er, greatly distressed?'

'I don't know, Signora Prioni,' replied Gabriella awkwardly, not wanting to betray the little she had been told about the husband's elopement.

'Of course not,' said her hostess quickly. 'I shouldn't ask such questions, but it caused such a scandal locally when Prince Emilio arrived at his villa with the Duchess – usually we get little sensation,' she added, with a flash of her sharp, inquisitive eyes. 'Now, do you like your room? Will you be happy here, do you think?'

'Oh yes, Madame. And the pansies are so pretty,' Gabriella said, appreciating the small vase of flowers which had been placed on the dressing-table.

'I am glad you like them,' said the small woman, her swift fingers pulling one velvety head back into position. 'I quite enjoyed preparing for your visit. My brother locks himself away for hours when he is composing; it will be nice to have a young person to talk to.'

'I'm very glad, Signora Prioni,' smiled Gabriella, though her head was beginning to ache from the sharp timbre of her hostess's voice. 'Does Madame Pasta live far away?'

'Oh no, her villa is just along the lake. It's quicker to go by boat. Andrea will take you tomorrow. Perhaps, when you've rested a little, you would like to take a walk with me in the garden before dinner?'

The next morning, Gabriella awoke with the most delicious feeling of anticipation. Today she was going to meet one of the greatest of dramatic actresses, the woman who her professor had said could imbue just one note with as many different shades as a rainbow or an artist's palette.

'And I, Gabriella Pepe,' she murmured, wriggling her toes as she stretched her arms above her head, 'I am going to meet her!'

Outside there was not one wisp of mist. The sky was a cloudless blue, as one with the lake beneath. For a long time she leant forward from her window and breathed in the crisp air as she looked across to the mountain opposite and followed its green ascent to the sky, noticing here and there the spire of a campanile as it thrust through chestnut trees to announce the presence of a village. So much to explore, she thought, her gaze catching the sun's rays striking what looked like a dome amidst the trees on a promontory across the water. With an exclamation of delight she hugged her nightdress to her and cast one final look at the mirror-like stretch of water and the mysterious dome. There was so much awaiting her!

At precisely half past ten by the Villa Rosa's clock, Gabriella set off for the villa of Giuditta Pasta. She was quite alone in the small rowing boat as Andrea Prioni, locked within his study, had barked at her to go away and not disturb him.

'It is ever so, once he starts to work,' Agnese Prioni had explained as she led Gabriella down to the boat-house. 'Meals, guests, all are forgotten. Wait here, I shall call the gardener, he will row you there.'

'Oh, that is not necessary,' Gabriella assured her hastily. 'I have often rowed on the River Thames.'

'Well, it's hardly seemly for a young lady,' demurred Agnese Prioni, looking shocked. 'But you're very young, I expect you would enjoy it.'

'Oh, I would, I would!' cried Gabriella, almost jumping up and down with excitement.

'Very well – you'll recognize Signora Pasta's villa by the green shutters and pink walls. Go beyond it and you'll come to her boat-house. It's then but a short walk back to the house. You could of course walk there, perhaps that might . . .'

'Oh no, I want to know the lake, and I can swim,' she added cheerfully, leaving before the shocked dame could change her mind.

It took Gabriella a little while to get used to the oars, for although she had been in boats with the boys at Blackfriars, it was not often they had let her do the rowing. But once past the gondola in the boat-house and clear of the entrance, she gradually established a rhythm. The air was fresh, it was the most magical place she had ever known and, gliding past a church at the water's edge, she paused and said a heartfelt prayer for so much good fortune.

As well as pink walls, she had been instructed to look out for two faces.

'You'll know when you come to them, I won't spoil the surprise,' the talkative Signora Prioni had said with a smile.

With the occasional glance over her shoulder Gabriella soon identified the pink walls; next she had to look out for two statues, for that was what she supposed the faces must belong to. Her boat moved parallel with the garden, whose bushes and overhanging trees trailed and dipped low alongside her into the water; now a magnificent magnolia tree appeared before an upper window, its waxen white laden branches making her shake her head in utter delight. And here came the faces! Large, grotesque, carved into the pink stone, one laughing and one looking extremely cross. Did Pasta look cross like that, she wondered, beginning to feel nervous as she rowed on towards the boat-house.

After securing her boat alongside several others, Gabriella walked from the boat-house through a long grotto lined with little pebbles. How deliciously cool such a walk would be on hot days, she thought, remembering the previous scorching summer in Milan. As she emerged from this shady corridor whose open embrasures looked out on to the lake, Gabriella saw a lady busy at work in the sunny garden.

'Excuse me, Signora,' she said, assuming from the old gardening hat and coat that she was a servant. 'I have come to see Signora Pasta.'

'Then you have found her.'

'Oh, forgive me, I didn't expect to find you, er . . .'

'You expected to find me dressed as a Druid Priestess or Anna Bolena perhaps?' asked the prima donna, her broad, good-natured face breaking into a smile. 'And you must be Gabriella, who Mr Lumley believes may cast my shadow when I am gone.'

'Oh, I hope so!' said Gabriella fervently, then, covered in confusion at the implication of what she had said, she blushed scarlet and wondered what she could say to make amends. She felt altogether disconcerted, for she had expected someone grander, someone more like Madame Grisi, whereas this lady was a little ordinary. As her short, stumpy figure limped alongside Gabriella towards the villa, it was difficult to discern that 'something' which had singled her out as the great artist of tragedy.

'You'll find the faces of the great sopranos in there,' smiled Pasta, as they passed another grotto set against the house. 'My dearest friend Malibran is there. Poor Maria died at the age of twenty-eight. So young.'

'Is Madame Grisi there also?'

'Yes,' smiled the prima donna, 'Giulia is there. She sang

Adalgisa to my Norma at its première, and she was only seventeen at the time.'

'She and Signor Mario gave several concerts to raise funds for Signor Mazzini's school . . . Madame Pasta,' said Gabriella, as they were about to pass the two carved faces on the front of the villa's walls. 'Who are these ladies? One looks so happy and the other . . .'

'The two emotions of the theatre,' explained Pasta. 'They are the symbols of *commedia dell'arte*.'

Giuditta Pasta's music room was on the first floor of the villa, and Gabriella found its window faced out on to the magnolia tree. Here the perfect blossoms were close enough to touch; it was a lovely sight, rivalling that through the other part of the window which offered a view of the lake either through plain glass or, lower down, through circles of purple and green.

'It's a lovely room, Madame.'

'Yes,' said Pasta. 'Donizetti wrote Anna Bolena for me here. Now, shall you introduce me to your voice?'

After Gabriella had run through her exercises, Pasta smiled.

'Like most sopranos, your head tones are stronger than the medium.'

'Yes,' replied Gabriella. 'Professor Mazzucato explained that in order to unite the two registers smoothly, I must strengthen the last medium tones and soften the first head tones – oh, and my chin and lips and chest should remain motionless,' added Gabriella, striving to remember all her professor's instructions.

The great singer smiled at the enthusiastic young girl, remembering her own struggles.

'It's a slow process,' she said. 'The voice is like a plant, you can't hurry things along. If you do, the plant will be weak and without substance. A little every day, that's how it must be. And now, let us take coffee in the garden, and you shall tell me all about yourself, for if I am to devote many future hours of my life to you, I must know a little of your heart.'

Blevio was the most delightful of places, with little streams and narrow, steep, winding pathways which led up under the trees to the mountain. The lake was so beautiful that at times Gabriella thought she was moving before a huge painting. On her second day, just after she had returned from Madame Pasta's villa, where she had met the prima donna's husband and her mother, Signora Negri, Professor Prioni emerged from his study and announced that he would take her and Signora Prioni on the steam ferry to Como.

'You must see the black marble at the duomo while you're here, and the visit will impress your priests at the Conservatorio. No doubt you're being indoctrinated with superstition every day!'

'Hush, Andrea!' scolded Agnese Prioni in a scandalized voice. 'You mustn't say such things before the girl. You mustn't interfere, just because you've lapsed.'

'I haven't lapsed, I never was!' snorted the grey-haired composer. 'I had the good sense to become a Free Thinker!'

It was the first time Gabriella had heard anyone speak so, and she was more interested than shocked, for the one thing she had disliked from her first day at the Conservatorio was the daily doses of Christian doctrine on the timetable. No one else seemed to mind, but they had been brought up in the faith since infancy, whereas Menotti had sent any black cassock-clad figure flying in fright – all, that is, she thought with a fond smile, but the black-suited figure of Giuseppe Mazzini.

Compared to the approach to the bay of Como, past golden and pink villas casting their sun-gilded reflections on the rippling blue waters, Gabriella thought the streets of the town very gloomy and dark. When she learnt it had been the headquarters of the fearful Inquisition, her imagination pictured terrible deeds. As they walked around the cathedral and her host pointed scornful fingers at petticoats and personal items draped on shrines, which were supposed to have saved the wearer from some horrible fate, Gabriella looked fearfully around to see if his ribald comments were being overheard. Despite the treat of sorbet, she found she was not sorry to board the ferry and leave the town to its past, and to the heavy presence of Austria's soldiers, about whom Professor Prioni was even more scathing.

It had surprised and slightly worried Gabriella that she had not been asked to sing again. On the last occasion she and Pasta met, they had again only talked and taken a walk through the garden along the side of the lake. The famous prima donna was so easy and kindly that Gabriella had to keep reminding herself that her future was partly dependent upon her companion; but she always felt so relaxed and carefree that she chatted away about her past and her opinions on the music she had heard at the Conservatorio.

'So, you will love nothing but Mozart!' teased Giuditta Pasta, as they passed by her conservatory and the villa which housed the servants.

'No, never! No one could be finer!'

'And Bellini and Verdi?'

'I do not know their music, but I do not see how they can be half as fine!' declared Gabriella passionately.

'Is that so?' murmured Pasta, stopping beside a huge cedar of Lebanon whose branches dipped out low over the lake. 'Do you not think it somewhat foolhardy to make such declarations from ignorance?' she scolded. 'Perhaps you should wait until you know a little more before you make rash judgements.'

'Oh dear,' gasped Gabriella. 'Have I made you angry? It's just that I feel so . . .'

'Passionate!' said Pasta, patting Gabriella's cheek and giving her an affectionate smile filled with understanding. 'I know just how you feel, and if you didn't I don't suppose I would be seeing you again.'

'Does that mean . . .?'

'Your professors must hear my decision first,' said Giuditta Pasta gravely. 'But Blevio and Bellini will be waiting.'

It was hint enough. Gabriella, unable to control her joy, flung her arms around the Pasta and kissed her passionately on the cheek.

'Oh, I wish it could be now! Now!' she cried.

'You have much hard work and growing up to do first,' said Giuditta Pasta as they reached the boat-house. 'Goodbye, Gabriella, and God go with you.'

Filled with happiness that she would return to Blevio and to

Pasta, Gabriella pulled on her oars with such enthusiasm that the small boat went flying outwards towards the centre of the lake. She was about to correct her course when the sight of the sunny promontory, over which the mountain never seemed to cast its shadow, beckoned to her across the water.

Every day since her arrival, her eyes had been drawn across to this spur of land and the golden villa which Signora Prioni had mentioned was owned by the Austrian Viceroy, the Archduke Ranieri. He had acquired it in mysterious circumstances.

'The owner died in 1841,' Agnese Prioni had explained on the morning they had first walked to the boat-house. 'And, as I understand, he left it to the hospital in Como. The next thing, the Archduke has it, with no public auction as the law demands. They do what they want in Lombardy, these Austrians!'

It was early summer, so there were few private boats on the lake. As there was no flag flying at the large villa, and its windows were shuttered, Gabriella assumed that the Viceroy was not at home. Nevertheless, for safety she decided not to leave her boat at the landing quay, but at a little iron gate more out of view further along the wall.

To her delight this gate was open; inside it Gabriella found a slipway which led her upwards between stone walls. After a few steps up this cool, dark path she could see sunlight striking into a garden at the top. So, abandoning caution, she ran the remaining distance. As she entered the garden, though, she suddenly noticed a gardener sweeping leaves from the close-clipped ornamental lawn. He was some distance away, and at the moment had his back to her so, anxious not to be spotted, she took the path upwards to the right, resisting a long terraced walk heavy with the scent of jasmine, for the gardener was now down below, and if he were to look up he would surely see her. Her path was gradually taking her away from the buildings, but she didn't mind, for the parkland was beautiful, with majestic trees so numerous and high she could not see their tops or guess their names. Often there was a choice of paths, some of which no doubt led to a lower level of the grounds but, having set her course, and filled with a growing certainty that it was leading her to the mysterious dome, she kept straight on. Finally, after about fifteen minutes, around the corner of a high hedge, she found it, standing in its own clearing. This was what she had seen thrusting upwards through the trees: a family mausoleum, she realized. Pleased with her find, Gabriella walked around the circular stone wall and found several steps at the front leading up to a black iron gate. Curious to see what was inside, she mounted the steps and pressed her face against the cold bars: the stained-glass window in the gloomy interior was brilliant; the Madonna a vivid, breathtaking blue. Transfixed, Gabriella stared at the white-clad baby Jesus on his mother's knee and she began to feel a stir of emotions, like distant vibrations that she could not quite hear. Her heart began to race; she felt such a strong sense of recognition within that she spun around and, pressing her hands against her temples, tried to calm her mind; she could not understand why she should be affected so powerfully. She turned and pulled at the gate to enter but it was locked. In the dim interior she could just make out one name on a tomb: Balziano. Balziano. The name rang in her head over and over as the bars cut into her hands under her grip. Inexplicably, a feeling of dread came upon her as her mind reached out to she knew not what.

All she could think of was to get away from this tomb in the silent clearing. She turned and ran, panicking, not choosing her route, rushing down a steep path which led her into the garden where the gardener had been. He had moved away; instead, between Gabriella and the opening to the slipway stood a young man who was looking at the panting girl with some surprise. Still upset and overwrought, she didn't care a fig that she was trespassing. Glaring fiercely, she made to run past this Austrian who had grabbed Italian property.

'Please wait!' he cried and, as she took no notice, the Austrian stepped forward and she felt his hand touch her shoulder.

'Let go, *tedesco* thief!' she cried, as she thrust his arm away.

Taken by surprise, losing his balance on the wet ground

in front of the fountain, the man slipped and, reeling backwards, fell into the round ornamental pond. At another time, Gabriella would have collapsed with laughter, but appalled and frightened at what she had done to this high-ranking Austrian noble, she fled towards the iron gateway through which she had come.

On gaining the boat, Gabriella jumped in and, yanking free the rope, pushed hard away against the wall. Her first frantic stroke caught only at air and she bit her lip in irritation and anxiety as running footsteps sounded down the slipway. Though her heart was pounding and her thoughts still in a whirl, somehow she managed to co-ordinate both oars in one slow, deliberate stroke. The boat moved away from the boundary wall of the villa. Two, three, four more and there was a safe distance between her and the tall figure which had appeared at the water's edge. Thankful that there was no boat in which he could give chase, Gabriella ignored the calls to return. Now certain of escape, she eventually released the oars and leant forward to regain her breath.

To her surprise, she found she was trembling all over and her face and hair were wet with sweat. After a minute or so of respite she looked up: the figure at the iron gate had disappeared; all seemed unoccupied, undisturbed as before, only now, deliberately, she stopped her glance short of the mausoleum amongst the trees. Bending over the side of the boat as if to wash its memory away, she scooped up a handful of water. Like the icy droplets of a fountain, the water splashed against her face; in her mind she recalled the stranger falling backwards into the liquid white plumes; but then, blotting out all else and making her heart inexplicably race, all she could see was his face.

# Chapter Five

Upon her return to the Conservatorio, Gabriella was besieged with questions from her friends about her trip to Como. She was happy to describe in detail everything that had happened to her – everything, that is, except her visit to the Viceroy's summer residence. Very soon she herself forgot all about it as studies totally absorbed all her thoughts. Some weeks later, though, when she was doing her laundry with Giuseppina, something which her friend said nearly made her drop the hot coal she was putting into her iron.

'Do you mean that someone like the Viceroy could ask me to go and sing at his home?'

'Of course,' replied Giuseppina, surprised at the sound of dismay in Gabriella's voice. 'More often it is the Contesse Clara Maffei and Giuseppina Appiani who request students to perform at their salons, but it can also be members of the Austrian court. It's a great opportunity to show what one can do. Don't look so worried,' she laughed. 'It's not likely to happen to you yet. Anyway, Archdukes don't eat music students at their dinner parties!'

'But if one had pushed him or one of his family into a fountain . . .' murmured Gabriella.

Giuseppina Verenese stared at the thick downsweep of lashes which concealed the expression in Gabriella's eyes. She knew her to be far too boisterous at play in the garden, and she was always in trouble for running down the corridors; but to push someone into water – surely even Gabriella wouldn't do such a thing.

'What nonsense are you talking about? Who would push any

91

Austrian into a fountain? Why, they would find themselves in prison if they did!'

'I did,' whispered Gabriella looking up, her expression tense with anxiety. 'When I was at Blevio . . . I was curious about Archduke Ranieri's villa. When I was leaving its garden a young man tried to stop me . . . I pushed and he slipped and . . .' Suddenly the laughter which had been denied at the time bubbled up inside and Gabriella started to shake with merriment, and as if she too could see the scene, her friend Giuseppina began to laugh as well.

'Did he go straight in?'

'Yes, yes! He made a very big splash, though I didn't dare look around. I was fleeing for my life at the time!'

'Oh, what if you'd been caught!' exclaimed Giuseppina, clasping her hands together as dramatic horror replaced laughter. 'And he must have known where you were from – your dress! Everyone knows the uniform of the Conservatorio!'

'Perhaps he could only see weeds and water lilies at the time,' laughed Gabriella, trying to ignore what had previously crossed her own mind. 'Whoever he is, though, I hope he won't remember me if I'm ever asked to perform in society.'

'Oh, I shouldn't worry,' replied Giuseppina, her earnest face filled with reassurance. 'By then you'll be different. You're much taller and fatter than when you first came here, so just think what you'll be like in a year or so!'

'Not fatter I hope!' laughed Gabriella, tugging one of Giuseppina's plaits.

Gabriella's own plaits now reached well below her waist. Having reached there, they grew no longer. But, just as Giuseppina had forecast, the hem of her dress had to be dropped twice and, when the time came a year later to change her summer dress for a warmer winter one, she had to request a larger size.

'You are quite right, Signorina,' Matron declared upon examining the inside hems of Gabriella's bodice. 'Two and a half years ago you were like a stick, but now there isn't anything to let out. Anyway, it's appropriate you have something new for . . .'

92

'For what?' enquired Gabriella, her eyes widening with interest.

A slightly guilty flush tinged the sallow face, but then the nostrils in the long sharp nose visibly tightened and Matron fixed Gabriella with a stern stare.

'You represent the Conservatorio when you walk through the city, Signorina. You should always look presentable – you might remind yourself that rough, violent movements place a strain on stitches and material, all of which causes expense to your patron! And speaking of the Princess Belgiojoso, I believe this letter which arrived for you yesterday may be from her.'

'Thank you,' said Gabriella, now understanding that guilty blush: whatever had nearly escaped from between Matron's thin lips would doubtless be contained within her letter; Matron was well known for her avid curiosity.

Outside in the Conservatorio garden the paths and lawns were still masked by the overnight frost, but now warmed by the weak rays of the sun, the translucent veil retained the three-pronged imprints of tiny feet. Apart from the birds it seemed that no one else had braved the garden since she had visited it earlier, so she had the wintry scene completely to herself.

Her letter was indeed from the Princess Belgiojoso.

I hope to arrive in Milan at the end of December and will look forward to calling upon you at the Conservatorio. Permission from Conte Borromeo and your Principal has been obtained for you to attend the Opera in my box should you wish to do so.

'Should I wish to do so!' shouted Gabriella, feeling she might explode with excitement and forgetting Matron's recent caution as she whirled around on the spot with the letter in her outflung hand . . . 'Should I wish to do so . . . I do, I do!'

The beautiful church of S. Maria della Passione had been dressed for Christmas, and now not even the two sixteenth-century Antegnati organs with their rich wood carvings and painted doors by Urbani and Dante Crespi could compete for attention against the simple, rustic crib. It was a special time and, for Gabriella, the most special of Sundays, for today she would receive a visitor just like other students. As she did every year, she renewed her vow not to fail the Princess or any of the other people who had helped her get to Milan. Christmas always made her think of Nico too: she missed him dreadfully, though the life they had shared seemed so distant now. But every year when she looked at the crib, she thought of the night when he had pointed out the star which had led the three wise men to the stable in Bethlehem. No doubt it had been just any star, Gabriella thought with a wry smile as she moved from the crib to light her candle, but he had always made things seem so real. Her small yellow flame added its light to the other candles, and tearfully she watched it burn, silent and steady, hoping that Nico would feel its warmth and her prayers, wherever he might be.

There seemed no change in the appearance of the Princess Christina Belgiojoso since Gabriella had last seen her: the same pearls hung from her ears and her dress was still a simple robe of grey. After their initial greetings were over, though, Gabriella noticed that her large black eyes were weary and her complexion was quite waxen. Gabriella's own appearance had, however, quite startled her patron.

'Why Gabriella, whatever happened to the rough little girl that came to me in Paris? You have grown into a graceful young lady.'

'It's due to all the ballet lessons,' smiled Gabriella, glowing with pleasure at her patron's evident approval. 'Will your stay in Milan be a long one, your Highness?'

'That depends on the flotation of shares in my newspaper.'

'Won't that be dangerous for you? My professor told me that the newspaper you started in Paris is banned here.'

'And in Florence, and Turin,' added Christina Belgiojoso with a sigh. 'As editor I endeavoured to make sure that the content of *Gazzetta Italiana* was not too provocative, but nothing will pass the censor here. I'm exhausted, my dear Gabriella, but I'm determined to keep the newspaper alive. I'm here to raise money; let the Austrians arrest me if they dare!'

'But will people support something which they cannot receive?' asked Gabriella, filled with admiration for the Princess's courage and determination.

'If they are patriots, yes. Italy's enslaved provinces need a mouthpiece.'

'Aren't you afraid of prison?'

'My arrest would expose Habsburg rule to the whole of Europe as a tyranny which suppresses free thought! When I take my place in my box at La Scala I hope it will inspire all good patriots!'

One of the daily rituals which society observed in Milan was the Corso, which took place on the high rampart walk between the Porta Nuova and the Porta Rense. In a low carriage called a bastardelle, from which society ladies took their sorbets in the Corsia dei Servi, Gabriella sat with her patron and looked at Milan's promenade as they completed the customary circuit before joining the two stationary lines of carriages.

'Before Napoleon brought us our Republic, only families of forty-eight quarterings might bring their carriages,' explained Christina Belgiojoso to Gabriella on the day set for their visit to La Scala. 'After his defeat, the Restoration imposed the old rules for a time, but I'm glad to say things are now much more relaxed: as you see, there are many carriages here without coronets.'

'Then my presence with someone of your rank is not so shocking,' smiled Gabriella.

'Ah, Milan expects anything of me. I long ago shocked the traditionalists by what they termed my eccentricities. Many still hold it a breach of etiquette to engage in conversation with acquaintances here; but I do not care to sit like a mute statue.'

For the next half-hour, until the *Ave Maria* began to sound, Gabriella watched her patron receive homage. She was pleased that her French was fluent enough to follow the rapid witty exchanges that her patron seemed to inspire.

'Ah, I wish I could talk like that,' she declared as they

departed to make ready for the winter start of half past seven at La Scala.

'All things come in time,' laughed the Princess. 'Though I fear,' she said with a gesture towards a carriage emblazoned with armorial arms, 'the Marchese Balziano will not see the dispute over his brother's palace settled in his lifetime. Things can take a very long time in Vienna, especially when property sequestrated on account of high treason is involved. The Villa Pizzo, which you no doubt saw across the lake from Blevio, was returned to the late Marchese when he was released from prison; but his Milan home, over there, was not.'

'Who lives in it?' asked Gabriella, looking away from the carriage and its haughty occupants towards an impressive façade.

'No one. The high-ranking Austrian officials are probably still arguing over it, while the Marchese's lawyers continue to send off their countless appeals to the Emperor in Vienna, where no doubt they gather dust along with all the other testimonies of injustice.'

Since it was a vital part of their education, and also served to inspire them to work harder, all the students at the Conservatorio had seats reserved for them at important productions. Although Gabriella was, therefore, quite familiar with Piermarini's masterpiece, its impact never lessened, nor did her admiration for the six elegant tiers of crimson draped boxes or Alessandro Sanquirico's spectacular chandelier, hung in 1823. She was, nevertheless, quite unprepared for what it would be like to step out into a box owned by one of Lombardy's noblest daughters. Only on first nights was there complete silence at La Scala: at other times people chatted and played cards and turned their opera glasses not towards the stage but upon each chandelier-lit salon, to see who was with whom and who had drawn their curtains for a tête-à-tête. The glint of glasses directed tonight upon the famous, newly-returned patriot – and thus upon herself – was almost blinding, and Gabriella felt as if she had stepped out on to the stage itself. At least the simplicity of the Princess's attire did not make her own seem inappropriate, she thought, envying the composed, languid way in which the Princess looked around the house and received salutations before reclining upon her couch.

'Don't look so anxious, Gabriella,' said her patron, as if realizing how self-conscious she felt. 'Would you like me to have all the candles extinguished in here?'

'Oh, I'm sure I'll soon get used to it. I feel a little under-dressed, there are so many gorgeous gowns.'

'Yes, well, perhaps it will give you more confidence if I tell you that many of the heads under those velvet and feathered hats are very short on intellect,' murmured the Princess, half turning as the first of her visitors entered.

Unlike the rest of the house, who only turned their attention to the stage to applaud patriotic lines and thus aggravate the Austrians present, Gabriella was much occupied in studying the soprano's superb declamation, when suddenly even her own attention was diverted, as a loud outburst in a box opposite developed into a quarrel which crescendoed for all to hear.

'You are a bungling fool!' shouted a man.

'It is not I who is the fool but you, blockhead,' cried another.

'*Zitti zitti!*' shouted students from the pit.

'What is happening?' Gabriella asked one of the gentlemen present.

'Just the usual little dispute over *tarocchi*. Do you enjoy cards?'

Gabriella confessed that she didn't know how to play the game and, as the quarrel was still at its height, she picked up her opera glasses to gain a closer view of the people who were causing the disturbance. One of the players had stood up and, to her surprise and delight, she recognized the angry face of the young Conte who had given her a ride in his carriage on her first day at the Conservatorio.

It couldn't have been the glint of her glasses that made the young man look towards Gabriella, for nightly attendance soon made one immune to blatant scrutiny. No, it was more a moment of exasperation, mingled with a loss of interest in

97

the diversion of a dispute, which led Conte Giovanni Forro to glance across to the boxes opposite. By the slender graceful neck and her slight, grey-covered shoulders he recognized the Princess Belgiojoso, even though she sat with her back to the auditorium. Not for the first time that evening, the young man's eyes rested on the Princess's enchanting companion. She was quite young – about sixteen, he judged – and quite deliciously forward, for he saw with a surge of excitement that not only was she smiling in the most familiar way, but also that she was actually beckoning to him. Without further delay, Giovanni Forro made his excuses to his hostess and left to call upon the Belgiojoso box. His mother the Contessa was on cordial terms with the Princess and, as she must be aware of his republicanism, he knew he would be given entry. To ensure a warm reception, though, and as it was almost the end of the first act, he decided to arrive with sorbet.

Just as Gabriella had hoped, it seemed that her past acquaintance had remembered her. He arrived within minutes bringing, to everyone's astonishment, a selection of pezzi duri, crepé and gelati.

'Why, how thoughtful of you, Conte,' exclaimed the Princess. 'But are you on the appropriate side of the house? Wouldn't your erstwhile companion appreciate something to cool his feelings?'

'Ah, that has been taken care of, Donna Christina.'

'Such generosity; why, I have never met the like of it before. You young men are freer with your money than my generation were,' said an elderly gentleman dryly.

'It is but a small tribute to pay to one of our greatest patriots, Prince Casati; and it is but a small tribute to pay to the beauty of the ladies,' rejoined the young man, his eyes darting from the Princess towards Gabriella as he sat down. According to the strict rule of etiquette, whenever a new guest arrived the first one had to withdraw, and so Gabriella watched the door with some impatience for any new arrivals who would eventually bring the Conte around to the seat next to hers. With someone of the standing of her patron, she did not have long to wait.

'Ah, at last I have reached my goal,' whispered Giovanni

Forro as he sat beside Gabriella. 'You are new to Milan, I think. Did you come from Paris with the Princess?'

Gabriella looked at the young man and realized it was not recognition of her that had brought him to her side. She decided to tease him a little.

'I hope, Conte, that your affairs go well with your friends at the Porta Tosa, and that your Marchesa's heart has warmed towards you.'

Giovanni Forro's jaw dropped, then Gabriella saw his eyes take in her uniform. Slowly his expression changed and understanding dawned in his brown eyes.

'It is too late,' she teased. 'Confess, you had quite forgotten me!'

'No, well, a little,' admitted the Conte sheepishly. 'But you had an unfair advantage, for you have quite grown up.'

'But so have you!'

'Not as you have,' sighed the young nobleman, his eager eyes engaged in an inventory of the charms before him. 'Though your eyes should have given you away. There's not another lady in Milan who has the dark violet of yours.'

'Not even your adored Marchesa?'

'No, Flavia's eyes are like shining jet,' murmured the young man, darting a look across the auditorium. Gabriella followed its direction and decided that a striking young woman wearing orange must be the adored Marchesa. She also saw with interest that it was the same haughty young lady who had been in the carriage which the Princess Belgiojoso had drawn her attention to earlier, on their return from the Corso.

'So that must be the Marchesa Balziano. No wonder you are smitten,' she said with a soft laugh. 'She is very beautiful.'

'There are many like her in Lombardy,' flushed the young man irritably. 'It is you that I wish to talk about. Will you allow me to call upon you?'

'At the Conservatorio?' teased Gabriella.

'Can you never escape from your prison? A note, perhaps, when you are going for a walk with your friends, or to church. Will you let me know, Gabriella?'

Before she could answer, the arrival of a new guest forced

the Conte to vacate his seat. Casting a furious look at this interloper, he moved on.

Gradually, as other arrivals displaced those present, the conversation turned to the flotation of shares of the *Gazzetta Italiana*. Feeling she ought not to listen, Gabriella picked up her glasses to look at the ballet. First, however, she swung them along the tiers of boxes, just in case she could spot any more of the young men she had met at the house at the Porta Tosa. Would they recognize or even remember her, she wondered? As her glasses caught the faces in the boxes, Gabriella suddenly sucked in her breath. It was him! Worse, the young man of the Villa Pizzo was staring directly at her! Quite flustered, Gabriella put down the glasses. Then, to make sure she had not mistaken the hateful *tedesco* for another man, she picked up her glasses and took a second look. Within the circle of magnification the curve of the man's lips widened into a smile, and then his thick black brows lifted and the corners of his lips pulled down slightly in a quizzical expression full of humour. Held mesmerized in this silent communion, Gabriella's heart somersaulted; confused, then angry, remembering he was an enemy, she snatched the glasses away and reversed them, just as the ladies did to show disfavour to their suitors. Now she viewed a reduced figure, but not so small a one that she missed the mocking salute as he turned away.

'Princess, forgive me interrupting you, but who is the Austrian in that box?'

Caught in mid-sentence, Christina Belgiojoso looked sternly at her protégée. She glanced distractedly to where she thought the young woman had pointed.

'That is Conte Giacomo Levati. He's not Austrian, my dear Gabriella, although he does have a high post in the Civil Service. Poor man, he is penniless; he had to take it. Don't ever talk politics when he is around, though. He is expected to spy for his salary.'

Her patron's words overwhelmed Gabriella with dismay, and all the joy of the evening fled.

# Chapter Six

The discovery that the young man of Pizzo was not a hated Austrian but, even worse, one of their creatures, filled Gabriella with dismay and disappointment. An enemy was one thing, but to think that such a face masked a cowardly, traitorous heart, ready to betray his own countrymen for money, made her feel utterly miserable.

Nor, it seemed, was Gabriella the only person to experience disappointment, for it clearly showed on her patron's face when, some weeks after the visit to La Scala, she called at the Conservatorio to bid farewell to Gabriella.

'I shall be leaving Milan soon for my casino at Locate. There perhaps I can do something for my peasants and be appreciated. The apathy amongst the Lombard nobles has quite drained my energy for politics.'

'I am very glad you were not arrested, Donna Christina,' said Gabriella, walking along one of the cloisters with her patron. 'Teachers and students here admire your courage very much.'

'Glad! I assure you, Gabriella, that I am bitterly disappointed. Perhaps if the Governor Count Spaur had taken such action, my martyrdom might have roused a few consciences. As it is, very few shares in the newspaper have been bought – yet Prince Emilio and I were always generous in aiding patriots like Mazzini. Conte Balbo's open appeal to the Princes urged them to link themselves with the movement for national liberty, and in coming here I was prepared to go to Spielberg for the rest of my life if it served the cause. Instead I have been ignored and thus humiliated!'

Spielberg! Gabriella's heart contracted with shock and the remainder of Christina Belgiojoso's words went unheard.

'What is Spielberg, your Highness?' she enquired, trying to control the feeling of fear which was growing within her.

'It is a terrible prison in Moravia . . .' Christina Belgiojoso looked at Gabriella with concern. 'Are you feeling unwell, my dear? You have become very pale. Surely you do not know someone who has gone to such a place?'

'No,' mumbled Gabriella. 'I . . . just felt a little faint, I have been studying very hard.'

'Yes, I know. Professor Frasi is most pleased with your progress and you have not disappointed my faith in you. Nor, I hope, will you do so in the future.'

Gabriella could hardly bear to return the Princess's grave smile, for as strongly as she felt she had seen the stained-glass window in the family mausoleum at the Villa Pizzo before, she knew she had heard the name of Spielberg. Was that the key to the secret of her past? Had her father been a thief, some low criminal, caught stealing and imprisoned there? In London the tiniest of children were used . . . Gabriella glanced anxiously at the haughty profile of the Princess Belgiojoso walking beside her and her mouth went dry with fear. What would happen if some terrible secret from her past were to be uncovered?

Expression, phrasing, giving light and shade, swelling the sounds, portamento, the executing of the different embel-lishments of singing: these were all part of the knowledge that she was acquiring to make her ready to begin her studies with Giuditta Pasta in the summer.

'Good morning, Gabriella,' said Professor Mazzucato look-ing up with a smile as she entered for her lesson one morning. 'Let's get that brain working. What is an appoggiatura?'

'It is a small unharmonized note placed above or sometimes below an ordinary note, Professor.'

'Would you change key for it?'

'No. If above, it stands either a tone or semitone higher than the adjacent note, and the key it was found in remains the same;

102

below, it always stands a semitone lower, and sometimes it is necessary to change the key to achieve this.'

'Said like a pretty parrot.'

'Just so long as I don't sound like one!'

'Fishing for compliments this morning are we, Signorina?' said the professor, who was always as much cheered by the sight of one of his favourite students as by the sound of her voice. 'Think Merelli is waiting outside with a contract for you?'

'Oh, do you think I'll ever be offered a contract?' sighed Gabriella, taking up her usual position in readiness to begin.

'If you were relying on your ability on the pianoforte, the answer would be a certain no . . . Now to work, young lady, if you hope to leave us in June for Bellini, Blevio, and Giuditta Pasta!'

Bellini's music was new to Gabriella. Seated before the window which looked out on to the magnolia tree and the lake, with the score of *Norma* on her knee, she proceeded to follow the sequence of notes of the 'Casta Diva', but soon she leant back and closed her eyes, her senses totally captured by the haunting majesty of the music and the rich voice gliding upwards, touching notes of sublime beauty, twirling, spiralling downwards into playful cascades, then onwards, borne aloft once more to such intensity that tears glistened in Gabriella's eyes as the last golden shimmer of Pasta's voice disappeared. After a while she felt the hands of her teacher on her shoulders.

'I know what you're thinking, but don't be afraid of it as I was.'

'You were afraid?'

'Of course,' smiled Giuditta Pasta sitting on the other chair before the window. 'When I first saw the "Casta Diva" I was afraid I could not do it justice – I cannot count the hours I worked on it. On the night of the performance I sent Bellini my lampshade and a bunch of silk flowers; my note said: This lamp by night and these flowers by day witnessed my studies of *Norma* and the desire I cherish to be ever more worthy of your esteem . . . I'll never forget writing it.' She sighed. 'Nor my terror when learning the role . . . Poor Vincenzo, he died so young. Some say Heinrich Heine frightened him to death when he told him in Paris that he would die young because his gift had made the gods jealous; but he was always delicate. And that is something you cannot afford to be if you wish to do justice to Norma. It's one thing to sing one aria, but to play the leading role week after week . . . that requires strength and stamina. See, take a look at my performance diary,' said the prima donna, handing Gabriella a tiny little blue-backed book. 'Some weeks I sang the part of Norma three times: that strain on an immature voice would be fatal.'

'They say Giuseppina Strepponi's voice never recovered from *Nabucco*.'

'Quite so. Remember what I said last time we met: the strongest plants are those which have not been forced.'

Gabriella was once again staying with Agnese and Andrea Prioni at the Villa Rosa. After the strict regime at the Conservatorio, life with them was very relaxed, and when her daily lesson with Giuditta Pasta was over, Gabriella was free to do as she pleased. Often she walked up to the high meadows which were a delight of flowers and herbs: there she would lie for hours in the shade of a chestnut and think about the music which they were studying. To study the composer and reflect upon the role one was playing was essential, Pasta had said, otherwise one's interpretation would be shallow and soulless.

One afternoon, having returned from such a mountain walk with her arms filled with wild flowers for Agnese Prioni, she found that she had had a visitor during her absence.

'Conte Forro?' she exclaimed in astonishment.

'Yes!' laughed Signora Prioni. 'He called on us and left his card. Such a splendid boat he arrived in; he requested that he might visit tomorrow afternoon. A most charming and very eligible young man – I took the liberty of saying yes, was that all right, dear? He did say that he met you at La Scala in the Princess Belgiojoso's box, and you see so few young people here, I thought it might break the monotony of your life.'

'It's not monotonous,' laughed Gabriella. 'It's a wonderful life; but it would be fun to see the Conte, though they would be scandalized at the Conservatorio!'

'Yes, I suppose they would be,' rejoined her hostess with a girlish giggle. 'I see no harm as long as I don't let you out of my sight. It will be the first Conte that I have received here – and he was so very charming.'

The following day, Agnese Prioni rushed to greet Gabriella the moment she returned from Pasta's villa. She had donned her best silk, and now insisted that Gabriella should change into the high-necked summer dress of the Conservatorio.

'After all, dear, you are the protégée of a Princess, and she would feel I had failed in my duty if you appear before a Conte in that old skirt and blouse.'

'I don't see why Giovanni should mind if Signora Pasta doesn't,' said Gabriella cheerfully. 'But if it pleases you I shall change immediately, just in case you decide to take these clothes back.'

'Perhaps I should,' replied Agnese Prioni nervously. 'For the skirt looks very odd with a different coloured hem.'

Terrified of losing her glorious freedom and the comfortable old skirt, Gabriella fled, grasping in her hands as she raced up the stairs the bottom section which had been cut from another old garment. The added piece was necessary in order for the skirt to reach her ankles, for now, of course, she was much taller than her little hostess.

Gabriella waved when Giovanni Forro stepped ashore at the landing stage, and would have raced down the sloping garden to meet him except for her chaperon's whispered reminder that it was more proper to remain seated under the shade of the wistaria.

'Good afternoon, Signora Prioni,' said the young noble, kissing the dame's hand with exaggerated gallantry. 'And good day to you, Signorina Gabriella,' he added, acknowledging Gabriella with a stiff bow. Such formality, thought Gabriella, trying not to laugh.

'It is very agreeable to see you, Conte,' she remarked with what she hoped was the cool air of a hostess accustomed to receiving numerous such calls. 'Would you care for lemon tea? It is something which Signora Prioni and I enjoy.'

The young man accepted the tea, and with assumed calmness made small talk with Agnese Prioni, until at last he became obviously restless and Gabriella found his gaze increasingly turned upon herself.

'You have a delightful garden, Signora Prioni, which would seem worthy of closer inspection. I would not wish to disturb you yourself,' the young man added hastily, 'but perhaps . . .?' He inclined his eyes towards Gabriella, who watched her chaperon melt under a smile loaded with persuasive charm.

'Yes, it is lovely,' purred Agnese Prioni, 'and from here it is so advantageous to be able to see every corner of it. Perhaps,' she continued, having made her meaning clear to all present, 'perhaps, Gabriella, you might like to show the Conte my lovely azaleas.'

'Ah, at last!' whispered Giovanni Forro, as soon as he and Gabriella were out of earshot. 'I could not believe my good fortune when I learnt that you had left Milan for Blevio. But why did you not let me know?'

'I should let you know?' laughed Gabriella in astonishment. 'And who told you that I was here?'

'I have friends in the Conservatorio!'

'Ah, the student Mario, who was present the first time I met you and your friends. He always smiles at me and my friend when we attend Mass.'

'Oh, does he!' said the young Conte fiercely.

'Well, I think it's directed at my friend Giuseppina,' said Gabriella hastily, as the young man seemed on the point of a jealous outburst.

'You have caused me great unhappiness, Gabriella. I have not had an hour's sleep since I saw you at La Scala!'

'Then you look remarkably fresh on such suffering!' she chuckled, unable to take such exaggeration seriously.

'Do not mock me,' snapped Giovanni petulantly, then, as if seized by fresh passion, he tried to take hold of her hand.

A discreet cough from the top of the garden reminded them both of the watching sentinel. 'Perhaps you will be allowed to come with me on the lake tomorrow so that we can be alone,' he whispered.

'I don't think you will lose Signora Prioni that easily,' smiled Gabriella.

'You smile!'

'I'm sorry, Giovanni. It's kind of you to ask me, your boat is beautiful and it would be fun,' Gabriella said regretfully. 'But there are other people who would not wish me to be alone with you, especially a gentleman by the name of . . .'

'You have a lover!'

'No, of course not.' She blushed.

'Then who is this man?'

'Bellini.'

'Bellini? He is dead!'

'Not his music,' she said with a smile, 'and it is that which I have started to study with Signora Pasta.'

'How can that have anything to do with me?' exclaimed the young nobleman, quite bewildered by her response.

'You would distract me,' responded Gabriella calmly.

'Of course I would want to distract you . . . divert you with compliments, with kisses . . . with all the soft caresses of love. Do you not want that?' he said, his brown eyes gleaming with confident invitation.

'If I think of you I shall not think of Bellini, and that would waste the hours that Giuditta Pasta is giving to me,' explained Gabriella, not wishing to be hurtful. 'She says that to find the essence one must shut out everything else; there is only room for the composer and the librettist.'

'Then I wish you enjoyment of your solitude,' said Giovanni Forro sarcastically. 'Perhaps you would feel more at home singing in a convent . . . Pray, do not let me keep you from your composer a moment longer,' he added, striding away to where his oarsmen waited.

Sadly Gabriella watched him. She hadn't wanted to make him angry. Perhaps she hadn't explained it well enough. But she was so close to her goal now and nothing, no matter how pleasant, must tempt her away. The music was taxing and difficult and she well understood the desperation her teacher must have experienced when she studied it all those years ago, and how heavy a burden it must have been for her to carry the music to its audience for the first time. But she could imagine too the power and joy such an experience would bring, whilst realizing how much she had yet to learn. So, although the flattery and attention paid to her by the handsome young Milanese gave Gabriella a thrill of pleasure, it was nothing compared to the moments she spent in Pasta's music room, nor the resolve which each day tightened like a spring of steel within her as she prepared for the great moment when, one day, she would walk out before her first audience.

Gabriella did not tell Agnese why Conte Forro had departed in such haste, and thought that that would be the end of the matter. However, two weeks later, despite her rebuff, Giovanni Forro appeared unexpectedly when Agnese was at church.

'Signora Prioni will be cross that you have called unannounced,' Gabriella told him as his oarsmen moved away from the Prioni landing stage. 'I should not let you stay here. She will be back soon.'

'No she won't,' replied the young man cheerfully. 'She has only just arrived. All wise Catholics are praying hard for the election of a liberal Pope, so doubtless she will be away for some time! I only hope the white smoke won't appear from the Vatican until the very end of summer, so that I can introduce you to far more exciting things than singing.'

'Will the election of a new Pope change things much?' asked Gabriella, looking away to hide the blush which these words had caused.

Giovanni Forro glanced at the profile of the girl beside him and sighed. It was no time to think and talk of serious matters when a fraction away were lips which promised to be soft and moist.

'Well, if they did elect a liberal, things should improve in the Papal States; but I doubt they'll do that, so the church will continue its divine suppression and tyranny over its subjects . . . But I refuse to speak of something so depressing on such a lovely day; besides, I came to tell you that I am interested in your singing . . . I've been telling a friend of Verdi all about you. Ah, that's much better!' laughed the young man, as Gabriella turned to him, her eyes gleaming with delight. 'I thought that might be the path to your cold heart. Verdi has been resting for health reasons: usually he is disinclined to write anything for a singer, but he is republican in belief and, as you are a friend of Mazzini, who knows, he may be persuaded to write a little showpiece for you.'

'Oh, Giovanni,' exclaimed Gabriella, amazed at such a proposal. 'You're teasing me!' she laughed.

'No, I'm quite serious. You'll soon be asked to the salons – Mario told me that Professor Mazzucato thinks you're exceptional – and my friend sometimes collaborates with Verdi and Conte Maffei, so I could possibly persuade him to speak on your behalf . . . But first, of course, I might have to be persuaded,' said the young man, moving dangerously close to her.

'Giovanni! You are a scoundrel!'

'No, I'm just as single-minded as you are,' he said, darting his hand around her waist. 'Except that my worship is given to flesh and blood.'

The sudden contact as he pulled her to him was exciting but alarming. Like stepping out under a harsh noon sun, she immediately wanted to escape back into shade.

'Gabriella! Gabriella! You are keeping me and the pianoforte waiting!'

The impatient voice of Andrea Prioni was answered by two sighs, one of relief, the other of thwarted desire. With a low gurgle of laughter, Gabriella twisted away from the young man and ran towards the villa to play the promised duet with Agnese's brother.

'But my boatmen will not return for another half-hour,' called a plaintive voice.

'Then you will have plenty of time to explain your presence here,' Gabriella answered with a laugh as she saw that Agnese had returned from church and was advancing upon them. With a parting wave, she abandoned the young man to his fate.

★　　★　　★

109

Gabriella's study of Bellini's demanding work continued throughout the summer months. By dint of constant application, Gabriella was beginning to approach the degree of control required by the piece, but during the last few lessons, Pasta had cautioned her that her pitch was sharp. The first time she had accepted it, but on the last two occasions the interruption had caused her acute distress, for she couldn't detect it herself. Was she losing her hearing? she wondered each night as she lay awake. So panicked had she become that, the moment she set off for her lesson, her rate of breathing increased to such a degree that it seemed impossible to reach deep within her chest for breath. Every day it seemed to be getting worse. Finally she spoke to Agnese. To Gabriella's surprise she seemed very knowledgeable about the matter.

'Why the remedy is simple, dear girl. You just put a brown paper bag over your head.'

'Oh, Signora,' spluttered Gabriella, seized with laughter. 'You can't be serious!'

'But I am,' said the little woman, giving her skirt a swish as she moved towards a cupboard.

'It's all to do with inhaling the air you breathe out. One of Andrea's friends – a doctor – explained it to me. Try it when you feel anxious: it will work, you'll see,' she said, passing a bag to Gabriella.

Still laughing at the picture of herself appearing before Giuditta Pasta wearing a bag over her head, Gabriella nevertheless carried Agnese's treatment in her hand as she made her way by foot to the prima donna's villa the next day. On the way, so that she might relax, she studied the leaves and stones in her path and tried to identify the various birds by their song. But as soon as she reached the steps which led to the kitchen at the rear, the anxiety began and, as she crossed the wooden bridge over the little waterfall, something like terror gripped her and her breath started to come in rapid, shallow puffs. 'Oh, if I do not sing pure notes today, I know it will be the end of me,' she gasped.

Just a few yards away from the villa, Gabriella saw that the little coffee-house overlooking the lake was empty so, clutching the brown paper bag and far too desperate to feel foolish, she hastened over to it. With her back to the villa so that she should not be seen, she faced out over the water and popped the bag over her head. Gradually, to her amazement, her intake of air slowed and deepened. It really worked!

'What an intriguing way to view the lake!' commented a voice whose timbre sent a thrill through her. Behind her brown paper shield, Gabriella's eyes widened with shock and horror at her situation – for she hadn't missed the repressed laughter; indeed, she could sense the man was shaking with it! Quite motionless, she wondered whether she should walk away, thus keeping her identity unknown and her dignity intact. But she knew if she did, whoever it was out there would dissolve into gales of laughter.

'I am regulating my breathing,' she said with as much dignity as was possible through a bag. Then, assuming a look of great aloofness, her fingers lifted it clear. 'You!' she gasped.

'Your German thief?' enquired the man, raising a black, quizzical eyebrow.

In the confusion of her emotions, Gabriella glared speechless at the man in the boat.

'Oh, you are no German thief,' she spluttered eventually. 'And you would do well to wear this bag to stop you spying on your countrymen . . . I suppose you are on your way to make your report at the Villa Pizzo!'

Her words, Gabriella saw, were as effective as when she had pushed the traitor into the fountain three years ago, and her own reaction was just the same: flight!

# Chapter Seven

Whether it was due to Agnese's daily devotions alone that Cardinal Mastai, Bishop of Imola, was elected as Pius IX, or to the prayers of all liberals, only the divine spirit could tell. Certainly, when the news reached Villa Rosa, it made far less impact on Gabriella than the invitation which had arrived for her that day. Professor Prioni, eager to discuss the election with anyone, found that his sister and Pasta's pupil were only interested in frivolity.

'The Contessa Wiera Forro,' murmured Gabriella, looking at the letter yet again. 'She wants me to sing at her villa, Agnese . . . just imagine. Do you think Signora Pasta will agree?'

'As the Contessa says that she has arranged the matter with the Conservatorio, I do not expect she will object,' replied Agnese, touching the fine quality paper with approval. 'I'm sure she will be delighted for you: there are bound to be important guests who will be able to help you. It's so important to move in the right circles and make friends with powerful people.'

'But I have a powerful friend in the Princess Belgiojoso.'

'Yes, well, one can't have too many. And this invitation must surely come through the Conte – who knows, he may be falling in love with you. We must make sure you dazzle him!'

'Oh Agnese!' laughed Gabriella, turning pink as the bright, bird-like eyes ran over her. 'The Conte may have called here to flirt a little, but I know he is in love with a beautiful Marchesa named Flavia. Anyway, I intend to be a prima donna, not a bride.'

'Flavia,' mused Agnese. 'I expect that must be the Marchesa

Balziano's daughter. From what I've heard she is promised to the *elder* son of the Forro family . . . But it's a wealthy family, dear, and whilst I don't want to raise your hopes, men are often prepared to overlook rank for beauty in a love match. Marriage into such a family would be a great honour; far better than trailing around the theatres of Europe all your life!'

A comfortable relationship had sprung up between them, and Gabriella would usually have hotly debated Agnese's words; but the name of Balziano intrigued her and, after a moment, she thought she remembered where she had seen it.

'Balziano, is that the family which once lived at the Villa Pizzo?'

'Yes dear,' answered Agnese Prioni. 'Flavia is the niece of the late Marchesa — I expect she will be one of the guests at the Forro villa . . . Are you absolutely sure you have to wear your uniform?' She chattered on. 'Couldn't I buy you something pretty? It would please me, I never had the opportunity of having a daughter . . . Somehow marriage never arose. It's always puzzled me, for much plainer girls than I . . .' she broke off to dart a glance of approval at her reflection in the drawing-room mirror. 'Of course I would not have married just anyone,' she continued, 'and then after Mother died, Andrea rather took it for granted that my duty lay with him. That is why it would be such a delight to see you . . . a lovely dress is what you need!'

'Oh Agnese, you're very kind to me,' said Gabriella, touched by the longing in the other's voice and realizing how many unfulfilled dreams she must have had. But the rules were strict about such things. 'Perhaps when I leave the Conservatorio, if you felt able then . . . For now I'm afraid it must be my usual dress.'

The Forro launch which collected Gabriella was the one in which Giovanni had paid his visit. Its canopy was blue and white striped and, like those which plied to and fro between the large villas along the lake's shoreline, its oarsmen wore smart livery and straw hats. Compared to her own solitary

113

efforts, the muscular stroke of the rowers made the boat fly, and Gabriella took delight in the rhythmical precision of the blades as they fell and dipped into the sky-blue water.

The Contessa Forro's villa was further north than Blevio, so the boat passed Giuditta Pasta's pink villa where, as usual, Git was in her garden and her husband Giuseppe was taking his coffee in the little house at the lake's edge. Gabriella gave them both a cheery wave. Though she couldn't see Git's broad, kindly face clearly, Gabriella knew that she would be smiling, just as she had done when she had given her approval for this engagement.

'Such occasions provide experience and are an excellent introduction to society,' she had said. 'And it will be fun for you. Ah, what parties I used to have,' she had reminisced. 'I haven't always been the quiet gardener, you know. Once I played the hostess and the garden was alight with lanterns and a band played all my arias from a boat on the lake . . . It was all quite magical . . . Go, and enjoy yourself.'

The flight of wide marble steps came right down to the water's edge. Until the launch had swung towards the shore-line, Gabriella had not imagined that the beautiful building she was admiring could be her destination. When, with military precision, the oarsmen glided alongside the wide curving steps and a footman walked forward to help her ashore, she suddenly felt very shy and nervous.

'Signorina Pepe, the Contessa is waiting to receive you, if you would be so kind as to follow me.'

The marble steps led up to a large central fountain, on each side of which were others leading upwards to a small terrace. Above this, where the air was fragrant with the scent of roses, double steps led on to a wide terraced walk which ran along in front of the house. Here large pots of orange trees were placed at regular intervals, and along the low wall twined the small green leaves of the plant which Gabriella had grown to adore since she had come to Lombardy.

'Jasmine,' she said with a smile of pleasure. 'It's beauti-ful.'

'Then you will enjoy your evenings here, Signorina Pepe,'

114

responded the footman. 'For it is the Contessa's favourite plant and you will find it all over the grounds.'

The decor of the room into which she had been ushered impressed Gabriella at once by its cool blend of colours – grey, lemon and white. These were reinforced by the upholstery and large bowls of camellias and lemon roses. From a grey and white striped Empire couch, the Contessa Wiera Forro stretched out a graceful hand in greeting as Gabriella walked across the ornamental terrazzo floor.

In contrast to her surroundings, Wiera Forro wore widow's black, but its severity was a dramatic foil for her pretty femininity. She was in her middle years: her face, below tiny black curls at the hairline, had the delicacy of a china doll's. The slightly heavier set of her lips and chin seemed to convey a haughty air, but now, as she smiled, every trace of arrogance disappeared.

'Welcome to my home, Signorina Pepe . . . My son did not tell me how lovely you were. He has, however, excited my interest in you, for I believe that not only is dear Giuditta Pasta guiding your development as a singer, but that your patron is the Princess Belgiojoso.'

'Yes, Contessa, that is correct.'

'She is a remarkable person, as is Prince Emilio – he also has a most beautiful singing voice. I heard him take part in The Creation with Verdi conducting. All the singers were amateurs, of course, but the standard was excellent. I hope you won't feel anxious at all about performing here. All my guests understand that you still have a year or so before you have completed your studies but we are all interested in the talents that Milan is nurturing for the future. There is no need to feel afraid: I want you to be happy here, Gabriella.'

The use of her name and the warmth in which it was spoken sent a glow of pleasure through Gabriella. Her blue eyes shone. 'Oh Contessa,' she said, her heart brimming over with pleasure at finding Giovanni's mother so informal and appealing. 'I shall be as happy singing here as when I am with Signora Pasta.'

'Then I could ask for no higher accolade,' smiled the Contessa. 'Now I shall arrange for someone to show you to your room, after which, if you would like to walk in the park or try the piano in the library, please do so. My other guests will be arriving soon. I know they are going to be charmed by you even before you sing.'

Contessa Wiera Forro had spoken from the heart, inspired by an immediate liking for the young singer her son had persuaded her to invite. Usually he kept his mistresses in the background, but she had wondered at the time whether his request was double-edged. Now she hoped his interest was purely confined to providing an informal setting for a promising young singer; she would be cross if it were otherwise, she thought. This protective, almost maternal feeling startled Wiera Forro as much as the feeling she had had when the tall, shapely young woman had entered her drawing-room. Perhaps she had missed having a daughter more than she had realized.

The bedroom to which Gabriella was taken overlooked the terraced walk and the lake. Her brief stay at the Princess Belgiojoso's residence in Paris had given her some idea of how the nobility lived but, even so, she felt quite overawed by the splendour of her surroundings. It seemed more like a palace than a villa. Gabriella had half supposed that she would lodge in the servants' quarters, but clearly she had been given what surely must be one of the loveliest of rooms, with its pinkish marble floor and elegant rosewood furniture. And just as Agnese Prioni had welcomed her with a bowl of pansies, here she was greeted by a bowl of pink roses on the dressing-table. Despite being captivated by the beauty of her room, Gabriella remembered the Contessa's words about the arrival of guests, and she decided that she would feel less nervous once she had introduced herself to the acoustics of the room where she was to sing.

From below came the sound of a piano: could it be her accompanist also taking advantage of the moment? Perhaps, Gabriella thought, they could go through her programme together. As she freshened her face with a little cold water and dabbed cologne at her wrists and temples, she heard the opening notes of her chosen piece, Mozart and Donna Elvira's aria, '*Mi tradi quell' alma ingrata*', and began to hum the tune. The music was so joyful that she could not resist its call: she left the airy bedroom, singing as she descended the curved marble stairs towards the melody's source. Instantly the pianist responded with a verve that was flirtatious. Like birds swooping and circling around each other in an aerial ballet, voice and piano interwove, followed, answered; and all the while the music grew louder, drawing her closer to the unknown hands, until outside a carved door she delivered her last notes and flung wide the door.

With bent head the pianist executed the last bar with a flourish and, as his hands flew up into the air and his laughter joined with hers, he looked up. Gabriella's laughter dissolved and she stared at the pianist in disbelief and disappointment.

'The Contessa has asked you to play for me?'

'That is so,' replied the man gravely, and Gabriella saw his hateful dark eyes were filled with laughter. He is remembering the brown paper bag, she thought, turning pink with irritation.

'I hope you found my playing accommodating.' Again there was the gleam of amusement as the thick black brows lifted in a quizzical fashion and his voice caressed the final word. 'I have never enjoyed Mozart so much before: you give it due brilliance; but then it is not so surprising for one who takes her art so seriously.'

'Are you mocking me, sir?' flashed Gabriella.

'I would not be so bold, especially with a fountain but a few paces away.'

Gabriella glared: a miserable informer had no right to look so confident and relaxed, or to make her feel so foolish.

'Signore, I have to say that I find it extraordinary that Conte Forro, who arranged for me to come here, should choose you as my accompanist.'

'So, Giovanni invited you here,' mused the young man, leafing through the rest of the music on the piano. 'Are you disappointed with the standard of my performance, Signorina Pepe?'

'Oh no, that is excellent. It's because . . .'

117

A rustle of silk announced the Contessa a brief moment before she appeared in the open doorway.

'That was glorious!' she cried, advancing towards Gabriella with a smile. 'Luciano said I would not be disappointed, and now I know why he was so impressed when he heard you taking your lesson with Pasta, and why since receiving your programme he has spent so many hours in here – when usually nothing will take him away from his writing. You look surprised, Gabriella. Didn't you know my son Luciano was going to be your accompanist? Ah, it sounds as if dear Flavia and her parents have arrived.'

Astonishment, embarrassment, a whole succession of emotions swept over Gabriella while the Contessa was talking. As the elegant black figure hurried away, though, she had no time to collect her thoughts; for the grey eyes of her hostess were replaced by the darker grey-green eyes of her son.

'Isn't it time you told me why you are so angry with me?'

So close; the powerful current she felt between them mesmerized her. With Giovanni she had been in control; now she felt as she had done the first time she had heard Bellini's music and she was afraid, overawed.

'At first I thought you were an Austrian, then I found you were even worse . . .'

'Worse?' murmured the man, his thick brows knitting together as he stared questioningly down into her eyes.

'I . . . mistook you for the spy Giacomo Levati,' she whispered reluctantly.

The firm curve of the Conte's lips tightened slightly, but apart from this and a fleeting coldness in his eyes he made no comment, which made Gabriella feel much worse. Giovanni, she knew, would have flown into a rage, and she would have welcomed the chastisement. Her cheeks turned scarlet as she remembered their various encounters. Why, he must have thought her quite deranged. Worst of all – though it was not entirely her fault – was to have thought him a base spy. This must be unforgivable!

'Don't become distressed, Signorina Pepe,' said Luciano Forro gently. 'For you have filled my life with mystery and excitement. Besides, if you begin to overbreathe, I regret I would not have about me the proper equipment.'

Gabriella knew exactly what he meant, and unable to resist his teasing tone and the kind concern in his eyes, she burst out laughing.

'So, I have caught you flirting with your mother's singer!' exclaimed a languid voice. 'At least you are not locked away in your study, Luciano.'

Like an exotic flower, the Marchesa Flavia Balziano filled the room with her perfume and colour. Her movements seemed as devoid of energy as her voice, yet the insinuating force could not be missed, nor the air of possessiveness as she glided up to the Conte and held out her gloved hand. As Luciano Forro raised it to his lips, Gabriella turned away, feeling intrusive and somewhat slighted by the Marchesa's words.

'Don't go,' said the Conte, who had noticed her making her escape. 'Signorina Pepe, let me introduce you to the Marchesa Balziano, who seems to think you are going to spoil us the entire weekend with your singing. Whereas we both know that part of that burden is to be mine . . . I hope you enjoy Chopin, Flavia, he is mandatory with the Contessa. My mother is Polish,' he explained, turning to Gabriella with a smile.

'Luciano, you haven't welcomed my parents yet. Come out on the terrace. They're taking refreshment there, and I am terribly thirsty after our journey,' said the Marchesa, completely ignoring the presence of Gabriella. 'It's . . . so impolite,' she chided, making to take Luciano Forro's arm.

'Flavia, you are a delightful distraction,' the young man laughed. 'But you must make my apologies to your parents. Signorina Gabriella and I are looking through her repertoire: as an amateur accompanist I need all the help she can give me. And, as she is first and foremost my mother's guest, I do not wish to keep her a moment longer than is necessary from our other guests.'

The black, almond-shaped eyes of Flavia Balziano flicked towards Gabriella with interest, and this time they did not dart away as from a servant but lingered, studying in every

119

detail the young woman responsible for thwarting her wishes. At first she didn't like what she saw at all, but then her sensual lips curled in satisfaction; after all, here was a mere commoner, and what was the use of a shapely figure if it was enclosed in a cotton uniform, or dramatic eyes if their owner exuded proud reserve? Luciano liked fun, laughter and sharp wit.

'Well, don't let the Conte keep you too long,' purred the Marchesa. 'Luciano becomes so intense about the most boring things: politics, silkworms – we hardly ever see him in Milan.'

'If it were not for the Lombard silkworm you would not be wearing that pretty dress,' scolded Luciano Forro.

'Oh yes I would,' retorted the Marchesa, arching her neck and looking up provocatively at the Conte from under narrowed lashes. 'I'd have silk from China, and better quality too . . . Oh, there, I've made you angry . . . I'm sorry. How can I make amends?'

As startled as the other young woman by the stern expression which had appeared on Luciano Forro's face, Gabriella saw his features suddenly relax and he was once again all careless charm.

'My dear Marchesa,' he said with a helpless gesture. 'How could one be angry with someone so deliciously feminine? And why should you concern yourself about such dull things as cocoons . . . Of course, perhaps that could be your penance . . . yes: you shall be made to see what makes our province so profitable, and why the Habsburgs will never willingly let it go. Tomorrow I shall take you to see the insects which give their lives to keep you in dresses. Would you like to come too, Signorina Pepe?' he asked, turning towards Gabriella.

'Why yes. I think that would be very interesting.'

'Yes, so do I,' rejoined the Marchesa hastily. 'I can't think why you have never invited me before,' she added over her shoulder as she glided from the room.

'Do you wish to continue?' asked Gabriella.

'But of course,' said the young man, taking his seat before the grand piano. 'Sometimes Flavia is quite impossible, but she is very amusing. Now, shall we run through everything?

120

You must tell me what pleases and what does not. It's the first time I have ever done this,' he said briskly, opening out the music before him. 'Usually I never play a piece of music the same way – it depends on my mood. But tomorrow evening I will have to submit my will to yours . . . it will be a new experience for me!'

'Then I hope, Conte, that it will not be too painful,' she teased.

It was Gabriella's first real social occasion on her own, and she was relieved that at least she would knew Giovanni, for whilst in the time they had worked together on her programme she had felt at ease with the Conte, once they had finished and his earnest, concentrated expression was replaced by a quizzical smile, Gabriella's nervousness had resurfaced.

During the latter part of the day, Giovanni arrived from Como. The news he brought created such a hubbub that any fears or self-consciousness which Gabriella might have felt on going down to dinner were completely banished by the noisy chatter of the guests who stood drinking apéritifs in the salon.

'Why, I don't suppose Prince Metternich will be at all happy with this! It's the last thing the Court at Vienna will want: a reforming Pope will not be to their taste at all,' laughed Giovanni Forro.

'It could mean Gioberti's dream could come true.'

'What do you mean, Luciano?' asked Flavia Balziano, touching the young man's arm, her scarlet lips parted and her dark eyes feigning bright interest.

'He means,' said one of the men, meeting Luciano Forro's eyes, 'that by granting a political amnesty on 17 July for all exiles and those in Papal prisons, the Pope has declared his support for liberalism and, as Gioberti of Piedmont envisaged, the unity of Italy could be achieved under the Pope, who would be the head of all liberated states.'

'But the Habsburgs will have to be kicked out!' exclaimed Giovanni Forro passionately. 'Will this Pope go that far? Will he place himself at the head of an army and lead it into a holy war?'

'Not unless he rids himself of the Gregorians and brings in more liberals like Cardinal Gizzi,' replied his brother. 'Still, it's wonderful news. Let's drink a toast to Pius IX.'

'Pius IX!' cried everyone, raising their glasses. 'Our new battle cry against the double-headed eagle!'

For the rest of the evening, during supper and afterwards, the talk was all of politics. Though there was chatter and laughter from some playing cards, and the entertainment of a fast and furious piano duet played by Luciano Forro and a Conte Manara, for the most part the men grouped together on the terrace, the tips of their cigars glowing in the velvety darkness. And in the low murmur of their voices, Gabriella heard they were still discussing the amnesty.

'Rome is where the influence is – Lombardy's interests lie there,' she heard Luciano Forro say.

'Then will you go, Conte Forro?' asked someone.

From where she sat, Gabriella strained to hear the answer, but a burst of laughter from Giovanni at the card table drowned the reply.

The next morning, the Marchese Balziano expressed the wish to join the visit to the silk mill. He was a gentle-faced man, whose brown eyes were sad and wavering in their glance. There was something about his submissive manner which reminded Gabriella of her life at Blackfriars and the feelings of unworthiness she and the boys had endured. But who could have made a wealthy man feel so? In Gabriella's mind, the face of Flavia Balziano's mother suddenly appeared: tyrants came in all forms, she decided; clearly the black-eyed woman with the iron-grey hair and the impatient, sarcastic manner, was the cause of her unfortunate husband's wary diffidence.

The Forro launch pulled away from the marble steps, and the Marchese pointed back towards the gardens around the villa. 'Well, Luciano,' he said. 'When you spoke to me a few years ago about removing your terraces of olives I thought you mad.'

'Yes, I know you did,' laughed the young man, a stiff breeze lifting his black hair back from his forehead. 'But now do you see how the trees and shrubs are progressing? I'd always been attracted to the English style of gardening, and I was finally persuaded to change things when I saw what Ettore Villoresi had done for the Viceroy at the Villa Pizzo – it was a visit I shall never forget . . . in more than one sense,' he murmured dryly. 'What a drenching I got that day. I have often wondered whether I should take revenge!'

'Viewing a garden on a rainy day can often be an advantage,' observed the Marchese innocently, unaware of the mocking glance turned upon Gabriella, or the discomfort she felt under the challenge of the green-grey eyes.

During the trip across the lake, Flavia Balziano had studiously ignored Gabriella, but when they transferred to the carriage, she began to ply Gabriella with questions, all posed with sugary sweetness. Luciano Forro, who had ridden ahead, was not present to divert the Marchesa, and Gabriella began to feel like a fieldmouse being stroked by a kitten's paw.

'So you were parted from your parents when young,' breathed the dark-eyed Marchesa, shaking her head sorrowfully. 'Did you hear that, Papa, poor Signorina Pepe is the protégée of the Princess Belgiojoso because she has no parents? What is even more dreadful is that she does not know who they were. Why, fancy,' Flavia said with a wave of her fan towards a group of peasants who were walking along the road with sacks on their backs. 'They could be here, tending Luciano's mulberry trees.'

Gabriella looked away, angered and upset by the taunt which she knew had been meant to humiliate. Her eyes fell upon a man carrying a large wicker basket on his back. His sunburnt neck was arched back and, like thick vines, the veins and tendons bulged out, distended by the strain of his heavy load. Here was the beast of burden that Giuseppe Mazzini had talked about: she glanced back at Flavia lounging indolently against the carriage cushions. For a second Gabriella hated her: she would have liked to have seen her forced to labour in the fields, and nearly said so, but then with a shrug and a sad smile she looked out again at the peasants passing by.

'If I thought I could find my mother and father here today,

nothing would make me happier, Marchesa. But until I do, I shall have to be content with what Signor Mazzini told us orphans in London: that in the family of human beings, all are brother and sister.'

'Brother and sister indeed. Your Mazzini sounds a strange fellow,' yawned Flavia. 'Presumably he has the poor in mind, for kinship is no advantage to my class. How long would my parasol last if those ladies over there borrowed it from their new sister?' she trilled. 'Goodness, I'm parched . . . Why I agreed to come on this wretched trip I don't know. Ah, here is Luciano. I hope everything is in readiness for our arrival.'

After a lovely luncheon, offered to them by a smiling pro-prietor and his wife, the tour of the mill began.

'It is so big,' Gabriella said to the proprietor who had accom-panied them.

'Yes, the Conte installed much new machinery when he took over the lease,' said the man with pride. 'There is nothing more modern in the Como area or Lombardy. Of course, greater industrialization is needed to recapture the trade we lost during the Napoleonic wars: the British installed machines in Bengal and still import most of their silk from there, though the quality is not as good.'

'Did you notice the difference in our silk, Signorina Pepe, when you first came to Lombardy?' asked Luciano Forro.

'Is it heavier – why should that be?'

'Quality is dependent upon a lot of factors,' replied the young man. 'But particularly on what the silkworm eats. Feed it on the black mulberry and you will get cocoons which give a strong but a coarse thread. In here,' he said, opening the door of a large storehouse, 'is where the workers bring the white mulberry leaves. They can be kept for two to three days. As you see, they are being turned with wooden forks to let the air pass through. The temperature is important – too dry and they will lose freshness, too damp and they rot. The advantage of the white mulberry is its early leafing, which means you don't have to prolong the rearing of the worm too far into the hot season.'

124

'Where do they take the leaves from here?' asked the Marchese as the party walked back out into the sunshine.

'They are taken to the laboratory.'

'That sounds very scientific, my boy.'

'It's a precise art, sir. Conte Dandolo set it out most elegantly, and one of the vital things is control of temperature. I shall let Alberto explain the process: he handles things from day to day and his family have been rearing the silkworm for years. He's the expert!'

'Thank you, Conte,' said the proprietor, flashing a look of devotion and respect at his employer. 'Have you ever seen a silkworm, ladies?'

'No, and I'm not sure that it might not spoil the enjoyment of my dresses if I did,' laughed the Marchesa, applying a lace kerchief to her nostrils as they were led within another building.

'On the left,' said Alberto, 'is the room where the eggs are incubated. We start to do this in March. On the first day we set the temperature at sixty degrees, thereafter we precisely increase it, until by the twelfth day it has risen to eighty-two degrees; constant checking of the thermometers is necessary. Once the eggs have hatched, the trays are taken into this room here, where the worms have their first taste of mulberry leaf.'

'Do they eat many leaves?' asked Gabriella.

The proprietor laughed as he led them into the room.

'Do you hear that munching? Silkworms from five ounces of eggs can devour 975 pounds of leaves. As you can see, we chop the leaves up for them: this gives them more edges to bite on so the leaf is eaten before it can wither. Or, if you are not going to do that, it is better to give them small sprays of leaves, as a single leaf can lie heavy on the young worms.'

'Well, I wish I hadn't seen the horrid hairy creatures,' complained Flavia. 'Every time I touch my dress I shall imagine they are crawling all over me!'

'And nibbling your pretty ears!' teased Luciano Forro, laughing at her shrieks as he lifted up a small spray on which was a worm. 'Come now, Flavia,' he added. 'How long do you spend choosing a gown that you cannot admire this poor little chap for a few minutes?'

'Has he any hope of entering the world as a moth?' asked Gabriella.

'Well, he might be one of the lucky ones not to be stifled,' smiled Luciano Forro.

'Or?'

'His gift to the world will be the 700 metres of silk which he spins around his body in a figure of eight.'

'Like a winding sheet,' murmured Gabriella, touching the chestnut-coloured hairs with the tip of her finger.

'Yes, if you like,' laughed the young man. 'But I shall rescue this one for you. It shall complete its cycle, and the moth will emerge into the world.'

'Silk is strong – how does the moth break free of its prison?' asked Gabriella, as she and the Conte followed after the others.

'It emits a substance which makes a little hole in the cocoon. Nature takes care of everything, you see.'

'For me she did,' smiled Gabriella. 'She gave me my voice and it allowed me to escape from my cocoon of poverty. Others were not so lucky, though.'

'And if you stopped singing?' asked the Conte, giving her a sidelong glance as they walked towards another building.

'I suppose I would have to creep back in, for my voice is the only thing I have.'

Luciano Forro halted and turned to the young woman beside him. Under the shade of her parasol her eyes were like soft, dark pansies and their expression was so vulnerable that his heart contracted.

'Love could set you free.'

'Not like music,' retorted Gabriella. 'Love is transient, people go away . . . In the end one is alone. But music is always there! I will never let myself fall in love.'

Though her initial words revealed the depth of her loneliness, the latter were voiced with such assurance that Luciano Forro burst into laughter as he recalled his brother's recent outburst of bewildered frustration to be competing with a dead

126

composer for some lovely signorina's time. He looked again at the calm, assured face and noted the sensuality of the full lips; nothing could conceal the vibrations of her inner nature, for it exuded passion. He had seen music lay bare its depths; was it there for a man?

'I wonder,' he murmured under his breath.

The last part of their tour took them into the part of the mill where more than a hundred women were employed in handling the cocoons.

'It's rather noisy in here with all the machinery,' said Alberto. 'Down at that end they are all steam-driven, but here we still use the older treadle machines.'

'I can't believe it!' exclaimed Gabriella in delight as she noticed cradles beside many of the operators' machines. 'Why, they are all hooked up to rock in time with the machine. Do you see?' she said, turning to the Marchese who also smiled at the domestic sight.

'It was the Conte's idea,' grinned the proprietor, picking up a cocoon from one of the wicker baskets beside an operator and giving it to Gabriella. 'He thought our women should be able to look after their babies at work.'

'Alberto, you're giving me false credit,' interrupted the Conte. 'I stole the idea from an ingenious silk master in Pinerola called Michele Bravo. If we are to encourage more women to work in factories we owners must make some provision, otherwise the iron cradles hanging in the foundling hospitals' doors will never stop revolving with the unwanted: my mother told me that over 3,000 babies were abandoned in Milan last year.'

The time in the reeling mill had passed very quickly, for the enthusiasm of the Conte and his proprietor had made every aspect of the process interesting. Apart from the rocking cradles, Gabriella had been surprised to see how airy and large the workrooms were.

'No wonder you never have time for socializing, Luciano,' complained Flavia Balziano, looking up at the young man as he rode beside the carriage on the return journey.

'Well, it was different in my day,' commented the Marchese

stiffly. 'One didn't dabble in such things. All these new machines you're installing in Milan . . . and your brother tells me you're going to build a factory to make railway parts. Is it fitting for a nobleman to do such things?'

'Yes, I believe it is. If we're to improve the lives of our peasantry, we must steer Lombardy towards economic growth: we must industrialize or we will be left behind. And we can do it for our people in a way that will not throw them from the fields into the hell of somewhere like Britain's industrial north, but gradually, in tune with the life they have known for generations.'

'I say leave things as they are,' stammered the Marchese after Luciano Forro had dropped down the shade and ridden ahead with his dogs. But neither his daughter nor Gabriella heard him as the heat of the day lulled them into drowsiness.

Light fingers touched Gabriella's bare shoulder and on opening her eyes she found the maid smiling down at her.

'It's time to dress, Signorina Pepe. I've prepared your bath. While you're taking it I shall go and fetch the hairpiece I have prepared. I thought it would set off your evening wear perfectly.'

'That was very kind of you,' said Gabriella. 'Would you also dress my hair? I'm very clumsy in such things.'

'Certainly Signorina, it's one of the pleasures of my work: you will find I am quite skilled.'

With a deep yawn, Gabriella stretched out her arms. As she did so, her keepsake rolled out from under her pillow. With a smile she picked up the golden cocoon and raised it at arm's length above her head, remembering the rows of slumbering infants oblivious of their mothers' busy feet on the treadles and their swift fingers twisting three cocoons into one.

When the maid returned, Gabriella saw that she had not exaggerated about her skill, for spread on a piece of damp napkin was the most delicate arrangement of violets and jasmine, caught as if in a spider's web of fine black net.

'Oh, how tiny your fingers must be! It's beautiful,' exclaimed Gabriella in delight.

128

'Well, I had plenty of practice as a child,' smiled the woman. 'In the winter, when there was no work on the land, my family used to weave baskets and hats. So I started very young. It was heavier work than this, of course, but once your fingers become nimble they adapt to anything.'

As soon as her stays had been tightened, Gabriella sat down in front of the mirror with a light wrapper about her shoulders. In her mind she rehearsed her programme and, as the maid brushed and braided, Gabriella felt an inner desire to make a change.

'There!' said the woman at last, lifting her fingers away. 'Do you like it?'

'Yes,' said Gabriella, clapping her hands in delight at what had been achieved, for as the maid held up a hand mirror, she saw that she had been given a large bun of braids at the nape of her neck. This had been covered over with the tiny netted flowers, whilst at the front two heavy looped braids had been left to hang over one shoulder with a camellia above them. 'It's very chic . . . I don't know whether my principal would approve,' she said with an impish smile.

'Well, I see no harm in a few flowers when others are all bedecked in silk and jewels,' remarked the middle-aged woman firmly.

Downstairs, rows of little chairs stood waiting for the guests who would be arriving from the villas around the lake. Gabriella was seized with a sudden fright, for soon they would be occupied and all eyes would be upon her. An urge to flee gripped her, and to calm herself she walked over to the piano and ran through a few scales. As she was finishing, Luciano Forro entered the salon wearing white tie and tails. Earlier, in his large round black hat and riding clothes, he had looked very much the sportsman; now with his shoulder-length hair swept back from his clear, wide forehead and an expression of anxious gravity on his features, he seemed very much the intellectual.

'Why am I so nervous?' he said, flexing his fingers. 'After all, I could ask Luciano Manara to play: you would only have to change a surname to find the better pianist.'

'No, I'm happier with the first Luciano,' she said softly. 'For I want to sing "Casta Diva" at the end.'

If she had pushed him into the fountain again, the young man before her could not have registered more shock.

'You're surely teasing me.'

'No, I feel I want to sing it for the first time here, tonight.' She wanted to add, with you, but that feeling was only half formed in her own mind. 'Are you afraid?' she asked, looking up into the greyish-green eyes. 'Perhaps, after all, Conte Manara . . .?'

'No!' said Luciano Forro, his eyes glinting dark with excitement. 'I think I now know you well enough to anticipate your needs . . . but as your partner in music tonight, might I advise you to leave the art of coquetry to Flavia: she is an expert in such things.'

Gabriella opened her mouth to protest as efficiently he proceeded to wipe the borrowed rouge from her lips. For an instant his hand under her chin retained its hold and his contemplative gaze lifted from her lips to her eyes. 'Now, isn't that more fitting for Norma, High Priestess? Shall we run through it?' he said, raising an eyebrow in enquiry.

Outside the sound of laughter announced the early arrival of guests.

'It is too late,' she gasped. 'Perhaps we should leave things as they were.'

'No!' said the Conte. 'I know the "Casta Diva" well. It will be all right.'

'Let us hope the wind is not blowing in the direction of Blevio, and may Pasta forgive me if I make a mess of it,' breathed Gabriella.

'You won't, I won't let you. We will pretend we are quite alone, discovering it together.'

Glittering like the diamonds she wore, Flavia Balziano stood surrounded by several young men at the reception on the terrace.

'I do hope the dust of the journey has not affected your throat,

Gabriella,' she said in passing. 'We're all looking forward very much to hearing you.'

'Thank you,' said Gabriella, giving the vibrant young woman a wide smile for the warm and sincere wishes.

'Ah, why do you not smile more often at me like that?' complained Giovanni, who had not left her side since the moment she had gone out on to the terrace.

'But I do, Giovanni. It's just that whenever I do, you seem to be admiring a young lady!' Gabriella teased.

'You force me to prove that I have eyes for no one else, so after you have sung I shall sit with you at supper, and after that I shall show you the garden by moonlight and you will let me kiss you,' he said, reaching for her hand.

At the door, Luciano Forro appeared. Gabriella saw that his face was serious and tense.

'We are ready!' he said.

Because there had been no opportunity to rehearse the 'Casta Diva', the Conte positioned himself so that Gabriella could easily see him. Her mind devoid of any emotion, she waited calmly for the introduction to her first selection. Though immersed in her music, as the joyful harmonies of Rossini, then Mozart, filled the room, she could feel the atmosphere changing, as if the people there were drawing closer to her. Then the moment for the Bellini had come!

Gabriella looked across at Luciano as he commenced the haunting, slow, melodic harmony; his face was serious and intent and she knew in her heart that somehow she had wanted to share this moment with him. All control, she started the slow, languorous ascents, gliding on to the notes of poignant intensity, winding higher, then spiralling down the shimmering chromatic cascades of golden notes, her voice and her being indivisible from the essence of the music. Not once did she consciously see the dark eyes, but the rapport between them was as strong as if they had been in each other's arms.

The almond-shaped eyes of Flavia Balziano blazed jealously, and she wished now that the singer had choked on dust during the carriage drive. She saw that Gabriella's shy reserve, which she had so quickly mistaken for coldness, in fact concealed a smouldering passion which now erupted like flames out of a volcano. At that moment, Flavia knew that Luciano Forro had been burnt.

In the stillness which followed the vibration of Gabriella's final note, Flavia applauded loudly and enthusiastically to destroy the magical hush which had descended. But both performers were unaware of her: the tension and union of the moment was still between them.

There was no time for reflection, though, for it seemed a hundred questions and compliments were being launched at her.

'I understand the English impresario Benjamin Lumley discovered you. Did he offer you a contract when he came to see Verdi last autumn?'

'Oh no!' laughed Gabriella, realizing Conte Manara was teasing her. 'But he did come to see me and check my progress.'

'You're destined to become a great coloratura,' said another young nobleman named Emilio, who stood with the Conte Manara and his older brother, Enrico Dandolo.

Like the heady scent of the jasmine, the compliments and Giovanni's flirtatious attention sent Gabriella into a whirl. She would have liked to have thanked Luciano Forro, but just as Giovanni was not prepared to give anyone the opportunity of taking her away from him, so at a table further along the terrace, the bright orange of Flavia's dress never left the side of Giovanni's brother.

Despite Giovanni's pleas that she should stay a little longer, Gabriella happily retired to the villa with the other ladies. After the maid had helped her to undress, she lay down on her bed and thought about the evening from start to finish. Down below, as on the previous night, the men were sitting over liqueurs and coffee. She imagined one of them taking out a cigar, his strong lower lip emphasized as he directed the tip towards the flame of a match, his chin rounding and eyes narrowing as he drew upon it.

For an hour or so she tossed and turned but could not sleep, and when at last she heard footsteps entering the villa and all fall silent, she rose and padded softly across the cool marble floor

132

outside on to the balcony. Down below in the middle of the lake, she could see the lanterns of the boats which were taking their masters home. Above, the moon was a huge white orb with a wisp of grey lacy cloud at one edge. In such cold purity of light, the Druid Priestess had cut the mistletoe; Gabriella raised her arms and held them aloft as though she were Norma; bathed in such light her arms became like marble and her nightdress a floating, translucent veil. Had the moon powers like the sun, she wondered?

From below a deep chuckle broke her reverie and a voice spoke: '"Chaste goddess, who dost silver these ancient sacred trees, turn upon us thy fair face unclouded and unveiled."'

Gabriella peered startled down into the darkness below, feeling foolish, yet unable to prevent a gurgle of laughter; for the voice was Luciano's, and he knew what she had been doing.

'I hope I did not misquote,' he said, emerging from the shadows and looking up at her.

'No,' she replied, meeting his smile. 'You must think me very fanciful!'

'Intriguing . . . and quite shameless. Would you like me to come and talk to you?' he asked, his voice filled with laughter.

With a cry, Gabriella suddenly realized how naked she was, and she stepped back hurriedly out of the moonlight.

'Too late, my lovely Priestess! Too late!' laughed Luciano Forro.

# Chapter Eight

Agnese Prioni demanded to know in detail everything about the weekend; what the villa was like inside, what they had eaten, who were the guests, and what the ladies had worn. As best she could, Gabriella painted the scene for her inquisitor. But she made no reference to the intriguing discovery she had made in Luciano Forro's study. She had gone there to collect her music, since the Conte had apparently taken it there the previous night. Luciano Forro himself was no longer at Como but had left early for Rome, and whilst she was relieved not to have to meet him after her embarrassment in the moonlight, she could not help feeling a small twinge of disappointment that he had gone away.

She entered his private retreat, and saw that her music had been left on his desk; but apart from a sheet of paper with a few brief notes on the sequence of arias, there was nothing else. And why should there be? she thought impatiently. Had she really expected a farewell note?

Compared to the reception rooms in the villa, the small study, with its faint smell of cigars and leather, had a cosy, masculine feel which tempted her to linger awhile. Was it only poetry the Conte wrote in this room, she wondered, thinking of Giovanni's confession of the previous evening that the friend who had influence with Verdi was in fact his brother.

'I hadn't quite got round to speaking to him about it,' the young man had confessed during supper. 'But now that he is obviously impressed by your voice, I'm sure he could be persuaded to write a poem to inspire and tempt the maestro Verdi. Luciano heard you during one of your lessons when he was on the lake, and managed to invite you here first. But you do believe I have your interests at heart?'

'Of course, Giovanni,' Gabriella had reassured politely. Now thinking of the younger brother's adept and persuasive tongue, Gabriella shook her head and smiled; any invitation from Giovanni would be confined to meeting him tête-à-tête in some secluded rendezvous!

Would his brother write something for her, she wondered, as she contemplated for a moment the vast collection of books lining the three walls of the study. To her surprise, many of the volumes were English and French. She had been in Lombardy long enough to know about the strict censorship of books; did the Conte smuggle them in? With interest she saw, side by side, the names of two famous patriots whom Signor Mazzini had told them about at school. Ugo Foscolo, the exile poet, had died in London: she had visited his grave at Chiswick with Mazzini and some of the organ-grinders. During this pilgrimage Mazzini had talked too about the young poet Silvio Pellico, who had endured imprisonment for enquiring about the Carbonari in a letter to a friend. And here was his book, *Le Mie Prigioni*, on his sad days in prison. As Gabriella pulled it from the shelf, curious to know more about him, she saw the creased corners of pages protruding from behind the next book along and, thinking that it might be a book which had become dislodged in some way, she removed further volumes. It was not a book but a manuscript. For a moment she stared at it, not liking to touch something which now she realized had been concealed. But in order to put it back flat against the wall, it was necessary to touch it; then the green, red and white ribbon proved too enticing and, overcome with curiosity, Gabriella pulled it out and read its title. *Austrian Oppression within Lombardy*. There was no need to read further to know the content would be treasonable; the tricolore ribbon itself should have been sufficient to warn that it bound a man's death sentence. If found, its author, named Larius, would face certain death.

Speedily she had thrust the manuscript back into position, replacing the books in front of it. Was Larius a pen name?

she wondered. If so, poetry was surely not the only literature created in this study. For the true author of this work must be Luciano Forro.

Like migrating birds, Como's summer residents were departing its shores, leaving their pink and cream villas shuttered, windows blinkered and blind to the approach of autumn and the sight of the lake. Not for another year would their caiques criss-cross the lake, or their parklands resound to laughter or witness a lovers' tryst.

It was September, and as Pasta was not wintering at Blevio, Gabriella left also to resume her studies at the Conservatorio. At the landing stage, Agnese waved goodbye as the ferry took her away.

'It will not be long before it's summer again!' she shouted, seeing Agnese's handkerchief fluttering near to her eyes. 'I will write very soon.'

'So, you sang "Casta Diva",' said Professor Mazzucato, adjusting his green gown as he peered out of the window. 'A little risky for your first appearance but then caution has never been your strongest quality, has it, Gabriella? That's why Verdi, not Bellini, is your natural master.'

'Attila of the Voice!'

'Yes,' chuckled the professor. 'That is what some call him. I don't agree, though his demands do single out the faint of heart and the second-rate. His is the music of the age that says what we dare not. Why, at the première of *Attila*, when the Roman general sang "*Avrai tu l'universo, Resti l'Italia a me*", there was nearly a riot in the theatre. What a rallying cry that is against the Austrian occupation.'

'"You may have the universe, but leave Italy to me",' sang Gabriella.

'That is it all right,' said Professor Mazzucato, thundering the bars out on the piano. 'Nor is it any good them banning the words, for if they are not sung there is even more commotion.'

'How the exiled patriots would applaud,' said Gabriella, thinking of the letter which had arrived for her from London.

136

'Well, let's see if I applaud the inclusion of "Casta Diva" in your programme at Como,' said the professor, bringing her mind back to the lesson and motioning for her to commence singing.

It had been well over eight months since she had heard from Giuseppe Mazzini, or rather Joseph Martin, as he always signed himself; for whilst the content of the letters was perfectly innocent, Mazzini's name alone was enough to place any recipient under suspicion with the authorities. During a free period, Gabriella was able to read her letter, which gave news of the school and her old companions; but in answer to her own enquiries about Nico, her old teacher had little information. 'Some of the boys say he and his friend Angelo took a job aboard a ship bound for South America,' Mazzini wrote. Well, no doubt that would provide the life of excitement which he had always craved, thought Gabriella with an ache in her heart and a feeling of sad resignation that now they would never meet again. Mistakenly enclosed with the letter was a blank piece of paper, which she set aside for her own use, wondering as she laid it down what Mazzini's postscript meant: 'A second errand would be of great service to me, and the delivery of interest to my friends.' The friends could only be the young men she had visited at the Porta Tosa when she had first arrived in Milan, but what was she supposed to deliver? Nonplussed, Gabriella looked at her letter and then after a moment's thought opened the drawer of her desk and looked at the large sheet of unused paper. Was it really blank, or had Mazzini written to his disciples in something like lemon juice? The warmth of a candle would provide the answer, but that could be more safely done at the Porta Tosa by the young men to whom it had been sent. But how was she to get there, she wondered anxiously. Last time she had tried she had been hauled before Matron, and although Matron's inquisitive eyes no longer took interest in these letters from England which she was unable to read, her severity towards those who broke rules remained just as great. But she could not fail Mazzini, nor dare she entrust or endanger one of the more amenable inspectors with the errand. For the possession of seditious material would bring certain imprisonment or even death. The dangers were very real, she thought, thinking of what lay so casually hidden in Luciano Forro's study.

Later that night, after everyone had retired for bed after prayers, Gabriella slipped into Giuseppina's room. She had not wanted to involve her, but the girl's help was vital to her plan.

'Why, you're dressed and in your coat!' gasped the student after she had lit her candle. 'Where are you going? Are you eloping?'

Despite her anxiety at the risk she was about to take, Gabriella burst into laughter.

'Giuseppina, you are such a romantic. Who am I likely to be eloping with?'

'Well, where else can you be going at such an hour . . . Is it a Conte?'

'Certainly not!' exclaimed Gabriella. 'Do you think I'd risk my place here for a man . . . Well, I suppose I am in a way,' she said, thinking of Mazzini, 'but not in the way you imagine, Giuseppina. I have to deliver something tonight and it's for Italy that I do it. Will you help me?'

'You want me to come with you?' whispered Giuseppina, looking very frightened.

'No, but if you could distract the doorkeeper so that I can slip out I would be very grateful. I shall be away for about two hours . . . well, let us say in two hours precisely I shall be at the outside gate.'

'But how shall I distract her?' asked Giuseppina, biting her lip in anxiety.

'What about a mouse . . . it goes away and then it returns a second time? Say you'll scream the place down if she doesn't come to look.'

For a whole hour as sleep descended upon those within the Conservatorio, Gabriella waited with Giuseppina, hoping that the doorkeeper would also be asleep in her small office. Then, when all was quiet, they crept downstairs together. Thankfully, as they had hoped, the sound of snoring reached their ears as they drew near the sleeping guardian of the door.

'Don't forget,' whispered Gabriella. 'Two hours from now I'll be waiting outside. If you can't lure her away, don't worry, I'll have to think of something else. I don't want to get you into trouble.'

On the street outside the sanctuary of the Conservatorio, Gabriella felt quite nervous as she looked around. As a child in London she had run through the darkest alleys, had felt no threat from drunks or the roughest of beggars. But for a long time she had led a most sheltered life, and so now she hurried along, keeping to the shadows. In the distance came the sound of raucous singing, the words were almost indistinct but the sound was guttural, harsh; it would be German soldiers, she thought nervously. Soon her surmise was borne out, and she did not linger before the lighted window of the drinking-house. But in the alley next to it there was a soldier urinating and, before Gabriella had time to avert her glance, he turned. On seeing her, with a drunken laugh, he directed his flow to spatter her.

'Why, you disgusting, filthy beast!' she cried out over her shoulder as she ran away. A bellow of laughter and a voice echoed after her. 'Italian whore . . . you're all whores, and your men are cowards!'

When she was certain that there was no pursuit, Gabriella stopped. For a moment she thought she was going to be sick. She had not been physically violated, but the foul dampness of her skirt made her cringe with distaste. Near to tears she removed a small handkerchief from her pocket and made a few futile dabs, then flung it away in disgust and walked on, her lips tightening as anger replaced revulsion and fright. She was no stranger to drunks urinating in corners and alleys, nor had the boys been very modest, but tonight the swaggering display had filled her with a cold rage. She was not dressed as a ragged beggar, she now looked like any other young Milanese lady, and that is what the contemptuous act had been directed against. What were these foreign soldiers doing here?

There was a game of cards in progress when Enrico Facini admitted Gabriella into his room. On seeing her there was an outburst of laughter from the young men present, and suggestions of a discovered assignation.

'Mario will tell you I visited you all some years ago,' said Gabriella, seeing the two students who lodged out of the Conservatorio were present. 'And I bring you something again from Mazzini. You must excuse my appearance,' she said, seeing some of the players looking at the front of her dress which showed below her short coat. 'That was a baptism from a white jacket.'

'What!' cried the young men, springing up in a fury. 'Where is he?'

Gabriella looked at the angry faces before her and remembered the coffee-house crowded with armed soldiers.

'He'll be long gone by now,' she said, with a smile and a shrug of her shoulders to calm the irate feelings. 'If you've a little water I'll sponge myself down. While I do so, perhaps you would like to examine this. It came enclosed in a letter from Mazzini, and he directed me to bring it to you.'

By the time Gabriella had dealt with her stained skirt, the paper held before the warmth of the fire had yielded faint writing.

'He wants us to set up guerrilla bases in the hills so that when the day of revolution comes they will be able to harass the Austrians and come to the aid of the towns,' said Enrico Facini, looking up with glowing eyes.

'Does Mazzini mean us to go and live in the hills over winter?' gasped one of his companions.

'No!' snapped Enrico impatiently. 'He wants us to recruit, train and supply these forces with firearms.'

There was an immediate hush in the room and Gabriella saw shock depicted on every face.

'But we haven't even got guns ourselves.'

'I've never fired one.'

'My father has two fowling pieces,' volunteered the rather feminine-looking music student named Angelo.

'That's good,' jeered his companions. 'Now we can start the revolution to liberate Italy!'

'If we haven't got guns, then we have to steal them!' snarled

140

Enrico, glaring around the circle of faces, who by their shifty exchange of glances showed they were little impressed by this suggestion.

At this tense moment there came a series of soft knocks at the door.

'Thank goodness for Giovanni!' said Enrico looking relieved. 'At least he has some imagination.'

'*Mon Dieu!*' cried Giovanni Forro, seeing Gabriella. 'Shouldn't dedicated students be in bed dreaming of Bellini?' he teased, gesturing for the young man sitting beside Gabriella to move one along so that he could sit beside her.

'Now perhaps we can get on with things,' said Enrico. 'Who knows the frontier around Como?'

'I do!' said Gabriella and Giovanni Forro simultaneously. 'Well, not as well as you, Giovanni,' she added.

'You're not a member of our group,' declared Enrico Facini.

'I've taken risks twice to get Mazzini's messages to you,' declared Gabriella sharply. 'And I am his friend . . . Whatever it is you want doing, wouldn't a young lady be less suspicious?'

'Have you thought about what could happen if you were caught?'

'No, and I don't want to,' she said. 'But I will not let what that soldier did tonight pass. Will you let me help you this time with your work against the Austrians?'

'Very well,' said the fair-haired young man, ignoring Giovanni Forro's cry of rage as someone whispered to him what had happened to her. 'What you brought here this evening must be given to the courier from the Capo Lago press. As soon as they send word that they have printed work ready for distribution in Lombardy, you and Giovanni shall take it. Meanwhile, Giovanni, you could think about how a number of pamphlets could be smuggled from the frontier to Milan.'

'If the delivery could be made when I have to return to Blevio it would be easier for me,' said Gabriella, reddening as everyone looked at her. 'It would be difficult for me to leave the Conservatorio otherwise . . . and . . . I don't want to lose my place.'

'Personal interest cannot be put above one's country's needs!' declared Enrico Facini, so fiercely that Gabriella's blush deepened.

'You're quite right, Enrico,' declared Giovanni Forro. 'But you know how thorough the searches are at the city gate, and how diligent the spies are in checking everyone's movements. A lady student, though, going for tuition to a famous prima donna, would never be suspected. Besides,' the Conte said, directing a swift wink to Gabriella, 'couldn't you work out some code, Gabriella, and transpose whatever else we have for printing into music? That way it could be included with your music.'

'Yes, yes, I'm sure I could,' she said, flashing a grateful smile at the artful Conte.

When it came time for her to leave, just like the first time it was Giovanni who drove her back. She was glad of it, for the streets were filled with carousing soldiers.

'Look at them: they swagger like fattened turkeys,' snorted her escort. 'One day we'll kick them out, but until then,' he said with a carefree laugh, 'life should be enjoyed. Just think what you have to look forward to, Gabriella. Danger, and who knows what else, on your future excursion with me.'

'Danger is quite enough for me to worry about,' she said sternly as the young man helped her down from the sediole and brushed her cheek with his lips.

'I'll wait until you get inside, just in case you have to spend the rest of the night in my arms!' Giovanni Forro called after her as she approached the door.

'Keep your voice down!' hissed Gabriella, as she turned the handle and pushed gently at the door. With her heart in her mouth, she peered around its edge. Her breath was expelled in one great sigh of relief, for somehow Giuseppina had not failed her. Turning around she gave a farewell wave to Giovanni, and then stealthily made her way upstairs and hid until a grumbling inspector emerged from Giuseppina's room and came forward towards the stairs.

'And did you find your mouse, Signorina Verenese?'

'There are no mice in here,' replied Gabriella's friend, endeavouring to look serious as she embraced Gabriella. 'But there is a huge rat that has twice appeared and required every piece of furniture to be pulled away from the wall to find it. I fear I am no longer popular in some quarters . . . so I think next time we are at La Scala you will have to buy a very large sorbet!'

Trivial though the soldier's action had been in comparison to some of her memories of childhood, the coarse contempt he had shown had in one brief moment given Gabriella experience of the humiliations people must endure within a system not so harsh to make them rise up, but which in robbing them of responsibility gradually erodes all pride. As she lay in bed after saying goodnight to her friend, Gabriella thought about how she had involuntarily involved herself in protest. Was Luciano Forro involved too as the writer Larius? But if he were, wouldn't he be involved with Giovanni and his republican friends?

From her bedside table, she picked up the cocoon which she had brought back from his silk reeling mill, shaking it next to her ear to hear the rattle of the chrysalis inside. That is Lombardy, she thought, around which Vienna has wound its silken skein of censorship and repression to hold everyone captive in a cocoon of apathy and acceptance. The only thing that offered brief release from the cocoon was the music at La Scala: there Vienna's subjects rebelled for as long as the patriotic lines lasted. Would Mazzini and his young followers be able to unwind the silken figure of eight, she wondered as she drifted off to sleep?

As Gabriella and Giovanni Forro approached Milan's gate to the north, they were stopped by the police.

'What have you got in that trunk?'

'Clothes,' stammered Gabriella.

'Let's see what your girlfriend has. Open up, Conte!' ordered the bewhiskered official. Hastily Gabriella smiled to try and make up for the dark, scowling looks of her companion.

'It's very empty!' remarked the man as he lifted the lid of the trunk.

'Yes, I keep most of my things at Como,' lied Gabriella, trying to remain calm. 'I study singing there with Giuditta Pasta, and Conte Forro is kindly giving me a lift.'

'Singing, eh!' said the policeman, eyeing Gabriella suspiciously and lifting up her music case. 'Patriotic songs, have we?'

'A little Mozart!' she replied faintly as he drew out the music and leafed through it, stopping at the very copies she had written out herself. Then she observed that the hard, knowing eyes were looking at her crochets and quavers upside down, and it was all she could do not to laugh with relief as, losing interest, he waved them on.

In silence Giovanni Forro drove on at speed, his face still dark with anger.

'How they enjoy humiliating us,' he said at last. 'But these reforms of the Pope's – granting freedom of the press to the Papal States for one – are really going to embarrass Vienna.'

'Is your brother still in Rome?' she could not resist asking.

'I believe he is between there and Turin, collaborating with Massimo d'Azeglio,' Giovanni answered with a frown. 'And I'd rather you kept that to yourself. Certainly you must never breathe a word of it to Enrico or my credibility will be questioned.'

'What do you mean? I don't understand. Who is this d'Azeglio?'

'He is a Piedmont liberal writer with great influence. He writes for your patron's paper in Paris, for example, as Luciano does.'

'But why would it upset Enrico? Doesn't Luciano want liberty and unity also?'

'Yes, but he does not believe in a revolution to achieve it. You see, he and others are in Rome to show that Lombardy is looking to the Pope for help.'

'But we are outside the Papal States. How can the Pope help us?'

144

'Ask yourself who the Archbishops of Austria are answerable to . . . Pius has great power, not only in Italy but throughout the world. Anyway, we don't want him to make too many reforms or we'll not get our revolution.'

'But wouldn't it be better without bloodshed, Giovanni?'

'You're beginning to sound like my brother,' the young man grinned.

Like Milan, Como was garrisoned with many soldiers. There were regular patrols to try and stop the smuggling that went on over the frontier, which was only two miles away from the town. So although all sorts of people were tempted to slip over the border for a desired luxury, Gabriella and her companion hoped that the patrols would dismiss them as a young couple seeking romantic seclusion away from parental eyes.

'Don't forget,' said Giovanni when at last they glimpsed the still waters of Como from the top of a hill. 'If soldiers approach at any inconvenient moment, you are to rush into my arms and press your pretty lips to mine. I pray the whole garrison will be combing the area tonight . . .' he laughed.

'Don't say that or it might well happen,' scolded Gabriella. 'Though I'd probably feel much safer with a whole regiment than with you! Just remember I'm here for Giuseppe Mazzini, and after tonight I go back to being a student.'

'Very well, prima donna,' grinned the Conte.

Darkness had come by the time they had left the town of Como behind, and Gabriella realized how superficial her knowledge of the surroundings were.

'Don't forget,' said her companion, 'I have spent every summer here since I was a baby, and Luciano and I have hunted in the mountains since we could walk. We're going to take this small track as far as we can go and then wait.'

'What for?'

'Our goodly mountaineers with their gifts of fine prose.'

Advancing up an ascending track, Giovanni Forro led the nervous horses forward by the bridle until they were a little distance from the road below.

'This will do,' he said. 'They may even be here; just keep your eyes sharp for a signal.'

'What sort of a signal?' she whispered close to his ear.

In the darkness lips touched hers.

'I couldn't resist,' the young man chuckled as she protested. 'Admit you liked it?'

'I did not come all the way to Como to kiss you, Giovanni,' she hissed. 'And if you do it again, I shall slap you.'

Suddenly, a little way up above them, the glimmer of a light showed, then instantly was gone. Beside her, Giovanni gave two short whistles. All went silent, then came the sound of a stone falling and, following it, more definite sounds of footsteps approaching. Suddenly, three, four men loomed out of the darkness. Pausing only long enough to say the agreed password, the men transferred what they had been carrying in the baskets strapped to their backs to the empty trunk on the back of the carriage.

'Thanks, we can do the rest,' said Giovanni Forro, replacing the dress and petticoats which Gabriella had brought to conceal the pamphlets. 'These are for you to take back for printing. You'll need someone musical to make sense of it, and the code is written invisibly at the top of the first page.'

'Very well,' said the courier from the printing press. 'You're all keeping ink on the printers' fingers – we were here last night too. Goodnight. *Viva l'Italia*!'

All seemed to be going well, and with due caution they made their way back down to the road; but just as they were about to get back into the carriage they heard before seeing a group of horsemen bearing down upon them.

'Oh heavens, let's make a run for it,' cried Gabriella.

'No, we'd never outpace them,' replied Giovanni, his voice sharp with anxiety. 'Give me your hand!'

Without asking what he was intending to do, Gabriella followed him to the edge of the roadway. The next thing she knew was that she was being pushed hard up against a sloping boulder, and that he was kissing her as though he would eat her.

'Stop it!' she gasped outraged as his hands started to raise her skirts. But both lips and hands assaulted her with vigour, until in a wild fury she thrust him back and slapped his face with such force that he staggered backwards.

'You're disgraceful, Giovanni!' she cried, then gasped with fright, for the soldiers she had momentarily forgotten had halted before them.

'It's late for you to be out, Signorina,' said one with a chuckle. 'I won't ask what you are both up to, but if this young man is bothering you we will be happy to escort you home.'

'Oh no, officer,' replied Gabriella breathlessly. 'We were, er, just having a little tiff!'

'Then your quarrels must be well worth hearing: I am sure the priest will enjoy your next confession,' declared the officer, and with a roar of laughter he and his soldiers went on their way.

'By all the saints!' exclaimed Giovanni Forro. 'You can certainly slap. If only you had concentrated on the kissing, what must that be like?'

'That you'll never know!' Gabriella responded. 'And you'd better concentrate. They're not the only soldiers out tonight, and next time I will bite you, very hard!'

With a laugh, the young man turned the carriage to the left, away from the direction of Como.

'Where are we going?' she asked, as they moved along with the silvery glimmer of the lake to their right.

'To a spinning mill.'

'Your brother's?'

'Yes. From there they send the hanks of silk to the factory in Milan. I thought it was an ideal way of smuggling in the pamphlets.'

'Does Luciano know?'

'No, but I think it's time he lent some practical help to the national cause. All this diplomatic talk in Rome and Turin won't get us anywhere. It's action we want, like the French had!'

'Do you think it's right to lay him open to danger without telling him?'

'Do you think I'd let Luciano pay for what I do? It is I who am the patriot!'

For the rest of the journey, Gabriella was filled with misgivings about what they were doing. All excitement had drained away, leaving only anxiety.

How Giovanni managed in the darkness, she did not know, but she knew they were drawing close to the spinning mill by the ever increasing sound of the powerful force which swept down from the mountain to the lake.

'Signor Alberto is still up,' Giovanni observed, irritation sounding in his voice as he opened the gate leading into the estate. 'We'll have to hope the dogs don't bark. Don't speak, voices carry.'

From one visit it was impossible to remember where they were but, after moving for some time at snail's pace, the young man took her by the hand and led her through a doorway. As soon as a lamp was lighted she saw they were in a large storeroom, whose shelves were stacked with the dull gleam of small hanks of silk.

'Look, those baskets over there are obviously ready for transporting to Milan,' said Giovanni. 'While I unload, remove some of the hanks from them.'

It did not take long to remove the top layer. Giovanni had left for a second armful of pamphlets, and she had just made a start on the next layer, when her fingertips came into contact with something hard. She parted two of the hanks, and saw the spine of a book across whose leather binding, boldly emblazoned in letters of gold, was a title that made her gasp in surprise. Behind her she heard footsteps, and instinctively she scooped up the hanks of silk and laid them back into position.

'What are you doing with that basket?' The voice was familiar, but it was imbued with an anger she did not recognize.

'I was going to remove some of the silk for . . .' Gabriella faltered, hardly able to meet the stern gaze of Luciano Forro as he confronted her. She saw he was wearing riding breeches and boots, but though the night was chilly he wore no jacket and the sleeves of his white shirt were rolled up, as though he

148

had been working at something – or packing something, she suddenly thought.

'It's all my fault. Gabriella is only doing what I told her to do,' explained Giovanni as he re-entered the room. He seemed not in the least put out by his brother's appearance. 'Perhaps you would like one of these for your library, Luciano, in return for the loan of your excellent transport system.'

Luciano Forro's face became pale with rage as he looked at his younger brother.

'You would have endangered my people without telling me. And for something that none of us believes in!'

'Do you not believe in liberty and unity for Italy, brother?' asked Giovanni sarcastically.

'Not by the methods some of your leaders would advocate – but then revolutionary leaders care little for the human cost of the glorious revolt, so long as they obtain power,' declared the Conte, his tone harsh and biting. 'Can't you see, Giovanni, that war always hurts the poor? Plantations that have been soaked with honest sweat for generations are ruined in a day, crops are burnt, the people starve. Do you want to see that in Lombardy?'

'There sometimes has to be a sacrifice. Your way, the moderate's way of reaching the mind, is too slow!'

'But it is less painful. More important, what is changed by consent is permanent. Won't you at least take that way first? I don't want to see you throw your life away like other followers of Mazzini in some ill-conceived plot that's doomed to failure before it's begun.'

'Giuseppe Mazzini's ideas are worthy and noble,' Gabriella interrupted in defence of the kindly man that had brought a light into the lives of her and other poor children.

'Some of his arguments are admirable,' responded Luciano Forro politely. 'But he is in London: he does not always have control over some of the more zealous of his followers, as was demonstrated by the Bandiera brothers. So far, everything done in the name of Giovane Italia has led to the loss of young lives.'

'Well, Conte,' said Gabriella coldly, 'I see that the pamphlets which were entrusted to us tonight are written by Mazzini. If you do not wish to help, I will have to carry all of them to Milan myself; and I will do so, rather than let down someone who gave me my chance in life.'

Luciano Forro looked at the stubborn expression on the face which was usually so gentle. Why – how – had she become mixed up with the hotheads in Milan? Was his brother the attraction? The supposition caused an immediate, unexpected stab of jealousy which he instantly strove to suppress for, after all, was it not likely she should wish to help a man who, according to the Princess Belgiojoso, had raised her from the lowest of lives? It was curious, in many ways Christina Belgiojoso's story seemed hardly believable, for even in her plain uniform the young student could hold her own with the loveliest women in Milan; but when she started to sing, yes, that was what betrayed all. Then there was nothing of the lady making sweet sounds for the drawing-room; like an assassin she took her listeners by the throat; all the earthy, courageous driving force of the survivor was there.

Luciano Forro picked up one of the pamphlets and read out loud:

'Like two distinct branches springing out of the same trunk, men and women spring in differing forms from a common base, which is humanity. No inequality exists between them, but, as often happens with two men, a difference of tendencies, of special vocations. Are two notes of the same musical chord unequal or of different nature? Man and Woman are the two notes without which the human chord is not possible.

'I can quite see why a young lady should wish to save these thoughts of Mazzini,' the Conte said with a wry smile. 'Please leave them here. I will see they reach Milan. Are you expected at this late hour at Blevio?'

'No, Gabriella is staying with me at the Villa,' said Giovanni, beaming with relief that his brother was not going to abandon him.

'But Mama does not arrive until next week,' said Luciano Forro looking slowly from his brother to Gabriella.

'As you say, it's late, and Signor Prioni expects me tomorrow . . . I didn't wish to compromise them tonight,' whispered Gabriella as Luciano Forro's expression grew bleak and cold.

'I rather think that it is you who is compromised, Signorina Pepe!' remarked the Conte icily as he turned on his heel and strode away.

'"*Avrai tu l'universo. Resti l'Italia a me!*" Is that what the Pope is going to tell Radetzky?' Gabriella giggled as Andrea Prioni literally danced with excitement as he related the news from Como.

'Well, dear ladies,' he beamed. 'I had my doubts about this cleric's intentions – I thought perhaps the amnesty was just a bid for popularity – but after further reforms and now this happening in Ferrara, well, I am one of Pius's greatest admirers.'

'But aren't the Austrians legally entitled to garrison their troops in that border town? I don't understand,' said his sister.

'It may be,' declared her brother impatiently. 'That doesn't give them the right to march in reinforcements of 600 Hungarian infantry, three guns and cavalry. There they were, artillery matches burning, marching up and down ready to blow the town sky-high when citizens of the Papal States were out on the streets celebrating the first anniversary of the amnesty. It was a deliberate act of aggression in a foreign state. Anyway, the Papal Legate, Cardinal Ciacchi, has been ordered by the Pope not to find billets for them; now we will see how things are going to go. Will Pius IX back down, or will it be Field Marshal Radetzky? Aha, the whole of Italy will be watching Ferrara!'

It was good to be back at Blevio and escape the summer heat of Milan, to enjoy Agnese's gossip and play duets with Andrea and listen to his impassioned views on politics. To wake and see a flimsy streamer of mist suspended below the dark mountain like some bride's abandoned veil; to lie on one's back and see an edging of cloud gilded by the sun into a meandering, glittering stream; to watch eagle and hawk wheeling high above the wooded slopes. Nothing could keep her from the mountain those first weeks, and Agnese, thrilled and happy to have her back, sent her off with a smile and something delicious to eat for a picnic.

It was a perfect day for walking, bright and warm but with a little breeze which stirred the long grasses and gently moved the leaves of the oak and chestnut trees. As she mounted higher, passing by some of the little villages, Gabriella sang the local song about the chestnut flour which makes the polenta. Wearing Professor Prioni's battered straw hat and the old rough skirt, she felt truly released from school. At a green meadow, near to the ruins of a little church, she decided to have her luncheon.

What a gypsy I feel, she laughed, touching where the restraint of her stays should be – and what a gypsy I now look, she thought, unrolling her stockings and flinging them on to the grass. Above, the eagle that she had spotted from a meadow lower down was still executing his solitary patrol. Perhaps he can see my picnic, she smiled, laying out the dark shiny black olives, creamy cheese and fresh baked bread. Barely a crumb did she leave for the aerial spy and, feeling quite guilty and so full that she might burst, she leant her head back against the basket and drifted off to sleep.

The next thing she knew something like a warm wet flannel was attacking her face. With a shriek of alarm, Gabriella opened her eyes and found herself looking up into the friendly face of a large hound. Beside him another was wagging his tail, while a third was gobbling up the treat she had been saving for later.

'Why you monster!' she cried, and then dissolved into fresh laughter as the dog beside her licked her ear. 'Will you stop kissing me!' she shrieked as she pushed the slobbering creature away.

'How I envy him,' murmured a voice that made her whirl around. 'I'm sorry, have they eaten your picnic?'

'No, that's all right. There was just a little cake left, nothing really,' said Gabriella, standing up and feeling acutely embarrassed as Luciano Forro's dog greeted him with one of her stockings hanging from its mouth. Was she always to be caught so with this man? She blushed, remembering the brown paper bag.

'Yours?' queried the Conte, eyes gleaming with raillery which Gabriella pointedly ignored. 'It's a little wet I'm afraid,' said Luciano Forro apologetically as he picked the stocking up from the grass. 'As you could see, he did not really want to part with so unusual a find.'

'It doesn't matter,' said Gabriella, thrusting her bare feet into her shoes.

'But it does. We have eaten your cake, spoilt your stocking, and interrupted the peace of your day.'

'No, I'm . . . glad to see you again,' she said awkwardly.

'Do you mean that?' Luciano smiled, handing back the stocking. Their fingers touched, and the brief contact made her tremble. She turned swiftly away to hide her feelings.

'That night, you made me hate my brother,' Luciano Forro said quietly.

'There was no cause,' she said, not daring to turn around.

'Look at me!' he said, his melodious voice not letting her be calm.

'I can't,' she whispered. 'I . . . I must go.'

Gabriella stooped to pick the basket up and, as her fingers touched the handle, the Conte's hand closed over them. Gently he drew her upright.

'Why can't you?' he murmured, his dark grey-green eyes glistening with humour and a desire that made her tremble as he drew closer. Her lips parted as she tried to speak and she was hardly able to breathe, knowing the moment was upon them as he lowered his lips to hers. The kiss made her sigh with pleasure as his lips moved on hers like the caress of silk, and when, too soon, the contact ended, she was filled with regret. For a moment he just looked at her, holding her face between his hands, then he leant towards her again. This time she could not stop herself responding: filled with wonder, curiosity, her mouth clung to his; but then he drew away with a lazy smile.

'It's time to go, my little priestess.'

Gabriella smiled back in response and then her eyes caught sight of the line of solemn spectators.

'Oh see!' she said, her laughter spilling over. 'Your little family look most disapproving.'

'Jealous!' laughed Luciano Forro, looking at the sad brown eyes of his gun dogs. 'Come, young lady,' he said. 'If I stay here a moment longer I'll not be able to let you go – and one should only pay homage to mountain flowers.'

Before they parted Luciano Forro took Gabriella's hand in his. 'You will probably find an invitation from my mother when you return,' he smiled. 'We have a guest coming to a supper party tomorrow who is most anxious to meet you. But I shall not tell you who it is, so that out of curiosity you will have to accept.'

There was no need of a mystery guest to entice Gabriella to accept the invitation, for her heart was in a whirl, and all she could think about was those warm lips touching hers and their owner's closeness. The following day, performing difficult scales with Giuditta Pasta, she either left notes out or added them, so that the famous prima donna, with a sigh and a knowing smile, sent her away to visit her daughter Clelia who was painting in her little studio perched high above the garden. Never had Gabriella been so restless, each hour seeming like two as she waited for the moment when she was to be collected by the Forro launch.

'I am always dressed the same,' she sighed, as she watched for the arrival of the boat.

'So are lovely flowers,' reassured Agnese. 'Besides, I think you'll find the old nobility are careful with their money. It's only the merchant classes that constantly flaunt their wealth. Besides, wearing the dress of the Conservatorio is a distinction!'

He was waiting on the illuminated flight of marble steps

154

leading down to the water's edge, and she saw there was a boyish eagerness about his studious features.

'How lovely you look,' he murmured. 'Can you really be the young priestess I met in the sacred grove yesterday?'

'I thought I looked more the gypsy.'

'Come, I'll not share you with the Dandolo brothers,' he said, as laughter and greetings sounded from an approaching boat.

Up to the first of the terraces they walked, where the perfume of the roses hung sweet and cool on the vapour from the fountain beneath. Not once had he touched her, but the vibrations between them were so strong that, when they reached the upper walk, simultaneously they halted and turned towards each other. As she raised her lips shyly to meet his, the Conte's arms closed about her, and for the first time she felt his body as he gathered her to him; the heady moment was as pungent as the scent of the jasmine about them and her senses surrendered.

'Are you going to let me love you?' he whispered, as he moved his lips down the line of her throat.

'I . . . I am afraid.'

'Do you wish me to go away?'

'No,' she whispered, trembling, desire dominating her thoughts as the handsome face looked questioningly down at her. Then once again his lips were on hers, and this time the fierce pressure and the deepening contact of the kiss made her gasp and pull away.

'Oh Gabriella,' he said softly, with laughter in his voice. 'We are going to enjoy each other hugely – and see,' he said stepping back, 'as if the stars are not enough, our fireflies are paying you homage as well.' Gabriella looked around and above and laughed too in delight to see the pretty lights of the insects dancing against the dark blue of the sky. 'I would like to whisk you away right now,' Luciano Forro sighed as footsteps sounded behind them. 'But a certain person is awaiting your arrival.'

Never had her son looked so happy, thought Wiera Forro as he entered the drawing-room with the Princess Belgiojoso's protégée. The Contessa watched as her tall, elegant son bestowed on the young woman a look such as those which his father had once thrilled her with, and the memory brought tears to her eyes. Shaking off her thoughts, the Contessa moved quickly forward to greet new arrivals and, as she did so, caught sight of Flavia Balziano's face in a mirror. There was no mistaking the emotion on the dramatic features, nor which couple had inspired such jealousy. A premonition of future trouble seized Wiera Forro, and she regretted sending the invitation to the young singer, for all her instincts had been alerted when she had seen Luciano and the young woman perform the Bellini. It wouldn't do, offending the Balzianos: they could bring disaster on Luciano. But it was more than that: despite her own romantic nature, Wiera Forro had been brought up to put duty first. Luciano was breaking all the rules of good behaviour by embarrassing the young Marchesa.

'Gabriella, my dear,' she said, hurrying forward. 'I'm so glad that you were able to come, but I must steal you away from my son to meet Miss Fuller . . . Perhaps, Luciano, you might see if Flavia is being looked after.' Wiera Forro gave him a meaningful glance that produced an expression of irritation on the Conte's face.

Gabriella had no idea who Miss Fuller might be as she accompanied the black-clad figure of the Contessa. Nor, when she was introduced to a blonde American lady, was she any the wiser.

'I won't keep you in suspense, Signorina Pepe,' the stranger said. 'I have recently been in London, where I was privileged to meet Mr Giuseppe Mazzini at the residence of Mr and Mrs Carlyle in Chelsea. I found him very charming, and when I told him that I would be coming to Lombardy, he naturally asked me to give you his greetings. I was going to call upon you personally, but when I spoke to the Contessa she said she would invite you here this evening.'

'Did you see the school in Hatton Garden, Miss Fuller?'

'Yes, I surely did and I was most favourably impressed. Education is everything. I myself was reading Latin when I was six, and by the time I was thirteen I had read your Italian poets,

Berni, Pulci and Politian. Unfortunately however, I still find it difficult to make myself understood on my travels here.'

'There are so many dialects, it is not easy,' said Gabriella politely, feeling intellectually out of her depth with a mind that seemed as piercing as the glances that the blonde-haired woman darted at her. Her voice was unmusical and her manner slightly overbearing and, when she spoke, her fair lashes punctuated every phrase by closing, which after a while began to irritate. Nevertheless, she had been thoughtful enough to seek her out, so Gabriella persevered and tried to conceal her impatience to escape.

'Do you miss London, Signorina Pepe?'

'I sometimes miss its mad clamour, the excitement of the river,' replied Gabriella, 'and of course my friends; but as to the rest – I am thankful to have been given escape . . . I sometimes think of those who weren't so lucky and wonder what they might have become if they had had my opportunity. And I long one day to become financially independent.'

Margaret Fuller laughed, displaying the most beautiful teeth. 'That applies to most of us, my dear young lady, I assure you. Nothing is more irksome than to travel with slender means, but in Italy it is worth it, for one is storing up many treasures in the mind. In Brescia, I was fever-stricken, wretched and lonely in a foreign land, but what will I remember? Why, the Titians, the exquisite Raphael and the Scavi. And have you ever considered how free you are compared to the daughters of the nobility? Look at them, look at me, travelling where I please. If I lived in one of these lovely palaces, would I ever want to write for the *New York Tribune*?'

Gabriella looked with admiration at this independent young woman, whose spirit was obviously so valiant. 'I don't think anything would ever suppress your thoughts, Miss Fuller, but Lombardy does have a Princess who sets an example to all the women here, for she does not let her sex or rank stand in the way of her fight for nationalism or the running of a newspaper.'

'The Editor of *Ausonio*?'

'Yes,' smiled Gabriella. 'The Princess Belgiojoso.'

157

After Miss Margaret Fuller had excused herself to go and speak with other guests, Gabriella stepped forward into the open doorway to enjoy the freshness of the evening. There were two people standing before the balustrade just beyond the light of a paper lantern. It looked like the Marchese Balziano and his wife, and indeed, as the woman spoke, Gabriella recognized an older version of Flavia's voice.

'What has she invited that little opera student here again for?'

Gabriella started at the words, knowing the Marchesa could only mean her. The woman's tone of voice made her shiver.

'Perhaps she is here to sing, dear,' responded the weary, resigned voice of the Marchese.

'Not by the look on Luciano's face. It is one thing for him to entertain mistresses in Milan, but to flaunt one in front of Flavia, especially as it's so near the time he will be asking you for her hand, is outrageous. I will not be slighted so. You must speak to him! And remind him where his duty lies . . .'

She had heard much, much too much! Her chest heaved and she leant against the wall, but it was impossible to quell the overwhelming feeling of hurt and the hot tears that were flooding her eyes. Without caring who saw her, Gabriella ran out on to the terrace and fled towards the steps leading down to the boats. Behind her she heard pursuing footsteps and a man's voice calling her name. But she neither stopped nor looked around. At the Rose terrace, she heard the man taking the steps two, three at a time and, as she reached the final flight, Luciano Forro seized her from behind.

'What is the matter, why are you running away? Who has upset you?'

'You have upset me,' she choked, trying to thrust him away.

'I?' he cried in astonishment, holding her fast as she struggled. 'How? – I will not let you go until you tell me what I have done! Can't you see how unhappy you are making me?'

Through her tears, Gabriella looked up at the desperate expression on the Conte's face. Could she have been mistaken? she wondered, clutching at any straw that would make everything as it had been.

'They said you are to marry the Marchesa Flavia,' she whispered, her voice jerky with emotion.

Luciano Forro tightened his arms around her and cradled her head against his chest. After a moment, as she became calmer, he raised her chin and kissed her long and with great tenderness, his lips finally coming to rest against the delicate skin beneath her ear.

'Can't you see I tremble for you?' he murmured. 'You will be everything to me, and the fact that Flavia is my wife will not alter our love. The Balziano family and mine have long ties: no one expects people of our rank to marry for love. Let me make you happy, my darling,' he said, seeing the fresh glint of tears in her eyes.

'I can't,' she gasped, pushing him away. 'It has to be otherwise. Everything!'

# Chapter Nine

It was September and the whole of Milan was bedecked not only in the Papal yellow and white befitting a welcome to a new Archbishop, but also with banners of red, white and green for this native of Bergamo. Archbishop Romilli had arrived on the fourth, and six days later the demonstrations of welcome were still continuing, for the Milanesi were taking full advantage of the occasion to cheer for a Pope who had shown the wisdom to appoint an Italian as Archbishop and, more importantly, who was still maintaining a firm line against Austria at Ferrara.

To their delight, the students of the Conservatorio had been permitted to join in the celebrations and, as part of a chaperoned group, Gabriella was standing next to Giuseppina before the Archbishop's palace, waving small flags. Alongside, with coloured ribbons in their black jackets, were the male students from the Conservatorio, who had started to chant Rossini's hymn to Pius IX.

'Hurrah for Pio Nono!' everyone shouted with a roar when the singing died away. Then, as if further encouraged by the applause, the singing broke out again. But somehow, thought Gabriella glancing about her, the atmosphere was more tense than joyful on this occasion, for the military presence watching them closely was enormous.

'There's going to be trouble. I can feel it,' whispered Giuseppina, who was obviously of the same mind. 'Look, Matron is signalling for us to go.'

'Pretend you haven't seen her,' urged Gabriella, intent on not missing anything, for it seemed as if the whole of Milan were here and every rank and age had come out to sing Pius's Hymn, which had become the battle-cry against the Austrians. 'Why, it's just as if the chorus of La Scala were here,' she laughed. 'And they can't do a thing to stop the encores. Don't those great whiskered faces look furious!'

Suddenly, as if the military could endure this act of defiance no longer, an order rang out. The sudden shocked silence of the crowd was broken only by the clink of metal as bayonets were fixed and swords drawn. Frozen with disbelief, unable to grasp what they meant to do, Gabriella stared. She was aware of a thunderous roar as the soldiers charged. Then all erupted into pandemonium.

'Giuseppina, hold on to me!' screamed Gabriella, but like sheep scattering before a pack of wolves, the people in front pushed and shoved in all directions in a bid to escape, and Gabriella, helpless to resist, was forced apart from her friend and fellow students. To right and left there seemed to be white jackets swinging out wildly with the flat of their swords at anybody blocking their path. More concerned to escape the swinging steel than to be reunited with her party, Gabriella concentrated on trying to get out of the hysterical mêlée. Nearby, a university student raised his fists against a soldier, and immediately he was ruthlessly smashed to the ground. Then, to her horror, Gabriella saw the Croatian raise his sword above the writhing, defenceless body.

'No!' she screamed, pulling at the uniformed arm before she knew what she was doing. Glancing towards her, with an indifferent, stony stare, the huge man smashed his fist up against her jaw and all went black.

As she drifted back into consciousness, Gabriella became aware that she was being carried by her feet and shoulders, but her head was splitting with pain and the jogging motion, together with the sound of uproar, made her feel dizzy and sick. At last the jerky movement ceased and there were low murmurings as she felt herself being set down. Slowly she opened her eyes, and found the Contessa Forro looking down at her in concern.

'My sons brought you here. You're not badly hurt, but the

brute could have broken your jaw if Giovanni had not pulled you away from him. You'll be a little bruised, I expect, but my physician will look at you to make sure that there is nothing more serious.'

Gabriella nodded her gratitude, but couldn't speak, for she could hardly comprehend what had happened; and when the Contessa's physician administered a sleeping draught, she quickly drifted back into unconsciousness once more.

The next time she opened her eyes it was morning.

'I fear I put you to trouble yesterday, Contessa,' croaked Gabriella, looking over the rim of the sheet of her bed as the tall, elegant woman entered.

'It's no trouble,' reassured the aristocrat, laying a cool hand against Gabriella's brow. 'I should have been angry if Luciano had taken you anywhere else.'

'Were many hurt?'

'Yes, I fear so. The troops had no right to charge an unarmed and peaceful crowd: it is monstrous! And I for one shall send my protest to the Vice-Regal. Anyway, my dear, I'm relieved that no great damage has been done to you. A day of complete rest is what you need. Perhaps you might like to sit in the garden? The roses are still lovely and the birds will provide a lively distraction.'

'It's most kind of you, Contessa,' said Gabriella. 'But I think I should leave. They will wonder what has become of me at the Conservatorio, and I have intruded upon your kindness long enough. I feel fully recovered. As you see, I only have a little bruising. So, may I go?'

The pretty lips of the Contessa parted and her silvery laugh shimmered on the air. 'Gabriella, you sound like a schoolgirl wishing to escape the schoolroom . . . Is my home and company so unpleasant that you wish to abandon it in such a hurry? No, I shall not hear of you leaving so soon. What would your patron think of me! And as for the Conservatorio, that has been taken care of, for I wrote to the principal myself to say you were in our care. Do you embroider?' she asked, just as she was leaving the bedchamber.

'Not very well,' replied Gabriella, remembering her feeble attempts for the fund-raising bazaar at Mazzini's school.

'Well, that doesn't matter, it will provide a pleasant distraction from yesterday's events. I shall bring my basket of silks out into the garden.'

Gabriella would have preferred to have left the moment she had dressed. But a will just as strong as her own had deemed otherwise. Not wishing to give offence, and hoping that the Contessa's eldest son would be absent, Gabriella made her way downstairs to the garden.

'I hope that missing your classes won't be too serious,' said the Contessa, looking up with a smile as Gabriella emerged on to the terrace.

'Not so much now that I'm in my final year,' smiled Gabriella. 'Though I don't think my maths teacher would agree. But it would not be wise for me to sing today. My jaw really is quite painful, and I cannot help but think of all the injured people.'

'That's why I suggested a little embroidery. I always believe in keeping the mind occupied when one is sad,' Wiera Forro said, a faraway expression touching her soft grey eyes. 'There were times immediately after my husband died when I felt just like a puppet performing social duties – but every distraction helps. They're like cogs in a wheel, clicking over one by one, getting you through each day, each week, until the pain begins gradually to lessen and one day you realize you have not thought of your loss once.' She paused and gave a little rueful smile, the corners of her lips turning down in the way of her eldest son. 'You think you are over it, a year goes by, and then you look at something, touch something . . . and like a razor the pain suddenly cuts you, takes you by surprise.'

'You were deeply in love, Contessa!' said Gabriella softly.

'Yes, I was fortunate to have a love match. It's not often possible amongst our rank – I was only sixteen when I married and I was so proud of him. He fought with Napoleon at Waterloo and survived, only to die of typhoid when Luciano and Giovanni were still babies. Ah, he looked so dashing in his uniform: he was but a boy himself, just nineteen. Of course many of the older families were glad to see the Restoration, and hoped that things would be as they had been before Napoleon; but it's never possible to turn back the clock completely. Napoleon did so much for us, he really revived the concept of nationalism . . . the Kingdom of Italy. Did you know he placed the Iron Crown of Lombardy on his own head, the Crown of St Helena with the nail from the cross?'

'How strange that Napoleon should end his days on St Helena,' reflected Gabriella.

'None of us knows our fate, and perhaps that is as well. When I think what happened to my dear friend Giulia and her little girl . . . so many loved ones gone,' whispered the Contessa, turning away with tears in her eyes. 'A moment by myself, my dear,' she said, rising abruptly from her seat and walking away down the garden.

Gabriella stared after the slender figure in black, and wondered whether to leave her to the solitude of the garden, but Giovanni Forro had appeared.

'Thank you for looking after me,' she said, as the young man flung himself into a chair beside her.

'Think nothing of it,' declared the young man, his tone flat and bitter. 'If we had been armed, the brute would not be breathing today. And if you had not collapsed into our arms, neither might my brother, for he was ready to try and run him through with his walking cane. Still, it's as well it happened. We'll make many more converts now . . . Good morning, Mama, is that for me?' Giovanni Forro asked, rising to greet his mother.

'Certainly not,' laughed Wiera Forro as he kissed her cheeks. 'It's for Gabriella. Are you going to stay and keep her company, dear? I have my charity committee to attend.'

'I don't mind sitting on my own,' said Gabriella quickly, realizing from Giovanni's sudden flush that he had other plans for his morning. 'The garden is so lovely, and with the embroidery I will be quite content.'

'Very well,' smiled Wiera Forro. 'I will have a little light lunch served to you here.'

'Thank you, that would be lovely.'

'Thanks,' said Giovanni as soon as the Contessa had departed. 'I would have stayed with you, but I do have a prior engagement. I thought it might take my mind off events.'

'I understand,' said Gabriella with a mischievous smile. 'Please don't keep her waiting on my account – oh, and Giovanni,' she said reaching up and squeezing his hand. 'Thank you for saving my jaw and my future career!'

After Giovanni had departed and the Contessa had bade her goodbye, Gabriella settled back. She felt more relaxed now that she was alone with just the servants in the house, and having learnt that Luciano Forro was visiting the silk weaving factory in the city. Not since the time she had sat with Mazzini's landlady in Chelsea had Gabriella embroidered, and it took a little thought to remember some of the stitches. In London the object had been to raise money for the bazaar, so there she had worked as fast and as long as her inexperienced fingers would allow. It had seemed very tedious work then. But here, with a lovely vista of flowers and shrubs, and the quick darting flight of birds, ever choosing new branches from which to serenade her, the occupation of embroidery seemed a delight, taxing the mind only with one decision: which colours best captured the exquisite rose on the table beside her.

Perhaps she had dozed for an hour, maybe only minutes, for her needle and silk were still between her fingers, resting against the abandoned material. But on the table a light luncheon had been left. Like the colours of the flowers in the garden, the artistically arranged platters were a delight to look at, a visual overture to stimulate anticipation and curiosity.

From the villa came the sound of a Chopin prelude. She had only heard him play twice, but she recognized his decisive touch at once. Gabriella smiled as he took the ending a little too fast: here was a man with much to do, but not so much that he did not pause to linger awhile. Now his reflective mood had changed, and he threw himself into the Polonaise with energy and rage, bringing alive Chopin's protest against a country's subjugation in a passionate release of his feelings.

Gabriella saw there were two glasses on the table, and with

a feeling of dread she anticipated that he would be joining her. How could she cope with seeing him when she had spent so many sleepless nights trying to rid herself of his memory? At the sound of his approach she glanced around nervously. His face was relaxed but grave.

'Perhaps the last bars . . . a trifle fast?' she teased, to hide her agitation.

'I've a great deal to fit into my day,' laughed the Conte, pouring out wine for them both. 'And your ears are too critical. Remember I am but a poor amateur.' Taking a sip of wine, he leant against the end of the table and looked down at her. 'You've a little more colour in your cheeks, but you have a bruise, I see.'

'I was very lucky . . . but for Giovanni and yourself. . . .'

'Indeed! Was it wise to attack a soldier? It's not usual for young ladies to take such action . . . but then, you're not at all usual,' he added, meeting her eyes for the first time. Their quizzical dark contact was brief, shadowed by a reserve which she had never seen before. At the silk mill, when he had learnt she was staying with his brother, they had become cold, devoid of any warmth; now, in his eyes and manner she felt warmth and affection, but also a control and a reserve similar to her own. It was not that his physical presence had lost any of its effect upon her: when the piano lid had closed and his footsteps had echoed on the marble floor, her heart had lurched and raced; when he had offered her the wine glass she had made quite sure that her fingers were well away from his. Had each of them taken up a fixed position? Certainly she could not and would not fit into the role he had envisaged for her, even if society did find it acceptable!

Until now, she had shied away from talking in detail about her life in Blackfriars, merely saying she was an Italian orphan whom Giuseppe Mazzini had looked after. Now, like inflicting self-hurt, she decided to make it easy for the aristocrat to keep to his family's neat arrangement, and for her, the student, to keep to her one true path.

'Let me tell you what has made me so unusual!'

Gabriella left nothing out: she spoke of the loft where she

had slept with the organ-grinders, of the rats and the stench and the beatings given out by Menotti. She told him of the icy-cold mornings when they had been sent out with nothing to eat, terrified of returning if they had made no money, yet being forced to for fear of losing the only home they knew.

'Then came Signor Mazzini to change all our lives, to lift us from ignorance and hopeless obscurity. He made us feel we were important and that we belonged to the family of Italy. Now perhaps you will understand what I owe him.'

Throughout her story, Luciano Forro had not interrupted once, merely moving to replenish his glass with wine. Now that her tale was done he stood up and, obviously moved, laid his hands on her shoulders in a brotherly fashion. Then, too soon, the comforting warmth lifted away and he walked a few paces away from her.

Luciano's swift mind considered what the young woman had told him as he stared at the ornamental pots of orange and lemon trees along the garden walk.

'The tree is known by its fruit,' he mused in a voice so low it could not be heard. 'Tell me,' he said, striding back to Gabriella. 'Why were you at the Villa Pizzo that day? You have never explained. Were you looking for something . . . for someone?'

Gabriella stared at him, searching for an explanation; for it was difficult to know herself what had drawn her there rather than to any other of the lovely villas.

'I . . . went there because I was curious.'

'And what kind of impression did the villa make on you? Did you feel you might have been there before; that you . . . belonged there?'

'Why no!' she laughed, startled by the question and the casual yet expectant way in which it was posed, as if he were hoping for something. But what? she wondered. 'I seem to remember I was rather frightened at the time. It was sad and lonely there. Why do you ask? Is it important?'

'Yes, it could have made things otherwise . . . It was just a wild fancy,' he sighed, the hopeful speculation fading from

his clear eyes and his mellow voice flattening with disappointment. 'Mama and myself had such a feeling . . . you reminded
us of someone we loved very much, someone I played with
when she was small. I gave her a doll to take on her journey to
Vienna,' he said with a short bitter laugh. 'We have so much
to thank the Austrians for. Shall we walk a little, and I will
tell you about the Scientific Congress in Venice.'

'Giovanni tells me it's very important for nationalism. You
are to speak, he says.'

'Yes, I'm to speak after Cesare Cantù. Perhaps you met him
at our villa . . . though perhaps there wasn't time,' he added
with a note of irony, as he touched upon her flight from him
for the first time.

'I'm sorry if I spoilt your evening,' she said in a low,
intense voice.

'It was a little more than that!' commented the man drily as
he led the way into a trellised arbour hung over with wistaria.
Suddenly he swung around, barring her way. 'Tell me you ache
as much as I.'

'Yes,' Gabriella whispered, unable to hide the feelings his
closeness was arousing as his hands reached forward and encircled her waist. His fingers tightened their grip but she did not
cry out, for the naked desire in his eyes was her own, and she
could hardly wait for his firm, generous lips to meet hers. As
their mouths collided there was no time for tenderness, only
an explosion of desperation. With hunger she answered and
returned deepening kisses until they alone were not enough.
Swiftly his hands worked, claiming each part of her that had
never felt the touch of a man before, and she moaned with
pleasure, her senses subject to each sensual sensation.

'Do you want me?' he whispered as he entered into her; with
a desperate, urgent cry Gabriella tightened her arms around
him to pull him deeper within her.

'Ah, I've dreamt of holding you like this so often,' he
whispered, as afterwards she lay trembling in his arms. 'From
the moment I looked up and saw every line of your beautiful
body exposed in the moonlight, I've lusted for you . . .' he
murmured, starting to rebutton her dress.

'I was pretending to be Norma,' she remembered, smiling.

'You were lucky that I did not arrive at your room. Would you have allowed me in?'

'Certainly not!' she exclaimed in shocked tones, reaching up to pinch his cheek.

'I thought not,' he grinned boyishly as he pulled her up and kissed the tip of her nose. 'Ah, we will have such fun in Venice, *cara*; moonlight on the Grand Canal, and a gondola to La Fenice where you will sing one day. Let me spoil you, let me shower you with gifts and kisses.' He swung her around, his eyes as excited as a schoolboy's. 'Say you'll come!'

Gabriella trembled, wanting to say yes, yes, despite the lunacy of the idea – but the face of Flavia Balziano got in the way.

'I can't,' she whispered. 'I will not become your . . .!'

Luciano Forro took hold of the thick looped braids of her hair and pulled on them gently so that she had to stand on tiptoe.

'Come now, will you still wear the English cloak of respectability after what we have just shared?' he murmured, his lips capturing hers in persuasive kisses which started to weaken her resolve. 'Come to Venice. I need you so much, more than anything!'

The conflict within her almost rendered her speechless, and with every second that passed she was slipping closer to the cliff-edge where disaster lay. Gabriella dared not trust herself to answer, so instead flung out a challenge which she knew he must refuse.

'No, you must stay with me in Milan!'

The thick black brows lifted in surprise at the request, and Luciano Forro's expression became grave.

'I have to speak at Venice, it is too important. It is the coming together of all the men in Lombardo-Venetia who seek reform. My paper is on the proposed routes for railways: they must be built if we are to survive economically and our people are to have better lives. The whole of Lombardy . . . Italy's very future depends on it!'

'And the whole of my future is dependent on my application to studies!' flashed Gabriella obstinately.

'Your refusal is purely selfish.'

'Perhaps,' she admitted. 'But I'll not fail Signora Pasta – and others who have given their life's time and money – just to become . . . a mistress!'

The Conte's face paled and his lips tightened in frustration.

'You make impossible demands on me,' he snapped, and he raised his hands in a gesture of haughty dismissal; but instantly he shook his head then pulled her to him, his dark eyes imperious and wilful as his lips consumed hers in a kiss that was savage with passion. Gabriella stiffened, forcing the whole of her body to resist, though it screamed to respond.

'But I know now you want me!' he said, his eyes glowing with excitement. 'Don't be afraid!'

'I want my career!' she sobbed, shaking all over from the strain of resisting her desire. 'I will not throw away everything I have worked for. One day I might even be able to use my voice for Italy.'

'So, the high priestess of patriotism,' mocked the Conte. 'Perhaps I should put your courage to the test – certainly you should read *Paracelsus* one day.'

'Why should I?' she retaliated angrily, not understanding.

'Because it is about conflict: love, which is self-forgetting, or knowledge, which is self-assertion. How sad that you have chosen the latter.'

'And haven't you?'

Like two adversaries they glared at each other, and there was no raillery in Luciano Forro's eyes when he spoke. 'Now it is not a question of whether, Gabriella, but when you will be mine completely!'

'Never!' she cried.

Then they had parted and she did not see him again. And the next day she left the palazzo.

News of her ill-treatment by the soldiers had reached everyone at the Conservatorio and everyone – even Matron and the inspectors – came up to her to express their sympathy for her and hatred towards Radetzky's men.

'This time they have gone too far,' said her professor. 'There is much feeling within the city. But of course it will do no good, for without weapons there could never be a rebellion, and the defiance that the young men attempt is as useless as a gnat's bite.'

'Well, gnats can drive one mad,' smiled Gabriella. 'And the police looked positively purple when we passed the Piazza del Duomo yesterday.'

'Ah yes, my son was there along with all the other young hotheads. What a lack of humour these officials have: a hundred or so young men brush their beaver hats feather fashion, and today there are proclamations all over the city forbidding the practice. It's too ridiculous – it can hardly count as sedition. What next?'

'Well, I'm told on good authority,' said Gabriella, who had managed a few minutes' conversation with the student Mario at Mass, 'that the students intend to keep the authorities busy. As soon as one thing is forbidden they'll think of something else, and there will not be a building that hasn't got Pio Nono written on it – one building in particular will bear his name, though I cannot reveal any more.'

'Or which young man it was who spoke to you,' said her professor with mock severity. 'Now perhaps if we could make a start on "Abigaille"!'

Gabriella needed no urging. The aria from *Ernani* was a favourite and, since her unhappy parting from Luciano Forro, she needed work as never before. Now more than ever it was everything to her: it was all she had, all she would ever need to achieve fulfilment and peace within. She did not need him or miss him at all!

Like a reflection of the city, the atmosphere in the Conservatorio had changed. The bell still tolled its demands, but there was an excitement and expectation, and news of the latest affront to Austrian dignity was quickly flashed around the old cloisters. First came what Gabriella had only hinted about to her professor, and it brought laughter from the young, and triumphant smiles on older lips: Archduke Ranieri, in seeking the sanctuary of Como from the unrest in Milan, had been pursued by patriots, serenaded from boats on the lake with Pius's Hymn, and woken to discover not only the Villa Pizzo's walls, but also its quays – even the trunks of the trees in the park – emblazoned with the name of rebellion, the name that stood for reform: Pio Nono.

Then Mazzini had shown his hand in an open letter, tossed into the Pope's carriage by one of his agents: 'Unify Italy', it urged. 'To achieve this you will not be called upon to act, but merely to bless those who act for you and in your name.'

'I expect the Pope was no more happy about Mazzini's offer than Torresani is about this writer Larius's opinions,' remarked her professor one day at the end of a lesson. 'Larius's latest pamphlet, championing Lombardo-Venetia's right to self-government, must have caused considerable fury. I expect every effort will be made to find out who he is, for he has not pulled his punches. It's all there: concise, hard accusations of press censorship, police abuse, the eight-year conscription of our young men, the price of salt, and so on. Let us hope – whoever he is – that he is not becoming careless.'

'Do you have a copy of it, Professor?' asked Gabriella, trying not to look too interested.

'Why, it's probably with its twentieth reader by now. You know how precious such things are – people risk their lives smuggling them into Lombardy; but then you wouldn't and shouldn't know about such things, even though you once lived under the same roof as the great Mazzini.'

'No, of course not,' said Gabriella, hiding a smile as she gathered her music together. 'Oh, by the way, Professor, I nearly forgot. I have received something far more exciting than any pamphlet. Will you play it and tell me who wrote it?'

'Well – it's Verdi!' exclaimed Mazzucato in surprise, peering down his reddish nose at the sheet of music as he set it before him on the piano. 'It's new to me, how did you come by it? It's a pity it has no words,' he said, humming as he played it through for a second time. 'It would make a striking

172

showpiece to slip in between scenes at La Scala, and Merelli has indicated his interest in featuring you next season. Tell me more about this?'

'I can't, but I wanted you to verify what I thought.'

'Definitely Verdi, and recent too: it's more melodic than some of his earlier work. Hold on to it with your life . . . all the sopranos in Italy would like to get their hands on such a gem!'

'Oh, I will, Professor! Do you really think Signor Merelli is interested?'

'Of course! He knows how you arrived here, and he'll seize you before Lumley or anyone else. You impressed some influential people at Como, and it seems they have also promoted you.'

The arrival of the sheet of music had at first alarmed Gabriella. She had thought it might be some coded message from Enrico Facini, but it had taken her experienced eye only a second to realize that she was holding a stirring, passionate piece of music. Where it had come from she had no idea, for on waking one morning she had found it slipped under her door with no note attached, only her name written at its top. And no amount of casual enquiry had revealed anything. Bearing in mind what her professor had said, Gabriella had tried, for several days, in odd moments of free time, to fit words to the music, but it proved much more difficult than she had supposed. And then she had had to abandon her attempt for a while since, besides the usual school work, she had several engagements to sing at various salons together with Mario and a fine tenor student from Bergamo.

The last of these engagements she was to undertake alone, which was a pity, for it had been great fun to be part of a team. The boys in their best green jackets had looked so smart that they had all begun to feel quite professional as they set off together for each venue. However, at least her host and hostess – the Conte and Contessa Manara – were familiar to her, since she had sung in front of them at the Forro villa at Como, so she didn't feel too nervous when she was collected by their carriage. And during the ride she began to wonder if they might know something about the music, for the Conte was, according to her professor, a close friend and admirer of Giuseppe Verdi.

Gabriella was not sure where the Conte lived, and for a time did not look to see where his carriage was taking her; but when it stopped outside one of the houses close to the city walls in the Porta Ticinense, she was somewhat surprised. The carriage, it seemed, had been watched for, as even before her feet touched the pavement, a manservant hurried forward. Like the undistinguished door he had emerged from, he wore no identifiable livery.

'Signor Boscoli will be with you presently, Signorina Pepe,' said the man, leading her through a softly lit hall into a comfortable drawing-room.

'Signor Boscoli? I don't understand!' uttered Gabriella in astonishment as the man withdrew. Then her eyes widened as the door opened moments later.

'Good evening, Gabriella. I'm so glad you could come,' said Conte Luciano Forro, striding into the salon and politely taking her hand to his lips before she could snatch it away.

'How *dare* you do this to me! How *dare* your manservant deceive me?' she cried, feeling totally confused.

'Did he? And how was that?' asked the Conte, with an aggravatingly charming smile.

'He told me a Signor Boscoli lived here. Where is he?'

'At your service, Signorina,' said Luciano Forro with an elegant gesture of his hands.

'But I am supposed to sing before Conte and Contessa Manara tonight . . . Oh, I understand,' she said, her eyes flashing with fury. 'The Conte and Contessa are not expecting me at their home, are they? You have lured me to some cosy retreat which only mistresses see. I do not suppose the Marchesa Balziano would be so honoured?' she flashed sarcastically, her cheeks burning with anger and her eyes filling with tears.

Luciano Forro looked at the wild expression in the dramatic blue eyes. Slowly he walked towards the smouldering young woman, daring her with his eyes to strike him. He could see her emotions were deep and needed release – as did his own,

174

he thought wryly. But it was too soon; he must be patient. She was more independent and stubborn than any woman he had ever met.

'So much passion, Gabriella,' he murmured, halting before her. 'I thought music was the chosen channel for your emotions. Aren't you wasting them on me?' he teased gently. 'But you are right, Flavia has not been here. Nor do I think she ever will.'

For one moment Gabriella thought she would throw herself at him, but she knew if she did she would end up in his arms and she would be lost, so somehow she managed to walk away towards the piano with contrived dignity. For a moment she stared down at the keys and then picked out a few notes.

'It was you who sent the music,' she said slowly. 'Is it for me to sing?'

'Yes, it is,' replied the Conte. 'That is why I invited you here tonight – to see the poem I have written. Forgive my deception, but I could think of no other way. I thought you would not come, and I knew the Conservatorio would not give permission. I wanted to hear you sing it, and I wanted your company for what I hope will be an evening of pleasure,' he said, an ironic little smile pulling at the corners of his lips.

At that instant, the sound of a doorbell echoed in the outer hall, followed by the sound of men and women's voices.

'Conte and Contessa Manara and the Marchese and Marchesa Gavazi,' announced the manservant.

Almost in disbelief, Gabriella stared at the other four guests, feeling her cheeks burning with shame that she had so misjudged him. As he turned to introduce her to his friends, she saw his eyes were filled with laughter.

'Why, Gabriella, how lovely to see you again,' said the pretty Contessa Manara. 'Luciano told me that he was hoping that you would come this evening, for I believe,' she whispered, 'you might be singing a new piece after the Carnival. I couldn't worm more than that out of him.'

'Did you say after the Carnival?' asked Gabriella, hardly able to keep her voice low as she stood with the vibrant little Contessa.

'Oh dear, hasn't he told you? Oh, you won't say I told you, my own dear Luciano would be so cross,' she said, turning to her husband who bore the same name as his host.

Across the room, Luciano Forro stood chatting in his usual relaxed, equivocal way, and Gabriella sighed, hearing his rich male laugh. She realized she was hopelessly lost.

Far from being a place of seduction, it was apparent from the happy supper party that entertaining guests here was a usual occurrence, and that the host thoroughly enjoyed serving the wine himself while they helped themselves to food from a cold buffet. Inevitably in such private, intimate surroundings, the talk turned to politics and the suppressed ferment in the province.

'Your speech in Venice, Luciano, received wild applause,' said Conte Manara. 'Have you noticed increased interest in your movements since you returned?'

'The secret police, you mean,' said Luciano Forro. 'Yes, I think they're sniffing around more than before . . . you took the usual precautions coming here?'

'Yes, but you must be especially careful, Luciano. They're ready to make an example of a few people, as they have done before. They are as repressive as they were in Confalonieri's day: you don't want to end up in Spielberg like him or Balziano. I have read everything in your name, and it's subtle enough to keep you out of jail; but those who write under pen names – Larius for example – are in great peril.'

Again that derisive little smile which she found so disturbing when directed at her, but as he shrugged indifferently, Gabriella felt a shiver of fear, for she had not missed the intonation of warning in the Marchese's words.

'Well, let us toast this Larius,' said Luciano Forro gaily as he filled everyone's glass with champagne. 'And let us also hope he has the sense to keep his work within a stone's throw of a convenient frontier! Now, Gabriella, perhaps you should proceed with the mission which the Conservatorio sent you on: to sing for Conte and Contessa Manara!'

At the end of the evening they had sung and chatted and played cards, and Gabriella felt as soft and loving as a kitten.

But as the other guests made their departure, the manservant, complying with his master's request, brought in her coat. And it was all she could do not to blush and betray her sense of shock, for she had expected Luciano might have wished some moments alone with her. But when his unmarked carriage rolled to a halt near to the Conservatorio, he still made no move to touch her, despite the fact that they were so close she could feel his breath on her cheek. She found it aggravating, but still she did not want to leave him.

'How did you choose the name of Boscoli for your private life, Luciano?' she asked, enjoying using his name in a way which she had not done before.

'Pietro Paolo Boscoli,' said Luciano Forro lightly, 'was a gentleman of the sixteenth century with whom I feel a bond: he lived at a time when the Italian republics were being destroyed by Austria and Spain; he was a man of letters, and he was accused of conspiracy and decapitated.'

A chill ran through Gabriella, and impulsively she reached out her hand. 'But isn't such a name likely to draw the authorities' attention to you?'

'Perhaps . . . only if they heed history,' and as her fingers tightened their grip, a tender note entered his tone of banter. 'Would you care, *mia cara*? Would you?' he whispered, raising her hand to his mouth and caressing the palm with his lips.

'Yes,' she replied, trying to control the intensity of her feelings. 'Please be careful!'

The urgency in her voice matched the increasing tension between them but, in a deliberate, matter-of-fact way, he returned her hand to her muff.

'Goodnight, Gabriella Pepe,' he murmured.

As an unknown she was not to be given the honour of Carnival week, but what did that matter? She was to make her first public appearance, and with a patriotic Hymn by Giuseppe Verdi himself. Gabriella, who had been thinking only in terms of trying to win one of the Conservatorio's end-of-year prizes, couldn't believe her good luck – and it was all due to Luciano Forro.

The moment she said his name, thought of his words, she saw in her mind the enigmatic expression beneath the thick black brows, the little creases that appeared at the corners of those grey-green eyes when he smiled, and her heart somersaulted. Yet at the same time she was terrified by her loss of control – if she should give herself to him, what would happen when he tired of her, what if she followed in Giuseppina Strepponi's steps and had a child? Could she ever play a secondary role to Flavia Balziano? Over and over she debated these things as the weeks went by. And though there was no lessening of intensity in her work, there was a difference, and her professor noticed it.

'You know, Gabriella, you are gaining a new warmth,' he said as he walked through the Conservatorio with her after a lesson. 'It seems due to this new work: you obviously like it very much, and it is a great privilege that it has been written for you. Conte Forro must have great influence with Verdi, for he hasn't put anything on at La Scala since his disagreement with management. And he never panders to singers – I know for a fact how hard Sophie Löewe tried to persuade him to write a showpiece aria for her in the finale of *Ernani*. Still, like Conte Maffei, I believe Forro collaborates with him; and being the republican Verdi is, I suppose he could not resist Forro's poem. Its patriotic flavour could have been stronger, I feel, but then he would not have got it past the censors, and no doubt he did not want you to end up in a cell. Anyway, it will still cause a stir, and when the time comes we will all be there to support you.'

Eight million lire from lotto and five million from tobacco went each year directly to the Austrian Government from its two state-owned monopolies. But at the start of the new year of 1848, the Milanesi struck! The singing of Pius's Hymn and the writing of his name on walls and in roadside dust had annoyed, the resulting ban on lotto and smoking hurt! How long the men could endure life without their cigars was debatable, nor was their enforced abstinence helped by the deliberate provocation of the NCOs of the Austrian army.

The effects of the ban were brought dramatically home to Gabriella when, together with the priest who was in charge of Religious Doctrine, she and one or two other seniors were returning with the younger girls, whom they had taken to view Leonardo da Vinci's *Last Supper* in the Cenacolo of Santa Maria delle Grazie. At the head of their usual orderly crocodile, Gabriella was trying to explain why a door had been cut into the fresco at Christ's legs, when she saw a number of young Austrian officers coming towards them.

'Isn't that the sin of gluttony, Signorina Pepe, for the monks to want a short cut through to the kitchens?'

'What, Lucia?' said Gabriella, keeping a wary eye on the approaching men. 'Yes, I suppose it is,' she answered with a laugh as the little girl repeated her question.

Though she had hoped the men would move to one side to let them pass, as the whiff of brandy assailed her nostrils, Gabriella knew they would not.

'Why look, Signorina Pepe!' giggled one of the girls. 'That soldier has two cigars in his mouth!'

'Yes, Roberta,' said Gabriella, moving her wards over. But as she tried to side-step them, all four NCOs moved with her to bar her way and simultaneously blew cigar smoke in her face.

'Have you given up cigar smoking, pretty one?'

Not answering, Gabriella stepped off the pavement and tried to hurry away from their leers and intimidation.

'Give her a little whiff of what she is missing, Franz!' laughed one of the young men.

'Please, you're frightening the students,' gasped Gabriella, choking as billowing smoke invaded her nostrils and stung her eyes.

'Leave her be!' cried a tradesman rushing up.

With a bellow of coarse laughter, the men turned upon Gabriella's rescuer and directed their smoke against him as he clenched his fists in rage. Significantly they loosened the hilts of their swords, then with contemptuous laughter turned back to plague Gabriella. But within seconds a cold hard voice spoke and, as she wiped her eyes, she saw a senior officer had joined the group.

'Go back to barracks immediately!' he snapped. Then two ice-cold grey eyes were turned upon Gabriella. 'I apologize, Signorina, Father,' he said, clicking his heels as the priest came hurrying up. 'This tobacco ban has made my men over-excited. I shall personally escort you back to the Conservatorio.'

Such protection was not welcome, even though as they proceeded the streets were alive with strutting, bewhiskered NCOs, all of whom were flamboyantly smoking cigars and puffing the smoke into every face they passed. They want someone to attack them, thought Gabriella. They want a riot. And it seemed an ever-increasing likelihood, for students and citizens of all classes were growing angrier every moment, and the streets rang with their chant of 'Fuori, fuori!'

'So, you study with Giuditta Pasta,' said the officer, no longer displaying any interest in the agitation about them. 'Does she not live at Blevio where the ballet dancer Taglioni also has a villa?'

'That is quite correct,' said Gabriella coldly.

'I too am a student,' said the man with a small private smile. 'And it is the birds around the lake that interest me. Indeed, I go to search for one today.'

'Are you going on a hunting party?' asked Gabriella, with a sense of unease at the nasty smug tone of his voice.

'Yes, I suppose you could call it that,' smiled the officer. 'I'm interested in the lake's own bird, the Larius.'

At these words, Gabriella's blood turned to ice, for she knew exactly what he meant, but feigning ignorance she shrugged indifferently. 'It is a very common bird of Como's shoreline.'

'Not the one I intend to pluck and hang!' laughed the man as he saluted and strutted away.

There could be no doubt to whom he was alluding, and the fact that he was going to Como meant surely that the identity of Larius was discovered! As the last of the students entered the Conservatorio, Gabriella hesitated, wondering what she must do. At all costs Luciano must be warned, immediately.

'Giuseppina,' she said, calling her friend back. 'I have to go somewhere urgently.'

'But we are due at classes in . . .'

'I know,' interrupted Gabriella hastily. 'Tell them that I dropped a glove and I've gone back to search for it. Yes, I know I will get into trouble, but what I have to do is a matter of life and death.'

Then before Giuseppina could protest further, Gabriella hailed a passing vettura.

'To the Via dei Bigli, as quickly as possible,' she ordered its driver.

Throughout the ride, Gabriella kept a watchful eye on passing carriages in case she should see any member of the Forro family — although she had not quite decided whether she should tell the Contessa or Giovanni of her suspicions. However, when she reached the palazzo, this problem was immediately resolved, for not only was the Contessa absent, but also the gentlemen, who had, it seemed, left early that morning with a large party of friends for a day of hunting. None of them was expected back until late.

'Where to now, Signorina?' asked the driver, as a troop of dragoons trotted past. The sight of gleaming sword hilts and plumed helmets sent a feeling of dread through Gabriella, reinforcing the sense of danger she had had since the Austrian officer had left her.

'Where do you wish to go, Signorina?' asked the driver again.

Gabriella bit her lip, trying to stem the feeling of panic as she thought what to do. The only person she could think of who might assist her was the manservant at the house in the Porta Ticinense; was he a party to his master's work? Gabriella supposed he must be, but already valuable time was passing, and if she delayed by going to him and he was absent, she might miss the train: that would put the intelligence officer hours ahead. Yet to go herself would mean her ruin at the Conservatorio: how would she be able to explain that to Christina Belgiojoso? Into Gabriella's mind surfaced a story her patron had told her of how her mother had saved her stepfather by burning his papers.

'Go back to the Conservatorio!' she ordered firmly, knowing that no matter what it cost it was the only course left open.

'Tell Matron I will be back tomorrow and no one should worry. I am visiting a friend,' Gabriella said as she rushed past an astonished inspector after collecting the remainder of her pocket money from her room. Then, regaining the carriage and ordering it on she fell back against the seat, relieved that the agony of decision was over.

Although the railway line had been open for several years, it was the first time Gabriella had ever travelled by train. She was glad to find a compartment to herself, for she knew trains went at the alarming rate of twenty-five miles an hour, so at least on her own she wouldn't make a fool of herself if she panicked. She was also anxious about bumping into the Austrian officer whom she anticipated must also be on the train. She had no idea what she would give as her reason for travelling if he saw her. Suddenly a whistle blew, and immediately all other fears were quite forgotten as the great iron monster rattled and lurched forward. In her corner Gabriella shut her eyes and prayed as the motion steadily increased, but as it seemed nothing terrible was going to happen to her, she soon opened her eyes and smiled to see how quickly trees and bushes flew past the window, yet how smooth and comfortable the ride was compared to a diligence. She would have enjoyed the novelty if she were not in dread of what would happen to her on her return to the Conservatorio, never mind what dangers lay ahead at Blevio. Monza was reached so soon, however, that she had no more time to dwell on her own predicament. As the passengers alighted, some laughing with relief after the new experience, a tall white-jacketed figure stopped outside her window. She shrank back, terrified: if she were seen, Luciano would be lost. She dropped her bag down on to the floor and, with her back to the window, made a pretence of searching.

'Can I be of assistance?' enquired a helpful voice. 'You seem to be having the same trouble as I had, for it has taken me several minutes to pick up a sheaf of notes I dropped when the train stopped.'

'Thank you,' said Gabriella without looking up. 'But I think I can manage. Nothing seems to have dropped out,' she said, raising her head very cautiously as the voices outside the window went away. 'It's my first time on a train: it was very comfortable. Now comes the shock of completing the rest of the journey by coach. If only the train went all the way to Como!' She said with a smile as a smartly-dressed young man stretched out his hand to help her rise.

'Well, it soon will,' he said with a smile. 'But for petty squabbles over routes there could be more lines by now, especially if there were more entrepreneurs willing to risk their money as Conte Forro did in the company that built this line. What we need is a national railway route, as Carlo Petitti advocates. But forgive me,' he said as Gabriella looked anxiously towards the exit. 'I am delaying you. Once I am on the subject of steam engines I lose all sense of time . . . If you would not think it presumptuous, perhaps I could offer you a seat in my flying chariot!'

'Well, if it flies, there is nothing I'd like better, for I'd love to overtake everything on the road between here and Como! Could you do that?'

'I will think of it as a mission of life and death!' responded the stranger gaily.

Outside the station there was no sign of the military party, and Gabriella supposed they had already set off. She cast a grateful look at her guardian angel, for without him there would have been little chance of reaching the Forro villa before the Austrians. And even now, her greatest hope lay in their reporting first to military headquarters at Como.

Like Giovanni Forro and the other young nobles in Milan, the young man who accepted the reins and whip from a waiting groom was a reckless driver.

'Where do you live in Como?'

'I don't,' cried the girl holding on to her bonnet. 'If you would take me to the lakeside, I will be able to take the ferry to Cernobbio.'

'I can do better than that,' grinned the young man. 'I shall drive you there.'

During the fast pace of the journey, Gabriella learnt that her rescuer was married and that his home was in Monza. The reason he had not stopped off there was because, after giving a series of lectures in Milan, he was to speak at Como, then afterwards at Bergamo and Brescia.

'Engineering is the noblest profession,' declared the young man as they raced along. 'Look what the hydraulic engineers have achieved in the Lombardy plain: we have rice fields, and fruit in winter. Why, the sight of that glittering water moving in total control over the lush green of clover can almost make me weep . . . Far better than weeping over a painting: artists don't feed and serve people as we engineers do; though of course Leonardo da Vinci managed to combine both disciplines. Of course our aqueducts and canals don't please the botanists,' he laughed. Then a note of irritation entered the engineer's voice. 'If we were only free from this suppression. It hinders all progress . . . Ah well, I must not become angry: that leads to indiscretion.'

'Have no fear, sir. I'll not betray you,' said Gabriella.

It was a great favour to proceed an extra four miles after Como to Cernobbio, but true to his word her driver did so. They had both lapsed into silence and, darting a quick glance at the plump, cheerful face alongside her, Gabriella wondered if she might trust this man, for during the journey another anxiety had entered her mind: what about the silk mill? Was there anything incriminating there? The more she thought about it the more she was convinced she must warn the proprietor. As for Milan, she had dismissed the idea that there would be anything incriminating there, for hadn't Luciano Forro joked that any cautious writer would keep his work near to a frontier? And surely any delivery to Milan would be immediately distributed? Nevertheless, she had to make sure.

'Where would you like to go?' asked the young man, Paolo.

'By the church please,' Gabriella said as they approached the village. 'Do you love Italy?' she impulsively asked, taking hold of the engineer's hand and staring at him earnestly.

'Yes I do!' declared the young man, his brown eyes full of fervour.

'A patriot's life is at risk. Will you help?'

'Tell me what you wish to do and I will do it!'

'I want you to take a note. No reply is required, nor is there any need to say who gave it to you. In fact, for your own safety, it might be better not even to speak. I will give you directions, you should be there within the hour. But keep an eye out for soldiers.'

'And you, are you safe?' the engineer asked anxiously.

'Yes, I will be – and pray God so will my friend.' Gabriella tore off a leaf of paper from a tiny notepad she kept in her handbag. As soon as she was done she pressed the paper in the man's hand; their eyes met, hers anxious and questioning, his filled with reassurance.

'*Viva l'Italia!*' he said with a wave of goodbye.

As soon as the carriage had disappeared into the dusk, Gabriella walked down to the lakeside. She was well known to the Comasque fishermen who were still about, so apart from a few cheery waves, no one made any comment at seeing her. Any one of them would have taken her up the lake to the Forro villa, but she did not want anyone to know where she was going. So, waiting until everyone started to drift away for their meals, Gabriella seized her chance and took away a small boat.

It was a long pull to the Forro villa, and she was soon quite hot. She was glad of the wind that was getting up, though it didn't bode well for the return journey, for if it were the feared Tivano which blew from the north, it would be no time to be out on the water. As she drew level with Villa Pizzo, Gabriella undid her coat and cast a look of satisfaction at the villa whose walls the patriots had daubed with the words of rebellion.

'*Viva l'Italia,*' she muttered, and as her eyes caught sight of the dome already silvered by the moon riding high above the trees on the promontory, impulsively she whispered the words again, as if for the dead patriot Marchese Balziano and his family. What had become of his family, she wondered suddenly, filled with curiosity about the little girl to whom Luciano Forro had given a doll to go on a journey to Vienna with her mother. A little girl who had reminded him and his mother of herself. Gabriella smiled wryly. She knew how they must feel, for she sometimes found herself looking for Nico in the face of a passer-by or in a group of young men.

The steps which she had mounted with such a beating heart in the summer were now dark and silent like the gardens above the terraced walks, but Gabriella rowed past, for not only might the caretaker be taking a stroll, but when the Austrian officer arrived with his patrol, that was where they would tie up their boats. So as soon as she was a good distance away from the steps and just beyond the family boat-house, she secured her boat firmly to the overhanging bough of a tree and hauled herself up on to the sloping bank of the park. In her pocket she had a candle, matches, and a knife with the thinnest blade she could find which she had bought on her way to the station. If she had ever considered her years at Blackfriars wasted, now she realized the art of breaking and entry was indeed very useful.

As she had expected, all was shuttered at the villa. After a cursory inspection of all the lower windows, Gabriella bit her lip and tapped the flat blade of her knife against her hand with a feeling of great frustration. Where are you now, Nico, she thought, knowing by now her old friend would already be inside. Gabriella sighed in exasperation and studied a small ornamental window, recalling as she did so the words of one of the young ruffians who used to play in their alley: 'If you can get one arm and your head through, you're in.' Well, it would be a tight squeeze, but she felt certain she would be able to wriggle through – while the advantage of breaking in here was that if the soldiers did come it would be less noticeable than if she used one of the large shuttered windows at the front of the villa.

The knife she had selected proved ideal: its flexible blade slid easily into the chink along the edge of the wood; now she had to bend it backwards very gently. She held her breath as the tip of the knife touched the catch, then, with a flicking movement it pushed against the metal; well, that was easy, she exclaimed, but now came the difficult bit.

Hurriedly her fingers tore open the fasteners of her clothes until she was down to her stays and bloomers. God help me if the soldiers arrive now, she thought as she gathered them up into a bundle and ran to hide them behind a bush. She thrust one arm through the window, then her head: it was tight and she tried to ignore the painful grazing of the wood on the skin of her shoulders and upper arms as she pushed and wriggled forward. After her shoulders it became comparatively easy, until she came to her bottom: once again she had to push forward in small, jerking movements while pressing her hands against the inside of the villa wall to give leverage. Then she was through and groping for the candle and matches which she had flung in before her.

Her small wavering light produced an eerie effect as she stole through the silent villa, casting every dust sheet into a flickering, ghostly shape that might have made her feel jumpy but for her sense of urgency.

Once in the study she made straight for the bookshelves, running her fingers along until she came to Silvio Pellico's volume and the poems of Alfieri. In one go she pulled out several books: there was nothing there; she had come all this way for nothing! Feeling relief, exasperation, Gabriella was about to turn and restore the volumes to their proper place when, in the light of her candle, her eyes caught the gleam of the finest of gossamer threads hanging through a crack in the wood. She pulled on it gently but it came away between her fingers. Now she knew her journey had not been in vain, for there must be some hiding place behind the wall.

For a moment Gabriella considered whether to give herself more light, but decided to make do: if visitors arrived, heat in the room would immediately arouse suspicion. So instead she relied on the sensitivity of her fingertips, and soon they discovered that a slat of wood at the back of the shelf was loose. And when she lifted it away, what she was looking for was revealed.

'You have been busy, my Conte,' she murmured, astonished by the number of manuscripts and pamphlets piled within the long, low cavity. 'And I shall need more than a handbag to carry it away.' After considering a moment, Gabriella removed the dust sheet from Luciano Forro's writing desk, and with care transferred everything from the secret cubbyhole on to it. Having made certain there was nothing else left, she was about to put the wood back into position when a thought struck her: the Austrians were thorough people; if the hiding place were found, wouldn't they be suspicious of what might be kept in it . . . With a wicked grin, Gabriella moved to the desk and, picking up a box of cigars, thrust it into the hiding place. 'Now they'll think that either you don't trust your servants, or that you're breaking the smoking ban!' she giggled.

At least the worst is over, she thought – although by the way the shutters had started to rattle, the journey back down the lake would not be so calm, for the wind was beginning to sound alarmingly wild. As she stood listening, trying to gauge its force, her ears also picked up something else; something which made her freeze with fear. The soldiers had come! And already the fast tramp of feet was clearly audible as they passed by the window outside.

Terror seized hold of her. She wanted to fly, but already her hand was pulling open a drawer in Luciano Forro's desk. Inside were envelopes; she slammed it shut; one after the other she wrenched the rest of them open, her eyes frantically scanning their contents. Much, she saw, had to do with business matters, but then she came upon letters, the first of which was signed by the Marchese Massimo d'Azeglio, the liberal writer; outside, a gruff voice complained loudly, and she realized it must be the caretaker being made to open up; there was no more time, so in one swift movement she tipped the entire contents of the drawer on top of the manuscripts.

The grinding crash of the front hall shutters assaulted her terrified ears but, as if her legs were controlled by a separate brain than the one which was telling her to flee through the study window, Gabriella moved towards the door which led on to the corridor and opened it with caution.

188

'Where is the Conte's study and library, old man?' rasped a voice.

'I only look after the security of the villa, I do not know about such things. It is up to intruders to find their own way.'

By his sullen voice, the family caretaker had obviously only opened the villa up under duress, and silently Gabriella saluted his final words of courage. She knew he was old, and how frightening it must be for him to be surrounded by soldiers. His courage helped her to overcome the trembling fear which had begun to affect her, and which was robbing her of the will to leave the room, but if she didn't do so soon, they would have more light and she would be found and Luciano would be as good as dead. The thought gave her all the courage she needed, and she glided out into the dark and stole across the corridor, holding her arm out before her to feel her way. She had moved none too soon, for as she gained the little window the sound of boots on marble and the swinging light from a lantern were coming towards her. Out went the dust sheet, quickly she followed, this time feet first, using her hands on the upper section of the window to propel herself forward. In one movement she was out. There was no possibility of securing the catch so instead she reached up from where she was crouching and, with one finger, pushed the window to, just as its coloured panes gleamed briefly with a soldier's passing light.

Outside the trees were swaying and groaning under the driving force of the wind. There was no time to dress, nor did she want her movements to be restricted, so just slipping on her coat, she stuffed the rest of her clothing into the dust sheet. She hoped that all the soldiers were inside the villa; nevertheless she looked anxiously about as she stole quietly along the terraced walk and onward into the park.

Unlike the trees, whose leafless branches bent to survive, the lake had become a heaving, jubilant creature of the wind. It was lunacy to set out, she knew, as she looked at the boat below, lifting and falling on the powerful swells. But the need to put as much distance between herself and the soldiers impelled her to proceed. Trying to remain calm, she dropped her bundle down into the boat and, at the first opportune moment, holding tight the mooring rope, she slid after it. Reciting a silent prayer, she struggled to undo the rope, then took hold of the oars and tried to manoeuvre the craft into the wind. Within seconds she was drenched as spray whipped up all around her. At least they'll not be mad enough to set off back to Como until this quietens down, she thought, slitting her eyes against water and wind as the boat pitched away from the security of land.

Driven at speed as she was, Gabriella determined her safety lay in keeping close to the shoreline after she had passed the villa's landing stage. But as she struggled to make some use of her oars, she sensed rather than saw that she had already gone beyond the villa's steps. Many times she had felt lonely but never before had she experienced this isolated terror of feeling completely lost to the rest of the world. And it seemed as if she had become the focus for the elements' rage. She shouted a few curses learnt from her old friends at Blackfriars, but instantly the wind snatched her voice and bravado away.

'I will not drown, I have too much to do!' she sobbed, as water poured over the side of the boat. In reply, the wind howled about her ears and a wave crashed against her face, sending her reeling backwards off the thwart. The water swilling about the bottom of the boat had soaked through to her bloomers: it was the final outrage and her temper snapped. In a terrible rage she hauled herself upright and gripped the oars as if they were mortal enemies, struggling on with the wind tearing and screaming at her like a hateful witch. Suddenly, with a force that robbed her of breath, the wind took everything before it. Her oars were wrenched out of her hands and, as the boat lifted, she was hurled sideways. Icy water and black, mindless terror engulfed her.

'Mama! Mama! Help me, Mama!'

Before her Gabriella saw a woman smile and stretch out her hands towards her; then her lovely face became a mask of agony and despair as the water lifted her up and bore her away.

'Mama! Mama!' With screams of fright, Gabriella thrashed

about in the darkness, kicking out her legs and arms like a dog. A wave took her sideways and her hip hit against stone. Spurred on by the will to live she kicked on, finally finding with her outstretched hand the sinewy branch of a trailing vine. Bit by bit she pulled herself along until there were steps. Somehow, from somewhere, she found the strength to fight her way forward and stagger up to safety. With a cry she collapsed and lay sobbing. In her mind's eye she could see only a boy's brown eyes: Nico's eyes, as he pulled her from the river that had taken her dear mother away.

# Chapter Ten

Luciano Forro studied the girlish handwriting on the small piece of paper.

'You say a stranger gave you this?' he asked, turning to the manager of his estate. 'And he would only say a young lady sent it?'

'Yes, Conte. I acted upon it instantly. The pamphlets were half-way up the mountain before the devils arrived! Do you think they went to the villa?'

Luciano Forro paled. 'I must go there straightaway. If they went there I'm lost. With this new Imperial Rescript, the trial for high treason starts on the spot – with no appeal against the death sentence.'

'Be careful, Luciano!'

'I will. I only thank Providence that I came to you first. Otherwise I might have walked straight into a trap.'

'What about Milan? The factory is clear, but your home?'

The Conte leapt up on to his horse and smiled down at the anxious, weathered face as he gathered the reins in his hands.

'Don't worry, there is nothing at Milan. Thank you for your prompt action, my friend!' Then, making a farewell salute, Luciano Forro wheeled his stallion around and galloped away.

Just as Gabriella had arrived at night, the Conte also delayed his approach until it was dark. There was considerable movement in the lake and his boat rose and fell on the white-tipped swells, so that by the time he climbed ashore his clothes were soaked. But he hardly noticed as, alert for every sound, he glided silently through the trees of his park. There had been no boats at the front steps, but he realized it was not beyond the wit of the *tedeschi* to hide them, so he proceeded with all caution to the caretaker's house and knocked very softly at the door.

'Who is it?' a frightened woman's voice quavered.

'Costanza, it is I, Luciano.'

Immediately bolts were withdrawn, and the door opened to reveal an elderly woman holding a candle.

'Come in quickly!'

By the urgency of her tone, Luciano Forro wondered if he had misjudged the situation and unwelcome visitors were about after all. But in effect, the nervousness of the old retainer's wife had been caused several days earlier.

'Oh Luciano,' quavered the old lady, tears starting to her eyes as the young noble embraced her. 'We tried to stop them going into the villa but they threatened to shoot Nino. They said they'd smash the door in.'

'You were very brave,' soothed the Conte, keeping his arm around Costanza's frail shoulders. 'But I don't want either of you to take such risks again. You must hand over the key next time, Nino.'

'I've been too long with your mother the Contessa to do that,' grumbled the old man. 'And if I'd been younger they wouldn't have ordered me around so. We got the parish priest to write to you in Milan; we didn't know what else to do. Did you get the letter?'

'No, I've been away in Piedmont. But don't fret,' he reassured them as the old couple crossed themselves. 'All will be well in Milan . . . Now, I must go and look over the villa.'

'Everything is in order,' said the old man, taking down a large bunch of keys from a hook. 'I looked over everything after they'd gone. Funny, you couldn't tell they'd been there.'

'Good!' said Luciano Forro, concealing his anxiety. 'There's no need for you to come out in the cold, Nino. I'll manage. You both go back to bed.'

At first glance, just as the family servant had said, everything was in its usual order. But it was not the external things which concerned Luciano Forro as he went to his study. It was the place of concealment he was worried about, and its damning contents which, under the new regulations, would mean death within fourteen days.

The relevant book titles seemed in order, except for two, and observing which ones they were the Conte's eyes narrowed with anxiety. His mouth was dry. He lifted down eight books from the shelf, then his fingers went to the panelling. Even before he lifted it out, he expected the worse.

The dark, empty space stared back at him; he groaned and leant his forehead against the upper shelf. After a moment he moved away to his writing desk, his expression grave and resigned, for here he had carelessly left letters which would complete the case against him. Unlike Gabriella's frantic search, his hand went straight to the drawer: as expected it was empty.

Despite the smoking ban which all Lombards were observing to damage Austrian revenues, the Conte opened his cigar box and took out the one remaining cigar, idly wondering who might have smoked the rest. Then his eyes fell upon the ashtray which Nino had obviously not noticed and which, apart from the missing papers, betrayed the visitors.

As he leant against the corner of his desk, his brow furrowed in thought, Luciano Forro calmly reviewed the various options. Then with a deep sigh he stubbed out the cigar, stood up, closed the empty drawer, returned the books to the shelf and left the study. With a feeling of sadness, for he realized he might never see his home or Como again, he walked down the hallway, intent on packing a few belongings.

He had reached the little window in front of the servants' quarters when, from the bright light cast by the candelabra, he saw something white fluttering outside the small panes of glass. Mildly curious, he bent forward to see what it was, and discovered that it was a scrap of lace whose end had caught on a splinter on the inside frame of the window. It seemed strange, but he shrugged and was about to move away when he noticed the catch of the window was not secured. Instead of closing it he thrust it wide open, and took hold of the fine lace trimming, studying the window thoughtfully as he fingered the material. Had some maid's petticoats caught in passing? Had Nino forgotten to secure it at the end of summer? Both scenarios seemed unlikely. The Conte leant forward and thrust his head out of the window. It was impossible to get his shoulders through afterwards, so it wasn't a break-in, although . . . a child could perhaps squeeze through – or even a girl might . . . a girl! A young woman stripped down to lacy underwear . . . Was he being absurd, enlarging on the idea which had touched his mind earlier when he had studied the familiar writing on the warning note? He withdrew his head and, after securing the window, reached into his pocket and read the large, feminine letters again: 'Visitors may come – Alberto, see your master is not betrayed!' A fierce feeling of exultation swept through Luciano! The frontier and safety were less than three miles away: if he were wrong about who had removed the manuscripts then Milan meant death! But with a burst of joyful laughter the young man pressed the folded paper to his lips. He was not wrong. With every fibre of his being, he knew it could only be she!

Retribution was awaiting Gabriella at the Conservatorio, but it could not strike her down immediately, for she had collapsed outside the church of S. Maria della Passione and had to be carried into the old convent by two of the students.

'I cannot imagine where you have been and what you have done, Signorina Pepe. Your clothes feel waterlogged and your hair . . . it's as if you have been walking through rain,' chided Matron as she bandaged Gabriella's hands. 'How could you have blistered and skinned the palms so, and your arms? You've a lot to answer for when you have recovered. No one has ever behaved so badly before. What will the Princess Belgiojoso say about this?'

Gabriella did not care. She felt so ill and cold that she thought she would die. And she was willing to let go, for at least she knew she had saved him.

Somehow she had survived drowning, had endured the cold

hours of darkness. At daybreak, when the winds of the night weakened and fled, she had seen the boat afloat nearby, still with the dust sheet wedged under a seat. She had found just enough strength to row on to the Prionis' boat-house, and there she hid the wringing wet bundle in the old gondola that was never used. How she got back to Milan afterwards she could hardly think, except that she knew it was the last thing that had to be done. The moment she had come within sight of the Conservatorio walls, like the final grain of sand in an hour glass, her willpower left and her legs buckled beneath her.

Complete exhaustion and a heavy head cold were the only after-effects of her adventure, for she had not lost the hardiness of childhood. So, after three days, though she still felt wretched and unwell, the fever had broken and her mind was clear.

'Oh, I wish I had been consumed with malaria,' she said to Giuseppina who had called in to visit her. 'I might have aroused enough pity for them to forget and forgive.'

Giuseppina Verenese looked down at Gabriella's bandaged hands resting on the sheet.

'I think it's obvious you were not out on some giddy outing. I know you don't want to discuss it, Gabriella, but you must have had a very good reason to go away as you did. They know how dedicated you are . . . could you not speak in confidence to Professor Mazzucato?'

'I can't – it's not my secret,' said Gabriella, trying to smile. 'Don't worry, Giuseppina . . . there goes the bell, you mustn't be late.'

From her bed, Gabriella watched her friend depart with some relief. It was a strain trying to be cheerful when in all likelihood she would soon be asked to leave. Down below in the cloisters she could hear the rush of feet and, soon afterwards, a male voice ascending a scale and, from elsewhere, a bow being drawn across a cello. All these familiar sounds; of Mozart, Donizetti, Rossini. As a final year student she would soon have had to leave this strict intense life anyway. It would have been hard enough to succeed in her chosen career, but to leave in disgrace, without the recommendation of her professors . . . Where was she to go, how would she survive? Would the impresario of La Scala feature a singer who had been expelled from the Conservatorio?

It was all too taxing; nor could she bear to think of him or contemplate asking his help. Besides, what nagged her mind even more than what lay ahead was what had gone before! Gabriella closed her eyes and conjured up the desperate memory that she had brought back with her: her mother. The face that was so like her own, whose stricken, brief, maternal smile had been wrenched away in a turbulent moment of parting. Mixed with her terrible joy at finding a parent was a sense deep within that her mother must be dead. The thought was too cruel. Burying her face in the pillow, Gabriella wept, trying to reach through the barrier that had only partly opened. There had been a carriage too, she remembered, and . . . The memory eluded her as she strained to grasp it, and Nico's boyish face appeared again, staring at her over the edge of a grassy bank. Where was Nico now? He would remember; only he could rid her of the troubled, turbulent feelings that had surfaced during the storm.

As though Matron had pre-empted the decision of the Conservatorio's governing body, the trunk with which Gabriella had first arrived had been carried into her room. It was a depressing sight on the morning she was to appear before Felice Frasi, and she could not bear to open it, knowing that she would find inside the small white organdie dress which she had worn in Paris with such excitement, such hope and such pride. A lump rose in Gabriella's throat as she walked past the portrait of Liszt and on towards the principal's office.

'Good morning, Signorina Pepe,' said Felice Frasi, rising politely from his seat as she entered. 'Please be seated. I hope you are fully recovered?'

'Yes thank you, Professor,' answered Gabriella a little thickly.

'Good, good,' said the professor looking grave. 'Now perhaps you feel able to explain your behaviour to Professor Mazzucato and myself?'

'I can't,' murmured Gabriella feeling tears start into her eyes as she saw compassion rather than anger in her singing professor's eyes. 'I can only say I had to help someone and that the last thing I wished to do was to fail to attend my classes and break the rules . . . but there was no alternative.'

'Even though you know that no one is permitted to leave without written permission from the president, Conte Borromeo, and the authorities. You knew what it would lead to?'

'Yes.'

'Well,' sighed Felice Frasi. 'Nothing can take your future away, Signorina Pepe. You are as gifted a singer as our young student Amilcare Ponchielli is at composition, but I am afraid . . .'

There was a knock on the door, and one of the inspectors entered.

'I am sorry to disturb you, Professor, but Conte Borromeo wishes to see you urgently. He is waiting outside.'

'Please do not keep him waiting – I shall send for you later, Signorina Pepe,' said the principal, his green gown rustling as he stood up.

'Perhaps, Gabriella, you will accompany me,' interposed Professor Mazzucato with a meaningful look as if to say, I mean to get to the bottom of this.

The execution had been stayed for the moment, and in a way that made it worse, thought Gabriella as she rose to leave. At the door, Conte Borromeo, the president of the Conservatorio, stood aside with a bow to let her pass. It was then she saw his companion: elegant as usual in a velvet suit and spotless linen, with his black hair falling in negligent disorder about his shoulders and a smile lighting the clear, sparkling, grey-green of his intelligent eyes, was Conte Luciano Forro.

'Good morning, Signorina Pepe. It is a great pleasure to see you,' he murmured, inclining his head towards her in greeting.

'And for me to see you, Conte,' she said breathlessly.

'I hope you have recovered from your chill . . . my brother Giovanni learnt from a friend who is a student here that you have been quite indisposed. Naturally my family and I were most concerned.'

Their eyes met briefly, then Gabriella passed on with her professor, carrying with her Luciano Forro's look which made her tremble with the intensity of its emotion.

'Neither Felice Frasi nor I are fools, Gabriella,' commented Professor Mazzucato when they had entered the privacy of his room. 'You have been one of our most determined students – you are ambitious, too. You would not have risked your position here for a frivolous whim. And I never forget that you were lifted out of some slum by Giuseppe Mazzini. We don't want details: if your disappearance was, say, for some national cause – just give us something to go on,' he urged.

'It was not frivolous, and I know you would have acted in the same way in my place. That is all I can say, Professor.'

'Well, that is at least better than silence. I will not press you further. Go back to your room and I will see you later when Conte Borromeo and Conte Forro have gone. I suppose they are here to discuss your appearance at La Scala.'

'Will I still be permitted to sing?'

'You still have a fine aria and a voice – don't abandon all hope yet,' said the gifted man, shaking his head and waving her away.

Gabriella waited restlessly for the next hour in her room, but she was not sent for, and when the bell went for the half-hour lunch break an inspector popped her head around the door and told her that she should attend classes as usual. It was over! With a deep sigh she leant her hands against her writing-desk top and stared down at its worn surface, feeling a mixture of relief and anxiety.

'You have told them,' she whispered. 'You have made yourself vulnerable for me.'

Lombardy's day of mourning, 3 January 1848, had been the day Gabriella had set forth for Como. Pestered herself in the morning by the cigar-smoking soldiers who were defying the Lombards' self-imposed smoking ban, things had erupted later in the day. Soldiers with drawn swords had attacked an unarmed crowd; amongst those who died was a four-year-old child.

'Now we have Danton's river of blood!' said the student Mario, who openly came up to speak to Gabriella after Sunday Mass. 'And it has washed the lethargy and moderation away; they now can feel everyone's hatred. In Venice they have locked the patriots Manin and Tommaseo up, but it's too late: Metternich in Vienna cannot hold Lombardy and Venetia down forever when they see other provinces in the peninsula gaining reforms.'

'Some say Vienna would let go of Lombardy if they were compensated with something else,' said Angelo, who had joined them. 'Like Conte Balbo proposed in "The Hopes of Italy". Give them some interest in the Balkans.'

'Enslave other peoples for our freedom!' snorted Mario. 'You know that is not Mazzini's way. Our hope lies in ourselves: that is why Mazzini has been encouraging all the groups of Young Italy throughout the peninsula to urge their townsfolk to press for a Civic Guard. Once they have arms they can come and rescue their brothers in Lombardy and Venetia.'

'Anybody feel hungry?' suddenly shouted a voice amongst the throng of music students leaving the church. 'There are two fine looking *polli* coming this way.'

Immediately everyone adopted the new method of baiting and mocking the police. Like a farmyard, the piazza in front of S. Maria della Passione resounded with the sound of clucking chickens.

'Keep moving everyone, or we'll be accused of a breach of the peace,' cautioned a voice. 'But keep up the serenade.'

With the female students – amongst them some little seven-year-olds who were giggling at the sounds their seniors were making – Gabriella made her way towards the Conservatorio's entrance. It might be childish what they were doing, but it was the only safe way to display hostility when a breach of the peace could result in a death sentence within two weeks. It seemed monstrous that all these foreign troops could make everyone feel so afraid.

At last the news which she had been waiting for came; her

appearance as a soloist between scenes at La Scala was arranged for 16 March!

'What are you going to wear?' was Giuseppina's first question.

'The Contessa Forro is arranging everything,' admitted Gabriella, her face suffused with pleasure. 'She has arranged for her own dressmaker to make my gown. It is her way of . . .'

'Of what?' asked Giuseppina as Gabriella abruptly fell silent.

'Well, I think she wants me to look the part . . . It is her son's words that I shall be singing,' explained Gabriella hurriedly, unable to reveal what the Contessa's note had actually contained, which was just five words: 'Thank you for my son.'

How much Luciano Forro had told her professors they did not reveal. And only at her very first lesson with Professor Mazzucato was anything made of the matter. He had risen, embraced her and had murmured, '*Viva l'Italia.*'

Then they had set to work on her aria. Like much of Verdi, it imposed great demands on the singer in the sudden leaps from the bottom of the chest register to a top D flat. And it required some courage and self belief.

'Remember the accent is Agitato,' said Professor Mazzucato as he sang the opening. 'Warmth, passion . . . No doubt,' he added with a dry smile, 'Conte Forro's, er . . . words are an inspiration.'

'I could croak like a frog and it wouldn't matter,' laughed Gabriella, trying to hide her blushes. 'They will cause more uproar than when the corps de ballet appeared in February with medallions of Pius around their necks and sent Fanny Elssler weeping from the stage.'

'If only we could send them all weeping back to Vienna,' remarked the professor. 'Though I don't think life can be very pleasant for any of them now. No one is receiving any families of the Austrian court socially. Even those families who through ties of marriage have always supported the Empire have remembered they are Lombards since our Day of Mourning in January. With thirteen thousand troops in the city under Field Marshal Radetzky, I don't suppose any of them sleep uneasily; but surely they must see that some form of devolution must be granted to the province?'

'Could there be an armed rebellion here as there was in Palermo?' asked Gabriella.

'With Field Marshal Radetzky in control of things, not a chance!' snorted her teacher. 'He may be eighty-two but he is fit and shrewd and learnt his craft against Napoleon. Anyway, as Professor Cattaneo of the University says, it is not for Milan alone to lead a fight against Austria, but for the whole of Italy.'

Despite this time of anger and frustration against the increasing police brutality, for Gabriella, attending her final rehearsal before Luciano Forro, it was a moment of great excitement. It was the first time he had attended, and she hoped he would be pleased. It was also the first time they had met since his visit to the Conservatorio, and she supposed he would wish to speak of her visit to Como. How had he known who it was? she wondered.

Standing on the vast stage where Grassini, Malibran and Frezzolini had performed, where Giuditta Pasta and Domenico Donzelli had interpreted *Norma* for the first time, where Milan had welcomed Napoleon, Gabriella felt as small and overawed as she had done so many years before at Her Majesty's in London's Haymarket. That moment had altered her whole life: it had led her here, to the greatest Opera House in the world.

From the back of the theatre where he was standing with the impresario Merelli, Luciano Forro watched Gabriella take her place to run through the 'Resurrection' for the first time with the orchestra. Just as Benjamin Lumley had found himself spellbound even before the unknown waif had begun to sing, Luciano Forro also could not take his eyes from Gabriella. He was aware that it was more than personal interest that held him hypnotized; it was a presence that seemed to reach out into every part of the darkened theatre. Then she opened her mouth, and the stillness which she herself had evoked was shattered. Like fire to gunpowder, so was music to her – especially the rough, robust music of his friend Verdi. Luciano

202

Forro's lips pulled into a self-deprecating little smile as he felt a twinge of jealousy. Yet it was there he had to be honest. He had taken her once and burned to do so again; but she had to be like this. He wanted himself to effect this passionate change that music wrought in her; he wanted to make love to her and see her face looking up at him, not just with the softness of love, but shining with that inner light which his words and Verdi's music had inspired in her.

'I must have that passion!' he murmured under his breath as the music faded and he began to walk forward. He called out to Gabriella: 'Your rendering and interpretation are magnificent, Signorina Pepe. The maestro would be very impressed.'

'I hope so,' said Gabriella, unable to restrain her pleasure at the compliment or the thrill she felt on seeing him. 'I understand now what a challenge it is to bring something alive for the first time, and what an honour as well.'

Luciano gave a boyish grin as he laid down his hat, gloves and silver-topped cane on a bench and looked up at her on the stage.

'I can see you will go far: you say kind things to please a librettist – but then, you are a very kind person, especially, I believe, where birds are concerned. You must tell me more about your mission of mercy to save such creatures!'

'How did you guess it was me?' asked Gabriella with a laugh as she joined him and walked away from the musicians.

Luciano Forro did not answer but, withdrawing a pocket book from a pocket of his dark green velvet jacket, he took out a scrap of lace.

'I recognized this!' he said with a look of raillery that turned her cheeks scarlet. 'You saw my books that night when you were about to unload the silk from the baskets at the mill. You guessed then that I was Larius, one of the thorns in the thick skin of the Habsburgs.'

'It confirmed my suspicions.'

'Confirmed?'

'Yes,' nodded Gabriella, as the last of the orchestra departed. 'I found your manuscript by accident when I was browsing amongst your books. You had not hidden it very well.

I learnt by sheer chance that the villa was going to be searched.'

'The sacrifice you made to save my life was not small . . . and you would have left the Conservatorio – Milan – without telling me, or asking me to speak for you?'

'I suppose so,' said Gabriella with a self-conscious laugh. 'And I am sorry if you have endangered yourself for me.'

'We both had to do our duty,' said Luciano gravely as he took hold of her hand. Dark with passion, his eyes commanded her to follow; the grip of his fingers reinforcing his will. Unquestioningly she allowed herself to be led up to the Forro box.

'Come and look down on your future world of make-believe where you will expose your inner self and win countless hearts,' said Luciano Forro with a gesture down at the stage. Then, like a box owner bored with a performance or intent on a tête-à-tête, he pulled the velvet curtains closed and turned to face her. 'But here is your real world,' he said advancing purposefully towards her. 'I will not share you, and I want you body and soul.'

'Here?' she whispered as he reached out for her.

'Here!' he said, the expression in his eyes making her tremble.

'I can't, Luciano,' she gasped, as his hands began to caress her body. 'The shame if we . . .'

'Faint heart,' he murmured, his lips brushing provocatively over hers to seek the soft skin behind her ears, then moving downwards, each kiss's imprint like a hot burning brand of possession. Sensuously his hands slid down Gabriella's body, until he was kneeling before her – her dress was raised, his hot urgent lips pressed against the flimsy cotton of her pantaloons. The kiss, long and unhurried, made her gasp and moan with desire; all sense of everything went but the burning touch of his mouth, and when his fingers loosed the drawstring and the cotton slid away, the ecstasy of the kiss continued and increased until she was pulsating with desperate, urgent need.

'Will the whole of you join with me?' he whispered, stroking her naked thighs and pressing his lips against her once more. 'Will you let your song of joy be when I move within you?'

Trembling with the intensity of the moment as he stood up and looked questioningly into her eyes, Gabriella nodded and raised her skirt. Like a fury, passion possessed them as they coupled. The constriction of their clothing went unnoticed as they joined in intimate ecstasy. Still only partly satiated, at last they sank down on to the couch and, in a different rhythm of avowal and committal, slowly and tenderly, they drew together once more, until that small part of her mind that she had kept back now confronted the drop over the abyss and, with the courage that his love had inspired, she leapt out into the unknown, leaving self behind and merging totally the essence that was hers with his.

'"The two wings of the human soul",' murmured Luciano, stroking Gabriella's hair as later she lay within his arms.

'That's Mazzini,' she said softly. 'You know, I was so afraid when I first sang the "Casta Diva" that I would not measure up to it . . . I felt that too, before . . .'

'And then you found we soared and hovered as one,' smiled Luciano, his teeth gleaming in the semi-darkness of the box. 'You have found your mate, Gabriella!'

With a joyful laugh he sprang up and, when they had adjusted their clothing, flung back the curtains.

'Oh,' said Gabriella looking out anxiously. 'I shall blush scarlet with shame if I look up at this box when I am on stage.'

'No you won't,' smiled the Conte, turning to her with an adoring look. 'You will look up and remember our love and be filled with joy! And you will share that real, not imagined emotion with your audience. Now, one last thing before we go. I am charged by my mother to give this to you.'

With surprise and pleasure, Gabriella accepted a small velvet box.

'Why, it's beautiful!' she gasped, as she raised the lid and found inside a sapphire butterfly brooch. 'But she has already done so much in providing my gown.'

'I am a much beloved son whom she would not have wished to lose to the Austrians,' teased the Conte. 'Even so,' he said, the laughter leaving his proud, distinguished face. 'She must love you to give you this. It belonged to her dearest friend, the Marchesa Giulia Balziano.'

'There was no need to tell her about . . . I cannot accept such a gift.'

'Yes you can,' said Luciano firmly as he snapped the lid shut on the box and pressed it firmly back into Gabriella's hand. 'You stir something in Mama's heart . . . as you have in mine,' he murmured. Then, almost shyly, he drew from his pocket a magnificent necklace. 'I hope you will wear this tomorrow for me. Do you know, young prima donna, there are hundreds and hundreds of sapphires and amethysts working very hard to outshine your eyes, yet now I see that they, like me, are only slaves to them.'

The whole world, Gabriella felt, would see the difference in her, for every bit of her body was bubbling like champagne; arms, legs, thighs, toes, all shouting, 'Look at me, I have been kissed and loved! I am come alive!' Certainly, on her way to the Conservatorio, people did seem to nod and smile at her more than usual, and it was confirmed by Giuseppina.

'I have never been in love, Gabriella, but I know that you must be!'

'How?' she laughed.

'You are glowing and you can't stop smiling . . . Is it the man who wrote the Hymn, the Conte? Has he kissed you yet?'

'Yes,' confessed Gabriella. 'But I will not tell you one thing more,' she laughed, seeing her friend about to speak. 'Except that he has given me this most beautiful gift.'

'Gabriella, it's exquisite. He must love you dearly,' said Giuseppina, her face quite grave and wondering.

'Yes, yes, I think he must.'

'Oh, you will be the most excited and happy person in the world tomorrow,' sighed Giuseppina enviously as she kissed and hugged her friend.

The next day, however, the whole of the Conservatorio was electrified with other news that continued to create a hubbub of excitement throughout the whole of Milan for the rest of the day: the Pope was going to grant the Romans a Constitution!

'You are going to need a big voice tonight, Signorina,' laughed one of the stage hands as Gabriella entered the theatre early in the evening. 'There will be an uproar, and I know now what they will be chanting.'

'*Benedite Gran Dio l'Italia!*' said Gabriella with a cheerful smile.

'Yes, that's it, "Oh Lord God bless Italy". When Pius said that in February he showed these Austrians that he was blessing the national movement. And now he has set the example . . . I say that if they don't give us a free press and a Constitution he should excommunicate the lot of them, starting off with that Prince Metternich. Anyway, good luck, beautiful lady.'

Her dressing-room was like a florist's shop, with so many blooms that Gabriella thought she might start to sneeze so heavy was the perfume in the air. But she felt a warm glow of security to see so many good wishes, from Giuditta Pasta and Agnese Prioni, and from every member of the Forro family.

'Are you ready for me to help you into your gown, Signorina?' asked the dresser assigned to Gabriella.

'Yes thank you,' said Gabriella. 'My hands are shaking so that I cannot do a thing.'

'Ah, that is a good sign. It would not be good to wait like a lump of dough,' said the woman, helping Gabriella to step into the gown of dark blue velvet. As the experienced, strong fingers pulled together the last of the hooks which closed the tight bodice of intricate, leaf-shaped sections, designed to follow the curves of the body like a skin of velvet, the dresser grunted with approval.

'You've a good body, Signorina Pepe. If you've a voice to match, they'll soon drop their cards and turn their chairs around. Is there anything else?'

'Yes,' said Gabriella with an impish smile. 'I know everyone will be talking politics tonight, so I thought this might focus their attention on where it should be. Will you be my partner in crime by helping to put this over my head?'

'Is that wise, Signorina?' gasped the short, sturdy woman.

'You'll bring the theatre police down on you for creating a disturbance.'

'La Scala's corps de ballet wore Pius's medallions in February.'

'A Holy relic is not the same thing as the tricolore.'

'Don't worry, Signora,' said Gabriella as the woman reluctantly lifted the red, white and green sash over the small blue velvet feathered hat which matched her dress. 'With the news today, I don't think the police will dare to interfere! And neither will the *tedeschi*!'

From the wings, Gabriella watched the first two scenes of the opera end. Then, almost sick with fright, she heard her entrance music begin. The moment that she had anticipated, that others had worked for, given their time and talent to prepare her for, was here. And though he was not here, for the sake of Mazzini and the brave patriots who had given their lives for Italy she wore the tricolore sash. Love had given her the courage of a lion, and she would sing as never before for the man who would be looking down at her from his box.

From the shadowy depths of the stage she heard as she moved forward the buzz of chatter and laughter above the sound of the violins. Then she was in light: there was shocked silence, a gasping, excited murmur, then a roar, ecstatic and approving, which crashed like surf against Piermarini's walls and ceiling. With a swift nod at the conductor, Gabriella indicated that she wished for the introductory bars once more. Then with that presence which was God-given, she demanded silence; the silence of a first night.

'"Arise! Awake! The hour is nigh! From their slumbers the Lombards must strike!"'

Straight towards the large Imperial Box with its crown and cross she directed her eyes, filling the house with Luciano Forro's passionate words and Verdi's glorious music of protest.

'*Guerra! Guerra!*' shouted the audience when she had finished.

The uproar was deafening, and she could see that a whole row of students from the Conservatorio, conspicuous by their

208

best green jackets, were on their feet and shaking their fists towards the officers of the Imperial army, who were returning the challenge by hitting their swords against the floor. On to the stage showered favours in the colours of the tricolore, then a Milanese noble threw down one in yellow and black. Gabriella looked up at the excited young man: she knew what he wanted her to do, so with the toe of her shoe she kicked the Austrian colours to one side. Immediately, the action brought a roar of approval, and from both sides of the theatre the police began to converge on the stage, but the cries for an encore were so loud that, with the usual helpless shake of his head, the conductor waved his baton to begin.

As Luciano Forro looked down from his box he felt a mixture of emotions: exasperation that the young woman had so endangered herself by wearing the tricolore, and overwhelming admiration for her courage. As a man his heart raced, knowing that this fearless, dynamic soprano had twined her body around his in love, and that he had made her cry out in joy and desire; yet now it was she who dominated him and everyone around with the golden power of her voice. As she accepted her applause for the second time, he threw down the bouquet of red and white roses which, with their green leaves, made the tricolore.

For the first time Gabriella looked up to Luciano Forro's box and she laughed, meeting his eyes. In mid-flight she caught the bouquet and, kissing the flowers, exchanged with the Conte a look as if they were alone. Then she made her exit and, despite the calls for her return, made her way slowly back to her dressing-room, receiving hugs and kisses and words of admiration on the way. As soon as she entered the lovely room with the woodland scenes on the tapestry covered walls, Gabriella sank down on to a stool. She realized she was trembling from head to foot. Pasta had told her what applause could be like, but no description could ever prepare one for the living entity of an audience, the power of all that admiration and approval blazing forth . . . Well, not quite all admiration and approval, she smiled, thinking of the Austrians present; not to mention the Marchesa Flavia Balziano, she thought, recalling the expression on the beautiful face in the box next to Luciano Forro's.

'I wish to speak to Signorina Pepe!'

At the sound of the voice, Gabriella's eyes widened in surprise and a feeling of foreboding swept over her.

'Tell Marchesa Balziano to come in, Maria,' she called out to her dresser. Straightaway, coral-coloured silk rustled and flounced into the room. The sight of the arrogant, haughty face effected a response in Gabriella that made her feel as if the rags of Blackfriars still clung to her: as if she could sense the shrinking feeling she had evoked, the aristocrat's lips curled in a superior smile.

'Your performance was a triumph, my dear Signorina Pepe – and what a clever thing to do, to ingratiate yourself with the audience,' she said, pointing with her fan to the tricolore sash. As she did so, Gabriella saw the young woman's eyes dwell on the Contessa's butterfly brooch and the heavy necklace of sapphires and amethysts. Flavia Balziano visibly paled and her black eyes flashed with such venom that Gabriella half stepped back.

'You have not come here to pay me compliments, Marchesa. Please come to the point.'

'Quite correct!' snapped Flavia Balziano, seemingly irritated by Gabriella's cold dignity. 'I will make it plain then, plain enough for the simplest beggar to understand. Leave Conte Forro alone!'

Gabriella looked in open-mouthed astonishment at the haughty young woman whose eyes glittered as hard as the diamonds and drops at her ears.

'I think, Marchesa, you should leave,' she said, eventually finding words. 'I do not think my friendship with the Conte is your concern.'

'But it is!'

Gabriella did not answer, looking away in embarrassment from the almond-shaped eyes flashing jealousy.

'If you do not obey me in this,' persisted the Marchesa, 'I will get my parents to use all their influence against your career . . .

On the other hand, if you were to find another lover, I would see that you are helped.'

'I do not want your help!' flashed Gabriella, unable to believe her ears.

'Conte Forro is meant for me, and I will have him!' stormed Flavia Balziano.

'Isn't that a matter for the Conte also to decide?' asked Gabriella mildly, realizing the other was losing control.

'He was promised to me!' cried the Marchesa petulantly. 'And you are ruining everything . . . I thought you were just like any other little opera girl . . . and that once he . . .' Again the dark eyes fixed on the butterfly brooch and then slid to the necklace. The feline face distorted with rage. 'Oh, I won't endure it, I won't be humiliated. I will *make* you give him up!'

'How?' The question was spoken gently, but it was as if a lash had struck Flavia Balziano. She sprang towards Gabriella, with her nails poised as if to strike. Her scarlet lips, like two snakes, lifted and writhed into an insinuating smile.

'You have sung in the salons like a chef cooks in a kitchen, but if he married you, do you think society would welcome a creature of the gutter? Imagine our distinguished Conte Forro dishonouring and degrading the family line with a beggar! Would you do that to him? Would you see his ruin?'

'Ruin?' flashed Gabriella, her cheeks burning with anger.

'Yes, ruin,' snarled the Marchesa. 'I will break him if he betrays me. Luciano is financially stretched to breaking point – I have heard Papa talk about it. He has poured his money into new factories and houses for his workers. The lease of the estates on which his new spinning mill stands, and on which a new factory is being built to make railway parts, comes up for renewal next year. When my uncle died, Papa as his heir leased them to Luciano, who has all these quaint ideas about improving the peasants' lot. Papa has no such interest, but he *is* interested in my happiness. He has never denied me anything, and Mama will not let a commoner like you make a fool of me. Give him up, or he will lose the Balziano land and you will see every member of his family suffer because of it! And they will come to hate you! Send him away!'

The door closed behind Flavia Balziano and Gabriella sank down on to a chair. She tried to stop trembling as shock overtook anger and outrage. She thought of the sharp, vixen face consumed by an inner fire as strong as her own and had no doubt about the Marchesa's resolve. Yet how could Flavia really ruin what she loved, destroy everything that a man had built up? It would be like destroying part of him, and would bring such unhappiness not only to the Forro family but also to the people dependent on him for their livelihoods. It seemed impossible that anyone could do such a thing . . . yet, as she remembered the night she had heard Flavia's mother speaking about her on the Forro terrace, Gabriella knew that both mother and daughter would not turn away from revenge. With a low groan she picked up Luciano Forro's bouquet and buried her face against it, feeling her heart would break.

'Quite a performance, Signorina Pepe!'

Hearing the joyful note in the loved voice, Gabriella could hardly bear to look up, let alone do what she must. Surely he would sense and see through the act? Oh please God, let him realize, she thought, kissing the petals of the roses; but she knew if he did that she would be the cause of his ruin.

'I'm glad you like it, Conte,' she said, looking up with a bright smile. 'Your Hymn touched the pulse of Milan tonight.'

'Indeed!' laughed Luciano Forro gaily. 'Another time and both you and I might now be being hauled off to prison . . . Instead I mean to make you my prisoner for half an hour before you meet your devotees. I want to speak to you alone,' he said, his eyes shining with love as he placed his hands on her shoulders and smiled down at her.

Feeling physically sick, Gabriella pulled away and started to undo the sapphire necklace.

'Oh, you mustn't take me away. After all, devotees are important to my future. One can't have too many of them.'

She could not look at him, but the effect of her words and the brittle way in which she had spoken them changed the atmosphere immediately. She felt him stiffen beside her.

'Don't you want to be alone with me for a little while, *mia cara?*' his mellow voice said.

'I think I'd prefer to see Signor Merelli. After all, he is the man who can offer me a contract. Please don't think I'm ungrateful: without your Hymn I wouldn't be here. But I have to look to the next rung for the sake of my career,' she said, forcing a smile as Luciano Forro's lips tightened and the hurt in his eyes changed to cold, proud contempt.

'Then I have already detained you too long. I wish you goodnight, Gabriella, and goodbye.'

'Your necklace . . .' faltered Gabriella, holding out the jewels.

'Keep it!' Luciano Forro almost snarled in reply as he turned to her from the door. 'I have no further use for it. Wear it for your next dramatic role!'

The black tails of the Conte's evening coat disappeared around the door and Gabriella, holding her fist to her mouth to stifle her utterance of grief, leant against the wall and wept for what she had lost.

# Chapter Eleven

'Metternich has fled Vienna! Manin has declared a Republic in Venice!'

It was the morning of 18 March 1848 and, in evidence to support this astounding news, the apprehensive authorities had put up notices that the Emperor had conceded a representative government to Milan.

Classes had been suspended and the sound of bells and cheering from the direction of the municipal government building filled the air from mid-morning onwards.

'Why, there must be thousands out on the streets,' declared Gabriella as she and the other women students walked in the Conservatorio's garden after lunch. 'All the men have been allowed to go. I wonder if it's worth asking?'

'I don't think so,' smiled a red-haired student named Lucia. 'You know what the call is?'

'Women to the windows, men to the streets!' chorused everyone together.

'Well, that is all right if your window happens to be in the right place,' retorted Gabriella with a defiant grin.

'Good, that is more like your old self,' murmured her friend Giuseppina as she linked her arm through Gabriella's. 'I've hated to see you so sad.'

Gabriella dropped her eyes, conscious of the remorseless pain that had been with her every day since the evening of La Scala. She hadn't confided in her friend, but she had been unable to hide her unhappiness. And the compliments, the proposals about her future, they had all flowed unnoticed over her head, for she could only think of the ashen face and the wounded expression in those proud dark eyes.

'I think I'll go back in and see if anyone has any news,' Gabriella said, giving Giuseppina's arm a squeeze of gratitude for her understanding. As she turned to go, above the sound of church bells and the continuing roar of Milan's citizens came the boom of a gun.

'Are the Austrians starting to shoot people?' piped one of the young girls.

'Surely not. It sounds more like the alarm gun.'

'Come on, Giuseppina,' said Gabriella in a low voice. 'I'm not waiting any longer. I'm going to join the men on the streets.'

Together with her friend, and with some of the more adventurous souls following, Gabriella ran out on to the street outside the Conservatorio and on towards the governor's palace. But they had barely gone a few yards when, to their amazement, they saw a group of people starting to pull up the pavement.

'What is happening?'

'We're in rebellion!' said a man, wielding a huge hammer.

'Rebellion!' gasped all the girls.

'Did they change their minds about letting us have a provisional government?' asked Gabriella.

'Oh no,' laughed the man. 'Things have moved on from there. Cernuschi, the republican, persuaded the Podestà, Conte Gabrio Casati, to march behind the tricolore from the Broletto to the governor's palace to demand the abolition of the police and the right to a Civic Guard. Anyway, it got a little out of hand; the crowd stormed the palace, and the acting governor, Graf O'Donell, was forced to sign agreement to our demands.'

'But why did the soldiers allow it to happen?'

'A good question, Signorina,' beamed the man, obviously relishing his story as he watched his companions working. 'We have our Conte Casati and the delegate Bellati to thank for that. Apparently they persuaded Graf O'Donell not to send his order for Radetzky to deploy his troops – why, the old bear must have

215

torn his hair out in fury. But he'll take his revenge soon, despite the fact we're holding the deputy governor hostage.'

'But how can we resist?' asked Gabriella, remembering the constant laments about lack of weapons and Milan being the headquarters of the Austrian army.

'Our only chance, the young leaders say, is to block the streets and build barricades.'

'Can we help?' asked Gabriella. 'Tell us how to do it and we'll start to build one.'

'Well, it doesn't seem right for young ladies . . .'

'We're patriots!' everyone shouted excitedly. '*Viva l'Italia*.'

'And you have a garden in the Conservatorio,' nodded the man. 'You need to build a bank of soil and then we'll come along and help with the paving stones – though you can pile anything on top. No one really knows how to do it, but it must be strong to stop the cavalry and a body of infantry.'

Hardly waiting for him to finish, Gabriella and her friends ran back to the Conservatorio. Work had already been begun by some of the men students who had returned from the demonstration and seizure of the palace.

The atmosphere was charged with excitement and a keen fear of what Radetzky would soon do. Every minute, they were told, was vital.

'Don't rest, gentlemen,' urged one of the professors. 'Our only hope lies in impeding Radetzky's cavalry and cutting his units off from the Castello. Once they have run out of ammunition, they'll be helpless.'

'But how will we manage until then?'

'With whatever comes to hand: flower pots, tiles, saucepans; anything that will smash a head. For every soldier who drops dead or unconscious, we have a gun.'

For well over an hour, everyone toiled. Just as they had started to carry out wooden benches to stack against the earth, the familiar figures of Mario and Angelo went running by.

'Where are you going?' someone shouted.

In response, the fragile-looking student of composition held up a very ancient fowling gun and made a pretence at aiming it.

'We're going to defend the Broletto! General Lecchi, the Napoleonic veteran, has been placed in command of the volunteers.'

'But what will everyone use for arms?'

Once again Angelo held up the ancient gun, and Mario waved a sabre.

'Anything that kills will do. Conte Forro has given over his gun collection to anyone who needs a gun, and we have the Ubaldi and Poldi Pezzoli collections too.'

'Why, they're priceless,' murmured one of the priests standing beside Gabriella. But she hardly heard, for the mention of Luciano's name filled her with anxiety and alarm.

Towards seven o'clock in the evening, as they were still labouring, the sound of fighting began and news came that Radetzky had sent about a thousand Croatians and Bohemians against the 300 volunteers defending the municipal palace. Throughout the next four hours, tidings of the desperate struggle continued: how so few could last so long against fully armed soldiers seemed a miracle. Then, as the rain started to fall towards eleven o'clock, there came the sound of cannon.

'Twelve-pounders!' spat the elderly porter, who always stood at the main gate and whose military bearing and single arm showed experience in such matters. 'They'll be trying to make a breach to reach our lads.'

The old campaigner's words filled Gabriella with dread.

'It's stopped,' she said hopefully as the cannon fell silent.

'That means they're in. It will be hand-to-hand fighting now.'

She thought, with terror, of the young men with their cologne-scented hair and velvet suits, whose only skills were in dealing cards and flirting. How would they survive against armed, ferocious Bohemians and Croats . . .

'How will they manage?' she whispered, not noticing the downpour which was beginning to douse the street lanterns.

'Men cornered in their own city have everything to lose. They'll not give way so easily,' explained the porter. 'Once the hotheads had killed the sentries at the San Damiano bridge, the die was cast. Even those men who sought the peaceful way could not distance themselves once the fighting started: it's all or nothing for all of us. Can you imagine what will happen if we lose?'

Half an hour passed, and the noise of gunfire died away. Soon afterwards came the sound of hurrying feet. From the light of the lanterns which they were using to light their work on the second barricade, they saw emerging from the blackness a group of students, carrying others who were wounded in their arms.

'Have they taken back the Broletto?' everyone shouted.

'Yes, their cannon blew the door down – we think Radetzky thought the town councillors were still holding the deputy governor there. Instead, we had him safely tucked up at the Casa Vidiserti. There have been quite a few of our men captured and some civilians standing near the Broletto were also seized, amongst them I think were one of Manzoni's sons and a member of the Trivulzio family.'

'Pray God they are not treated harshly!' said the old porter.

'Tell me,' said Gabriella, going up to one of the young men who was wiping blood from his brow. 'Do you know if Conte Forro is amongst those captured?'

'No, both brothers are unhurt. They've gone to see to the erection of barricades. Before dawn we have to isolate every police station, every barrack, the Palazzo Reale, the Palazzo di Giustizia, the headquarters of the Royal Engineers and the Palazzo del Governo. Tonight is no time for sleep, nor is one barricade in a street enough: there must be as many as five every hundred yards.'

Only the old and infirm were within doors: everyone else was out ripping up the streets in a desperate bid to protect themselves from the troops before daylight came.

By four o'clock in the morning, short bursts of artillery fire resounded throughout the city.

'Listen, it's increasing!' said Gabriella, halting as she and three others were making their way to the Piazza del Duomo.

'*Benedite Gran Dio Milano!*' said the priest as the church bells everywhere began to ring out rebellion.

In the main approaches to the sacred ground of the cathedral, there was still frenzied activity as people strove to strengthen the defences. Amongst the men Gabriella saw Enrico Facini working with Mario and other students from the Conservatorio.

'I expect our boys would prefer bullets to bread and cheese,' commented Gabriella as they approached the barricade which blocked off the approach to the duomo from the Piazza dei Mercanti. All at once, before they could hand over the food and drink, the alarm went up as artillery fire broke out close at hand.

'They're here!'

'Quick, you women – fill those baskets with stones!' ordered a young man. 'And keep bringing them to us.'

Activated by the urgency of his command, Gabriella ran with the others towards a wagon loaded with broken paving stones. Emptying the food on to the floor, they refilled the baskets with stones. Then, staggering back, they handed up the missiles to the boys perched on the barricade. Only two men had guns, whilst from the other side of the barrier the unseen enemy were pouring a deadly fire up at the defenders; yet although they could only reply with stones, somehow they were holding the troops back. Twice more Gabriella and her companions ran back to refill the baskets with the makeshift missiles. Then they heard a cry. 'Abandon! *Viva l'Italia!*'

Immediately the defenders were leaping down and running for cover behind the second defence. Once again the unequal struggle began, until the final barricade was falling apart.

'Get ready to run, we can't hold any longer!'

With bullets whining about their heads and the first sight of white jackets through the holes in the barricade, Gabriella and her companions took flight away from the duomo.

'See,' she gasped when they had reached comparative safety. 'Do you see, their marksmen are already moving along the gallery of the cathedral.'

'It's the cathedral more than the palazzo they wanted,' said the student Mario, who had cut his leg badly against a broken mirror on one of the barricades. 'Now it will be impossible to move about. They will have a clear line of fire at the whole of the centre.'

'What devils to use a sacred building for their killing. There'll be no bringing them down once they're high on the roof; impossible!' said Father Domenico, who was still with them.

'They'll get very hungry up there,' remarked Gabriella, looking at her empty basket. 'For even if they found our bread and cheese, there'll be no more offered.'

It had been a casual remark made half in jest against herself and the others who had thought a picnic was a way to keep the morale of the fighters up. But whilst the deadly Kaiser Jägers continued to rake the surrounding streets and kill every citizen that moved, in turn the Milanesi did indeed cut off their communications, ammunition and food.

All the time the building of barricades continued. And when a detachment of infantry smashed one down, it was rebuilt the moment they had passed on. And little by little, more guns were seized whose fire accompanied the deluge of tiles and boiling water constantly poured down on the soldiers' heads as they stumbled over avenues and streets that resembled huge earthworks decorated with carriages, pianos, and every conceivable household item.

No one slept, for the pressure had to be kept up all the time, the leaders said. To keep the fighters going, every palace had thrown open its doors to provide a buffet of food and drink; and every chemist was at work producing bullets and gun-cotton.

'We are going to fight to the death!' said Enrico Facini, who had come to fight with the students of the Conservatorio.

'Have you seen Giovanni?' Gabriella enquired, leaning against an upturned chair as they waited for any attack that might be launched.

'He is supposed to be joining me here, unless he has ridden after his brother to shoot him!'

'Shoot Luciano. What do you mean?' she gasped in astonishment.

'The Conte has gone to fetch the Piedmont army. He managed to get away before they closed the city gate. Giovanni

220

is wild with anger about it, calling him a traitor to bring the Piedmontese to our fight. Conte Martini has also gone.'

'I see,' said Gabriella slowly. 'You do not seem very upset about it.'

Enrico Facini smiled grimly. 'I'm a realist, like Forro. Radetzky has only to keep us captive within the city walls and we will starve to death. If he hears the Piedmontese army is coming to our rescue, he might leave.'

'So you, a republican, will accept the help of a king?' asked Gabriella with an ironic smile.

'It's the only army that can rid us of the Austrians. Once they've done it, well . . . we will be waiting in the wings to take over. I'll follow any cause if it serves our ends . . . Why do you suppose I cheer so loudly for Pius?'

'Because he is the hope of nationalism.'

'And he must fail,' said Enrico Facini cynically. 'We will see to that. In Rome our agents lead the crowds like choir masters to the Quirinale to applaud the reforms; now they also show disapproval as those reforms slow down. We are teaching them how to demand, and we've raised their expectations so high that soon Pius will find his back to the wall. When he fails, they will turn to people like the republican Sterbini.'

'How cruel,' said Gabriella.

'That's politics, dear girl. You give the mob the right shepherd and like sheep they will follow.'

'But surely Giuseppe Mazzini would not approve of your methods?'

Gabriella never got her reply, for there was a sudden warning yell from their look-out. 'They are coming!'

'*Viva l'Indipendenza! Viva l'Italia.*'

As the cries rang out, Gabriella scurried away with the other women to their posts. They bolted and barred the door behind them, then made their way upstairs into a chamber looking down on to the street below. All along the street the windows were opening and heads were craning out into the heavy rain to watch for the advancing squad. Beside Gabriella was a huge laundry basket of roof tiles, and she and another woman gathered up as many as could be held in their skirts. To their left was the barricade, and to the right, which almost stopped their hearts with fright, they saw the advancing soldiers with their bayonets at the ready.

'See, they're conscripts. Don't they look miserable,' commented the woman beside Gabriella as the householders further along started to throw down their deluge of missiles.

'It can't be much fun watching for a bullet and a flowerpot all at the same time,' agreed Gabriella, preparing to take aim.

The procedure was now well known by everyone: the idea was to try and stop the squads getting close to the barricade, especially when its defenders had no weapons.

'Go home, boys!' shouted a woman from the next window along as she hurled down a chamber pot. As if to reinforce the message, a bombardment from the upper storey began. A moment ago what they held for weaponry had seemed more than inadequate against armed men, but the frenzied screams of the women as they started to tip out pans of boiling water and oil on to the men brought its results! On her part, Gabriella hurled pieces of tile, aiming for faces and hands and ducking back when, in pain and rage, a soldier retaliated with an upward shot. It was a fantastic sight as stools and vases broke apart the orderly formation and the men staggered and reeled, trying to maintain their attack under the extraordinary onslaught.

'Who are your mothers? Which is your country?'

Suddenly, as if he had heard the accusation above the uproar of musketry and yelling, the officer of the Italian conscripts threw down his gun and, producing a large white handkerchief, shouted for the whole street to hear, '*Viva l'Italia!*'

Immediately his men followed suit and threw down their arms. With whoops of delight, the cheering students emerged from behind the barricade and ran forward to embrace their fellow countrymen. But as Gabriella and her companions applauded this moving sight, around the corner of the street swept a company of cavalry whose magnificent horses cleared the first of the barricades as though it were some low hedge on a country lane. They were a breathtaking and terrifying sight as they galloped forward with their sabres outstretched before them to deal out death. Once again, the students ran back to defend the barricade, now with their new allies. Only feet behind the laggards chased the leading two horses, whose riders – huge, athletic cavalry officers – grasped their sabres between their teeth and leant forward in the saddle as their stallions launched upwards into flight to clear the obstacle before them. For one moment, through the veil of rain, Gabriella thought the horses hovered motionless above the heads of the defenders; then, unbelievably, a patch of crimson showed, spreading out on the back of one of the white jackets. The rider slumped forward in his saddle, falling sideways as his horse landed and galloped on.

'*Viva la Repubblica!*' cackled a voice from somewhere above.

Gabriella looked up to see who had brought the rider down. She saw an old man whose wizened yellowish face and white hair set him at a great age. '*Morte ai tedeschi!*' He spat and nodded jubilantly to her. 'He'll arrive there before I do!'

The shot in the back was both cowardly and vindictive, and Gabriella hastily pulled back into the room without responding to the old man's laughter. For a moment she just sat and watched the scene below, but as a rider lashed downwards with his sabre towards a youth, automatically her fingers snatched up a piece of paving stone. It was no time to moralize, she thought grimly, watching her stone find its mark.

There was no way of holding such a number of troops, and within minutes the students had to retreat to the next of the barricades. With no one left to bombard the enemy, everyone ran down on to the street to rebuild and reinforce the barricade against the next body of troops that would try to pass.

Gradually the citizens were beginning to contain the movements of the Austrians, bringing heavy fire to bear on any detachments which tried to pass from the Piazza del Duomo and Piazza dei Mercanti towards the Broletto; like a vast spider's web, the barricades had caught and isolated each individual unit and garrison and, little by little, their ammunition and rations were running out. High up on the cathedral roof, the Tyrolean sharpshooters, moving about behind the statues, could have paralysed all movement in the centre of the city for days; but they too were running short of supplies and so, just over twenty-four hours after they had taken up their positions, the Kaiser Jägers found their retreat was as firmly barred and resisted as their attack had been. And for them and other units, attempting to obey Radetzky's command to retire to the bastions and circumvallations entailed a desperate, bloody manoeuvre.

A new, furious fight began, to gain access to the outside world. Courage amongst the Milanesi was plentiful, what was not was food: even the well-stocked pantries of the palazzi were almost bare. Things were becoming desperate and the university students were sending off dozens of balloons carrying pleas for help. Then the glad tidings flashed around: the Piedmontese army would come to the rescue of Milan. The news brought relief and acrimony: in the coffee-houses, on the streets and amongst the students, especially the supporters of the federalist-republican Professor Cattaneo, there were furious arguments.

'Carlo Cattaneo, Cernuschi, Clerici and Terzaghi are leading us to victory; the professor says we should be our own masters for once.'

But the fact that King Carlo Alberto's army was ready to cross the Ticino put fresh heart into everyone.

'Forward, boys!' directed Professor Cattaneo's proclamation. 'The town is ours now. The enemy is retiring on to the bastions to begin his retreat. Harry him! Leave him neither truce nor rest. Tonight all the gates must be unblocked; eight thousand men from the country are ready to join hands with us. The enemy asks for a truce; do not waste time in discussion. The moment has arrived when we can be rid of him for ever. *Viva l'Italia!*'

Everyone prepared for the final effort; people of all classes manned the barricades to release the active fighters for the attack on three of the city's gates. But seven guns and about two thousand troops were in position, ready to defend the Porta Tosa gate.

'If they put up a fight like the Imperial cadets did at the St Celso barracks, there'll be a lot of our boys who will never see the morrow,' sighed the old porter who was standing with Gabriella and Giuseppina outside the orphanage opposite the Conservatorio. 'I'd say it was impossible, but for this bright idea of using movable barricades on wheels. It will give them some protection and allow them to get in closer; even so, it will be a tough fight.'

During the ensuing uncertain hours, at the thousands of barricades throughout the city, people stood motionless, listening to the fierce fight raging at the Porta Tosa gate. And whilst the men of Milan tried to break out, those who had marched to their defence were trying to break in.

'Ah, Signor Mazzini, how you would wish to be here,' thought Gabriella, thinking how amazed he and the Princess Belgiojoso would be to know what was taking place at this moment. Then, in the next hour, news came that the Milanesi had triumphed!

'The gate is ours!' shrieked some schoolboys. 'And the Porta Comasine has been breached. The day is ours!'

Black, belching smoke and soaring tongues of orange flame dominated the sky above the castle later that night. The Austrians were burning their dead. They were still firing upon the town to hold the victors at bay, whilst for five long hours the exterior roads resounded to the sound of marching feet and the rumble of carriage wheels as the withdrawal took place. Wives, daughters, cooks, clerks, all were fleeing with their army, leaving Milan to the Lombards.

'Have you ever felt so happy?' laughed Giuseppina Verenese the next day, clapping her hands to her ears against the vibrating, clanging sound of church bells and the cheers of the crowds. 'What about the outside of La Scala. Doesn't it look like some strange production with all the trees and statues and thrones on top of their barricade? Just think, not one Austrian will sit in there; there will be no beastly soldiers and police there any more – and your Conte so brave . . . Oh, I'm sorry, I shouldn't have . . .' said Giuseppina, colouring at her indiscretion.

'It's all right, Giuseppina,' said Gabriella, pushing back the curtain inside the door of the cathedral. 'I've heard his name so often today I must begin soon to become immune. I'm thankful he is safe, as is Conte Manara, who led the charge against the Porta Tosa.'

'They were all so brave,' sighed Giuseppina. 'I think Sottocorno, the hunchback, will have free wine for the rest of his life for his part in the attack on the headquarters of the Royal Engineers. He is my hero, for it was one thing to hobble across to lay resin at the Genio gate, but to crawl back after having been wounded to set it afire – why, that must be the bravest of acts. It must have shown them how determined we all were.'

'They can no longer despise us,' said Gabriella, looking around at the motley defences. 'It seems unbelievable that thousands of troops have been beaten and that it only took five days to set us free – and without help from outside, although now support has arrived.'

'The university boys say it was because of their balloons,' laughed Giuseppina.

'Well, they would!' giggled Gabriella.

The whole of Milan was like some vast, muddy battle-ground, with its once beautiful broad avenues of pinkish stone ripped up and piled high along with grand pianos and church pews, chandeliers and dining tables. Those who had marched from the banks of the Po, from Lago Maggiore, Monza and Como to aid its citizens, inspected the great sacrifice, wide-eyed with admiration.

With the discoveries at the Castello of the horribly mutilated corpses of many hostages taken during the fighting, much of the euphoria was replaced with anxiety as to what would happen if Radetzky returned. It was too terrible to consider such a possibility and on Friday 24 March, the volunteers who had enlisted in the Army of the Alps, as it was to be known, marched out of Milan to make sure that such a thing should not happen.

King Carlo Alberto's demand for a formal request for help from Milan's Provisional Government had delayed Piedmont's entry into the war, but two days after the Lombard volunteers had left for Treviglio, a brigade of the Piedmont army, following behind a tricolore superimposed with the Cross of Savoy, entered Milan. With thousands of others, Gabriella had stood in heavy rain to cheer the infantry and cavalry of the Piedmont and Pignerol regiments. They were splendid troops and the sight of them filled everyone with hope, for they were going east to meet up with the volunteers.

In the days that followed, everybody waited anxiously for bulletins, familiarizing themselves with the map of where the campaign was taking place. The main body of the Piedmontese army was in the south on the left bank of the river Po and advancing towards the River Minchio, behind which Radetzky had latterly taken up a defensive position within the Quadrilateral. The four fortresses of the Quadrilateral, each garrisoning nearly a thousand troops, were Peschiera, Mantua on the Lombard frontier, Legnago, and Verona, where Radetzky had recently moved his headquarters. Between all these fortresses were nature's own defences: to the east the River Adige, to the north Lake Garda and the Upper Adige, to the south the river Po, and to the west the River Minchio, which the Piedmontese army must cross before reinforcements arrived to aid Radetzy. Meanwhile, the Lombard volunteers in the north were laying siege to the fortress of Peschiera, endeavouring to cut Radetzky's lines of communication to prevent help from Austria reaching him in Verona.

It seemed hard to resume a normal routine, for every day there was fresh news, and all the time new arrivals entered Milan. Amongst them was Giuseppe Mazzini. As he entered through the city gates, Gabriella saw him lifted shoulder-high like a conquering Caesar come to claim his people. From where she watched she cried unrestrainedly, remembering the first time he had welcomed her at the classroom door, remembering the dreams he had spun for them at Hatton Garden. Here, now, as the tricolore flags waved along the route, the exile had achieved his own dream: to come home. A few days later the streets were once more thronged to greet a returning exile: the Princess Christina Belgiojoso-Trivulzio.

Soon afterwards, Gabriella was reunited with them both.

'So,' said Giuseppe Mazzini, holding Gabriella at arm's length after embracing her. 'Whilst I have been growing old, the little girl with the broomstick arms and legs has grown into a lovely young woman.'

'You haven't grown old, Giuseppe,' said Gabriella, smiling through her tears. 'The silver in your beard is most distinguished. Tell me, how does it feel to be on Italian soil at last? Your dream is coming true as mine has done through you,' she said, squeezing his hands to show her gratitude.

'Ah yes, you sang at La Scala – and a patriotic hymn by Verdi, no less,' beamed Mazzini.

'And you know I have you partly to thank for that – Verdi admires you, and I expect Conte Forro told him of my connection with you.'

'Whatever,' the exile smiled. 'You have repaid all of us by what you did at La Scala. I'm sure the Princess was proud also. Did you see her entering Milan?'

'I thought she looked like Joan of Arc,' whispered Gabriella so that Christina Belgiojoso, who was at the far end of the room, should not hear. 'In her hand was the tricolore banner, and behind her the Neapolitan volunteers to whom she had given passage on her privately chartered steamer.'

'Christina is a remarkable woman,' murmured Mazzini. 'And it's good to see the Neapolitans coming to join the fight. It makes it Italy's fight.'

'Many of your followers are urging the declaration of a republic. Is that why you are here?'

'Partly,' answered Mazzini, fingering the smooth dark beard now tinged with grey. 'Though now I have listened to the arguments and seen the situation I am trying to restrain them. The most important thing is to win the war, and that means everyone has to work together. After victory is the time to decide such things.'

'Set the prisoner free before you decide which clothes he should wear?'

'Yes, something like that,' smiled Mazzini. 'At the moment Lombardy's liberation is the most important issue. Until then, I am trying to urge the young to have patience. It is not easy for them: I had to acquire mine in prison and in exile.'

The Lombard volunteers had covered themselves in glory in their daring actions around Lake Garda. This, along with Carlo Alberto's victory at Goito, forced Radetzky to withdraw his troops behind the Rideau fortifications before Verona. Things seemed to be going well: not only had the Neapolitans come to the aid of Lombardy, but Parma, Modena, and Tuscany had sent volunteers, and a force from Rome was marching towards the frontier, even though the Papal States had not as yet declared war upon Austria.

Milan had become the focus not only for all exiles, but also for the advocates of republicanism. Amongst those who came to urge for it was one who sought out Gabriella.

'I hope you won't disappoint me, Signorina Pepe,' Giuseppe Verdi said, shaking Gabriella's hand vigorously. 'There were several people pleading your cause to me in Paris, so I expect the extraordinary – however, I'll be frank and tell you it was my friend Forro's poem I was interested in – and its message for Italy . . . I hear you chose your moment well.'

'That was luck,' smiled Gabriella, liking this fierce man's directness. 'We weren't to know that revolution would break out in Vienna.'

'Well, let me hear what you made of it,' the maestro said, lifting up his coat tails as he sat down on the piano stool. 'You know I wasn't admitted to the Conservatorio. They turned me down on account of my poor technique on the piano,' he laughed as his fingers flew up and down the keys.

Gabriella smiled, then looked away, composed herself, and began to sing. When she had finished, the maestro slammed down the lid of the piano.

'Yes, I want you! You bear Pasta's stamp; you've learnt a great deal from her.'

'I'd like to sing *Norma* one day,' admitted Gabriella wistfully.

'You'll cast your own shadow, Signorina – with my music!' rasped the maestro looking at his pocket watch. 'You're the singer of tomorrow, Gabriella Pepe. This is the age of revolution, its music requires vigour and strength. You'll find I'm a hard taskmaster. When do you finish here?'

'July,' said Gabriella breathlessly.

'Then come to Paris. I am going to do a new opera for Rome next year – if you've nowhere to stay, my friend Giuseppina Strepponi will help you out for a while. She's a former student of the Conservatorio, who is now teaching singing in Paris.'

'You're like a whirlwind,' laughed Gabriella. 'I can hardly think.'

'There's nothing to think about, there is nothing for you here. You need my music and it needs you, and Paris is the place to be.'

As quickly as he had arrived the composer departed, leaving Gabriella with a mixture of emotions.

'Hasn't the reality of what this means sunk in yet?' asked Giuseppina as she sat with Gabriella and watched the gardener still trying to restore some order after the devastation in March. 'It means he will create a role for you, like Donizetti and Bellini did for Pasta. And you can be in Paris soon, and if Verdi wants you, so will its Opera House. Aren't you longing to go . . .? Frenchmen are very handsome and romantic.'

'And how would you know that, Signorina?' enquired Gabriella with a teasing smile which was meant to hide all other feelings. She knew what her friend said was right and that she should be elated by what had been offered. But her concern was only for the Lombard volunteers who, formed into a new company of sharpshooters, were now guarding the frontier up in the Tyrol. How could she go anywhere until she knew what became of them?

As the Lombards were looking down from the mountains on the valley of Chiese, the various political factions in Milan were quarrelling heatedly over the question of fusion with Piedmont. Feelings were bitter between republicans and Albertists. But on 8 June the provisional government announced the people's vote on the issue: fusion, and by a great majority. Then

Parma and Modena followed suit and, with Manin's approval, Venice also voted for fusion.

'This could give us another Kingdom of Italy,' said Christina Belgiojoso, whom Gabriella had gone to see. 'And Giuseppe is behaving with great restraint, though he and the republicans demanded the safeguard that, after the war is over, Lombardy should be free to decide its own political destiny.'

'People say your newspapers, *The Crusader* and *Cross of Savoy*, did much to influence the vote for fusion.'

'I hope so,' said her patron, smoothing down the folds of her grey robe. 'It is the surest way to achieve freedom, I feel. Now, have you set a date for leaving Milan to go to Paris?'

The question came as a shock, even though she herself had told the Princess about her interview with Verdi.

'No, I haven't,' confessed Gabriella, glancing away to avoid her patron's shrewd black eyes. 'It's difficult to think of such things when . . .'

'When the fate of Lombardy hangs in the balance,' interposed Christina Belgiojoso. 'I understand it is a time for all of us to set personal matters in abeyance . . . but don't leave it too long, my dear Gabriella. We don't want Signor Verdi's enthusiasm to cool for you.'

Her patron's words made Gabriella blush, for she knew it was more than the outcome of the war that made her reluctant to leave Milan. It was ridiculous, for she had cut herself off from him completely, and the deep hurt she knew she had inflicted had been confirmed by the cold unfriendly look the Contessa Forro had directed at her that very morning from her carriage as it passed Gabriella by on her way to her patron's residence.

Then something happened that made her forget everything.

Along with thousands of others she had gone to listen to Giuseppe Garibaldi address Milan. Up high on the balcony of the Albergo Marino stood the legendary fighter who had formed an Italian Legion in South America and brought glory to it and every Italian by its defence of Montevideo against the Argentinians. He was not covered in gold braid but, like his officers, clad in a simple red shirt.

'People of Milan,' he called. 'I thank you all for your enthusiasm. But this is not the time to talk and shout. We must act. The enemy has recovered courage and assurance. We must cut off his progress in this part of the land. The united Fatherland must not only present a bold front to the Austrians, but to the world in general. Long live Milan! Long live the independence of Italy.'

It was then it happened. Just as the famous guerrilla fighter altered his position to acknowledge the cheers and homage, Gabriella's eyes were attracted to the face of one of his officers standing behind. Like many of Garibaldi's men his face was bearded and his hair wild and dishevelled, and for some time as she examined him she was uncertain. Then, as if someone had said something to amuse, the man threw back his head and laughed. Then she was certain. She had found Nico at last!

# Chapter Twelve

The horse pounded towards her at a furious rate and she squealed in alarm as it swerved away within inches of her. Again the rider galloped away across the huge ground on which the Austrians had so recently paraded. Filled with irrepressible laughter and fresh alarm as the horse returned in a direct line towards her, Gabriella felt that she had returned to the past. He was just the same wild, carefree boy; only now he had the horse he had always wanted, and his lanky frame was solid with muscle, like that of a gladiator come to life. For the third time Gabriella steeled herself to remain still as horse and rider plunged towards her, but this time the game had changed and she saw he had started to spin a rope above his head. As the circle widened, with a flick of his wrist he was snaking it towards her. Open mouthed in astonishment, Gabriella watched as the circle dropped down about her head and bound her arms to her body like a trussed chicken.

'Are you a gaucho?' she laughed as Nico slowed his horse to a walk and pulled her towards him.

'We certainly lived like them, riding with Garibaldi in South America. We looked like them too, for without chaparajos the pampas grass cuts wickedly,' he grinned, jumping down from the American saddle whilst keeping his hold on the rope.

'Now, are we to say hello? After all, that is why I met you here,' she smiled. 'Or are you going to show me more tricks?'

For answer Nico tugged on the rope. Unable to keep her balance, she fell forward against his body.

'Hello, Lark,' he murmured gruffly. 'It's been a long time.'

For the briefest moment she looked up into the familiar brown eyes, moist like her own with tears; then, unable to help herself, she laid her face against his red shirt and wept as his arms held her tight and safe.

'We must never part in anger again,' she said at last, drying her eyes and laughing with happiness at being with him again. 'And there are such things as letters! Just one would have stopped me worrying about you.'

'I'm not sure about that,' retorted Nico, fingering a scar that ran along under his cheekbone. 'I've seen the gates of Hell more than once open up before me – and not a word about this to my friends,' he said, sheepishly wiping away the tears from his cheeks.

'Don't you Garibaldini ever cry?'

'Not with women. We're usually too busy kissing them,' he responded with a wide smile that showed off his teeth above the bushy black growth of his curly beard.

'You haven't changed at all!' she teased.

'Haven't I?' he said with some disappointment.

'Well, you're taller,' Gabriella reflected, narrowing her eyes as if to appraise him. 'And you are very brown. I think our old Master Menotti would be very frightened to meet up with these,' she said, touching his shoulders.

As her fingers came into contact with the hard, resistant mound of solid muscle under the red shirt, Gabriella's eyes widened in wonder. Seeing her reaction, Nico chuckled, his brown eyes narrowed and gleaming.

'You're with a soldier now, Lark, not some piano player.'

'I'm no longer Lark,' she said primly, annoyed at the strange fascination the contact with blatant masculine power had given her.

'You may have acquired fine manners and you may be the loveliest woman I've seen since we landed, but you'll always be my Lark. When our General told us we were coming here, I knew it was destiny that we should meet . . . I did wonder if you might have forgotten me.'

'How could you think that?' she said, seeing the vulnerable look in his brown eyes. 'Though how I recognized you under all this,' she teased, ruffling the shaggy dark hair and beard in order to lighten the feelings between them. '. . . What happened to your friend Angelo?'

'His sea legs were better than mine, he stayed on board. Me, I fell in love with Giuseppe Garibaldi, so I stayed in port at Montevideo. I'll stay with him until he sends me away or a bullet takes me from him.'

'Will you all fight soon?' asked Gabriella as they walked through the trees in front of the Castello.

'As soon as we get arms for all the men who are volunteering. We're having to make do with the uniforms the Austrians left behind: they'll have to be dyed.'

'Will you be leaving soon?' asked Gabriella anxiously.

'Any time . . . Why, will you come with us?'

'Fight with the army?'

'Why not? Garibaldi's Anita does. You'd love the life, it's so free. Remember those stinking alleys and courtyards – there's none of that, my love: you stretch out under the stars. You don't miss a family either when you have comrades in arms: they are everything to each other.'

His words prompted her to speak.

'And I had a family, Nico. I had a mother, and now I know she drowned. Didn't she?'

'Oh, are you still fidgeting your mind about the past!' he snapped irritably. 'What do you want a past for when you have the present? Is it because you hope to find you're more than a beggar girl?' he asked, his eyes filled with resentment. 'Have you met a noble who is disappointed that you are a commoner?'

'No, that is not it at all,' she flashed angrily. 'I want to know, I have a right to know her name . . . I nearly drowned at Como, and I saw her face above the waves – yours too, and your hand reaching out to me . . . Please Nico . . . please tell me, don't leave me in darkness. Why should it matter to you?'

'I . . . always thought it might part us,' he responded slowly, putting a cheroot between his lips. 'And it might have got my kin into trouble. If I tell you, I must first have your promise that you will never seek revenge.'

'Revenge? Was my mother murdered?'

'No,' said the soldier, throwing the reins over the head of his horse and letting it graze as he leant against the trunk of a tree. 'As you guessed, your mother did drown; so too would you have done, except that I pulled you out like a wet, frightened kitten. It's so long ago that I can hardly remember it myself. I was young too, remember.'

'But how did it happen? Did my father drown too?'

'No, there was just a coachman and postillion and some sort of woman servant: a maid, I expect. There had been a violent storm and the river was already swollen with the melted snows brought down from the mountains . . . I think I was sheltering from the cloud-burst when I saw the carriage crossing the bridge down in the valley. The next moment the carriage was falling sideways as the main supports of the bridge were swept away. Then all the passengers fell into the water.' Nico paused for breath, his dark eyes serious as he recalled the grim scene.

'It was no deeper than a man's armpits, but within seconds they were swept downstream. I ran as fast as I could but it was too late . . . Then, incredibly, I saw this little girl clinging to a spoke of one of the wheels. I think I called to you just as the current whipped you away. I shall never forget your bright blue dress – it ballooned out like the petals of a flower. That is what saved you. And when I leant out and pulled you towards the bank I remember the shock of seeing your eyes – the first blue eyes that I had ever seen, as deep as violets.' He turned to her with a look of tenderness.

'But why were you afraid to tell me this, Nico?' she asked gently.

The lanky, red-shirted figure beside her turned away and drew on his cigar. Then he shrugged. 'I have your promise?'

'Yes.'

'When they searched for the bodies, my uncles found the coachman unconscious on the bank further downstream – there were many valuables. You can guess what they did.'

'My mother also?' gasped Gabriella in horror.

'No, but I feared what might happen to you, so I ran away

236

with you that night. We ended up eventually at Genoa, where we met up with a party of peasant boys going to London to work as organ-grinders . . . you know the rest.'

'Did my mother have a Christian burial?'

'What do you think?' smiled Nico cynically. 'I didn't hold with what they did, but neither would I see them put to death for it.'

'Could you take me there?' asked Gabriella, feeling breathless with emotion. 'And my name, tell me my name, Nico . . . my father could still be alive.'

'Your family name is Balziano.'

Balziano. The name struck like a blow: it seemed incredible; she stared at Nico in disbelief. The Villa Pizzo flashed into her mind and the strange disturbing effect her visit there had had upon her. She remembered especially the beautiful window at the mausoleum where, childlike, she had peered through the black iron gate at the blue Madonna with the baby Jesus. It all fitted, in a sense it seemed obvious, yet still she could not quite believe it, could not comprehend the full import of Nico's revelation. 'This is extraordinary,' she murmured. 'Of all the families . . . yet he felt it.'

'Who felt what?' asked Nico sharply.

'Just someone who thought I resembled the Marchesa Giulia Balziano.' Gabriella's thoughts were racing. 'Oh Nico, will you come with me somewhere this evening? You're good at breaking in, and there are no Austrians to stop us. Say you will.'

It seemed a lifetime since the Princess Belgiojoso had casually pointed out the Palazzo Balziano to her. Later that evening, as Gabriella hurried to meet Nico outside its entrance, it was all she could do not to run. Since hearing Nico's story she had felt many different emotions. Now she just felt impatient to find the answers to what had been veiled in shadow for so many years.

It was still quite light, but no one seemed to be paying any attention to the Garibaldino officer pacing impatiently up and down in front of the long façade of the palazzo.

'You're supposed to be the eager one,' Nico commented when she approached.

'I'm sorry I'm late. I had to finish some Geography.'

'Geography at a time like this!' expostulated Nico with a roar of laughter. 'It's unbelievable!'

'It's unbelievable that I am here at all. Before March I was locked away like a novice. Do you think you can get in?' she asked anxiously.

'Not from here: it's too public. It will have to be over the wall bordering the park. Does the Contessa . . . Marchesa wish to remain here and enter by the front entrance?' he enquired sarcastically.

'Not without my coronet,' she giggled, still unable to grasp the reality, for with him it seemed as if they were participating in some childhood adventure.

The wall surrounding the garden was high, but with one throw Nico hurled his rope over a stout branch of a tree and, like a sailor mounting rigging, he was quickly on top of the wall and holding down his arm with a carefree grin.

'Care to join me?'

'It's impossible dressed like this.'

'Take it off then,' he said jauntily as he disappeared from sight.

Cursing all her petticoats, Gabriella approached the stout door in the wall. After a time the impatient curses from the other side of the wood ceased and the door swung open.

'It's like a jungle in here,' commented Nico, pushing back the door after she had entered. As he wrenched the rusty bolts back into position, Gabriella looked round, filled with curiosity and expectation. But, unlike her visit to the Villa Pizzo, as she and her old companion hastened past vine-covered statues and overgrown fountains, she saw nothing that stirred a memory in the abandoned garden.

Before the first green-shuttered window under a portico, Nico halted. Using brute force, he broke apart the wood with the point of a heavy dagger. Likewise he dealt with the window. Minutes later he opened the door into the darkness of the palazzo.

'There's probably a rat's ball taking place here,' he chuckled, as she lighted the two candles she had brought. As they sputtered into life, Gabriella saw that they were standing in a corridor off which was a large kitchen.

'Do you want me to hold your hand?' asked Nico, his voice echoing abnormally loud in the stillness. 'Because if not, I'm going to find the wine cellar . . . that is, with your permission, Marchesa.'

Before Gabriella could answer he had marched away, his laughter reverberating and shattering the silence. Enough to frighten any rats away, she thought, as she wandered along the damp-smelling corridors. Her candle gave only a poor light but, as she went through a door, despite the pressing darkness, she could tell she had left the domestic quarters of the palazzo.

'I must have more light,' she murmured, and walked around the edge of the room until she came upon a candelabra. As soon as she put her candle flame to the dozen or so wax tapers, the blackness fell away and her surroundings were suffused in golden light. She was standing in a long, richly decorated gallery, its walls hung with large tapestries and family portraits. Here I will find them, she thought, moving slowly along the dusty marble floor.

She thought she was prepared, but when the moment came her lips parted on a sigh of shock and wonder, for it was like looking up into a mirror. It really was true, then . . .

'Why, we could be sisters,' she exclaimed. Unhearing, unseeing, the Marchesa Giulia Balziano smiled down at her lost daughter. The moment was poignant with sadness; Gabriella moved forward and laid the palm of her hand against the canvas, as if to try and reach beyond the barrier of oils to the warm flesh of the woman. But the canvas of the image captured so long ago was cold like the chill of the deserted palazzo. She shivered and moved on to the next portrait and the ache in her heart deepened, for here was her father, Andrea Balziano, who she knew had been sent to Spielberg along with the other Lombard liberals.

'And today Milan is free, Papa,' she whispered. Tears

flooded Gabriella's eyes as she studied the scholarly, aquiline features of the father she could not remember. And she uttered a deep sob as the lively, intelligent eyes regarded her. 'Oh, it is too cruel!' she exclaimed out loud in a mixture of anger and grief. She remembered Agnese Prioni telling her the year that he had died; the bitter irony made her cry out again. 'I was alive when you were set free – we could have been together. Now you are lost to me . . . I will never know you!'

With relief she heard Nico's footsteps approaching the gallery. It was time to go, for she could not bear to stay longer; it was all too desolate and tragic.

'Are you feeling happier now?' he asked, holding up a bottle of wine. 'I am . . . why, have you seen this? It's the little fish I pulled out of the river.'

Wanting no more, Gabriella shook her head and showed no interest in going to see the small painting he had stopped before.

'Oh well, you might change your mind later, and I'm not coming back,' said Nico, taking the miniature from the wall and placing it within his shirt. 'I take it you want to go?'

'Yes,' said Gabriella. 'If I ever come back it will be to let in the sunshine.'

Outside the light had almost gone and, as Nico climbed back out of the window and pushed the shutters closed, Gabriella wondered why the palazzo had been left unoccupied for so long.

'It's strange the Austrians have kept it as it is,' she said.

'You should be grateful to them,' commented the young man as he walked through the grounds with her. 'Otherwise greedy relatives would have taken everything by now.'

Just as when he had spoken the name Balziano, the implication of what he had just said struck home, and Gabriella was gradually seized with silent laughter that erupted into bitter, hysterical mirth.

'I sent him away. I lost him needlessly! And I could have sent her away instead.'

'Lost who? What are you talking about?' asked Nico, seizing

her arms in a grip so painful that it pulled her up as sharply as if he had slapped her.

'Nothing,' she gasped, feeling that she would break apart with grief. 'I suddenly realized who it is who owns the Balziano land. It is I!'

The next day, Gabriella was preparing to go for lunch when one of cleaners came running after her. 'Signorina Pepe, there is one of Garibaldi's officers wishing to speak with you urgently outside. He says it cannot wait.'

It must be Nico, Gabriella thought as she picked up her skirts and ran hastily towards the entrance to the street. She was about to say, 'You shouldn't call here', when her eyes noted his bulging saddle bags.

'Was that you singing a while ago?' he asked. 'I'm impressed,' he said as Gabriella nodded. 'As you can see, we're moving out to Brescia. I've come to say goodbye . . . unless you'll come along?'

'That's not possible,' she said with a fond smile.

'No, I rather thought you'd say that, especially after listening to you. I thought you should have this, after all the effort I went to last night,' he said, placing the miniature in her hands. 'And, Gabriella Pepe,' he said, using her name with deliberation as his eyes bore into hers possessively. 'If the Piedmontese army cannot hold Radetzky away from Milan, I'm coming back for you!'

'I'm sure they'll not fail,' she said, reaching up and pressing her lips against his cheek. 'Take care, Nico. As always I will pray for your safety.'

Her childhood friend flung his strong arms about her and pressed her to him. Then, before she could protest, he had given her a kiss that left her lips bruised and her body gasping for air.

'The ladies are much more responsive in South America,' he laughed, leaping up on to his saddle. 'But it will keep me happy for a little time.'

And then he was galloping away, whooping like a schoolboy, with the feathers in his hat streaming out behind.

241

The fierceness of Nico's kiss filled Gabriella with alarm. She had been reunited with the only family she had known: finding that she was a Balziano had not changed that. But what had changed was Nico: she had deluded herself that he was still the boy of Blackfriars, whereas he was a Garibaldino officer who had lived life to the full. All the world knew that his master had seen Anita from the deck of a ship and, only hours after he had snapped shut the eyeglass, he had carried her away. Nico, she knew, was wilful too. If his boyhood desire were still alive, she realized he would not lift out his arms in invitation as he had once done from that barge on the river Thames; instead he might take her! If Luciano Forro were still alive, would he care?

News had come of victory at Custozza, to add to those at Pastrengo and Goito. After that, though, all news of the Piedmont army's progress was vague. Then, as quickly as revolt had broken out, news of disaster came. It seemed that hardly had the Garibaldini left with their recruits than, from the direction of Lodi, the Piedmontese army was falling back in disarray towards the city. Unexpected, unbelievable! People were wild with grief and terror as every hour was bringing the enemy closer.

'Oh, they'll bury us alive in quick-lime like they did to those poor folk during the *Cinque Giornate*,' wailed a woman with her apron clutched before her face. 'Oh, that feeble King has betrayed us all.'

'But he's coming to make a stand outside the city,' comforted the woman next to her.

'But is he? Can we believe in anything we are told?' grumbled others as they began to make barricades in response to Giuseppe Mazzini's appeal from his Committee of Public Safety.

There had been fear during the uprising, but it had been mixed with hope and an energy that had been born of countless years of frustration. Now the city seemd seized with a paralysis of fear, and the work on the defences was carried out in grim silence. Inside the city, fifty thousand National Guards were

242

standing ready. If the city were to burn around their ears it seemed a fate preferable to becoming the victims of the Croatian and Bohemian troops. On 4 August, the enemy, having repaired the cut bridge at Lodi, advanced. They made their attack on the Piedmontese army at about one o'clock in the afternoon. The noise was deafening, and the fighting was fiercest outside the Porta Romana, where an ever-increasing number of shells came flying over the walls into the city. No one could think of anything except that the enemy must be kept out!

'No capitulation!' people muttered as they ran to take cover every time an explosion sounded near at hand. 'A fight to the death! No capitulation!'

From three o'clock until nightfall, the cannons boomed, their sound mingled with the high-pitched screams of men and horses as they were killed or wounded. From the north a fierce storm approached to play like some terrible orchestra for the men struggling below. The air became oppressive and taut: huge jagged flashes of lightning lit up the skies and added to the terror of flames leaping upwards from houses hit by cannon in the suburbs. Word spread: the King had moved his headquarters within the walls to Conte Greppi's palace.

At first light, people tumbled into the streets to take over the work of digging the defensive ditches from those who had toiled all night. Suddenly, from outraged mouth to mouth, spread the news that during the night Carlo Alberto had made a convention with Field Marshal Radetzky: Habsburg troops would be entering to take possession of Milan the following morning at eight o'clock!

With their bare hands they had ousted Radetzky; now he had been offered the key of the city. Towards the Greppi Palace everyone ran to scream fury at the Piedmontese King.

'No capitulation! No capitulation!'

'No capitulation! To the death, to the death!' screamed Giuseppina, her face streaming with tears as she raised her fist in the air along with hundreds of others.

'*Tradimento! Tradimento!*'

Tall, sad, looking more like a priest or ghost than the royal head of an army, King Carlo Alberto looked silently down upon them. With a sad gesture he lifted thin white hands and tried to speak, then shook his head and turned to the short figure of Cesare Cantù who stood beside him. Suddenly both men on the balcony started back as a shot rang out; with a another gesture of despair, Carlo Alberto withdrew from the balcony.

The next day, Milan woke to find the King had slipped away in the night and that the provisional government had agreed to the armistice with Radetzky. The Piedmont army had forty-eight hours to cross back over the Ticino into Piedmont, and citizens wishing to leave had twenty-four hours' grace to do so. The news was like a bombshell; everywhere there were men and women weeping.

'What are you going to do?' asked Giuseppina, throwing her clothes into a valise. 'Will you come with me to my parents at Bergamo? Perhaps you might be safer there. If you do not leave Lombardy you might be arrested for what you did at La Scala . . . and heaven alone knows what the troops will do to women when they enter the city.'

'Thank you, Giuseppina,' said Gabriella with a grateful smile. 'I thought I could ask to go with the Princess Belgiojoso to Paris. She is sure to leave, for she will be at the top of Radetzky's list. I'm only a small fish in comparison.'

'Then at least you'll see Verdi,' said Giuseppina, sitting on top of the bulging leather lid to squash down her belongings. 'And you've finished here anyway, whereas I have five more years – oh, it will be so boring here without you . . . and even more boring with my parents.'

'Ah, but think of all the fine tenors you'll meet in Bergamo,' teased Gabriella, trying to cheer them both up.

Giuseppina was ready to leave, and the two women turned tearfully to each other.

'Goodbye, my dear, dear Giuseppina,' Gabriella murmured, putting her arms around the student's shoulders. 'I will write soon. When I am settled in Paris and you have finished your studies, I hope you will come to see me.'

'I will, dear Gabriella,' wept Giuseppina. 'And I shall pray that you will find happiness in France. Now go quickly and make your arrangements for leaving. I could not bear to think of you here when they march in.'

Taking Giuseppina's advice, Gabriella hurried from the Conservatorio. Outside there were anxious parents who had arrived to collect their sons and daughters. To those whom she knew she gave a wave of goodbye.

To witness the universal grief was terrible: all had been lost; all given away within hours. Not only would slavery begin again, but also retribution: one felt the fear under the heartbreaking scenes of grief as wives strove to comfort their weeping husbands as though they were small boys.

First Gabriella went to say goodbye to Mazzini. But she could not find him: she was told that he had gone to join Garibaldi's forces. Next, she went to the Princess's, where frenzied packing was taking place.

'Ah, good, you had the sense to come here. We shall be leaving within the hour,' said Christina Belgiojoso, leafing through a stack of papers. 'Did you bring your luggage or does it need collecting?'

'I can bring it, there isn't a great deal. Do you know if the Volunteers have been informed of what is happening in Milan? Where will they be sent?'

'I do not know,' said Christina Belgiojoso, concentrating on her papers.

'Could you find out?'

Christina Belgiojoso looked up in surprise at the urgency in her protégée's voice.

'I'm not sure that I can. The provisional government has left to seek the sanctuary of Lugano. Things are in chaos, Gabriella, but I'm sure someone has thought to notify their commanding officer.'

'You mean that if they haven't they could still be fighting?' gasped Gabriella, the blood draining from her face. 'Oh please, couldn't you see that someone deals with it?'

'I'll see what can be done,' said the Princess hurriedly. 'Now go and make ready. Do not delay, we shall be leaving soon!'

There was one more person that Gabriella had to see; one last person. She ran like the wind towards the Via dei Bigli. As she gained its entrance she heard a horseman coming up behind her, and for one wild moment she thought it might be him. But the rider was not wearing the uniform of the Lombard sharp-shooters; he was dressed in the red shirt of the Garibaldini.

'Nico!'

'I told you I would come! You're lucky I spotted you – what are you doing here?'

'I must say goodbye to the Contessa Forro.'

'You'll probably find she's fleeing with the thousands of others that are pouring out of the city gate.'

'No, I don't think so,' said Gabriella with certainty. 'Please don't delay for me, Nico. You should not have put yourself in danger . . . the Princess Belgiojoso says there is a seat for me in her carriage.'

'Good, I'll wait and take you there,' said Nico in a calm voice.

There was no time to argue or even to question, so she turned and approached Luciano Forro's home.

'Really, I am most surprised to see you, Signorina Pepe, and today of all days,' said the Contessa Wiera Forro with considerable coldness.

'I will not impose upon you any longer than is necessary,' said Gabriella, pained by the aloof manner of one who had always been so friendly. 'I know you hold me in a poor light, Contessa. But before I leave Milan, I must speak, because what I have recently discovered makes it possible for me to do so. What I did at La Scala I did out of love . . . I believed Luciano might be ruined if I did not break with him. But this week I discovered that Giulia Balziano was my mother. That means the danger to Luciano and his family does not exist. Things are so disordered that it probably does not make any difference now; but I could not bear you to think ill of me . . .' Gabriella could say no more. Her voice faltered and tears fell from her eyes.

Wiera Forro rose slowly from her chair and held her hands out towards her.

'Forgive me,' she said, her voice filled with emotion. 'How could I, how could Luciano have been so foolishly deceived? It was Flavia?'

Gabriella didn't answer. It didn't matter any more. All that mattered was that Wiera Forro had forgiven her. The two women embraced.

'Giulia's daughter!' the Contessa continued with tears sparkling in the depths of her eyes. 'I've always felt it every time you entered a room. I thought she had come back to me – that is why I gave you her brooch.'

'I should have returned it to you,' said Gabriella, taking it from her purse. 'But despite the fact I knew you were angry, I couldn't bear to part with it. And see, Mama is wearing it here.'

'You went to the palazzo?' asked the Contessa in surprise as Gabriella showed her the miniature of her mother and herself. 'But tell me, how did you discover the truth about your background?'

'From the boy who saved my life. He told me our coach fell into a river in the spring floods and Mama was drowned.'

'So that is what happened,' sighed Wiera Forro, looking down wistfully at the portrait of Giulia Balziano and the small girl that was Gabriella. 'No one knew: there were just terrible fears that you had been set upon by brigands on the way to Vienna – she was on her way to request a pardon for your poor father. Of course it broke his heart when he was released from Spielberg.'

'Poor Papa,' murmured Gabriella. 'Oh, there is so much I would like to ask you, but I am leaving for Paris with the Princess Belgiojoso within the hour. Will you not leave also?'

'Certainly not!' exclaimed the Contessa. 'I am Polish. I will not run from my home for *tedeschi*! And if any one of them threatens me, I shall shoot him,' she said calmly, her grey eyes filled with resolution. 'And if in return I am shot, they will have reunited me with my husband. We cannot all leave Milan, and I feel I have a responsibility to my staff and to the poor families who must stay and bear it. Besides, I'll not let them turn this palazzo into a stable for their horses.'

247

'Then I shall stay with you!' declared Gabriella.

Wiera Forro smiled and patted Gabriella's hand. 'No, you are young. Fly to freedom while you can. I only pray that Giovanni and Luciano will be able to do the same, but the way things are going I fear I may never see them again.'

'But won't they be given the same forty-eight hours that the main Piedmontese army has been given?' asked Gabriella, returning to the anxiety she had touched upon with the Princess Belgiojoso.

'*If* they are told – but that I doubt,' said the Contessa bitterly. 'I have letters from Luciano and Giovanni – so too has the Contessa Manara – and they all relate the same story of neglect and abominable lack of communications. And if once again they have been forgotten, and no word gets through, they are in danger of being cut off and surrounded.'

Gabriella looked at Wiera Forro and bit her lip in anxiety as she wondered whether the Princess had managed to do anything.

'I think I know who could help them,' she said slowly. 'He would get through to them when others would fail. He is the boy who saved my life, and now he is an officer of the Garibaldini. He is waiting for me downstairs. Nico could save the Lombard Volunteers!'

# Chapter Thirteen

The road leading out of the city was, as Nico had described, packed with traffic; thousands of people moving along as far as the eye could see. And it was not only nationalist leaders like the society hostess Contessa Maffei who were departing, but poor people, carrying their belongings in sacks and sheets. All were fleeing away from the horror of what the troops might do on entering Milan. For besides witnessing with their own eyes the evidence of recent cruelty, stories had found their way to the city of villages like Melegnano and Castelnuovo being burned. Progress was slow on the road and the atmosphere was dreadful: most people were sobbing their hearts out to have left their homes and the beautiful spires of their cathedral. Would any of them see it again, wondered Gabriella, turning around in the saddle to take one long last look.

'Your Contessa Forro is very persuasive,' declared Nico, who was riding alongside her.

'But not enough for you to go on beyond Bergamo.'

'I take my orders only from the General,' he said stubbornly.

'Oh, was it he who ordered you to come and find me?' she mocked.

'As a scout I can cover a lot of territory. It depends where I think is of interest,' Nico grinned, his brown eyes raking over her body. 'At least you have my protection and company for part of the way, whereas if I had agreed to be the messenger you both wished me to be, I wouldn't have had yours and you would be sitting with your Lombard Princess in her carriage and you would be very bored . . . Come on, admit it: aren't you excited?'

'No, I'm terrified, and that is not the same thing at all. I will probably break my neck falling off this horse before I get within a kilometre of either the Volunteers or the Austrians,' said Gabriella glaring at him. 'Still, many of the Volunteers are my friends, so perhaps I should try to reach them rather than you, a stranger.'

'Oh, I think you'll see the enemy soon enough,' said Nico, spitting away the butt of his cigar. 'But why you are willing to risk your neck to warn these aristocrats I can't imagine. If Garibaldi had been in charge right from the beginning, how different things might have been. I expect these Volunteers have made very poor soldiers if the Contessa's son is anything to go by. Too much book learning. I've never seen so many books – every wall was covered with them.'

'The Contessa took you into the library?' asked Gabriella, so surprised that she did not bother to defend the reputation of Luciano and his friends.

'Oh yes, she really gave me the confidence to face the insurgents! Made me sign a declaration before two wizened witnesses as to who you were . . . just in case I am foolish enough to get shot.'

'I didn't know,' said Gabriella. 'There was no need for that.'

'No, I didn't think so either: it made me feel that the finger of Fate was pointing at me. But she is a formidable woman. I thought she might shoot me if I didn't co-operate and, as you were still pulling on breeches, I couldn't escape. This is where we turn off: see how they stare; they think we are mad.'

With a wave and a nod, Gabriella acknowledged the warnings as they took the road towards Treviglio. Until now they had moved at walking pace. Now the test of whether she could handle the stallion that the Contessa had provided her with was imminent.

'Meteor will outpace anything a chasseur may have,' Wiera Forro had said when she had given Gabriella some of Giovanni's old riding clothes. 'Are you sure you must go? Let me send a groom.'

'No, I could not live with myself if I thought Luciano and

Giovanni and my friends from the Conservatorio had perished for want of a message. Do you have a copy of the armistice?'

'Yes,' replied the Contessa. 'I will give it to you before you leave. I would not let you go if I thought the Garibaldino was really intending to abandon you. I cannot think he will,' she added. 'But I hope you will be safe with him. He seems very wild.'

'Yes, I know. But I grew up with him,' reassured Gabriella.

'Ah yes, I was forgetting,' sighed Wiera Forro sadly. Then, placing her palms either side of Gabriella's face, she pressed her lips to her forehead.

'God protect you. None of us knows what tomorrow will bring. You may have to decide, Gabriella, whether you take upon yourself the burden of your rank, or whether you continue with your career. I know that you and my son found love in the past; what you are about to do is no more than I would have done for his father. Giulia was my friend and, no matter what happens, remember that I have taken upon myself her role as your mother. You have her brooch?'

As she followed after Nico, Gabriella felt once again for the butterfly brooch which was pinned to the inside of a silk scarf. She prayed that Wiera Forro would be safe.

'Time to stop day-dreaming,' interrupted Nico, calling back to her from where he was riding a few lengths ahead. 'Now, remember all that I have said. You must establish right from the beginning who is master. There is no time to bribe him with little delicacies like you did with that spoilt bear Pepe. You give him a taste of the whip. If he plays up, you give it to him again, only harder. After that he'll forget you're a novice with any luck.'

Since leaving the stables and the city gate, the stallion beneath her had become increasingly restive. Now Gabriella felt him positively trembling with excitement and impatience. It only took Nico's horse in front to break into trot and, without seeking permission, Meteor kicked back his heels and, with a whinny of delight, was off.

Somehow Gabriella managed to keep her seat, but she lost the reins and had to snatch hold of the tossing mane. She wanted to scream for Meteor to stop, but all her efforts were concentrated on staying on, and speech was impossible when every moment her insides seemed in danger of hitting her rattling teeth.

'You must go with him!' ordered Nico, snatching up the fallen reins and gradually slowing the pace until they were trotting. 'Grip with your legs and feel his rhythm.'

Gradually, under Nico's instructions, the strangeness fell away, and Gabriella began to feel more like a partner with the horse and not so much a bundle of bones being bumped and shaken about. She was just beginning to enjoy herself, when suddenly Nico swerved to the left and waved for her to follow.

'I don't need to rest yet,' she said, even though her brow was wet with sweat.

'Get down and put your hand over your horse's muzzle,' he directed urgently.

She didn't understand but she obeyed.

'Quiet!' he hissed as she was about to speak.

The drumming sound of galloping horses cut across the peaceful sound of bird song and the heavy breathing of their own horses. With her eyes fixed on Nico in case he wanted to communicate with her, she heard the hoofbeats drew nearer and sharper. She closed her hands gently over the muzzle of her horse and remained motionless as the jingling sound of harness and then the terrifying sight of metal helmets with waving horsehair plumes passed along the top of the brush behind which they were hiding.

'Chasseurs,' she gasped, when the sound had died away. 'You saw them long before they arrived.'

'If you wear a red shirt, you have to,' replied Nico, his tanned face creasing into a smile. 'It makes for a better scout.'

'Take this jacket, then. It will be safer for you.'

'I am a Garibaldino!' he exclaimed proudly. 'I won my red shirt in the defence of the Republic of Uruguay, and I'll be buried in it.'

During the next few hours, his prowess as a scout was

252

continually demonstrated, for the road was busy with the enemy and they constantly had to wait – sometimes for more than an hour – as baggage and supplies went by. In view of these regular dangers, Gabriella breathed a sigh of relief when Nico made no sign of leaving at the turn-off for Bergamo.

'Will your General be angry with you if you are away too long?' she enquired later. They were making camp for the night in the shelter of a stone wall bordering a plantation of mulberry trees.

'Likely have me shot,' laughed Nico, unwrapping what looked like a tent. 'I'll take my chance. You wouldn't have one out here on your own. As soon as we have got our message through to the Volunteers' headquarters at Preseglie we can return to Bergamo. Would you like a little supper?' he asked.

'You're very resourceful,' she smiled, accepting a handful of raisins.

'You have to be, riding the plains of South America,' he said, squatting down and pushing a little dried grass in between a criss-cross of twigs. 'You are definite in your plans?'

'Yes I am,' said Gabriella gently, guessing he would not like her answer.

'What if I did not let you go?'

'Then you would spoil my chances.'

'Do you think I care about that!'

The light banter had disappeared and she heard the ruthless note in Nico's voice. Gabriella walked away a few paces to break up the conversation, but he sprang lightly to his feet and followed her. In the darkness his presence was dominating: she felt as though a burning brand were behind her. She moved, but his arms encircled her and prevented it.

'Don't say goodbye. Don't let us part,' he urged, his voice breaking with tenderness. 'Think how happy we were together as children. What fun and laughter we shared. Do you remember our boat trips on the Thames . . . the night we stole the coal?'

'Yes, I remember,' she smiled, her eyes filling with tears as she thought of how he had made life endurable; of the nights they had lain close together for warmth and comfort when his voice, like now, had made her unafraid of darkness and danger. 'Remember the night you made us all line up and cut our wrists and swear to be blood brothers?' she said with a smile in her voice.

'You see?' he responded eagerly. 'There is too much that binds us – I've tried not to show how strongly I feel, but now . . .'

He whirled her around and his lips found hers with a force born of desperate passion. She moved backwards but, firm as a wall, his hands held her; her senses reeled as his strong, virile odour filled her nostrils and his mouth drew the life out of her.

'That is how I feel about you!' he gasped, pulling away. 'Tell me that you do not feel anything for me.'

Quivering, she could not reply, for the wildness of him, the primitive appeal of the taut muscular lines of his body beneath his thin clothing had set her body trembling. He felt it too for, lifting her to his mouth, he spun her round and round until she was so dizzy that she didn't know whether she stood or whether she was still, only that she must escape from the hot, torrid madness before it extinguished all reason.

'Ah, I could not believe how luscious, how ripe the curves of your body had become,' he said, his rough hands moving over the thin cotton of the shirt she wore. 'Lie with me in the grass, tell me you can love only me.'

'I'll always love you, Nico,' she said, pushing his hand away as it sought the bareness of her body through the torn material.

'That's not what I asked. Do you want to spend the rest of your life with me, bear my sons, be my wife as it was meant to be from the day God put your hand into mine?'

The rough, strong hands caught hold of hers, and Gabriella squeezed them in a helpless gesture. There was no denying that his world and his body, by its very maleness, had briefly aroused animal desires in her. But she knew it was not this alone he required. And she was no Anita to pledge herself to a soldier; her mind and aspirations could not be denied, and with a man like Nico both would be famished. Besides, she was consumed by a love that no other could challenge, and though she might never see him or hear his mellow voice again, there could be no other for her.

'It is not possible,' she said gravely, without prevarication. 'We are on different journeys. There will be someone else waiting to hold your hand and go with you.'

'But I know you love me!'

'I do. You were my father and my brother – now we are friends.'

'Your body was hot for mine!'

'It is not enough for either of us.'

'I don't understand – you want servants, baubles, a villa . . . Is that it?'

'No,' she said helplessly, for how could she make him understand about a man like Luciano Forro? 'I would not fit into your world. I would restrict you. And you could not help me to grow in the way that I need.'

'You have found love with another man!' he accused.

'Yes.'

'An aristocrat, no doubt!'

Gabriella sighed. 'It isn't that, Nico. I love because . . .'

'I don't want to hear!' howled the Garibaldino as though she had kicked him. He strode away, crashing his way through the undergrowth until darkness and distance hid his whereabouts. For an hour she waited for him to return, but he did not. Exhausted and miserable she wrapped herself in a blanket and went to sleep.

When she awoke, it was to the pale cold light of dawn. Her body felt as if the horse had kicked it all over the previous day. Not far away, the red-smocked figure of Nico was bending over a small fire on which was a tin canteen.

'Hello,' she said, feeling embarrassed after what had passed between them the night before. 'I didn't realize one could have so many parts of the body bruised with sitting a horse.'

'It will get better every hour once you're back in the saddle,' said Nico, handing her a small mug of coffee.

'Did you sleep?' she asked timidly.

'After smoking all my cigars,' he said with a small, rueful laugh. 'Don't worry: as soon as I cross swords with someone, I shall be my old self; especially,' he said meaningfully, 'if it happened to be with one of Contessa Forro's sons.'

There was nothing tentative in his assumption, and Gabriella made no attempt to refute it or tell him which of the sons had stolen her heart.

'I wouldn't blame you if you went on your way, Nico. I don't want you to take any risks because of me. There isn't far to go and I have got the idea of what to do now.'

'Maybe,' he said laconically. 'But nothing would keep me away from seeing what I must become.'

'Oh Nico,' she chuckled, unable to restrain her laughter as he minced towards the horses. 'Just because a man reads and studies, it doesn't mean he is an effeminate coward.'

'No,' he said, stopping the pantomime, his face filling with sadness as he looked towards her. 'I didn't think for one moment he would be – you couldn't love such a man. Come on, let's go and warn your Lombards. I'll not leave you: I couldn't bear to think of you captured and ending up as a thing of amusement for enemy troops.'

The headquarters they were heading for lay north of Brescia but, from a fleeing party of peasants whose dwelling had been fired that morning, they learnt that the Volunteers were at Gavardo, and that a force of some eight thousand of the enemy were encamped at Lonato preparing for an attack.

'So, they have not been informed!' cried Gabriella angrily, watching the little family continue on its way with their goat following along behind. 'And no doubt by now Carlo Alberto's army is safe. No one apparently cares what is happening to our soldiers here.'

'So let's forget headquarters and go direct to the fighters,' said Nico.

With a firm nod of agreement, Gabriella flicked the reins and prepared to follow on in the direction of Rezzato. As she did so something hummed past her cheek.

'Tyrolean chasseurs!' shouted Nico, uttering a curse in a language she did not understand. 'There are four coming from both sides. You'd better make a run for it and I'll divert them.'

'No, let's both go,' she cried, as another ball kicked up in the dirt beside her. 'I'll not leave you, Nico!'

The bearded soldier leant forward and grabbed the white silk scarf, yanking her towards him.

'You must, there are many lives at stake! I always thought it would be the General's blue eyes I'd take the bullet for. Instead . . . goodbye, Lark!'

Briefly the merry brown eyes, alive with audacity and daring, looked into hers; then, as he snatched a last kiss, he slapped the rump of her horse with the flat of his hand. Off Meteor shot, and like the first time she had experienced his full flight, Gabriella had to hang on for dear life. Desperately she gave little jerks to the right and left of the reins and, gaining control, she eventually managed to slow down the pace of the horse. Wiera Forro had given her a gun. Intending to support Nico in his stand, she dragged it out of the waistband of her breeches. As she wheeled the stallion's head around, she saw the chasseurs had completely surrounded Nico. His sabre glinted as it whirled and parried, and Gabriella raised her gun to take aim. But before she could even squeeze the trigger, the figure in the red shirt suddenly clutched at his chest.

'Nico!' she screamed, almost dropping the gun.

Horrified she saw her childhood companion fall to the ground. As the horsemen now galloped towards her, she realized he was dead. Hardly able to see for the choking tears that were filling her eyes, she turned Meteor and, bringing her hand down, urged him forward.

'Don't let them get me please!' she cried, filled with terror. 'Faster, please, faster!'

Her position was low in the saddle and she felt confident that she was putting distance between herself and her pursuers. But they were driving her west, and she was possessed by a nagging fear that she would never be able to get back, especially with such a large body of the enemy encamped near to the lake.

Suddenly, as she emerged through some trees, she saw a peasant boy cutting grass with a scythe.

'Are there *tedeschi* in your village?' she asked, slithering to a stop beside him.

The young boy shook his head and stared at her with his large soft eyes.

'They came and took all our food yesterday,' he said, swinging at the grass with a vicious blow.

'Will you do something for our army?' asked Gabriella, as the sound of galloping drew closer.

'Yes!' he said eagerly.

Quickly she pulled the copy of the armistice from her pocket. Unwrapping the silk scarf from her neck, she pinned the armistice and the butterfly brooch to the silk then dropped it down to the boy.

'Take this to Conte Forro at Gavardo and tell him the Austrians are preparing an attack from Lonato. Do you understand?'

'Yes!'

'Thank you, patriot. Now hide! *Viva l'Italia!*'

'*Viva l'Indipendenza!*' cried the boy, running behind a bush as a chasseur broke the cover of the trees.

At such a distance she knew she would not escape him. Her mouth went dry and her hand shook as she withdrew her gun. She held it up and pointed it before her. With a bellow of laughter the chasseur swerved his horse as she shot, and then he was upon her. She had nothing to protect herself with as his gloved hand reached out for her – only the whip. With a desperate cry, Gabriella lashed it across the man's face. He cried out in pain and grabbed her wrist as she pulled it back to hit him again. Terrified that he would wrench it from her grasp, she struggled with all her might, but his strength jerked her wrist back, though so quickly that he yelled in pain as the silver handle shot straight into his eye. She didn't lose the advantage and, remembering what Nico had done, she brought the whip down on his horse with all the force she possessed. It reared up in alarm and fright and she repeated the action. As it plunged away in terror, she applied her spurs and urged Meteor to fly.

Behind her was more danger than any obstacle that now

stood in her way, and she was riding the finest of beasts which took dykes and walls with ease. When her pursuers lost interest she had no idea. She just kept going until Meteor was covered in foam and both of them were near to collapse.

Throughout the hours of darkness, Gabriella lay shivering in her blanket and thought of Nico lying alone and cold in a meadow. She longed to return, to take him in her arms and weep over him, feeling it might ease the terrible pain of loss. As a girl she had cried as the widening waters of the Thames had separated them, but today she herself had led him to the banks of the River Lethe.

Hour after sleepless hour she tortured herself with the memory of their last moment together, and with the image of his body falling to the ground. At last the light of dawn came. Numb from cold and spent with grief she staggered to her feet and made ready to continue her journey.

In Milan, Gabriella had resigned herself to the fact that it might not be possible to say goodbye to her friends at Blevio. Now, like seeking the sanctuary of a nursery, she made her way to Agnese at Villa Rosa.

The door to the small, sand-coloured villa was always unlocked, but Gabriella nevertheless rang the door bell lest her sudden appearance should startle Agnese. Although, she thought wryly as brisk footsteps came towards the door, her wild, rain-sodden appearance was enough to alarm anyone. And indeed, as the door opened, Agnese Prioni cried out in alarm.

'Merciful Heaven! What has happened to you, child? – And there's Andrea only telling me yesterday that I should put a stop to worrying about you. Imagine, in times like these! Come at once to the kitchen and have something warming.'

Installed before Agnese's spotless white wooden table, Gabriella felt immediate relief as the dame bustled around and fussed over her. Here, nothing was expected of her, only an appetite and a willingness to listen. Despite the fact that all she really wished to do was to collapse into bed, she made a big effort with the hot soup which Agnese had instantly heated over her fire. Soon the little woman's chattering brought her brother down from his study. As startled as his sister had been, he nevertheless nodded in understanding when he looked at Gabriella.

'I told Agnese not to worry, but I see by your clothes you have done a little more than flee Milan. You travelled by horseback?'

'Yes, I left my horse with the owner of the Villa Besana.'

'No greater patriot,' commented Andrea Prioni with a nod. 'Did you know our lads drove out the Warasdiner Borderers and Hussars?'

'Yes, and they came to Milan to help us. So did the patriots of Monza; such joy there was that day! I left before the Austrians swaggered through the Porta Romana. It must have been a heartbreaking sight. With a friend I rode towards Lake Garda to tell the Volunteers about the armistice, but when Nico was killed by chasseurs I had to put my trust in a peasant boy,' she said, swallowing the last of the soup under his sister's watchful eye. 'Would you think me rude if I go straight up now, Professor?' she asked, suddenly feeling she might collapse with exhaustion.

'You shall go straightaway – and no more talk of politics,' said Agnese, directing a reproving glance towards her brother. 'Come along, Gabriella, rest is what you need. Rest and prayer. If the world prayed a little harder we might all be in a happier state,' she said, leading the way out of the kitchen and up the stairs to the bedroom. 'Do you remember the first time I led you up here, dear? You were all eyes and no body.'

'Well, you soon changed that, Agnese,' smiled Gabriella, pulling herself up by the banister, for she felt the last of her strength had gone.

'And I need to now, by the look of you,' scolded the spinster, turning around to glance over her shoulder. But, as she did so, somehow she missed her step, and the next instant she was falling backwards. Gabriella stepped forward, lifting up her arms to save her, but the body of the little woman bumped into her like a boulder, knocking her down the stairs as well.

'Oh I can't move!' Agnese shrieked.

'Is she all right?' asked Gabriella, hardly able to speak as Andrea rushed into the hall to see what had happened. From where she lay, Gabriella saw the elderly man kneel beside his sister. After a while, as her wails diminished, he helped her up into a sitting position.

'Everything functioning, dear?' he enquired. 'Just a little bruising, I expect. And what of you, Gabriella? Did she wind you?'

'Can you get help, Andrea?' uttered Gabriella, her lips twisting in agony. 'The pain is enormous.'

A broken leg at Blevio at the end of summer was akin to taking the veil. It was a bad break, and unless she wanted to risk limping like Pasta, she had to learn to be patient.

'I'm sorry to disappoint you,' said the doctor after he had examined Gabriella's leg for the second time. 'You will not be able to go to Paris. You must remain at Como!'

# Chapter Fourteen

Paris might have helped to divert Gabriella's mind from its gloomy thoughts, but the long stretches of solitude in her room did not, especially as her outlook gave her a view across the lake of the dome of Villa Pizzo's mausoleum. Constantly it made her think of the first time she had visited it, and that led her straightaway to him and the memory of the contempt in his eyes when he had departed from her that night at La Scala – departed from the rightful heir of Villa Pizzo. Gabriella's smile was ironic as she wiped away the condensation of her breath on the window pane. As yet she had not confided in Agnese about her discovery, nor did she really want to, for she suspected that their relationship might immediately change. For a moment she thought what being a Marchesa would be like: she would have her own box at La Scala, but so would she if she were a prima donna; she could wear expensive gowns and sit back in a lovely carriage for the Corso, but so could she as a prima donna; Gabriella pursed her lips, trying to think of the advantages, but what loomed in her mind more were the words of the American writer, Margaret Fuller, about loss of freedom. She turned away from the sight of the Archduke Ranieri's residence: between lounging around in a gilded drawing-room, or taking the stage in Paris, New York or London, there was no choice. As if to confirm this decision, the smiling face of Giuditta Pasta entered the room.

'I've come to say goodbye, *cara*. It's becoming a little chilly at Blevio.'

'Oh Git, will you desert me?'

'I'm afraid so, my dear, but I do have some news that will

262

cheer you. I have received a letter from Mr Lumley of Her Majesty's Theatre. He has invited me to consider a benefit concert the year after next.'

'Oh Git, I'm so pleased for you!' exclaimed Gabriella, her lips widening into a smile that lit up her whole face. 'I must be sure to book my seat to London for the year of 1850!'

'Yes, you must,' beamed the great prima donna. 'For he intimates that he is considering offering you a contract for that year.'

'You mean we would be together?'

'Yes: you for the season, and myself for one or two concerts. As you know, they would be a great help to me financially . . . Oh, that I were thirty years younger. I hope they will be kind.'

'How could they not be, for you are what you were: a giant!'

Giuditta Pasta's kindly face broke into a wistful smile. 'I fear I am but the shadow now; but in you they will glimpse my *Norma* as it was when I first sang it for dear Vincenzo. Did you write to Signor Verdi?'

'Yes,' replied Gabriella faintly. 'I explained that although I had intended coming to Paris to be available, I was compelled to stay here because of my fall – oh, he will think me so feeble!'

'Feeble! A broken leg feeble?' exclaimed Giuditta Pasta in surprise. 'Do you think Giuseppe Verdi would want you hopping about with a stick singing bravely through gritted teeth. Why, it would be worse than that poor tenor in Rome who, after tripping up on his entrance, ended his aria nursing the House cat in his arms.'

'With the audience crying, Meow, Meow,' smiled Gabriella, finishing off the anecdote. 'Did anyone ever discover what had frightened the cat?'

'A mouse perhaps?' suggested Pasta, showing her lovely teeth in a responding smile. 'Now,' she said, unwrapping the parcel she had brought with her. 'I have brought you something precious – well, two treasured possessions for you to look at while I am away. I want them back, mind you,' she said with mock severity.

'Vincenzo Bellini,' murmured Gabriella, looking at the small painting which had been given to Pasta by the composer. 'And Clelia's painting of the centre of the lake. Oh, how marvellous – each time I feel low I will look at them, my dear friend.'

'They were given to me with love: in the same spirit I am lending them to you. But this, my poster of *Norma*, I am giving to a pupil who will soon show the world what I am no longer able to do. Your *Norma* will make them forget Grisi and even Lind. Did you tell Agnese about your plans to go to Paris?'

'No, I didn't want to upset her. She still blames herself for what happened. I told her that my letter to Verdi was to thank him for the Hymn.'

'Has he responded yet?'

'Brusquely. Don't run to seed, was all he said.'

'That's not brusque,' laughed Giuditta Pasta. 'That's encouragement!'

On 26 September, while Milan was enduring Radetzky's harsh retribution, the last resistance in Lombardy came to an end as Garibaldi's depleted force was attacked at Morazzone by a Kinsky battalion and a squadron of Polish Kaiser Uhlans. And soon after, when d'Aspre threatened with Schwarzenberg's brigade, there was nothing else for Garibaldi to do but retire across the Swiss frontier.

Whether the young peasant boy had got through with her message, Gabriella did not know. She had never doubted that he would try, though he might be tempted to keep the brooch if he peeped at it, and one could hardly blame him if he did, she thought, realizing how such a thing could transform his family's life. Had Luciano been alive to receive it? If so, was he now marching with the Volunteers to Piedmont where they had been permitted to go under the terms of the armistice?

To pass the long hours, Professor Prioni – besides keeping her up to date with current gossip – had given her *The Betrothed* by Alessandro Manzoni to read.

'It's the first book written in the Tuscan dialect,' he had explained rather pompously, as if to a classroom, 'and thus it has become almost a reference book, a dictionary for the whole of Italy, one common, living language. It also illustrates perfectly the tyranny of the powerful against the weak. But you won't find it at all depressing: Manzoni's humour is wonderful.'

So Gabriella made a start on the story of Lucia and Renzo's struggle to marry and their flight from the wicked Don Rodrigo. And with the wind howling and the rain lashing against the window panes she sat for hours, totally absorbed and greatly moved when Lucia and Renzo were forced to leave their home.

'Listen to this passage, Agnese,' she said one afternoon when they were sitting together, she concentrating on her book and the dame on her sewing.

'What then must be the feeling of those who have never had a passing thought or a fugitive wish that went outside the boundaries of their mountain homes, who have made the hills the background for all their future plans, and yet are torn far away from them by a perverse fate; who, swept away from their most cherished habits, frustrated in their dearest hopes, have to leave the hills, to go and seek out unknown people whom they have never felt any desire to meet, without even being able to guess at a possible time for their return!'

'It's just like that for our exiles today, isn't it?' said Gabriella.

'Yes,' sighed Agnese. 'There are many who will never see Como again, or the inside of their cottages and villas.'

The winter months passed slowly. The first tips of green shoots had pushed upwards through the earth before Gabriella was able to walk without the support of a stick. With the first green of spring in March, so the hopes for liberty resurfaced when hostilities resumed between Piedmont and Austria on the 20th. And news came that the Volunteers were not with Carlo Alberto's main force at Novaro, but in position at the fork of the River Po and the Ticino. On 23 March an excited neighbour brought news of victory, unaware that at that moment it was being stolen away by Radetzky, Wratislaw, Thurn, and Appel. The end to Lombardy's hopes had come and with them Carlo Alberto's youthful dreams as his defeated army left the field of Novara and, bidding adieu to his throne, his heir moved forward from the wings.

It was time to return the portrait of Vincenzo Bellini: it was time to leave for Paris!

After obtaining the key of Pasta's villa from the caretaker, Gabriella lingered for a time in the garden, looking at it with the interest of a visitor or someone bidding farewell; beside the sweeping, silent lines of the cedar of Lebanon she leant against the wall and looked out over towards the promontory of Pizzo. How long ago seemed that bright morning when she had set off and found the young man before the fountain, not knowing that her rage would turn to another passion that would dominate everything, even her music. Perhaps I should never have gone there, she thought, then I would never have walked towards that door singing Mozart and found a pianist whose eyes had crinkled in laughter – would never have seen him lift a baby from its cradle at the mill, nor felt tender lips in a high meadow; Gabriella's heart ached as she thought of the moments when her life had begun to go out of control and she sighed, whispering Felice Piave's words: '"Bring back to me the peace and warmth of love!"'

Inside the drawing-room of the villa, Gabriella hung Clelia's *Centre of the Lake* back in place and then walked to the music room. In the little vestibule outside she touched the little cupids on the small rosewood cabinet with her fingertips and gave them a cheeky wink. But as her feet moved over the threshold into the salon, her mood changed as if she were stepping into a shrine. Here Bellini had stood, Gaetano Donizetti had composed. And here she herself had spent countless desperate hours striving for perfection. Here she had laughed and often almost cried in despair; until kindly Pasta would say, 'Patience, *mia cara*, you run before you walk.'

With a feeling of deep affection, Gabriella walked through the draped curtains into the recess of the room and looked up at the portrait of the great singer painted when she was young; she was not a stunning beauty but there was a stead-fast strength and gentleness about the face and there was no arrogance or vanity.

'I hope I'll do honour to your music as Pasta did,' Gabriella murmured, putting the portrait of the young Bellini back in its usual position. As she turned around, beyond the draping of curtains, the eyes of the child Napoleon stared across at her and she moved towards the portrait.

'Our Lombards should have had you to lead them,' she said, raising her eyebrows at the dark-eyed child. Near to the portrait, on the harmonium, lay Pasta's score of *Norma*. It was open, and her eyes caught the words and notes for Pollione: 'A purer heaven and holier gods I offer you, in Rome. I am going there now.'. . . I am going there now, the words leapt up at her as if they were printed in gold; Rome, where a republic had just been declared, a republic which would need defending . . . Was it possible? She picked up the score and took it to the piano and began to play and sing for the whole of Blevio and Cernobbio to hear. '"Ah! bring back to me the peace and warmth of love. And in that love I shall find again Life . . ."'

Like another omen, the Princess Belgiojoso's letter arrived the next day.

'I pray that you are still at Blevio,' she wrote. 'And if so come to Rome. I am here to support its Republic and I need patriots like you to help me . . .'

'I'm sorry you have to leave,' said the Professor as Gabriella laid her letter down. 'When you are here, I don't have to be tortured with Agnese's attempts at partnering me at duets. She seems to think that she is entering a race when she sits beside me. However, perhaps I should have kept her here more often instead of letting her go and pray so much for peace; perhaps it was her efforts that led the Pope to make his allocution. Once he said that as Vicar of Christ he could not declare war: it made a great impact on those who believed they were on a holy crusade. Anyway, dear girl, I hope your journey to Paris will not be fraught with too many dangers!'

'I'm not going to go to Paris, Professor. The Princess Belgiojoso urges me to join her in Rome.'

'Not to that wicked city!' exclaimed Agnese, throwing up her small hands in horror. 'What ungodly people are they, that our good Pope had to flee from the city?'

'Well, from what Princess Belgiojoso says, the Roman republic is behaving in the most exemplary manner; and Signor Mazzini, who has been elected as one of its triumvirs, has maintained order and calm.'

'Well, it's still the Holy Father's city, and there'll be good Catholics throughout the world who'll want to see it given back to him. I for one will pray for it!'

'You just give some regard to your arthritic knees,' warned Andrea Prioni, glancing over the top of his glasses which perched on the curve of his nose. 'Leave the praying to the prelates. That's what Pius should do, stick to the faith and leave other matters to the people. But no, he would rather remain with King Ferdinand, the supreme example of tyranny and cruelty.'

Gabriella picked up the letter and read it through once more as the bickering continued. A feeling of great excitement filled her: Rome's republic was calling to Italy's patriots. Would the Lombard monarchists also go to its aid? Would Luciano Forro too be there?

# Chapter Fifteen

Rome, the Eternal City, about which Mazzini, in the dusty schoolroom in Hatton Garden, had spun the golden stories that had made them yearn to see it. Gabriella's own response to the ancient remains of Empire was no different, she supposed, to that of other visitors: one of awe.

The Princess Belgiojoso had told Gabriella that she could be found at the hospital of the Trinità dei Pellegrini. Until the Pope's hurried departure it had been run by the monks, but now Christina Belgiojoso had been put in charge of its administration and that of all the hospitals in Rome.

'Gabriella, you have not failed me,' said the Princess, rising from her chair with a welcoming smile on her pale face. 'I was sorry not to have your company on the journey to Paris last year, and I have been most anxious about your safety, but how I applauded your brave, courageous act. I made it known to Signor Verdi.'

'Thank you,' said Gabriella with a grateful smile. 'Do you want me to help you here at the hospital?'

'Yes, my dear. It isn't that I am short of volunteers: nearly six thousand ladies have offered their help; but I will feel more calm if I have a few friends around me who understand my disposition to nervous attacks. I feel quite well, but the republic has entrusted me with an enormous task: it is the first time that we women will be able to show what we can do. I think it will be the first time too that ladies will have donned the nurse's apron – and I am to lead them!'

'Well, there couldn't be anyone more competent,' smiled Gabriella, realizing that the Princess's concern was about her epilepsy which could be brought on by overwork and stress. 'But will we have the stamina to keep up with you?'

As patron and protégée laughed together, the door opened, and a blonde-haired young woman entered. Gabriella saw it was the American lady writer she had met one summer at Como.

'I believe, Gabriella, that you met Miss Fuller at the Contessa Forro's?'

'Yes,' replied Gabriella, extending her hand in greeting.

'Mr Mazzini will be pleased to see you, Miss Pepe,' said Margaret Fuller with an approving nod of her head. 'He is showing the whole of Europe what a republic can achieve. Perhaps you have not had the opportunity to see this,' she said with pride, picking up from Christina Belgiojoso's desk a newspaper. 'How the French might have learnt from this programme, don't you agree, Christina? "No war of classes, no hostility to existing wealth, no wanton or unjust violation of the rights of property; but a constant disposition to ameliorate the material condition of the classes least favoured by fortune." And the people are keeping to it,' she declared, dropping the paper back on the desk. 'So you see, you have made the decision that all right-minded people must make. Rome's republic needs everyone's support; so much hangs in the balance for our dear Mr Mazzini.'

'It's what he has worked for and dreamt of for so long,' remarked Christina Belgiojoso. 'To unite the whole of the peninsula from Rome.'

'Why, I declare, Ma'am, not just the peninsula,' said Margaret Fuller. 'Mazzini sees the whole of Europe united. Just think of it: the whole of Europe united and looking to Rome for moral guidance.'

'It is far to go when so much has recently been lost,' commented Gabriella. 'Are you helping with the nursing, Miss Fuller?'

'I surely am, and will be supervising the hospital of Fate Bene-Fratelli. Did you come to help at the hospitals?'

'Yes,' said Gabriella. 'Do you really think there will be a conflict?'

'It's only a question of whose army arrives here first to claim the glory of giving back the Pope his throne: the Neapolitans, Spain, Austria, or the French.'

'Not France!' declared Christina Belgiojoso heatedly. 'Never against a new republic!'

Margaret Fuller's eyelids blinked slowly and her gaze was piercing and direct under the heavy lids.

'I cannot share your faith, Princess: a large Catholic vote, politicians trying to please; it will be hard for them not to support the Vicar of Christendom. And how is Milan, Miss Pepe?'

'I don't know from personal experience,' confessed Gabriella. 'But things are very hard, we heard, and Radetzky's troops moved into the Conservatorio. The students are having to visit the professors in their homes for tuition. The troops are doing everything they can to punish everyone. The poor people of Brescia have really suffered for their recent rebellion: the stories of what Haynau's men did afterwards is beyond understanding; people burnt alive, wives forced to cover their loved ones with pitch before it was set alight, and worse, much worse – and to little children! There is no animal that behaves with such vile cruelty as some men. I hope, Miss Fuller, that you will write to the *Herald Tribune* and tell the American people what atrocities the Habsburg troops have committed,' said Gabriella passionately.

'Rest assured: I am keeping a complete record of everything,' replied the Bostonian. 'And I know from the money contributions I have already received from the Americans here in Rome that their hearts are with you all in your struggle for liberty. Did we not have to struggle for our own?'

Like bright sunlight entering to dispel their gloom came Maria Belgiojoso. Her young face was impatient with excitement. 'Mama, quickly, we have to go to the Piazza del Popolo. There is news of troops!'

'Come!' said the tall, slender aristocrat rising from her chair. 'Let us go at once.'

The Piazza was crowded with people when they arrived. Following her patron's example, Gabriella – with Maria holding on to her hand – climbed up on to one of the benches.

'What is happening, Mama?' asked Christina Belgiojoso's eleven-year-old daughter.

'Hush dear,' she replied. 'They are about to put up a proclamation.'

Suddenly, piercing above the excited babble, a man's voice cried out. 'The French are coming! They are disembarking at Civitavecchia!'

Applause, cries of alarm, cheers and a few bars of 'La Marseillaise' erupted.

'You see, Mama,' laughed Maria. 'They are coming to help just as you wanted them to. Oh look, Miss Fuller is with her American friends. Have you met Monsieur and Madame Story, Gabriella? They are very kindly and they are raising lots of money for Mama's hospitals. I shall go and bring them over to meet you. You will find Monsieur Story very interesting, for he is a sculptor.'

As her young friend had described, there was a warmth and generosity of spirit about the American couple which Gabriella liked instantly. And though the state of affairs in Rome was not their own issue, their concern was genuine.

'We enjoy the freedom of a democracy, and so should Italy,' declared Mrs Story as, like every other group on the Piazza, they discussed what the arrival of the French army might mean. 'I hope we will hear you sing something patriotic, Miss Pepe. Miss Fuller tells us that you have trained with Giuditta Pasta . . . perhaps you should come to America to make your début?' she beamed, as she took her husband's arm to walk on.

'Oh no!' cried Maria Belgiojoso, twirling her small parasol coquettishly as the three Americans moved on. 'Mama says you must début in Paris, Gabriella. If they are friendly to Rome, that is!' she added with a giggle.

'France respects foreign nationalities. Her might will never be employed against the liberty of any people. So says the fifth article of the French constitution,' quoted Christina Belgiojoso bitterly the day after the French landing, when the visit of their Colonel Leblanc to Mazzini revealed they had not come to

272

support the republic, but to restore the Pope to his throne, with or *without* the consent of the Roman people.

'So there will be fighting,' said Gabriella.

'I'm afraid so,' replied the Princess. 'They have called to Garibaldi at Rieti.'

'And the Lombard division?'

'They were ordered in Piedmont to disband. I believe they have actually stayed together . . . but whether they will come to aid the republic I do not know. Many of our Milanesi went to join with Garibaldi of course, so I expect we will see many familiar faces: where they will all lodge I do not know. Our rooms may be small here, but at least we are certain of a bed.'

'Yes, I appreciate staying here. After buying my ticket here my funds are rather low,' said Gabriella awkwardly.

'My dear girl!' said Christina Belgiojoso. 'We must set that right at once. Things are so disordered that I was forgetting my responsibility towards you: of course everything was provided for you in Milan.'

'Well, I hope when all this is over I shall soon be financially independent . . . There is something else I have waited to tell you. Now that we are alone, perhaps this is the time. I have discovered who my family are.'

'Why, that is very good news,' said the Princess with a gracious smile of interest. 'Are they still alive, my dear?'

'Sadly no. My mother was Giulia Balziano.'

The white, wraith-like hand of Christina Belgiojoso lifted from the desk in a gesture of astonishment, and the large black eyes studied her as they had done that night when Gabriella had walked into the black-draped drawing-room to meet her patron for the first time.

'You are Gabriella Balziano, whose disappearance caused such scandal and sadness . . . But how did you come by such information?'

Quickly Gabriella related her story and then, asking the Princess to follow her to the small room she had been allotted, she showed her the miniature of herself as a child with her mother.

'There can be no doubt on this evidence alone,' murmured the Princess, examining the painting and looking from it to Gabriella. 'How ironic that fate brought you to the attention of Giuseppe Mazzini and then to me . . . all the time guiding you back to your heritage. But it will take a team of lawyers to make your claim, especially for those properties still under sequestration. Why, this means that Flavia Balziano is your cousin!'

'Yes,' said Gabriella turning aside to hide her wry smile.

'Did you know that Luciano Forro was promised in child-hood to you? Then, after disaster struck, it was always assumed that it would be Flavia.'

'No, I did not know that,' said Gabriella breathlessly. 'And I would be obliged if, like Contessa Forro, you would not reveal my identity to Conte Forro.'

'I cannot see why not,' said Christina Belgiojoso with a puzzled frown. 'But naturally I will respect your confidence.'

It did not take Garibaldi long to respond to Rome's cry. On 27 April he and his men arrived.

'He is coming! He is coming!'

If one could go back in time, this is what Palm Sunday must have been like, thought Gabriella as she looked right and left along the Corso at the radiant, hopeful faces.

'Oh, Mademoiselle Gabriella,' exclaimed the Princess's young daughter clapping her hands. 'Monsieur Mazzini's knight should be riding a donkey, for with his long fair hair and beard, does he not look like our Lord?'

'Yes, he does,' murmured Gabriella, as she looked at the gentle-faced enthralling guerrilla leader. 'Yet he is able to control all those men!'

'They look more like bandits than disciples!' laughed Maria. 'And look at the black man behind Garibaldi. I think the French will run away when they see him carrying his lance. I will too if he turns around and looks at me,' she giggled, taking hold of Gabriella's hand. 'Do you see how large he is? Aren't his clothes bizarre?'

'I think I should run with you,' agreed Gabriella, following the progress of the huge black warrior who wore a beret on his head, a black cowl and striped trousers of blue and green. 'I believe they call him Aguyar,' she said.

'Why look, Mademoiselle! Is that not Conte Forro?'

Gabriella's heart lurched at the name on her young companion's lips. Yet even before her eyes fell upon the horseman in the red shirt, she knew it must be Giovanni whom Maria had seen.

'*Evviva! Evviva!*' she shouted with the girl and the populace; but Giovanni did not see their individual waves, for he and the whole column seemed dazed by the ecstatic welcome they were receiving. '*Evviva!*' she shouted again, feeling tears prick her eyes.

'Why are you crying, Mademoiselle?' asked the young girl, taking hold of Gabriella's hand.

'For my brother who has missed this proud moment,' she murmured, her heart pierced with grief as she thought of Nico and how he would have revelled in this moment as Rome paid homage to the First Italian Legion.

With the arrival of Garibaldi a sense of urgency could be felt. As in Milan, all sorts of people took a turn with a shovel at the defences being built in the streets and at the walls.

Under Christina Belgiojoso's leadership, the lady volunteers were being organized into teams of attendants for the wards.

'The monks have left things in a terrible state,' sighed the Princess, who had asked Gabriella to come and meet some of the ladies who had formed the Committee for the Relief of the Wounded. 'Ladies, we are very short of linen for beds and bandages. Can I leave you all to organize an appeal for such things!'

'Will we be given any instruction in the care of wounds?' asked Gabriella.

'There surely will be doctors on hand for such duties,' commented a Roman lady in a languid voice.

Christina Belgiojoso looked up sharply. 'Signora, I hope you realize that your duties are going to involve more than arranging flowers at the bedsides of heroes. What doctors we will have,' continued the Princess, 'will be much in demand

and occupied with the severely wounded. You will have to learn to dress minor wounds and also take care of all things that the men cannot do for themselves. I hope you follow my meaning,' she said severely, her words making several of the women turn pink.

On the 29th, Gabriella accompanied one of the Committee to the home of a wealthy merchant to enlist his wife's support for the Committee's work. The patrician lady she accompanied was received with eager attentiveness, and they had just accepted the offer of iced drinks when a disturbing ripple of sound came from the Corso below.

'Shall we go out on to the balcony, Contessa?' asked their hostess, looking eagerly towards the open doorway as the murmur started to increase.

'Certainly!' said the aristocrat, following the merchant's wife out into the sunlight. 'What can they be cheering for?'

'Perhaps the French have changed their minds,' suggested Gabriella, marvelling at the number of people running towards the Corso from all directions. While, just like themselves, others were coming out on to balconies.

'It's the Aristocratic corps – the Lombards have come! They are marching into the city.'

Gabriella gripped hold of the iron railing of the balcony, hardly able to bear the suspense . . . dear God, let him be amongst them, she repeated over and over again under her breath. By the time the band came into sight the pavement below was thick with people. And just as they had welcomed Garibaldi, now they cheered for the Lombards who had been formed into a company of Bersaglieri in Piedmont.

'Oh, how proud they look,' declared the Roman Contessa beside her. 'Don't you agree, Signorina? Your countrymen look magnificent!'

'Yes,' agreed Gabriella, her heart lurching with relief and joy to see the tall, elegant figure striding beside Conte Manara.

Misty-eyed she watched the advancing, disciplined column. Were these the same young men who had gone to war from Milan in their velvet suits, hoping to be back at the card tables and salons within the month? Now, a year later, in their dark green tunics, with the sun glinting on the Cross of Savoy fastened to their sword belts, they looked like soldiers. The familiar faces beneath the broad-brimmed hats looked older, almost like children who had grown up too soon: long gone were the daring days of gobbling at policemen and writing the name of Pio Nono in the dust.

With her eyes fixed on the glossy green feathers which hung down from Luciano Forro's hat, Gabriella silently urged him to look up, but unlike the unruly, boisterous troops of Garibaldi, the Bersaglieri looked neither to right nor left, but marched along as professional soldiers. Some flowers were thrown down from the next balcony along, dropping in front of him and on to the brim of his hat. He glanced upwards with a polite smile; a smile that widened and became incredulous with joy. Gabriella laughed, wept and waved as he nodded and proceeded.

She turned to make her excuses, and knew by the look in the ladies' eyes that they knew exactly where she had to go in such haste. No doubt they are scandalized, she thought as she left the elegant apartment with their offers of hospitality for the officers sounding after her. But she didn't care, and the moment the leather of her shoes touched the pavement she was off, running just as if she were still the urchin Lark, weaving her way through the crowded thoroughfares of London.

'What is the hurry? Won't you stay a while, beautiful Signorina?' laughed a young man who wore the short jacket of Angelo Masina's Lancers.

'Forgive me, Signore, for pushing you so,' apologized Gabriella, pink with embarrassment to have knocked him sideways. 'I have seen a friend in the Bersaglieri.'

'Should I exchange my hat for one with bird feathers? Would that persuade you to stay?'

'Nothing, no one would make me stay,' she laughed, waving goodbye.

Suddenly, above the noise and din, a huge body of men shouted, '*Viva l'Italia.*'

'It's the Bersaglieri, swearing their oath of allegiance to defend Rome,' she heard a soldier mutter to his companion.

'Tell me, Signore,' she interrupted. 'Where are the men of the Bersaglieri billeted?'

'They've been told to bivouac on St Peter's Square tonight – give him a kiss for me, sweetheart,' the soldier bellowed after her as she hurried on.

The entrances to the great Piazza were thronged with Bersaglieri and Gabriella felt a rising sense of panic that she would never find him. Darting between the columns, she desperately scanned the huge crowd, searching for that face she knew so well. Oh God, where was he?

Suddenly she heard a shout from behind her. She spun around, scarcely daring to believe that it was really him. She was laughing, crying, running blindly into his arms.

'Oh, I thought I would never see you again!' he cried, burying his face against hers. 'Tell me you love me, desperately, completely.'

'Desperately,' she murmured, her lips touching his. 'Completely!' For a timeless moment they pressed close, thrilling to the feel of the other's body. Gabriella felt such joy that she thought she would burst. Luciano felt it too, for he suddenly hugged her as if he would squeeze the life out of her, then stood away from her, his eyes dark and shining with desire.

'We've marched in the heat all day, and I thought the most delicious and desirable thing in Rome would be a cold drink . . . but now . . .'

Gabriella laughed and took his arm. 'Then, Captain, I insist we find a shady place for you to have one. And I shall enjoy all the admiring glances you receive, for you look very handsome,' she murmured, touching the glossy green-black feathers which hung down from the brim of his hat. 'And I see you wear the Cross of Savoy to defend the Republic?'

'For Rome and Italy!' he said, answering the teasing note in her voice as they walked towards the brightly coloured striped awning of a café.

In a state of utter bliss, with her heart still racing with excitement, hardly able to bear even the intrusion of the table between them, Gabriella studied greedily every detail of Luciano's tanned face as he slaked his thirst.

'I needed that!' he said, putting down his drained tankard with a smile.

'You drank that like a soldier,' she teased. 'Did you know Giovanni is with the Garibaldini and that they are here?' she asked as he reached for her hand.

'Yes, I know,' Luciano Forro said, his voice edged with regret. 'He decided at Bergamo not to march with us to Piedmont, but to continue fighting with Garibaldi. They carried on a brave fight around Luino and Varese, from what we heard,' he murmured, looking at her as if he were seeing her for the first time, his speculative grey-green eyes dark beneath the brim of his hat. 'I have something to return to you,' he smiled, reaching inside his tunic and withdrawing the butterfly brooch. 'Your peasant boy arrived and I'll admit we wept bitterly when we read the armistice. Twice you have risked your life to save mine, Gabriella . . . why did you try to break my heart at La Scala?'

'I'll tell you one day,' she smiled. 'I hoped the brooch would tell you what my heart felt for you and that you would forgive me.'

'I had done that long before the butterfly arrived,' he said, caressing her hand. 'After my anger and hurt faded I realized it was unbelievable that you would ever act so – can't you explain?'

Gabriella shook her head and squeezed his hand. Her pride could not let her answer. She was still Gabriella Pepe. Whatever future they had must be based on that fact: she could not bear to think of herself valued more highly like a piece of silver with a superior hallmark.

'Let's speak about you,' she said. 'You look very tired.'

The corners of Luciano Forro's firm lips pulled down into a derisive little smile.

'More disillusioned than tired – none of us is a professional soldier, but it might have been better had we held the reins. It has been harrowing to see so many brave lives thrown wantonly away. I never felt from the first that we stood a chance, but I was wrong: we could have crushed Radetzky's forces before they reached the security of the Quadrilateral if

Piedmont had acted with speed. But having lost this advantage there was no point in wasting time laying siege to the fortresses: we should have come around behind Radetzky and isolated him from his reinforcements. And then in the second campaign we were separated from the main force when we should all have been at Novara. Bah, it makes me furious to think of it.'

'And what of Rome? The Austrians are marching south to the Romagna. What chance do we have against them or the French army?'

'Little chance, but I suppose we have all come to nail the colours of nationalism to the mast and affirm a people's right to determine their political future . . . We will show how Italians can fight and die for those rights, even though it is more in our nature to love,' he said, touching the crimson petals of the flowers on the table: his thick curved lashes lifted and the sensuality in his glance made her heart somersault, then it disappeared and his expression became whimsical. 'Perhaps there will come a day when nations and people will use intellect rather than the club to settle issues.' He shrugged. 'Here am I with a sword when all the time I thought Fate had me marked for a poet and silk master! Ah well, let us talk of more cheerful things. Where are you staying?'

'I have a room at the hospital; the Princess Belgiojoso is in charge of all the hospitals in Rome. But if you need accommodation, the Contessa I was standing beside on the balcony extends an invitation to you and a few other officers.'

'A most voluptuous Roman, I thought!' murmured Luciano Forro, his eyebrows drawing together and little creases of laughter appearing on his face as he saw the jealousy spark in Gabriella's dark-blue eyes. 'Would I be comfortable there?'

'Yes,' said Gabriella unenthusiastically as Luciano Forro's face assumed an air of intense interest.

'It sounds very tempting, don't you think?' he said. 'Of course, she might not approve of some of my friends,' he laughed, giving a playful tug on the thick looped braid which hung below Gabriella's bonnet.

'Oh you wretch!' she cried. 'Must you always tease me?'

'Only when there are no fountains about.'

'Then you'd best be careful . . . this is Rome, remember?'

'Come, let's go and look down on her,' he said, standing and handing her the pink parasol. 'And while we are there, we will say hello to that ardent young republican brother of mine.'

They climbed up to the San Pancrazio gate by the steep path and steps of the Via di Porta San Pancrazio.

'Garibaldi has established his headquarters up there at the Villa Corsini,' said the Conte as they walked out of the city gate.

'Wouldn't it be safer within the walls? They look very strong,' she said looking back.

'Yes, they are, but imagine French cannon here and along the Janiculum hill.'

'Their shells would drop on the city below,' she said, realizing how high they now were.

'Precisely,' said Luciano, leading her further from the city gates up the road towards the gates of the Villa Corsini. 'No, there is nothing vulnerable about Urban VII's walls, except that sadly the ground up here is higher: whoever holds the Janiculum holds Rome.'

The avenue which led up to the Villa Corsini was flanked on either side by a tall, stiff box hedge. Inside the villa's gates to the left was a small house, outside which a group of soldiers, wearing the blue tunic of the Italian Legion, were smoking their cigars. The country house, built by the Corsini family, was an impressive building, four storeys high, with an ornamental parapet on top and a balcony in front on the second floor.

'It has a good view of Rome,' said Gabriella, looking back down the avenue. 'But surely for our headquarters that is unimportant?'

'It is everything if it falls into the hands of a French general. Look back down at the San Pancrazio gate. Do you see how hard it would be to retake this villa if we lost it?'

'A clear sweep of fire,' she observed. 'There would be no cover except at the villa on the right of the road.'

'Villa Vascello.'

'And anyone firing from here down the avenue and towards the city could hide behind this wall.'

'Householders who were obviously nervous of mobs from Rome,' agreed the Conte as they moved closer to the low wall bearing ornamental pots of oranges which ran the length of the façade of the villa to the garden walls.

'I will go in and see if Giovanni is about, and introduce myself to the General. There is a seat in the shade just over there.'

After about ten minutes, Luciano Forro returned and shook his head with regret. 'We've just missed Giovanni. He's gone to familiarize himself with the layout of the city, although I wouldn't be at all surprised if there is some pleasure mixed in with it. Would you mind if I remind myself of the layout of the grounds while I am here, just in case we meet an attack here.'

But for the soldiers basking in the shade of trees and sitting beside the sparkling sprinkling of fountains, it was hard to imagine that the serenity of the smiling marble statues could be disturbed by fighting.

'It's so peaceful,' she said, smiling at a group of young men who looked up from their game of cards as they passed. 'So many flowers and shades of green, and the moment you are beyond people, you feel there could be no one here but the birds.'

'It would need several thousand troops to defend it adequately,' commented the Conte. 'See how wide an area there is here behind the villa for troops to wait in safety. If the French got as far as here they could keep sending their detachments forward to defend the villa, whereas anyone wishing to take it from the front has the acute angle of a triangle to squeeze his men through. Garibaldi has chosen the right place to base his defence.'

'Isn't it ironic?' said Gabriella as she surveyed the dappled green scene. 'Our Pope, who could not bring himself to declare war against Austria, is willing to let others commit bloodshed in order to give him back his throne.'

'A true example of expediency,' laughed Luciano, taking hold of her arm and leading her forward through the trees.

282

'What lies beyond the stream, Luciano?'

'The Villa Pamphili and its gardens. Do you see that long lush grass beneath the evergreen oaks? That is where Conte Forro made love to the loveliest soprano in Europe.'

His thick black brows lifted and she could not resist his quizzical appeal. Beneath fluttering leaves they ran over the criss-cross shadows and patches of sunlight to the secluded spot. Within their palisade of green rustling in the breeze, they lay concealed from all others in the deep grass.

Gentle and tender at first, their kisses were almost shy; but as their passion gradually increased, the mating of tongue and lips was not enough. His swift, urgent fingers disrobed her of dress and petticoats. Left only with her stays and long cotton pants, she felt naked, until his lips took hers with renewed urgency. Soon she longed to lose everything which came between them. With gasps of pleasure, she responded to his kisses at her ears and throat, and felt the excitement mounting as his lips moved along the top of her stays. The upward naked swell of her breasts strained to meet his mouth; slowly he pulled open the first two hooks and, as her breasts burst free, she heard him sigh with pleasure. For a moment he covered each with a hand and smiled down at her: his expression took her breath away, making her insides ache with need as his fingers slowly intensified their caresses. Then it was not enough for him and he leaned forward, his lips as hungry as the hands that slid away the fine cotton from the round of her hips.

After a long time, calm came. Quite spent, they lay apart, only fingers touching.

'Love is glorious!' she said, looking up at the canopy of sunlit leaves.

'There is better yet to come,' he replied, turning his head to look at her. 'And I see I have neglected a most important part of you.'

'Impossible!' she laughed.

'But I have!' he said. 'How could I have left undone what I have longed to do since the day I first desired you . . . I've always wanted to unbraid your hair, and watch it swing around your naked body.'

'You thought that?' said Gabriella, turning pink to know that he had looked at her so.

'But of course, it would be unusual for a man not to. If you thought a Canova or a Michelangelo was beneath a dust sheet, would it be so odd to wish to lift it aside, admire, and follow each lovely curve with an admiring hand? There, it is done,' he said, his fingers lifting from her hair. 'I have set free the last of the black silk.'

Gabriella laughed and raised her arms. As the sweep of the straight black hair made a backcloth to the lines of her creamy body, Luciano Forro narrowed his eyes as if studying a painting.

'At least if I am to die here, I shall remember I loved here,' he murmured, looking at her with such tenderness that her heart filled with pain.

'Do not talk of dying,' she whispered, 'when your love has filled me with life!'

# Chapter Sixteen

There were some 9,000 troops to face the French, who were expected to attack the north-west of the city from the direction of Palo. Given the defence of the right bank of the Tiber and Monte Janiculum, Garibaldi at the Villa Corsini had, beside his own legion of 1,000, 300 students and artists and 900 volunteers of the Roman States. Guarding the Vatican walls were troops of the Papal line and 1,000 National Guard. And if the citizens of the Trastevere quarter did not have the uniforms of the Bersaglieri, the Carabineers, or the cavalry on the Piazza Navona, the knives and axes they carried and their grim expressions as they rushed to the walls were military mark enough.

It was an anxious night and a watchful morning whose calm was shattered at midday by the firing of the cannon above the Porta Pertusa.

'It must be the French!' gasped a Roman matron who was helping Gabriella cut up linen for dressings.

Sharing her anxiety, Gabriella ran to the door and called to one of the young porters. 'Please go and see what's happening – and don't forget to come back,' she added, knowing how tempting it would be for someone of his age to stay. After nearly three-quarters of an hour, the youth returned, his face glowing with excitement.

'Do you hear the musket fire, Signorina?' he shouted gleefully. 'It's the National Guard: they are really giving the French a welcome. What a sight! You've never seen such uniforms: white coats, white gloves, shakos, braid, why they look as if they are coming to a ball – and I bet they're sweating like pigs! They thought they were in for a welcome, for they have no scaling equipment with them and they have had to unlimber their guns. Now they're attacking towards the Porta Cavalleggeri.'

'Good boy, keep us informed,' said Gabriella. It was in fact the last they saw of him for another two hours, but soon the casualties arrived and bit by bit they heard what was happening. At half-past four, after nearly six hours' fighting, a young artist who had been bayoneted in the thigh told Gabriella what part he had played.

'General Garibaldi sent us down through the Pamphili gardens to attack the French. I can't tell you how my heart was beating as I dropped down with my friends into the deep lane which runs along beside the villa grounds. Anyway, just after we had left the lane, we came upon eight companies of the 20<sup>me</sup> *de ligne* infantry. What a shock that was, but a friend shouted, "Drive them out, lads", and we flew at them with our bayonets. I was so excited I didn't know what I was doing: I just kept lunging at anything before me. They were so shocked they fell back, for we were like screaming devils, but not for long. There were many more of them than us – soon it was our turn to run,' he laughed, his excitement in recounting the scene making him forget his pain. 'I've never run so fast, I can tell you, with at least twenty after me. By the time we got back into the Pamphili the Garibaldini had come up to support us, but we couldn't hold our own and the French advanced right up to the Villa Corsini.'

'You were left behind?'

'Yes, I was with five others in a little outhouse. We thought we were done for, for we were completely surrounded; but the French suddenly turned their attention elsewhere and we saw Garibaldi on his horse, his poncho swirling, his gun smoking as he led the counter-charge. "Come on boys," he roared. "Put the French to flight like a mass of carrion. Take them with the bayonet!" We flew out of the hut and joined in the bayonet fight . . . I didn't do too well,' he grimaced. 'But as I lay there with my dead and wounded friends I saw our students charge, then charge again. Oh, it was marvellous: I felt so proud of them for it is a frightening thing, Signorina, for those who have never fought before. Then came the final rush, and they drove the enemy back over the walls.'

That night as sounds of rejoicing drifted through the open windows of the hospital, the volunteers worked on, frantically busy not only with their own but many of the French.

Finally Gabriella's turn to rest came but, even though she was exhausted, she set off for the Quirinale palace. It came as no surprise to find that Mazzini had selected the smallest of rooms: he had lived for too long in small rooms to feel comfortable in anything large and palatial.

'I had to bring flowers to the victor!' she laughed as he came towards her and embraced her. 'Did you think that this could possibly happen? Won't they be surprised in London!'

Giuseppe Mazzini laughed almost boyishly. 'I think our Assembly will say that this has not surprised us Romans, but it will astonish Paris!'

'I hope you found time to celebrate last night,' she said, starting to put the flowers into a jar for him. 'We were not able to leave the hospital, but we could see the sky was quite light from all the lights in the houses and we could hear singing and laughter until the early hours.'

'Yes, I walked around the streets: it was a marvellous sight. Our French prisoners are being given every courtesy, I hope?'

'Of course,' replied Gabriella. 'We treat them no differently.'

'Good,' smiled Mazzini. 'I tried to make Garibaldi see that having demonstrated our determination to resist, we should now try to pour salve on what has happened. He wanted to take the army out and crush Oudinot's force completely. It has caused great aggravation between us, I fear, but I am convinced that we must ameliorate the situation and call to the hearts of the French nation. This is such an opportunity to do things well for all the citizens.'

Almost immediately, a second danger threatened the infant Republic. King Ferdinand and his Neapolitan army had reached the Alban hills. Straightaway, Garibaldi's forces, supported by the Bersaglieri and Masina's lancers, marched away to meet the new foe. It was all very worrying, but Gabriella found herself so busy in the hospital that there was little time to brood on what was happening to Luciano and her friends.

The hand-to-hand fighting with sword and bayonet in the Corsini and Pamphili gardens had been fierce. Where the cut was clean there was a good chance of recovery, as the edges of the wound reunited by adhesive strips knit together; but the bayonet wounds inflicted on many of the students were deep and many had received more than one wound. On the first occasion that Gabriella had watched a doctor at work she had turned aside, her face ashen; but then, filled with shame, she had returned, reached out her hand and taken the bloody dressing from the doctor, assisting him as best she could.

'Will he recover?' she whispered one morning when she and the doctor had finished at the bedside of a young student who was no more than seventeen.

The doctor shook his head as they walked down the corridor. 'It's hopeless with such wounds: unless the bowel sticks to the abdominal wall and discharges out on to the surface, which is, alas, very rare, they will die. The effluents discharge into the abdominal cavity, you see.'

'But they are all so young,' said Gabriella, her voice hushed with shock. 'There must be something we can do for them?'

'Divert their minds and try to calm their fears. When it becomes too much to bear, I will prescribe laudanum.'

During May, while the Neapolitan army was twice put to flight, the negotiations between the French envoy Ferdinand de Lesseps and the triumvirate continued. And on the 31st, the day that the weary army returned, the treaty for peace was signed by the triumvirs and de Lesseps: French troops, bivouacked outside the city, would henceforth protect Rome against the Austrians and the Neapolitan army.

'Oh, I wish I had my lovely blue velvet gown with me,' laughed Gabriella as Maria fastened some flowers in her hair. 'This borrowed gown is very tight: I hope I won't burst the seams. Perhaps you should have pulled me in a bit tighter, Maria.'

'You look wonderful, Mademoiselle Gabriella,' smiled the young girl. 'Oh, I can't wait to go to parties. Do you think all the young men will fall in love with me as they do you?'

'That's quite untrue!' laughed Gabriella, pinching the young girl's cheek.

'No it isn't. Mama says Conte Forro is deeply in love with you.'

'Well, that's quite different to lots of young men . . . I think they are waiting for you to grow up!'

'Oh, do you think I will be a *femme fatale*?' asked Maria looking anxiously at her reflection in the mirror. 'Or do you think I will be clever like Mama?'

'You must be yourself, sweetheart,' said Gabriella, kissing her. 'And you could be both at the same time.'

To be going with Luciano to a party, in the knowledge that the republic had a strong ally outside its doors, made her feel almost ecstatic with relief. Perhaps the other two enemy armies would retire completely. And to be away from the hospital in beautiful surroundings was what she needed, for the agony of those who were slowly dying, the smell of their wounds and of gangrene was horrendous. And she had latterly found herself praying that Luciano would not be wounded; better the unthinkable than that.

'This was a great mistake to meet you here,' declared the Conte as he led Gabriella into the salon of their host. 'I can hardly hear myself think. Shall we go and find a quiet corner in a restaurant?' he asked, then laughed with her, for every café and restaurant was packed with merry-makers.

'Well, this is just what I need,' said Gabriella. 'And I shall drink lots of champagne!'

'Am I not distraction enough?' he teased, taking her arm and steering a path to where Conte Manara and the Dandolo brothers were standing with another young man of the Bersaglieri.

'Yes, but I also know you are all exhausted after your march to Rome. Consider: here you are protected from my wicked demands, though I am surprised you have not all collapsed into bed.'

'That's what we intended to do until we heard about the miracle . . . We'll collapse tomorrow instead,' he laughed.

'What was your most frightening moment?' Gabriella heard someone ask Conte Manara.

'I can tell you that straightaway,' interrupted the youth with the sweet and angelic face. 'It was when we slept the night at the Dominican monastery at Palestrina. We turned out for roll call in white robes carrying our tapers. That really frightened you, didn't it, Conte?'

'Yes, Morisini. I was afraid you might all start to chant,' joked Conte Manara. 'But I give you a serious toast, my friends: to all those who are not with us tonight, and who gave their lives in recovering the honour of Italy. Now, Conte Forro, shall we give our Roman friends a little Verdi? Will you play or shall I?'

'I think it is my turn,' responded Luciano, leading the way over to the piano. 'Will you sing for everyone, Gabriella?'

'It would be my pleasure,' she said.

As soon as Luciano bent his dark head over the keys and began to play, a hush descended in the noisy salon.

'What will you have me play for you?' he asked, looking up to where she stood at his side. 'A little Verdi, Rossini?'

Gabriella did not reply: there was no need, for his fingers had wandered into that music which had first brought their souls together. She began the slow, melodic 'Casta Diva', filling the salon with the golden melodic cascades that would always belong to Pasta. When it was done, she scarcely heard cries for an encore as her eyes met his. All else was excluded. Her music and her love had become as one.

On the following day, while many roused themselves from groggy sleep after the celebrations, the terrible news struck like a thunderbolt: General Oudinet had dismissed de Lesseps' treaty and had cancelled the truce; French citizens would have time to make arrangements for leaving before he attacked on

Monday 4 June. It was heart-breaking news, ending all happy thoughts and plans.

'We were too quick to celebrate,' said Gabriella as she walked with Luciano over one of the bridges spanning the Tiber. 'Are you surprised?'

'With hindsight, no,' he said, pausing with her to look down along the stretch of soft green water. 'Military honour has been with them much longer than republicanism. I suppose they were just playing for time until reinforcements arrived.'

'Many soldiers in the hospital say Garibaldi should have been allowed to push them back into the sea.'

'I don't think it would have made any difference. Nations don't like losing to a motley assembly such as ours. Why, they would probably have sent the whole French army here to retrieve their glory. A pity about all those goodwill cigars sent to the French camp,' he added, dropping a pebble into the water below.

'Does Rome stand any chance?'

'If we can hold the key positions; but even so, against an army like the French, it's only a matter of time.'

'Oh how I hate them!' she cried, striking her hand against the parapet. 'I hope our bands will blast their "Marseillaise" over the walls and down their disloyal republican throats.'

'Can you stay with me tonight?'

Above the slant of his cheekbones, the expression in Luciano's clear eyes was intense. The lines of his noble face were taut and grave. 'It will be the last time I can be with you before the killing starts again.'

Gabriella shuddered and held on to his hand, wishing that they could run away, whilst knowing neither of them would.

'Try to keep me away, Conte Forro,' she said, trying to stop her voice betraying the fear she felt.

For hours that night in soft candlelight they feasted on love, consumed each other. Outwardly, inwardly, caressing and touching over and over, crying out with delight and disbelief at each new heightened climax. At last they lay back, half asleep, blissfully satiated. Suddenly, down below, they heard the sound of running feet and a loud hammering on the door.

'What can it be?' Gabriella asked, as Luciano sprang from the bed, ran towards the window and flung it wide.

'What is happening?' he called.

'It is I, Ripari, Garibaldi's doctor. Let me in, I must rouse Masina. The French have attacked!'

In two bounds, Luciano's naked figure had left the room. Gabriella started to drag on her clothes.

'But the agreement was Monday!' she cried as he raced back in and started to pull his breeches up over the curve of his thighs.

'I cannot believe such treachery!' he snapped as he buckled on his sword belt and the bells of alarm began to peal out over the city. 'It goes against all the rules of war. And it seems our Commander in Chief Roselli left but few forces at the Villa Corsini. It's been overrun.'

Downstairs, as Luciano raced away to rouse the other officers of the Bersaglieri, Gabriella hovered as the doctor appeared followed by the Commander of the Lancers.

'Do you want me to take any messages?' she asked.

'If you've the stomach, take this to the field hospital for me,' directed the doctor, holding out an instrument case. Gabriella nodded and set off for the church of San Pietro in Montorio. All around there were soldiers tumbling out of their private quarters and racing away to join up with their comrades. The sound of the alarm drums and the panic and confusion were terrible. Strings of horses galloped past, led by frantic orderlies looking for their officers; civilians armed to the teeth rushed across the Tiber to go to the city's defence; soldiers who were racing to gain the height of the Janiculum screamed for them to let them pass.

'What is happening?' cried Gabriella, stopping two men who were about to return with a wheelbarrow up the Via di Porta San Pancrazio to the city gate.

'The French breached the south wall of the Pamphili about three o'clock; before anyone knew what was happening thousands were pouring into the grounds to take the villa and the

Villa Corsini. Most of our men were asleep, not expecting anything until Monday. Garibaldi's launching attacks to get it back.'

As Gabriella entered the church which was serving as a field hospital for the severely wounded, her breath caught in her throat. Transfixed, unable to advance or retreat, her petrified eyes and ears took in the harrowing scene. Hundreds of men, their heads and bodies shattered and covered with gore crowded every available space. From the shadows echoed the restless, distressing sound of suffering. Nearby, the morning rays of the sun piercing through the stained-glass window suffused the stoical faces in pools of red and blue as the young men waited their turn on the stout operating tables to her right. Around them the surgeons were at work, their aprons bloody, their faces streaming with sweat. She squeezed tight her eyes and turned to the wall with her hand pressed against her mouth, trying to stem the tide of nausea. She was no stranger to amputation and knew how the four-ended bandage called the Malta Cross could be adjusted to bring more pressure to bear against the surface of a thigh stump. And receiving such a patient in hospital she knew the stump must be pinned by a bandage to the mattress to prevent shaking and spasm. But to see what grisly work went before, and discover what the fainting young men had to endure, their faces paler than the roll of calico around their loins, was terrible. She knew too that they would only revive to suffer more torment.

'Why are you here – this is no place for you, Signorina,' said a rough voice at her side. 'Such sights are not bearable for ladies.'

Gabriella composed her features and turned around to find one of the medical orderlies looking at her in a mixture of surprise and sympathy.

'If they can bear it, so can I,' she said in a low voice. 'Tell me what to do – I'm not going away.'

The man took in the determined set of the young woman's face and nodded. 'Try and bring some comfort to the dying – it's going to be a very hot day: a sponge soaked in water gives a little relief.'

'Is there nothing they can give them?' asked Gabriella as an agonized cry of '*Viva l'Italia!*' sounded from the operating area. 'I . . . I thought such things would be quicker.'

'When they used the guillotine method of amputation, some surgeons could take a man's leg off in fifteen seconds,' commented the orderly leading Gabriella away from the surgeons' tables. 'Then it was on with the hot pitch. But now things have progressed: the nerve ends are dealt with and our surgeons cleverly create a flap of skin; it's trying for the patient, of course, but can prevent pain in the future.'

Gabriella nodded as if in understanding, though in truth all her mind could ponder on was the terrible inadequacy of his word, 'trying'. As directed, she moved along the rows of men: many were unconscious; others lay with eyes open, staring with pain and bravery.

As the time went by, more and more casualties poured in. Even if Luciano had not pointed out the difficulties of retaking the Villa Corsini, the sight of the wounded and the young lives expiring all around her told what an unequal struggle was taking place up on the Janiculum.

'Oh, where is the good Pope now to give his blessing to this boy,' she thought savagely, seeing the light fade in the eyes of a young man as he wept to go to Jesus. 'Soon . . . I'll not let your hand go until then,' she soothed.

'Is the General here?' he gasped.

'No, but his chaplain is. He is coming over to you now,' she said, seeing the red-smocked figure of Ugo Bassi nearby.

As the priest took her place, Gabriella kissed the forehead of the Garibaldino, then turned, uncertain who to attend to next – there seemed so many. At that instant a doctor seized hold of her arm. 'Get some dressings and follow me!'

Swiftly Gabriella did as she was bid and accompanied the young man towards the precipitous ascent up the Via di Porta San Pancrazio. It was alive with people, just like a never-ending column of soldier ants. Some were running up shouldering guns, others were coming down, their bodies splattered with blood.

'Mario!' she shouted in disbelief as a familiar figure ran past her clutching an arm oozing blood: pushed on by those from behind, she had to continue up; all she could do was turn her head and acknowledge the student singer's wave.

'I couldn't miss the finale!' he boomed after her. 'Give them a verse of the "Marseillaise" while you're up there.'

Hoping that he might still be at the hospital when she returned, Gabriella heard the stirring strains of the 'Marseillaise' as they passed the Villa Savorelli to the right of the path.

'What irony!' commented the doctor as he looked towards the musicians on the right of the San Pancrazio gate.

'*Avanti!*' '*Avanti!*' shouted a large crowd of civilians urging forward a detachment of soldiers as they marched out under the gate. Then, as some of them stood to one side, a huge cheer and applause broke out as several litter-bearers raced in carrying wounded. Gabriella heard them joking with the soldiers who were about to take their place to face the onslaught beyond the gate.

'Over here,' directed the doctor as the cries of encouragement for a fresh contingent of soldiers were renewed. 'The stretcher bearers thought this lad would bleed to death if he was moved . . . I see they were right,' he murmured as he knelt on the ground beside the wounded soldier. 'Hopeless, we could not have done anything for him even if we had been on the spot – though speed is everything. Napoleon's head of medical services, Dominique Larrey, taught us that when he introduced his flying ambulance stations: never further than three miles from the army. He put his surgeons on horseback and they tended the wounded on the battlefield. Before him, men were left to lie in their blood until the fighting was over. Come on, we might as well go back down,' he directed picking up his instrument case.

But Gabriella did not heed what he said, for she had heard a sound which made her stomach lurch with fear. Despite the morning sun, she shivered, for the bugle of the Bersaglieri had pierced through the sound of artillery fire and the French Hymn of liberty which the Roman band was playing to rouse the consciences of the enemy. 'It's the round hats' turn to dine on lead,' observed the doctor grimly as he followed her to the gatehouse.

From where she stood with the crowd of cheering spectators, Gabriella saw the Bersaglieri approach from the mustering ground, their officers walking up to speak to Garibaldi who was mounted on his horse outside the gateway. As the officers turned to rejoin the ranks, Gabriella saw Luciano, so near that she could have touched him. She wanted to rush towards him, to bar his path, to warn them all of the bloody horror of amputation while there was still time to keep their young bodies intact. But it was no use: in each heart that passed through that gate the sacrificial words of Verdi's opera for Rome were ringing: 'He who dies for his country does not have a guilty soul.'

Gabriella turned aside: no matter how much she wanted to embrace him she knew she must not. In a frenzy of indecision she ran towards the Merluzzo bastion to the left of the gate.

'Please, let me see my love,' she cried, grasping an officer's arm.

'Perhaps it is better not, Signorina,' said the man gently as he eyed with respect the blood-stained evidence of her work.

'If it is the end I must!' she choked, her voice desperate and hollow with dread.

'Go up and stand behind the sandbags with the artist Koelman,' said the officer, taking pity. 'But be careful: the bullets are whistling through at a great rate.'

Looking out over the city walls, it seemed that she had always looked at things with lazy eyes; for never had a scene seemed so sharp in detail. Beside her, viewing it with the same intensity, the Dutch artist strove to retain the memory of what was happening with his pencil.

Ahead the enemy were clear to see, moving on the balcony of the Villa Corsini. Though she couldn't see them, she knew that there would also be soldiers behind the orange trees decorating the two-foot wall at the front of the villa. Now indeed their presence was betrayed by the smoke from their guns as they mowed down a small detachment of men who were running up the driveway between the six-foot box hedges which bordered the long avenue.

'It's sometimes called the Casa dei Quattro Venti,' commented the artist without looking around, 'but the wind today is in the cornfields: see it bending to our gunners' shot?'

Gabriella watched for a moment the crouched figures of the French infantry as the grape shot parted their cover and halted their advance. Then, as the bugles called, she looked back to the road and saw that the first company of Bersaglieri, waved on by Garibaldi, were making the advance out of the city. Straightaway, as the poncho-clad figure rode up and down encouraging his men, the French battery sprang into action and the open road was raked with fire.

'Why, this is terrible!' she said dully, seeing men fall just a few paces away from the walls and all along to the Villa Vascello on the right of the road.

'You've seen nothing yet,' sighed the artist. 'They are relatively lucky. You see they are turning left towards the Vicolo della Nocetta to the Casa Giacometti? That is a little safer in comparison to what this company will face.'

With the glass which the artist thrust into her hand, Gabriella looked at the column of some four hundred Bersaglieri marching out of the city to the attack. She could not see his face, but she knew the man beside Conte Manara was Luciano. She started to pray. Down the road sped the soldiers towards the Villa Corsini gate, set in the apex of the triangular garden. Here began the problem of the assault, for at once its impact petered out as the men were forced to enter no more than five at a time, while all the time – from behind the row of orange pots and from the windows and balcony of the villa – a never-ceasing fire was directed at them.

'No cover!' she said out loud, watching the Bersaglieri start to run up the avenue between the stiff hedges. In the mêlée she had lost sight of Luciano: all she could see were the men falling.

'Oh, it is murder,' she moaned.

'It's been going on all morning,' retorted the artist. 'And if they manage to get into the villa they cannot hold it, for there are thousands of French reserves in the grounds of the Pamphili just waiting to move up.'

'If I have to die here, I will remember loving here,' he had whispered when they had lain in the long green grass. Gabriella pressed her hands against the barrier of sandbags, then uttered a low sob as those Bersaglieri who had survived the angle of death reached the top of the avenue. As if they too had a protecting wall, they knelt, raised their guns and discharged their fire, the officers standing erect behind them. It was mad: sheer, flamboyant courage; and with all her heart she wished she could cover the distance and be beside him to meet death; for now the Lombards were reeling as the bugle sounded the recall. Like distant puppets whose strings were being cut by unseen hands, the figures spun and fell forward as they ran down the avenue. Arms outstretched, some turned back for wounded friends; but such hesitation cost their lives as they jerked backwards, clutching at their hearts. Unable to bear the sight any more, she climbed down from the wall, hardly able to see for the hot tears streaming from her eyes. At the bottom near the San Pancrazio gate, some twenty Bersaglieri reserves stood waiting, ashen-faced, as they glimpsed the slaughter of their friends and comrades beyond the gate.

When dusk fell and the day fled, it took with it hundreds of brave men, amongst them Enrico Dandolo, the dashing Masina of the Bolognese lancers who, when wounded, returned a second time to the attack to give his life for Italy.

As the days wore on, so the trenches of the famous French engineer, General Vaillant, drew nearer to the walls and bastions. There was no hope, only a determination not to surrender.

During the long hours of the night Gabriella, like the other ladies, sat and talked or read to those soldiers who could not sleep. She could only pray that Luciano was still alive, for the wounded and dead were so numerous it was impossible to know for certain.

'How are you bearing up, Signorina Pepe?' asked the doctor as he came to administer the precious and eventually lethal laudanum to the young Florentine she had been reading to.

'Not as well as the Princess,' she smiled, looking towards the bent dark head of Christina Belgiojoso who sat reading Charles Dickens beside the bedside of Mameli, the war poet.

'Mameli bears his suffering bravely,' said the doctor in a low voice. 'Sadly his knee wound has turned gangrenous. Ah, here comes the General. That will ease their pains more than anything I can prescribe. Some have clung on to the thread of life just to bid him adieu.'

Still outside the walls, the Unione regiments were fighting like tigers to hold the Casa Giacometti, as was Medici at the Villa Vascello. During the day the French batteries hurled down multitudes of shells at them, whilst at night, along their trenches, hundreds of night raiders launched bayonet attacks against the weary defenders. On 21 June, Rome learnt that the enemy was on the walls: they had taken the Casa Barberini to the west and the Central Bastion. Now the French batteries began to work in earnest. Sheets of yellow, crimson flames raged upwards to the sky as more hovels of the Trastevere quarter were set alight. Soon, every family would be homeless, thought Gabriella, as she paused to watch the frightening scene. Her eyes began to smart as a breeze changed the direction of the smoke and, as she closed her eyes against it, she heard something thud on the ground nearby.

'Another gift from Pio Nono!' shrieked a group of children and, before she could stop them, the ragged urchins, darting forward, scooped up the live shell and hurled it down into the Tiber as if it were a ball. It was not the first time she had witnessed such foolhardy courage, for the descending shells, far from cowing the Romans, were filling them with an even greater will to resist. The sight of the children's courage and the daily worsening situation made up Gabriella's mind. 'I must go to him, I must know if he is alive!' To attempt to reach Garibaldi's headquarters she knew was almost suicidal but, despite the danger, she could bear the agony of uncertainty no longer. Past the burning houses, whose fierce heat now added to that of the day, Gabriella hurried through the groups of people cursing and shaking their fists in the direction of the French batteries. From these issued forth ceaseless flashes and billowing blue-grey smoke, as the gunners directed their fire at the Roman positions, which answered back from the high ground of the terrace of San Pietro in Montorio and the Pino hill. The roof of San Pietro in Montorio had been blown off and, as Gabriella drew nearer to the Villa Spada, which lay within the second defence of the Aurelian wall, she saw that it was taking a terrible pounding. Under her feet the ground shook with every explosion, and all around huge clods of earth were being hurled high into the air. She tripped and, unable to keep her balance, fell, grazing her cheek against a pile of rubble. Badly shaken she put her hands over her head as a shower of earth and rubble rained down upon her. She staggered to her feet and climbed over the branches of an uprooted olive tree, watching as she went the timing of the French guns; she must get it right if she were to make it inside the Villa Spada's door. She lifted up her skirts in readiness, then, as a huge piece of masonry fell away from the villa with the last gunner's efforts, thinking of Luciano and trusting herself to God, Gabriella ran, love and fear lending wings to her feet.

Garibaldi stood before an open window looking upwards to the Janiculum. To either side of him were Manara, now his Chief of Staff, and the Dandolo brother who had survived the third of June.

'Forgive me, General,' she blurted out breathlessly as the men turned and looked at her in amazement. 'I came . . .' Her voice failed her as terror seized her at not seeing him. She swallowed, her heart contracting with fear. Then, from another room, carrying a telescope in his hand, Luciano appeared. With a cry of relief she ran to him.

'I had to come,' she said, her eyes filling with tears of joy as she looked up at him. A beautiful smile lit up Luciano's tired, ashen face, as he gathered her into his arms.

'Oh, this is too good to be true. Are you real?' he murmured after a time.

'Quite real, and thinking and praying for you every moment

of the day and night,' she said, with her cheek pressed against his chest and her arms tight around his waist. Then her eyes lifted to the bandage around his forehead and, as always, her heart did a little somersault as his lips pulled into the whimsical little smile that was his alone.

'A farewell from the Villa Savorelli,' he explained. 'And the way things are going here, the French don't care for the architecture here either. How is Rome?' he asked.

By his brittle tone, she knew how desperate things were: one only had to be inside the building to know it, for with every hit a deluge of plaster and dust showered down.

'Well, the city is getting ready to show the French that we're not in the least bit demoralized: there are going to be Roman rockets in the sky on the Feast of St Peter and St Paul, and the fireworks will be red, white and green.'

'And what of the people in the Trastevere? I suppose many have lost everything,' he said sadly.

'Yes, they're homeless, although the Assembly has housed them in the palaces of those owners who are away – on the strictest understanding that everything is to be treated with great care and respect. Mazzini has inspired everyone not to let the republic down. They are all longing to meet the French at the barricades and do what we did to the Austrians in Milan.'

'That will never happen, Gabriella. When they break through the Casa Merluzzo, and once their guns are on the terrace of San Pietro in Montorio, they will have Rome before them on its knees. I'm only amazed we've held them so long: Medici at the Villa Vascello has been their hindrance.'

'Is it still in our hands?'

'Yes, despite their worst: they knock down the walls and we shovel them back up,' he laughed bitterly. 'The French will undoubtedly take Rome for the Pope, but when he returns and lifts his hands to bless all his people, they will see blood on those hands – for he could have stopped this!'

'Will we surrender soon?' she whispered. 'While there is still . . . a chance.' For you to survive, she had meant, and she felt he understood by the way he did not answer, holding her close as if it would be for the last time.

'Oh, let me stay and fight by your side,' she urged.

His reply was a kiss: long, unhurried, his lips declaring his love and his farewell. He looked down upon her face as if to recall every line and detail. She knew she should be savouring this moment too, but she could not: she felt a confusion of terrible emotions inside. She pressed her lips against the warm curve of his to prolong the moment, but he gently pushed her away.

'One of the soldiers shall escort you back,' he said firmly.

'Don't worry about him, Gabriella,' said the young Emilio Dandolo coming forward to say goodbye. 'As an attendant you should know,' he said, pointing to his wounded thigh. 'Bullets are like mosquitos: they either like your flesh or not.'

'And we have two secret weapons here,' laughed the handsome Conte Manara, lifting a small statuette of Verdi from his pocket.

'And the other?' she asked, trying to be brave.

'When you leave, *cara*, you shall hear it!' replied Luciano, touching her hair in a wistful parting gesture.

The bombardment had not slackened as Gabriella stepped away from the villa, but barely had she and her escort gone twenty paces when a piano burst into life. Moved from tears to disbelief, she looked at the young soldier as the men's voices hurled out cheerful defiance.

'How mad the French must think us,' she shouted, envisaging the three Lombards grouped around the piano, just as they had been so many times at their beautiful palatial villas in Lombardy.

'It has to be!' said Giuseppe Mazzini, his face filled with agony when Gabriella, in desperation, had visited him to make her individual plea. 'The sacrifice must be made. From the first the victory was in the human sacrifice. Every man who climbed up to the Janiculum, who dashed through the Corsini gates knew that. There are golden threads in a people's history, and the youth of our country came to Rome to make one. We cannot give way to brute force: monarchies may capitulate, republics die, and bear their testimony even to martyrdom.'

'*Orsù! Questa è l'ultima prova!*' cried the voice of Giuseppe Garibaldi.

It was, at last, the final fight. On the night of 29 June the dome of St Peter's glittered like a prize bauble for the French to lust over as it glowed first red, then green, in the lights of the fireworks. Along the Corso, the lanterns hung from the branches of the trees, their tricolore colours and swinging gaiety making it seem as if a carnival had arrived. From the cafés and piazzas, songs and laughter filled the air; above, in the darkness, men held their muskets and wondered whether they would see the morrow.

It had begun to rain and at Santa Maria della Scala field hospital where they waited for the attack to begin, Gabriella shivered with cold and fear. Suddenly, like the outbreak of an electrical storm, the attack started. Up on the slope leading to the Janiculum, the Cavaliers of Bologna, the Legionaries and the Garibaldini were engaged through the dark hours in desperate hand-to-hand fighting.

'Has the Villa Spada fallen?' Gabriella asked a wounded Bersagliere brought down from the bastion of Merluzzo.

'No, but Morisini is mortally wounded,' he gasped.

So young to die, thought the girl, remembering the sweet young man of seventeen whom they called the guardian angel.

Frantic to save lives, they strove to follow the surgeon's shouted instructions as he moved down the rows of wounded men. Suddenly Gabriella gasped out loud as she saw young Emilio Dandolo wheeling a handcart in. On it lay the Conte Manara, pale as death.

'Luciano?'

The young man, clutching a wounded arm, shook his head in a dazed way as Dr Bertani rushed in and knelt beside his friend.

'Oh, Bertani,' sighed the Conte. 'Let me die quickly.'

Wild with terror, Gabriella turned away from the weeping Emilio Dandolo who knelt beside the dying Conte Manara. Without asking leave, she ran outside and turned towards Villa Spada. Behind her she heard shouts for her return, but she took no notice. Above the Janiculum the sun was climbing high, shining down on Rome's burial ground.

'Luciano! Luciano!' she called, staggering forward over the broken earth. Everywhere were the dead: French chasseurs and, in the garden and within the damaged shell of the villa, the Bersaglieri. In various attitudes, the dead defenders were sprawled upon the floor. She knew that she would know him instantly, but still frantic with fear, she began to turn over every body.

Suddenly she heard the jingle of harnesses and voices speaking French. Seized with fright, she peeped through a crack in the wall of the villa and saw three French officers in magnificent uniforms. They were riding around the villa, inspecting the damage their guns had wrought. Gabriella wiped the tears from her eyes as she saw one of them dismount. Desperate to stay and continue her search, she hesitated, but then as another of the officers also leapt down from his horse, she knew she must go or she might be taken as a prisoner. With great caution she crept back through the shattered remains and ran through the garden, snatching up a bloodied hat adorned with the glossy green-black feathers of an officer of the Bersaglieri.

# Chapter Seventeen

They left Rome by the Lateran Gate at night, heeding the order of no talking; for they were with the army, and the French would destroy those who had not surrendered. The retreat was fast and at one point Gabriella stumbled; immediately unseen hands dragged her up on to her feet and she trudged onwards with the fugitives over the silent countryside.

Gradually dawn lifted away the darkness from the land, and the sun began to cast its rosy hue: ahead, glimmering grey and palest amethyst, Gabriella saw the line of the Sabine hills.

'Tivoli,' said a soldier, raising his finger.

She could see no town then, but as the hours went by, the lush green hills disclosed their towers, gleaming and winking in the sunlight, while beneath the vine-clad slopes lay the ancient ruins of Hadrian. At about seven, the head of the column reached the old town, and by the time Gabriella arrived, the army was camped out at its southern gate.

Like many around her, she dropped where she was and listened to the roar of the Anio as it leapt down the mountainside. But as soon as some strength had returned to her legs, she got up and walked away, wanting to put distance between the encamped people and herself. She had left Rome because she could not bear to witness the French enter: that had been the only thing her numb mind had been able to decide. Now Rome lay across the silent countryside and, like a child, she wondered why she had come with those who were here to carry on the fight. She was sick of the stench of death and the sounds of agony. And because she had not found him, she cared for nothing.

Two Garibaldini in their red blouses were galloping towards her. Torn from her gloomy despair, Gabriella jumped aside as the riders raced at her, holding her hands up to shield her face from the dust. Their wild approach made her think of Nico, and she started to weep.

'That's no greeting for a fellow student of the Conservatorio!' boomed a voice.

'Oh Mario, Giovanni,' she cried, wiping her eyes and then weeping again at the relief of seeing them alive. In a trice, Giovanni leant down from his horse and lifted her up to his saddle.

'I have an antidote that will cure those tears,' he grinned. And offering no explanation, he galloped towards the old town with Mario following behind. There, outside a villa, the Garibaldino set her down. With a burst of merry laughter, as if he were once more driving his sediole through Milan, he departed at speed.

The gate to the villa was open, and the profusion of wild greenness drew her inside. Neglect and riotous nature beckoned, and with a beating heart now filled with excited hope, she set out along the walks of tangled vines and leafy shade. Everywhere there seemed to be water, trickling over mossy stones or shooting up into the sky in plumed rockets, erupting into millions of sparkling gems. But there seemed to be no one about: she walked around the edge of a pool and towards the downward noisy rush of its fountain, entering within a dark damp way that led her as if to the back of a waterfall. Here the walls ran with water, and all she could hear was its roar blotting out the sound of the outside world, the memories of the cannon's boom and the terrible cries of suffering. Her clothes were stiff with sweat and dried blood. She stepped forward.

From a distance the Bersagliere looked towards the fountain and watched through its curtain of water the slim figure of a girl raising her arms like some nymph come to life. Out loud Luciano Forro groaned in despair that his men had carried him unconscious from the city. He had resolved that, though it might cost him his life, he must return to find her. Feeling he